THE LUCIFER COVENANT

THE LUCIFER COVENANT

PHILLIP ELLIS JACKSON
R. A. VARGHESE

PUBLISHING COMPANY
P.O. Box 220 • Goleta, CA 93116
(800) 647-9882 • (805) 692-0043 • Fax: (805) 967-5133
www.queenship.org

Library of Congress Number # 2005909435

Published by:
Queenship Publishing
P.O. Box 220
Goleta, CA 93116
(800) 647-9882 • (805) 692-0043 • Fax: (805) 967-5133
www.queenship.org

Printed in the United States of America

ISBN: 1-57918-290-9

CONTENTS

PROLOGUE

For centuries, there were rumors of a "contract" between God and the Devil.

The Hebrews believed that God allowed Satan to enter the Garden of Eden to test primordial humanity. The Book of Job chronicled the divinely-sanctioned tribulation of a holy man administered by the Devil. The New Testament Gospels speak of the Holy Spirit leading Christ to the Three Temptations of the Evil One. And, climactically, the Book of Revelation shows God releasing the Beast from the Abyss to put the human family to its ultimate test.

These rumors took a new direction in the nineteenth century. In her famous apparition at La Salette, France, the Virgin Mary warned of a time when "Lucifer together with a large number of demons will be unloosed from hell." Then the renowned Pope Leo XIII witnessed a celestial encounter in which God allowed Satan to do his worst for a hundred years before his final defeat.

The enemies of God called this the Lucifer Covenant.

But for the faithful it was a sign of the times, a warning that the world would soon reap what it had long sown. Now only a last stand against the Powers of Evil would avert the Wrath of God.

It was a time for truth.

It was a time for action.

Chapter 1

Dallas

Little Miguel hid in the shadows of the narrow, cluttered hallway, crouching noiselessly behind a partially opened door that led into his parents' bedroom. Inside, a portrait of the Virgin Mary, its edges frayed and surface color tarnished with age, seemed to look back at him as if taking pity on the frightened, eight-year-old child.

The small, one-story house was only five miles from the heart of downtown Dallas, but it may as well have been on the other side of the world. Indistinguishable from the other homes dotting the southern shore of the Trinity River, the ramshackle wood and stucco structure was badly in need of a coat of paint. Missing patches on the gray shingled roof were covered over with thick coats of black tar, giving it a curious checkerboard appearance. But to Esteban Guerrero and his wife Marisol, for all its imperfections, their little house in the barrio was a source of immense pride. Living in the shadow of a modern, twenty-first century city, it both protected them from—and allowed them access to — a culture that was at once foreign and familiar. Since leaving Mexico ten years earlier they had devoted themselves to building a future for themselves and their child while holding on to the values and traditions of an earlier time. But now, in this house where their son Miguel was born, something dark, cold, and threatening had forced its way in. A terrible pall had settled over them, reaching into their very souls. The fight had begun to exorcise the Beast, and in doing so restore a spiritual balance to their lives that had been fiercely tested.

Peering out from the imagined safety of the old tattered door, Miguel struggled to comprehend the shrieks and noises that drew him closer to his parents' bedroom despite his fear; strange guttural sounds mixed with haunting cries, sinister cackles and Latin chants. His eyes were riveted on his father Esteban and uncle Zacarias who were locked in a struggle that sent furniture crashing and glass breaking. Across the room another man, short and stocky in a black cassock and cleric's collar, read aloud from a thick careworn book, his words strange and alien, rising and falling in rhythm to the surrounding chaos.

An icy cold seemed to envelop the room, chilling the breath of those it touched, and turning their shouts into tiny puffs of escaping vapor backlit against a mid-day sun that fought its way through the partially drawn drapes. Amid the chaos the crucifix over a simple, wood frame bed threatened to tear itself from its anchor and come crashing down on the two struggling figures. Like every other room in the house, it was filled with religious icons and other manifestations of Catholic piety. Placed there in homage to a God of peace and serenity, they now seemed curiously out of place as the battle to control the writhing, thrashing man went on around them.

"I'll kill you!" Zacarias shouted, his arms flailing like a madman, his voice sounding like the fearful roll of thunder escaping from the halls of Hell itself. "Let me go! Let me go!"

Redoubling his efforts, Esteban pinned his brother's arms behind his back and threw him onto the bed. The full force of his weight was used to press him against the mattress. Zacarias snarled and growled as he spat out a torrent of obscenities. He fought to rise, but Esteban's grip was too strong.

"Holy Lord, almighty Father, everlasting God and Father of our Lord Jesus Christ," the cleric prayed over them both, "who once and for all consigned that fallen and apostate tyrant to the flames of hell, who sent your only-begotten Son into the world to crush that roaring lion; hasten to our call for help and snatch from ruination and from the clutches of the noonday devil this human being made in your image and likeness."

"You will not defeat me!" Zacarias roared. His eyes distended in rage, and a strange, primal sound worked its way out from somewhere deep inside him. Like a fearsome beast his features almost seemed to transform, but Esteban held firm, using every ounce of strength to keep him restrained.

Watching the battle through unblinking eyes, little Miguel steeled himself against the impulse to race into the room and help his father. Esteban Guerrero had warned his son away from their house, and it was only through an act of almost unthinkable defiance that the eight-year-old boy had ventured back inside. Miguel knew that his father would be furious at this bold rejection of his authority. But earlier that day he had seen Santos Machado, the short, stocky Filipino priest, hold his father transfixed in a whispered conversation that ended with a cascade of tears, the first time young Miguel had ever seen his father cry. Now Esteban was locked in a death-like struggle with his younger brother Zacarias. It was as if the Devil himself was trying to break free of his grasp, and only Miguel's father could hold him back.

"Strike terror, Lord, into the beast now laying waste your vineyard. Fill your servants with courage to fight manfully against that reprobate dragon, lest he despise those who put their trust in you."

"I will *not* … submit!" Zacarias screamed, foaming at the mouth.

"Zacarias," Esteban wept for his brother. "God forgives you for your sins. Let go of the Beast."

"NOOOO!" the screeching wail was piercing.

Instinctively, Miguel covered his ears and turned his head away, then forced himself to look back again. The priest Santos was now methodically tracing the sign of the cross on his uncle Zacarias' forehead. Zacarias reacted as if each touch of his thumb, dipped in exorcised water, was a knife slicing through flesh. It drove him to struggle harder, but he was kept pinned against the bed only through Esteban's exhaustive efforts.

"I command you, unclean spirit," Santos prayed, "whoever you are, along with all your minions now attacking this servant of God, by the mysteries of the incarnation, passion, resurrection, and ascension of our Lord Jesus Christ, by the descent of the Holy Spirit, by the coming of our Lord for judgment, that you tell me by some sign your name, and the day and hour of your departure."

Zacarias quieted, death-like. "I am Quetzelcoatl," he finally hissed in a gruff, menacing voice. "I serve Lucifer, the creator of all things in heaven and earth, the master and lord of the universe."

Esteban gave a look of utter disbelief while the priest Santos smiled triumphant, like a hunter closing in on his prey. "Audacious deceiver," he announced. "Feathered serpent demon who deceived the Aztecs. Don't you remember that your master was cast out of heaven into the outer darkness? I command you to bow before the Lord of all things that I might send you to the abyss."

Santos touched the man with his stole — a slim silk strip that he wore around his neck — and breathed into Zacarias' face. "I command you to show your presence infernal spirit."

Almost immediately an unseen force pushed Santos to the ground. Zacarias wrested himself loose of his brother Esteban's grip and ran for the door.

"Stop in the name of God," Santos shouted, retrieving his prayer book. He continued to read. "Leave him at once. I command you to obey me to the letter, I who am a minister of God despite my unworthiness; nor shall you be emboldened to harm in any way this creature of God, or the bystanders, or any of their possessions."

Zacarias wheeled around. *"He is mine,"* he grunted in a strange new voice, his face now contorted in a hideous grimace. Whining, pleading, it sent chills through Miguel. "Let us be!"

Santos pulled himself to his feet. Ignoring the pain from his injured leg, he made the sign of the cross. "I cast you out, unclean spirit," he intoned, "along with every Satanic power of the enemy, every spectre from hell, and all your fell companions; in the name of our Lord Jesus Christ. Be gone and stay far from this creature of God. For it is He who commands you, He who flung you headlong from the heights of heaven into the depths of hell."

With a terrible shriek Zacarias fell, limp as a rag doll. Esteban rushed to his unconscious brother's side and cradled his head in his arms. Sobbing with joy, he lifted Zacarias in his arms and carried him to the bed, gently laying him down. The priest Santos, exhausted, felt his own legs begin to weaken, and he let his weary body seek needed relief in a nearby chair.

"Papa," Miguel spoke softly, emerging from the shadows.

Esteban snapped his head around to face the voice. He could see the fear and confusion in his son's eyes as he stood paralyzed in the doorway. Forgetting his anger at Miguel's disobedience, he beckoned him closer, embracing Miguel and kissing him on the cheeks while caressing his head.

"I'm sorry Papa," Miguel whispered. He stared at the sleeping man lying on the bed, and grasped his father tightly. "Will uncle Zacarias ... be all right?"

"He's in God's hands, Miguel," Esteban said, stealing a glance at Santos. "The Heavenly Father will protect him now."

"What made him do those things Papa? Speak like that?"

"It was a malefice," Santos announced, still sitting on the hard-backed chair with his eyes closed.

"A spell?" Esteban could barely speak the words aloud.

"Your brother Zacarias has enemies. Tell me who they are."

For a long moment Esteban thought. "There's a gang from Old Mexico living in the barrio. Black magic people, from Coahuila. I heard Zacarias speak of them. He warned them away from his wife and children."

"A hex then, yes," Santos nodded. His eyes opened, and he let his gaze drift over toward Esteban. "They used black magic to steal his soul. A simple photograph, or strand of hair, is all they would need to place a curse. Their power is great, but it cannot withstand the visage and countenance of the Lord our God."

"How do you know this?" Miguel couldn't resist the question.

Esteban frowned at his son's innocent challenge, but Santos took no offense. His grim face broke into a smile. "My angel told me," he said with a wink.

The quirky Filipino priest rose from his chair, closed his prayer book, and made his way to the bed. With a light touch he again traced the sign of the cross on Zacarias' forehead. "Your uncle is now free of this wickedness," he spoke to Miguel. "When he awakes, make sure he goes to confession, and receives communion often. That's the best protection against the dark arts."

"I will," Miguel answered seriously.

Santos patted the young boy on his head, smoothing his hair with the palm of his hand.

"Good boy. The Devil's power is no match for an innocent heart. Your uncle will be safe now. Your purity and devotion will keep him away."

For the first time in hours, Esteban Guerrero allowed himself to smile. He put his arm around Miguel, whose eyes never left Santos' piercing gaze, and gently led him from the room.

***

The small kitchen hummed with conversation. Miguel, sitting opposite his father, had said very little since leaving his parents' bedroom earlier that day. His father had remained at the young boy's side watching over him carefully, both to gauge Miguel's state of mind and to ensure that no harm would come to the child from any evil presence still lurking nearby. Other than a natural, reflective introspection on the day's events, Miguel seemed to have weathered the events with little outward effect. Bright, always curious, he had absorbed the strange happenings as best he could. Now it was time to put those thoughts to the back of everyone's mind, and enjoy a meal with family and friends.

Next to Miguel sat Santos Machado, looking slightly out of place in a wild Hawaiian shirt and light blue polyester slacks, his cassock and cleric's collar set aside for a private evening with friends. Outfitting himself with second-hand garments purchased from any number of local Goodwill stores, he focused more on comfort than fashion to compensate for the heavy, sometime cumbersome priestly garb he wore over his clothing. His choice in attire had often been the butt of friendly jokes between Santos and his fellow priests, who saw them as an extension of his unique, and somewhat odd personality. Santos accepted the teasing good naturedly, and almost seemed to seek out the most flamboyant clothing to burnish his image.

"We give blessings, oh Lord, for thy bounty," Esteban prayed over the steaming plate of rice and chicken his wife Marisol placed on the table, "and for your servant, Santos Machado. May you bless him and the good work he does, in your Name."

"Amen," Miguel said reverently, ending the dinner prayer as he did each night, bringing a smile to his father and Santos.

"Now, we eat," Esteban said in a hearty voice.

Santos lost no time in busily spooning a generous portion onto his plate. The day's bizarre events had obviously not affected the priest's appetite. He savored each bite with almost carnal delight before returning to the plate for another big helping. Two other places were set at the table, but not occupied.

"Come sit, Marisol," Esteban beckoned. "We have much to rejoice this night, and many memories to share with our good friend Santos."

"I should check on Graciela," she said. "She's been sitting at Zacarias' side since this afternoon." Fixing a small plate of food, she wiped her hands on the frayed cloth apron wrapped around her waist, then placed her hand on Santos' shoulder. "Thank you, Santos," she said, kissing him lovingly on the cheek, for the good works you've done, and for blessing our home with God's presence. *Mi casa su casa, amigo.* You are always welcome here."

Esteban nodded approvingly as his wife covered the food with a cloth, and left the room.

"Your wife is as beautiful and gracious as the day we first met," Santos said, reaching for another dish to sample. "And her *arroz con pollo* is still the best I've tasted. But I must now try some of this!"

"You know my Mama too?" Miguel asked incredulously. The strange little man who walked with a limp and carried a cane had come to their home the evening before with an armful of books and a small black satchel filled with holy water and anointed oils. In the torment and confusion of Zacarias' possession, it wasn't clear to Miguel who Santos was, or where he had come from. All he knew was that Esteban, his father, had prayed for his brother's deliverance from the evil curse that befell him, and somehow Santos Machado was the instrument God had sent them.

"Father Santos baptized you, Miguel," Esteban said. "And before that, he married your mother and me."

"And before that, your father and I were friends; dear friends," Santos placed his hands on Esteban's shoulder.

"I'm sorry to have doubted you, Santos," Esteban's voice was a whisper. "I did not believe before today. How different my life would have been, had I had your faith in Father Aurelio and the Priestly Society of the Holy Cross, the priests of Opus Dei."

"God has a plan for each of us, Esteban. Some of it, we can see. But much of it, we can't. Had you followed the calling and become a servant of the Lord, as did I, you would not have been blessed with a fine wife and son." He smiled at Miguel. "Those who marry in the faith and bring blessed children into this world are as honored by God as those who preserve and propagate His Holy Word."

"Will you stay with us tonight?" Esteban asked.

"No, my friend," Santos replied sadly. "I must take my leave once we finish our meal. But fear not, your brother is surrounded by the love of God. No harm will come to him, his family, or yours."

Reaching for a bottle of wine, Santos poured himself another drink. Esteban watched his friend of twenty years rinse his mouth with the drink, savoring the sweet aftertaste. He thought about their time together at the seminary, before he left and Santos remained. Even as a young man Santos was immersed in the supernatural world, always talking about angels, spirits and demons. They were not metaphors to illustrate a parable from Christ's teachings. They were real, tangible manifestations of good and evil that pervaded everyday life. For Esteban, it was too much to embrace the reality of the occult, especially when the theologians of the Church seemed increasingly to push such extreme beliefs to the sideline. But now he had witnessed the adjuration of the Devil with his own eyes. It was not a metaphor that possessed his brother Zacarias. It was evil in its rawest form.

Today Esteban became a believer with the same intensity as his friend Santos. His world, from this point forward, would never be the same.

Just as it had forever changed for his son.

Chapter 2

Dallas nine years later

Over two hundred and fifty people filled the tightly packed room in the Oak Cliff Manor, a once proud hotel located in a low income suburban Dallas neighborhood. Most were dressed casually; some wearing t-shirts and jeans, others in pressed slacks and buttoned down shirts, and a few sporting suits and ties. Mixed throughout were a smattering of truly odd-looking men and women distinguished by their long hair and black, occultish clothing, adding to the carnival-like atmosphere. Several newspaper and television reporters were also present, though the bewildered expressions on their faces made it clear that they didn't quite know which story to cover. With the possible exception of a Star Trek convention, few had ever seen such an odd collection of humanity assembled in one location.

"Man, did I ever draw the short straw on this," Wynn Colgate mumbled to his cameraman Felix Ortiz, who was busily setting his equipment on a tripod in the back of the room. "Felix, let's grab a few establishing shots, then move closer to the podium and get a close up of this Mercado guy when he starts to speak. We'll close with a head shot of me wrapping things up so I can hustle back to the airport and catch my five o'clock flight. It's going to be close, but I think I'll make it."

"Machado," Felix corrected.

"What?"

"'Mercado' means 'market'. His name is Father Santos Machado. He's a very famous priest who—"

"Yeah, okay," Wynn glanced at the papers in his hand, cutting him off while he scribbled a note in the margin. "Machado, Machado," he repeated to himself, then grunted toward the cameraman. "If I screw it up Felix, we'll do a voice over in the car after you shoot the tape."

"Hey Wynn," a pleasant female voice called from behind. The stately looking reporter turned to see an attractive, twenty-eight-year-old woman approach, dressed provocatively in a tight skirt and gauzy blouse showing a hint of cleavage. "I haven't seen you since the Shuttle went down over Nacogdoches. What's Hastings Communications' national science reporter doing at an exorcists' convention in Dallas Texas?"

"I've been asking myself the same thing," Wynn shook his head mournfully. "You're looking beautiful as ever, Gina. Still doing local color, I see."

"You say that like it's some kind of disease," she chuckled. "If it's quirky, it's for Gina. You know three of my last five stories have gone national? In fact, I'm up for a spot on ABC's new weekend morning show. I figure this freak show will put me over the top once and for all, if I cover it right."

Felix Ortiz cast a disgruntled glance in the woman's direction, but said nothing while her mindless prattle continued.

"Have you ever seen such a bizarre collection of humanity?" she struggled to suppress a giggle. "Someone must really be looking out for me to drop this in my lap!"

"Well, it may be great for you, Gina. But I figure I must have really gotten on the bad side of old man Hastings himself. He assigned me to this personally … whatever it is. One minute I'm sitting in my office, deciding whether to do my next report on new microsurgery techniques or look at current advances in the human genome project. The next thing I know I'm on a plane to Dallas with instructions to do an in-depth report on this Mercado Machado guy. I can't even figure out how to pronounce his name, let alone take him seriously." Pulling a green Xeroxed flyer from his folder of notes, he waved it in Gina's direction. "Have you seen how they're promoting this so-called symposium: '*The Devil in the Modern World; A Personal Odyssey of Truth*'. This guy sounds like a real crackpot."

"Like I said, right up my alley," Gina smiled, surveying the crowd. "Well, I'm sure Roger's finished his wide shots by now. I'm going to pull a few of the real oddballs here out for a little chat so I can wrap up my story. I think I'll start with that guy over there, the one with the nose rings and dagger tattoos on his forearm."

"You're not staying for the main speaker?" Wynn looked at her askance.

"Wynn, darling," Gina touched his hand seductively. "Take a good look around. I already have my story."

"Yeah," he muttered, shaking his head. "And to think I did two years of post-grad work at MIT. Well, it's a paycheck."

"Look me up when I get to New York," she waved, smiling while he watched her sashay away.

"I'm married, Gina."

"Yes. There seems to be a lot of that going around," she purred before disappearing into the crowd.

For a moment Wynn stood silently, his gaze lingering on the vanishing, well-rounded form of Gina Lewin. "That," he grinned, half-grimacing, toward Felix, "is a very dangerous woman. Well, let's wrap up these shots and move closer to the stage. It looks like this thing is about to start."

***

A low buzz of excitement swept through the crowd as the rotund little priest in his black cassock and cleric's collar limped his way to the podium. Santos Machado looked out at the audience, his eyes distant and unfocused, until gradually the room quieted. A single light illuminated the podium, and he gripped the sides of the lectern. His demeanor began to change as a broad grin slowly worked its way across his face.

"Okay folks, are you ready for a sparkler?" he quipped in a voice that rang over the hotel's struggling PA system.

"Yes," came the reply, neither loud nor clear. Santos smiled and leaned forward impishly.

"Who came first in the human race?" he asked. Heads cocked in puzzled contemplation. There was no reply. "Adam," he chortled to surprised, polite laughter. The joke was neither funny nor appropriate, given the setting of the seminar, but it achieved its purpose. Those who had come to see a fundamentalist religious diatribe by a stodgy, stern, Protector of the Faith would leave disappointed. The audience focused on him attentively as Santos launched right into his talk.

"Many people wonder if there's such a thing as the Devil. Psychiatrists say it's only in the mind. Scientists and philosophers find the idea amusing. Theologians warn against a belief in mysticism and the supernatural. Let me tell you brothers and sisters. The Devil does exist. I've met him."

There were a few titters from a group of college students who had attended the conference on a lark, but for most in the room his statement had the desired effect. People sat up straight and listened with rigid intensity. To Santos, the Devil was not some metaphor or silly ancient contrivance to scare the ignorant, and frighten little children. Evil existed in the world apart from man's own doing, and it was the Devil and his minions who led this war against the faithful.

"The Devil is not what most people picture him to be. He's not some creature in red tights with horns. There's nothing funny about the Devil. In fact, he hates laughter, and that's one of my favorite weapons against him. The Devil is a spirit, a most powerful and intelligent spirit. But a vile and malicious spirit bent on destroying us all."

Most in the crowded room were transfixed, hanging on the plump cleric's every word. Santos' voice rose and fell with each point he made, the passion of his beliefs evident to all.

"When I said I've met him, I meant this quite literally. We exorcists have an insight here that isn't available to the psychiatrists and theologians. We actually encounter the Devil and his minions in their most fearsome form on earth — when they actually "possess" the soul and body of a human being. And we have the authority to make them reveal their secrets and plans. We are the scientists of the spiritual world because we have direct contact with what we're studying. We're not mere speculators like the philosophers. You may ask, does the Devil really exist, and what is he doing here in our world? The Book of Revelation says the Devil and his demons have been sent here on earth. Their final destination is an everlasting abyss in which they are frozen out of contact with anyone else. But until the Final Judgment they are allowed to stay here distracting themselves from their miserable state by drawing human persons down with them. Luke tells us when Jesus drove the demons out of the possessed man, he sent them into a herd of swine because 'they pleaded with him not to order them to depart to the abyss.' So they're here with us until the end of time. This is where they're 'kept for judgment.' And they're desperate. 'Woe to you, earth and sea,' says Revelation 12:12, 'for the Devil has come to you in great fury, for he knows he has but a short time.' In our own exorcisms we find that the demons initially act arrogant telling us we can't touch them. Then, as we start making progress, they get more desperate and violent — afraid of being sent to the dreadful abyss. They start calling us killers and torturers. They only leave their victims because, as they tell us, the exorcism itself becomes more painful than Hell."

In the back of the room a young, seventeen year old boy slipped inside and joined the audience. Skipping school to attend the event, he found a seat and settled in as inconspicuously as he could. Like the speaker on the podium, he was a walking contradiction; bright, engaging and personable, but a social recluse and poor student. Questions of philosophy and theology were his main interest, but where these subjects were addressed at all in high school, it was usually among the ill-informed social dropouts who gravitated toward the dark side of religious occultism. Miguel Guerrero knew that another unexcused absence from class would infuriate his parents, for whom education was the only true path out of the barrio. But somehow, he reasoned, his father would forgive this particular transgression, as he did nine years earlier, when a frightened eight year old child watched from the shadows while Santos Machado chased the Devil from his uncle Zacarias' soul.

"To those who think the Devil is an abstraction," Santos continued, "I say, 'beware'. The diabolic is all around us. Movies, the Internet, music, your local bookstore, they all purvey the most dangerous vehicles of the occult. Right in their school grounds, your children are introduced to séances, white magic, witchcraft, ouija boards, you name it. These aren't harmless pastimes. They're sugar-coated poison pills seducing you step by step into the clutches of an enemy that seeks your soul. I can't tell you how many of the poor possessed souls I've exorcised were first enticed by these instruments of the Devil. At one time, the occult was reserved for eccentric characters at the fringes of society. I'm afraid it's now part of the mainstream."

"What a crock!" cried a voice from the back.

The insult reverberated like a gunshot through the room, shocking everyone because of its incongruity and its suddenness. Several in the audience turned in their seats and glared at the heckler while Santos peered owlishly out at the young man in his twenties, looking back at everyone with a smirk.

"That 'devil made me do it' crap went out a long time ago," the man said sarcastically. Boos and hisses from those nearby only emboldened him to continue. "This is the twenty-first century, not the Middle Ages! We have science and technology to guide us, not your fairy tales. You can't fool me. You're just some right wing fundamentalist who wants to censor our movies and take away my MTV."

Small arguments began to break out among the crowd as others voiced their opposition or support. The young man, who looked like a graduate student in college, was now arguing with a woman in a pink blouse and skirt, as well as a straggly haired man in what some might describe as Satanic garb. Both challenged his assertion that the Devil didn't exist, but for entirely different reasons. A few rows away another argument ensued among several people, some of whom supported Santos, and others who thought Santos was merely a charlatan whose reputation as an exorcist hardly proved the existence of the Devil.

As bedlam threatened to overtake the assembly hall, Santos spoke into the microphone and tried to regain control of the room. "I know there are skeptics, those who believe that the Devil does not exist, or if he does, has no influence over our actions in this world. But I challenge those who believe this way to account for a little child suddenly having the strength of four men? Or speaking in exotic languages without knowing any before? Or showing encyclopedic knowledge without a formal education? Not all of this behavior can be explained as psychiatric disorders. Scientists study the behavior of the physical world. Philosophers apply human reason, and theologians interpret biblical passages. Exorcists offer a new window of knowledge that comes from direct experience of evil and personalities from below. The Devil does indeed exist, and has made his presence felt here in this world. And he will win the battle to bring down humanity with him, soul-by-soul, unless we recognize this fact and take action to stop him. You have questions now. I will be happy to address them."

The first person to rise was a distinguished looking man in his fifties. "Frankly speaking," he began in a measured, self-assured tone, "I agree with that young man over there. I found this talk to be more dangerous than any mystical threat you raised in your presentation, Father Santos. He put my sentiments quite well. Your obsession with the dark arts is an invitation to return to the dark ages."

There was a burst of applause that again produced shouts and counter-charges from several in the audience. The gray-haired man, emboldened by the strong reaction of those who supported his position, continued.

"I'm Dr. Solly Cooper, a psychiatrist and clinical psychologist specializing in dissociative identity disorder. You may know it by its common term, multiple personality disorder. What you call exorcism is simply a pre-scientific attempt to deal with this medical condition and other disorders of the nervous system including schizophrenia, and the famous Tourette syndrome.

"Dissociative identity disorder has many of the symptoms you priests call possession. One or more identities or personality states that are entirely distinct from each other take control of the patient's behavior and speech patterns. Patients also roll their eyes in strange ways and have apparent seizures. Bodily symptoms can include wounds suddenly appearing on the patient. These patients sometimes show extraordinary abilities such as apparently reading people's thoughts or causing observers to feel cold.

The main cause for this condition is usually severe childhood abuse.

"Then there is schizophrenia which causes delusions and catatonic behavior. These delusions include the idea that a demon is speaking through the patient and that religious objects will cause harm. Facial and other bodily contortions are common. Schizophrenia and other psychoses are caused by malfunctioning of the dopamine system in the brain. Bipolar disorders are the main cause of the apparent superhuman strength shown by some subjects. Tourette syndrome, caused by another brain malfunction, results in such behavior as shouting obscenities and can also be treated medically."

A number of people who had listened to Santos in apparent agreement now seemed riveted on his words as Cooper pressed his position.

"Without putting too fine a point to it, I will call exorcism what it is; quackery, but positively dangerous quackery. We all know about clergy child abuse. Exorcism is a far more insidious form of abuse. Many patients owe their conditions to abuse in their earliest years. They can only be helped with pharmacological treatment and counseling. The ritual of exorcism is very destructive for them. You're dealing with highly traumatized people who've been terribly abused. They're very vulnerable. When you confront them with an exorcist and his high pressure tactics, you re-awaken memories of childhood horror and create in their minds the idea that they're possessed by some evil external force." With a stern look he continued, "These patients need to be treated by competent doctors, not by self-appointed witch-hunters. It's obvious we need to update our current laws to stop this nonsense. That and a few lawsuits will put the exorcists out of business."

Several additional voices in the audience were raised in support. Dr. Cooper, sensing that a number of people were now with him, began to speak with even more passion. "Also, this business of Hell. Please! What kind of God would sentence the creatures he supposedly loves to an eternity of torture?"

The final remarks were met by sustained applause from a vocal minority scattered throughout the hall. Others shouted their objection to what they considered his blasphemous remarks only to be met by a fusillade of counter-protests, giving the television cameras a front-row view of the circus-like proceedings.

Santos, alone on the podium, watched the unfolding scene with barely concealed anger. It was all Miguel could do to stop himself from running up to the stage and hugging the poor priest to shield him from further ignominy. Finally Santos put his face close to the microphone. Those expecting a humbled, contrite response were startled by the intensity of his remarks.

"I didn't come here for a debate," he said indignantly, hardly able to form his words. "Our Lord said, 'Don't throw pearls to swine.'" There was a hush, and then a chorus of boos, but this only seemed to energize Santos. "I'm a witness. I have looked into the eyes of the possessed. I have seen the demonic. No, this is not some creation of the victim's psyche. There was another intelligence, another being, sometimes more than one, at work in the victim's soul tearing it apart. What the good doctor has failed to tell you is that modern medicine doesn't claim to explain or even understand major symptoms associated with possession. Certainly there are personality disorders that can be treated with drugs and counseling. But we must be reminded that there is no consensus among the specialists about the actual causes of dissociative identity disorder. Anyway, these or other brain disorders are not the issue. The subjects of exorcism exhibit such behavior as levitation, knowledge of languages to which they had no previous access, penetration into the thoughts of observers. No respectable scientific theory can explain how a person can be suspended in thin air because this defies known scientific law. No amount of changes to the brain can cause a person to levitate in the air. Neither is there any scientific explanation for children suddenly speaking in languages they've never heard before or reading the thoughts of the people around them. For that matter, there's no explanation for the measurable reduction in temperature observed during exorcisms. These are all hard data. To say that the data are associated with one physical malady or another is simply a higher form of superstition. You're simply slapping a label on these data and calling it X without any evidence for your assumption and no idea how the X got there."

Finally, his voice trembling with rage, Santos leaned forward and spoke slowly and deliberately. "Regarding your comment about Hell, I would only remind you that Hell is not a punishment from God, but a choice we make to separate ourselves from God because we have the freedom given us by God. Many of the demons we've exorcised tell us that Hell was created by them, not by God, and that they would rather be in Hell than not exist."

The challenge was met with cat-calls of derision and cheers of support as the once staid conference degenerated into a near brawl. A cadre of Santos' supporters had begun to encircle the stage, as much to seek his continued wisdom as to protect him against the small but aggressive surge of protesters who were growing more vocal by the minute.

Miguel headed toward the stage, not certain what he was going to do, but feeling that he must somehow physically join the debate, only to be blocked by a man shouting obscenities at Santos and calling him a fraud.

"You don't know what you're talking about!" Miguel spun the angry man around. Several inches taller and fifty pounds heavier, the startled man looked down at the seventeen year old boy, whose fists were clenched and face contorted in anger.

"Get out of my face, kid, before I bust you in the mouth!"

"Father Santos is a great man!" Miguel did not back away. "You take back your words!"

"Or you'll do what?" the man laughed.

A strong arm on Miguel's shoulder pulled him back before the young boy could act. Miguel now found himself staring at his father, who unknown to him, had also been in the audience.

"Papa, I—" Miguel began to explain, but Esteban Guerrero stopped him. He led the young boy into the outer hall, away from the chaos inside.

"I thought we talked about this, Miguel. We agreed you would stay in school and finish your studies."

"I … I came to see Father Santos," Miguel tried to explain.

"Yes, I know. Had you asked me, I would have allowed you to come here today," Esteban spoke in a low voice. "But once again you acted only on impulse."

"I'm sorry, papa," Miguel said, bowing his head.

"Your mother and I are worried about you, Miguel. Your teachers say that you are worthy of the tasks they give you, but your grades are falling. They say to me 'Esteban, is your son in a gang? Does he take drugs or do other bad things?' I say 'No, Miguel is a good boy, one who is blessed with great talent by God, but who has no interest in developing those skills. He has but one obsession' — the obsession that drove him here today."

"I'm sorry for the shame I have brought you, Papa," Miguel fought back tears.

Esteban let a small smile tug at the corner of his mouth, and he put his arm around his son's shoulder. "You have brought me no shame, Miguel. Only great pride and happiness that you are my son. Come now. I have a surprise for you."

Making their way to the rear of the hall, Esteban led his son to a room behind the stage. Opening the door the young boy was startled to see Santos, safely secreted away from the crowd, resting on a couch near a large basket of fruit. Dressed in a lime green paisley shirt and jet black pants, the chubby little man was savoring the taste of a fresh ripe pear when his eyes met Esteban and Miguel. Rising with difficulty from his crippled leg, he braced himself with his cane and threw open his remaining arm.

"Ah, little Miguel! How you have grown!" Santos chirped. "I thought I would see you tonight, but here your father arranges a wonderful surprise for me. Come!"

Miguel rushed forward and hugged the little man like a familiar, favorite uncle.

"Well, did you enjoy my talk?" Santos asked with a wide smile, stroking Miguel's head once the embrace finally ended.

"Those people, the ones who said those terrible things—" Miguel replied earnestly.

"Yes, well, nothing too uncommon, I'm afraid," Santos returned to his seat and began picking through the fruit basket for another treat.

"Things are always like this?" Miguel replied, confused.

"At times a little more boisterous," Santos laughed. "It is always difficult to open your mind to God's teachings when your heart is corrupted by the perversions of this world. Still, I will admit that lately the Devil seems to be gaining the upper hand. There is much work we need to do, you and I Miguel."

"I don't understand," Miguel said, glancing at his father.

"We haven't spoken about your offer yet, Santos," Esteban replied.

"Offer?" Miguel's eyes flashed. Santos, still seated, opened his arms and drew the boy closer.

"I'm getting old, Miguel. The years are beginning to take their toll, physically. I need someone who can tend to my needs, help me get around and take care of me, but who is also more than that. I need someone who will learn all that I can teach, and one day perhaps succeed me in my work. Your father and I have had many long discussions about this Miguel. I am here not just to speak at this conference. I am here for you, Miguel."

Speechless, Miguel's mind raced. He had hoped one day to follow Santos, to be his protégé. But these were the dreams of a seventeen-year-old boy. He could barely reconcile the words he was hearing with the reality that, for him, another year of high school still lay ahead.

"Your mother and I have talked about this, Miguel," Esteban said softly.

"We know that these past few years have been difficult for you, son. You keep to yourself. You miss school. You immerse yourself in a search for answers that we cannot provide. We have prayed to *la Virgen de Guadalupe* for her guidance, and she has led Father Santos once again to us. If you want, your mother and I will sign the papers to make you an adult in the eyes of the law. Then you will be free to follow Santos, and through him fulfill the destiny that God has clearly chosen for you."

"Papa," Miguel choked as he embraced his father lovingly. "I will always love you and Mama. I will never forget this gift you have given me."

"It may not be a gift," Santos interjected seriously. "Together we must face the unholy powers of darkness that seek to possess the souls of all men, including ourselves. I need someone like you Miguel, strong of will and strong of body. But even your absolute faith in the Lord is no guarantee that the Devil will not find a way to steal your soul."

"I am ready to join you, Father," Miguel said earnestly.

"You must call me Santos," the little man chuckled. "After all, we are going to be spending a great deal of time together." Slapping his hands on his knees, he started to rise, this time with Miguel's assistance. "Now, Esteban, let us share the good news with Marisol. We must give Miguel an opportunity to pack his things, and say goodbye to his mother. Besides," he winked. "It's been too many years since I've sat down to supper with your family. I'm looking forward to another wonderful meal from your wife."

New York

"Mr. Hastings will see you now," the attractive young woman said, sitting at a desk outside the office of Ralston Hastings.

Wynn Colgate rose from his chair and walked toward a pair of ornately carved doors. A portrait of a grey haired, middle aged man graced one wall, imposing in both its size and extraordinary attention to detail. Like some grand, Old Master's painting, it showed a handsome, confident, but deeply lonely man standing amidst the trappings of his wealth. Orphaned at age eleven when a traffic accident took the lives of both his parents, Ralston Hastings inherited a real estate company built by his father; turning it several decades later into one of the most formidable communication empires on the planet. Diversifying into radio, television, newspapers, and the Internet, he used his Harvard MBA training to assemble a conglomerate of companies unrivaled in human history.

Information and opinions were shaped and controlled worldwide by Hastings Communications. Surviving numerous regulatory challenges to his near monopolistic power, he seemed impervious to attempts to limit his global dominance. Rumored to have secretly bankrolled the candidacy of at least two U.S. presidents, and extending his reach to overseas governments as well, he was irrefutably the most influential individual in the world. And yet, for all his wealth and power, there was a deep sadness manifest in his eyes that even the most skilled artist could not erase. Never married, without children or an extended family, he seemed driven only by his work, and a desire to exercise control over as many lives as possible.

Entering the room, Wynn saw Hastings standing at the corner window, looking out over an imposing view of Manhattan from the top floor of his massive office building. There was no acknowledgment of Wynn's presence while he closed the distance between them.

"Mr. Hastings, Sir," Wynn found his mouth suddenly dry. "You asked to see me?"

"Tell me what you saw in Dallas?" Hastings replied, his gaze still directed elsewhere.

"We're assembling the final piece right now, Sir. Should I have production send you the rough cut, or do you want to wait until—"

"I've killed the story," Hastings turned, fixing Wynn with a deep, penetrating stare that gave no insight to his innermost thoughts.

"Er, killed it, Sir? I-I don't understand."

"I'm not interested in publicizing the rantings of a lunatic fringe, not on my network."

"But, you sent me there Mr. Hastings, personally. Didn't you? I got a message from your secretary—"

"I want your assessment of Santos Machado," Hastings interrupted, his voice still devoid of emotion. "I like to keep track of these religious zealots from time-to-time, see what they're up to. This Machado fellow has something of a reputation following that business in Caracas last year where he supposedly performed a public exorcism. He fooled a lot of people with his act. Tell me what you thought of him, and his message."

"Well," Wynn began slowly, unsure how to reply. "He's an odd little man, but not without a certain charisma, if that's the right word. You could see that many of the people looked on him as a figure of some importance. And it wasn't just the Mexican community, though that seemed to be his greatest base of support from what I could tell. My cameraman gave me a real earful on the way back to the airport. He said Machado is like a cult figure in certain circles of the deeply religious, and maybe even beyond. I can attest to some of that. Discounting the weirdoes that always seem to gravitate toward things like this, I saw several executive types at the conference hanging on to his every word. In fact, he seemed to be hitting a receptive note with the crowd until some college professor challenged him and all hell broke loose."

"So when challenged, the audience rejected his message?" Hastings asked, almost as if making a statement.

"Well, not exactly. There were a number of people there who didn't buy into his 'the Devil is going to get you' speech. But I'd say a lot of them came for a fight, more than to hear what this Machado fellow had to say. A couple of opinions might have been swayed, but mostly the attacks brought out his vocal supporters. A few of them hustled him off to the back someplace when things turned really ugly. But no, to answer your question, a lot of people left persuaded that he was some kind of hero taking on the Devil. Not many minds were really changed, as far as I could tell."

Hastings walked over to his desk and sat in the large, overstuffed chair. Wynn wasn't sure whether to leave or stay while he brought up a new screen on his computer, and began to study it intently.

"If that's all, Sir," he mumbled, not sure how to complete his sentence.

"One more thing," Hastings said, his eyes still focused on the computer. "What did you think of Santos Machado's warning? Do you believe the 'Devil' is growing stronger with each passing day, and that we must fight him vigilantly?"

"Me, personally?" Wynn shrugged, pondering the question. "I'm a man of science, Mr. Hastings. The devil has no place in my world."

"Nor does it in mine," Hastings looked at him and smiled for the first time. "Thank you for your excellent report, Wynn. I'm sorry to have wasted your time, but I wanted a scientist to report on that charlatan, for exactly the reason you stated. If he had something useful to contribute to humanity, I would have aired your report. But as it was, I think we'll just leave this one on the cutting room floor."

"I understand entirely," Wynn fawned shamelessly.

"Now if you'll excuse me."

"Oh, certainly Sir!" Wynn backed away, retreating toward the door. Once he left Hastings' face again hardened. He tapped a silent buzzer on his desk, and a few seconds later Vincent Stout, a tall, distinguished looking man in a dark blue, suit entered the room.

"You wanted to see me Sir?" Stout asked.

"Yes. See that professor Cooper gets his research grant. Full funding. And take care of the others in the usual way."

"Yes Sir. And the Filipino priest?"

"He's no one of consequence. Just another misguided follower of Raphael Aurelio and his Holy Cross exorcists."

"Yes Sir," Stout nodded.

Hastings relaxed in his chair a bit, lighting up a cigar and savoring the taste of the fine illegal Havana Bolivar.

"So tell me Vincent, what have you found out?"

"We're still completing our backgrounder, Sir, but it's like you thought. This fellow Shaitana you wanted further information on is a complete whack-job. He thinks he's got supernatural or mystical powers, or at least a straight line to the demons and bogeymen on the 'other side'. But it plays right into the superstitions of his followers, and he uses it to great effect, I'll give him that. In three years he's built a strong base of support in the Orient, and now he's making some decent inroads in the West, mostly on the backs of traditional religious institutions. A number of churches, mosques, and temples have been ceded over to his 'Lumen Covenant'. People are looking for answers in troubled times, and he's supplying them. There's even a movement in San Francisco to declare Shaitaanism the city's official religion, if you can imagine that. With the help of Hastings Communications he could become a significant player on the world scene — if his enemies don't get him first."

"Can he be controlled?"

"He's charismatic, ruthless, and very politically savvy. He's got at least ten million followers so far, and that's just a conservative estimate. But he doesn't have the legitimacy he needs to go beyond being an interesting footnote in history. It's one thing to get the people of San Francisco on your side. It's quite another to do the same thing in Iowa, or London, or Madrid. These people aren't going to abandon centuries of religious tradition to flock to a Lumen Covenant or 'new ecumenical church', or whatever he calls it, just because the world's in a mess. They'll still seek refuge in their old rituals and customs. I'm convinced that Shaitana will remain an interesting, but ultimately non-influential side show unless you can bring him into the mainstream. The fact is, he's already become a victim of his own success. He's not only despised by traditional religious leaders, but some governments and certain paramilitary forces feel threatened by him too. His enemies are sharpening their knives, and it's only a matter of time before he shakes hands with Jim Jones, David Koresh, or any of the other religious megalomaniacs who also became a threat to the powers that be. Without Hastings Communications to legitimize and protect him, he won't last another year. That's how he'll be controlled, Sir. The more visible he becomes, the more vulnerable he is."

"Yes, I agree," Hastings took another draw on his cigar. "As much as I hate dealing with these religious fanatics, I must admit he's got a novel twist on an old con. Instead of sitting on the throne of St. Peter as God's chosen representative on Earth, or taking instructions from some burning bush, or carrying out the will of God by blowing up school busses full of children, he's trying to tone down these irrational beliefs in a God who constantly interferes in our world. I've seen enough of him to know that he wants to keep God out of our lives, which is fine by me. At least I can support that. I'll indulge his fantasies about all this supernatural garbage, Vincent. But only as a means to my own end. As soon as I have what I need, I'll cut him loose like a bad check."

"Yes Sir. Will there be anything else, then, Mr. Hastings?"

"Have my plane fueled and ready for departure first thing tomorrow morning. I'll be traveling to Washington for a private meeting with some of our friends, then to Nepal to meet with Shaitana. I want no record of either of these trips."

"I understand perfectly, Sir."

With an unctuous bow, Stout left the room. Hastings leaned back in his chair, setting his cigar aside and interlocking his fingers behind his head, and swiveled to watch the setting sun dip below the tops of the nearby skyscrapers.

Chapter 3

Kathmandu five years later

Tiny orbs of light descended from all directions while a shimmering haze enveloped the room. The strong aroma of in cense filled the air. The buzzing hum of low, rhythmic chants, falling and rising to a cadence of their own, echoed off the finely carved contours of the old Buddhist temple.

Flanked by two heavily muscled men, Ralston Hastings watched as the chants of a dark-cloaked figure at the center of the room reached a crescendo. "Asmodeus, I invoke your presence at this assembly of your faithful. Zebulun, I beseech you to enter our midst. Meridian, I implore you to visit us."

The sudden appearance of three luminous figures forced an audible gasp from Axel Olsson, Secretary-General of the United Nations. Squatting awkwardly in the lotus position, he looked at his colleagues Jacques Arnaud, President of the European Union, who was gaping in disbelief, and Colin Brown, Managing Director of the International Monetary Fund, who struggled to maintain his unflappable demeanor.

Their host, His Holiness Lord Shaitana, resplendent in black robes that matched his dark hair and impeccable goatee, abruptly stopped his invocations. Shaitana's eyes were unmistakable; greenish and snake-like, they seemed to read the soul. He stood to address his guests.

"What you are witnessing here, my friends, is the beginning of a new era. The forces of light will prevail over darkness, enlightenment over obscurity. I present to you the Lumen Covenant."

The three, shimmering globes began to coalesce, taking human shapes, their features not yet discernable.

"Modern science tells us that we are all condensed beams of light. In the beginning, there was nothing but photons created at the moment the universe began. Everything and everyone around us is simply a manifestation of this primordial light. Today, for the first time in the history of our race, the Masters of Light have come to help us fulfill our destiny, to enter the photon-belt of the higher spirits. I invite each one of you to invoke and accept as your Guide the Master who has selected you as his own. Together we enter into the Lumen Covenant."

The three amorphous, luminous beings came closer to each of the guests. Shaitana took Olsson by both hands and brought him toward one of them.

"Axel, repeat these words after me. 'I, Axel Olsson, invoke the great Master Asmodeus and accept him as my Guide.'"

Nervously at first, but then with sudden vigor, Olsson repeated the formula. Instantly the radiant, ghost-like figure next to him vanished. Olsson seemed to glow for a moment, then sat down, his head bowed in silent meditation.

With Shaitana's help Arnaud then Brown performed the same ritual. A calm, almost passive demeanor took hold of them too. Contemplative, their eyes closed and palms extended upward, they formed a tight circle, seeming to draw energy from each other's presence.

Approaching Hastings, Shaitana kept his hands hidden in the large, bilious folds of his jet black robe. The middle-aged man in a tailored western suit motioned to his bodyguards, who backed away a respectful distance

"The power of the human mind, when magnified and focused, can achieve unimaginable feats," Shaitana let his gaze drift back to the tight circle of quietly chanting men.

"How long until you're ready to act?"

"Soon. Everything is coming together, just as the prophecies foretold."

"Not good enough," Hastings replied, a sharp measure of irritation creeping into his voice. "I don't give a rat's rear end about your so-called prophecies. I've been funding your Covenant foundation for five years. I expected a return on my investment long before now. Parlor tricks and magic acts aren't a substitute for results. My patience is being tested, Shaitana."

Shaitana let his eyes play over Hastings' face. "Like most Westerners, your concept of 'time' is measured in minutes, hours, days, and months," he responded calmly. "These are but fleeting markers in the span of eternity. Like all matters of importance, the universe will unfold according to its own demands. We are but humble passengers whose deeds can affect the flow of history, but only within carefully prescribed limits."

"I'm not interested in a philosophy lesson," Hastings reacted. "I've subsidized your expansion from Nepal to Paris, and then to the farthest corners of the world. I've built you an international following through every media outlet I control, and directed the coverage of many that I don't through bribery and intimidation. I've brought you three of the most powerful men in government and industry. I positioned you to take the next step, and I expect you to do it now. There will be no more delays."

"To possess the soul, completely and without recourse," replied Shaitana, "the subjects must become hardened against the call to cast off the spirits who exercise this dominion. Even though they have given their souls willingly in exchange for the increasing wealth and power that will now accrue, we must cement this union through the celebration of a Black Mass. What you have witnessed today is only the first step. As the bond becomes stronger, so too will the energy that flows from this communion."

"I'm not interested in waiting," Hastings reacted angrily. "You forget, Shaitana. When I found you, you weren't a prophet, or the leader of a new religion. You were Sukoomar Thyssen, the bastard son of a seventeen year old servant girl whose own father wouldn't even acknowledge your birth. I know what you did to claw your way out of the cesspool you grew up in, and I know what you've done to hold on to every shred of power you managed to accumulate. You built a following that took you out of the mud shack your mother raised you in, but we both know that without my help you'd still be living in some obscure corner of this remote, godforsaken land, ruling over a kingdom of sheep herders and peasant farmers."

"You insult me once too often," Shaitana said, controlling his rage.

"Save the melodramatics," Hastings dismissed him with a wave. "I made you, and I own you. With my control of the media, I can bury you with a single broadcast. Perhaps you're forgetting that even with your devoted followers, you have more enemies than friends. Christians hate you for perverting their Mass with satanic offerings. The Buddhists and Hindus fear you for co-opting their followers and carving out an empire in the heart of their own base of power. The Jews think you're collaborating with the Muslims to stir up tensions in the Middle East, and the jihadists want you dead, like everyone else who isn't a 'true believer'". "If I withdraw my support, everything you've built, everything you desire but haven't yet achieved, collapses in the blink of an eye."

"Forgive me for my impertinence," Shaitana oozed with false sincerity. "I meant no offense to the generosity you have shown me, and I freely acknowledge the debt in which I am held."

Hastings watched the proud man bow slightly. He let a small smile tug at the corner of his lips.

"There's not much difference between us, Shaitana. God — or the Devil — has nothing to do with our success. We're both where we are today because we're willing to do what it takes to reach the top. That's why I agreed to bankroll your Lumen Covenant, and that's why I'm here today, to collect on that investment. Now I ask you again, how much longer will I have to wait?"

"The Black Mass will complete the transfer you witnessed today. After that, only one group still stands in the way of our success. Once they have been eliminated, nothing will stop you from having everything you want. You saw, with your own eyes, the power that can be summoned from beyond."

"There is no Devil," Hastings said somewhat dismissively. "Only men with weak minds who the strong control, just like you did with that little hocus pocus of yours. With twenty thousand dollars and the right special effects equipment, I could have made any god you want appear. I understand the power of suggestion. If people want to believe you have supernatural powers so they'll accept your authority, I'm willing to bankroll it. But don't ever confuse me with these sheep. I intend to leave humanity with the greatest gift any man has ever bestowed, the complete and total elimination of all fundamentalist doctrine. Once we substitute science and reason for ignorance and superstition, we can rid ourselves of the wretched excesses religion has brought to all of us. Marx tried it once and failed miserably, because he never understood that God must have his place in this world. We can't totally eliminate religion, but we can ecumenicalize it, and in doing so rid the world of its excesses. When the people understand that God owes his existence to man, and not man to God, we'll reach a new level of human development unmatched in history. That is the legacy I intend to leave."

Shaitana listened respectfully while Hastings continued his rant, his face never revealing his thoughts. Like most men who professed an unwavering belief in their own abilities, Hastings could not hope to understand that material wealth and power were but transient elements in the spiritual ebb and flow that truly controlled our lives. The universe was essentially a struggle between two opposing forces, the Force of Power and the Force of Love. The Force of Power was Lucifer. As Shaitana saw it, humanity was created to worship at the altar of Lucifer, serving his every need and command. Like drones in a hive, humans had no purpose other than to serve their Master. Certain individuals, like Shaitana, would be granted a higher place in this realm, and it was only this status to which one could aspire to distinguish himself from others through all eternity.

Opposing Lucifer was the Force of Love, what the People of the Book called *God.* These who followed God and his teachings believed that he had given them free will. Through the exercise of this gift every person would choose a different eternity. Surrendering to base human greed, the thirst for power for its own sake, or to any of the other deadly sins prohibited by most religions was a human choice, and therefore a response to the divine offer of love. Because of free will, in the war between Good and Evil, the fewer the restraints that held evil at bay the more fertile the conditions for succumbing to temptation, and thus losing one's immortal soul.

In the great conflict between the two Forces, Shaitana had chosen his side. He would rule over the liberated and the empowered as an agent of Lucifer, rather than strive for spiritual perfection as a slave in the realm of the meek and the weak. Hastings, who believed that both God and the Devil were solely and simply creations of the intellect, cared little about the afterlife. The only thing that mattered to him was the here and now — to increase his power over others in a demonstrable, tangible way.

Together they made the perfect, deadly instrument, each using the other for his own purpose; neither concerned, ultimately, for anyone but himself.

"Your Holiness," a bespeckled, shaven-head acolyte interrupted. "We are ready to proceed with the Black Mass."

"Very well," Shaitana nodded.

Hastings motioned to his bodyguards, who again drew closer. "Finish your ceremony," he said to Shaitana. "I have a board meeting in Zurich. Now tell me, when will you be ready to begin?"

"Seven months, in June. The last obstacles will be removed by then."

"Seven months," Hastings repeated, then turned and left.

***

An ornate Christian chapel, hidden deep in the recesses of the old Buddhist temple, was lit by a harrow of dimly burning candles. The sweet scent of incense wafted through the air, emanating from a gently swaying censer. The altar, forged from a single block of stone, was carved with ancient Latin inscriptions surrounding the distinctively-shaped cross of the early Roman church. Resplendent with fine linens upon which an ambo and lectionary rested for the readings for the Mass, it was framed at the center by a brilliant gold ciborium, a sacred vessel shaped like a chalice with a fitted metal cover surmounted by a Cross. Covered by a finely spun veil, an ancient sign of divinity, it held a single consecrated host, stolen from a Church in the remote Italian village of Belvedere Marittimo.

"Your Holiness," Rykaard Cardinal Hindriks bowed once Shaitana entered the chapel. A Dutch prelate who was the titular Archbishop of Arzignano, Hindriks was a student and ardent defender of the famous theologian Piet Schoonenberg who had rejected the key Catholic dogma that Jesus Christ was literally a Divine Person and by extension the Redeemer of Humanity. For this Hindriks was formally censured by Rome. He responded to the rebuke with a fierce denunciation of papal authority and arrogance coupled with an open challenge to the underlying foundations of Christianity. He went so far as to question the very existence of a benevolent, loving God. For his heretical pronouncements he was excommunicated from the Church of St. Peter and went into a self-imposed exile. Reemerging as the self-appointed leader of the new Catholic Ecumenical Church, Hindriks found an ally in Shaitana, who through Hastings protected his new church and helped it to grow as another bulwark in the fight against fundamentalist religious dogma.

Although skeptical about the supernatural, Hindriks was entranced enough by Shaitana's vision of an earthly utopia, and embittered over what he considered Rome's unfair and imperious treatment, to be particularly receptive to any opportunity to wreak vengeance on the Vatican. Bargaining away his own destiny as part of this calculation mattered little to a man for whom the quest for redemption had been replaced by an obsession with spiritual and temporal power. What Hindriks no longer found in formal religion, he embraced with vigor as an acolyte of the one man he believed would usher in a new era of human development, free from the shackles of Rome's theocratic repression.

All eyes were fixed on Shaitana as he strode to the altar, taking his place next to Hindriks who was cloaked in a red Cardinal's robe. Hindriks was now ready to perform the final act of sacrilege against the Church that he once helped lead. He would conduct a Black Mass to mark the beginning of Shaitana's ascent to total power.

"The hour has come," Shaitana raised his hand and spoke to dozens of men and women seated in the pews, Axel Olsson, Jacques Arnaud, and Colin Brown among them. "We celebrate the Rites of the Black Mass. Through it we reject the tired, misguided falsehoods perpetuated by corrupt men who claim to speak with the authority of God. We respond instead to a higher mandate, to liberate ourselves from the guilt and tyranny of religious oppression. To do this, we must look within ourselves and discover our own divinity. We do not blaspheme; we affirm. Join with me, my brothers and sisters, in ushering in a new age of human enlightenment the world no longer hangs on to the false hope of religion, but thrives in humanity's own grasp of the universe that we alone have created."

A bell tolled and the celebrants stood. Whatever doubts, whatever misgivings Rykaard Cardinal Hindriks may have had in surrendering the last vestiges of his faith did not show upon his face while he crossed the threshold, and committed himself to the Forces of Darkness in perpetuity.

"Belial, Leviathan," Hindriks intoned from the altar. "Awaken from your sleep. Enter this hallowed chamber and liberate us from the pious hypocrites who have subjected us to their cruel subjugation." Lifting a chalice, he drank the dark, sweet wine while bells tolled. "Join with me now, and with the apostates who assemble here in witness to your powers, as we prostrate ourselves before the mighty and ineffable Prince of Darkness. Repeat now with me, 'In the company of all the demons of the pit, I do hereby proclaim that Satan Lucifer rules the earthly domain. I promise to honor and respect him throughout life, without reservation, desiring in return his manifold assistance in fulfilling my desires and enflaming my passion for vital existence.'"

Sliding back the ciborium veil, Hindriks lifted the single, consecrated host, and broke off a small corner. Shaitana now knelt at the communion rail, waiting to receive the Body of Christ. With it he would begin a process that would gird him with the highest level of occult energy; enough to render him impervious to any physical attack, and ward off the remaining spiritual defenses erected by his enemies.

"O Mighty Lord of Darkness," Hindriks voice rose. "Come forth from Thy Great Kingdom! Honor us with you presence, and look auspiciously upon this sacrifice."

Hindriks held the wafer fragment to Shaitana's lips, who received it on his tongue as his final act of defiance against a faith he both respected and feared. The remainder of the host was desecrated in an earthen bowl filled with polluted soil.

"I reject the false teachings of the prophet, and defile the transubstantiated Eucharist. O Dark Lord, through this act I pronounce to all that I am Thy Faithful Child. Deliver me Lucifer, Lord of Light, bringer of enlightenment, from all past error and delusion. With the fires of Hell purify the void of my mind. For I walk upon the left hand path and have vowed myself to thy service."

The assembled began to chant, their voices cold and terrifying. "Hail Satan, Hail Lucifer, who liberates me in mind and heart!"

Shaitana opened his arms, blessing his followers who reveled in his presence. His coronation was now complete. Enthroned by a Prince of the Church — who, though excommunicated, still retained his episcopal and priestly faculties — as Lord of the World in the same way that generations of kings were crowned by popes heads of the Holy Roman Empire, all that remained was to take possession of his Scepter, the lance that pierced the side of Christ.

Hindriks bowed respectfully to his new Master and offered the spear of the centurion Longinus, a relic that was personally removed by Adolf Hitler from the treasure-house of the Hofburg, the ancient palace of the Hapsburg emperors in Vienna. As an occultist, Hitler believed that possession of the lance would enhance his power and protect him from his enemies. When the allied armies liberated Germany, the lance was secreted away by the Thule Society, members of Hitler's innermost circle who were steeped in the practice of Satanic ritual. Eventually the whereabouts of the lance came to Shaitana's attention, who with the help of Ralston Hastings acquired the artifact.

Now, only one last obstacle stood in his way, the seven 'divine remedies' or 'Secrets', the existence of which had been revealed to Shaitana by the Prince of Darkness himself. These Secrets, if discovered and implemented, would negate the elevated power of Lucifer, and render powerless those who acted at his behest. Only one institution was capable of deploying them. Although weakened from a combination of external assaults, internal dissent, and the decadence of many priests and bishops obsessed with power and money, Shaitana still feared the Roman Church. It was, after all, the Church of Peter, the Rock upon which Christ had bestowed his blessing blessing and about which he had prophesied "the gates of hell will not overcome it."

But now that he was enthroned through the Black Mass, Shaitana would take care of this problem too by invoking powerful demons to destroy the pope while crippling the work of groups like Opus Dei and, most important, decimating their deadly wards, the small cadre of exorcists.

But first he needed to gather them all in Kathmandu.

Rome five months later

Giovanni Battista Grippaldi came from a privileged family that lost much of its wealth by the sixteenth century. Through a combination of poor business investments, political intrigue, and a general incompetence borne of the expectation of continuing wealth without the corresponding hard work to secure it, his ancestors had managed to squander away one of the largest private fortunes in Tuscany. Arranged marriages and shady financial dealings helped maintain a comfortable lifestyle for the descendants of the Grippaldi family for the next three hundred years, but eventually that too passed. By the dawn of the twentieth century, the Grippaldis were nothing more than a family of struggling middle class merchants barely able to maintain any kind of social standing. It was a bitterly resented decline for some of their clan who longed for the halcyon days of their ancestors, now more myth than reality, but it was still a compelling image for young Giovanni Battista Grippaldi, born in the aftermath of World War II, for whom the re-acquisition of his family's former prominence was a paramount goal.

By happenstance or luck, where others in his family chose careers in business to make their fortune, or simply went about life raising a family and children with no pretense of social standing, Giovanni Battista Grippaldi entered the service of the Church. Not as a priest, for a life of celibacy and sacrifice was not what he desired, but as a member of the Curia, the Vatican's civil service. It was here he hoped to substitute great power for a lack of wealth, and in so doing apply a salve to the open wound that had brought him so much unhappiness.

Working his way through the Vatican's councils and tribunals, its agencies and commissions, he eventually rose to a position of great prominence within the Curia. It was here that he found himself able to influence the decisions of the various Cardinals who protected their favorites, particularly those skilled enough to navigate the complex structure, overlapping jurisdictions, and Byzantine procedures of the policy making body. It was also here that an emissary from an unknown party, purporting to represent the interests of "true Catholics" horrified by the harmful, superstitious practices of a fringe group of exorcists, offered this embittered old man an opportunity to correct a great wrong — and embellish his own financial account at the same time.

Giovanni Battista Grippaldi accepted the financial inducement not as a bribe, but as a reward for his loyal service in the interests of the Church. Power, he had come to discover, without the accompaniment of great wealth, was of little comfort to a man with great ambitions. Inside the Leonine walls that surrounded the Vatican, he made good on his word and convinced his superiors to sever ties with the exorcists who had brought so much ridicule upon their noble institution. The exorcists were formally notified that they were no longer permitted to meet in Rome. Feigning sympathy, Grippaldi notified them that an anonymous donor had, however, furnished the resources required for them to meet in Kathmandu, Nepal.

Now that he had managed to accomplish this task, Grippaldi's next mission was to go after Opus Dei itself, the sanctum sanctorum of the traditionalists the protector of the practitioners of this ancient superstitious art. But that would be another time — and would require many additional payments — for doing God's work as Giovanni Battista Grippaldi saw it.

Rome two weeks later

The papal secretary ushered the aged nun into the audience hall. She knelt at the Holy Father's feet and, somewhat impatiently, kissed his jewel encrusted ring.

"The time has come," she announced to the pope in her usual raspy voice, clearly in no mood for pleasantries. "You must ready yourself to fulfill the vision."

Pope Gregory XVI turned pale. "But the hundred years are over. The prophecies have not come to pass."

"No," said the feisty nun, her sharp eyes never wavering from the ailing pontiff's face. "When the St. Michael prayer was removed from the liturgy, the clock stopped. Since then the Satanic forces have multiplied in power and number. And now they're poised to strike."

Strangely, Gregory found both comfort and fear in her divination, confirming what he already knew deep in his heart, but had never voiced. Philomena was talking about the famous vision of Pope Leo XIII. After celebrating Mass in 1884 he fell into a trance, and heard a conversation between Christ and Satan.

"I can destroy your Church," Satan boasted to Christ

"You can?" came the soft reply. "Then go ahead and do so."

"To do so, I need more time and more power," the Devil replied.

"How much time? How much power?"

"One hundred years, and a greater power over those who will give themselves to my service."

"You have the time, you will have the power," Christ replied. "Do with them what you will."

It was following this vision that Pope Leo XII composed a special prayer that he decreed was to be recited after every Mass. *St. Michael the Archangel, defend us in battle. Be our protection against the wickedness and snares of the devil. May God rebuke him, we humbly pray, and do thou O prince of the Heavenly Host, by the Power of God, cast into hell Satan and all the evil spirits who prowl about the world seeking the ruin of souls.*

But in 1964, in the reforms following the Second Vatican Council, Church authorities struck this prayer from the liturgy. And in 1984, when the hundred years had indeed passed, the unholy threat had not lessened — quite the opposite in fact. The obstacles to the Church's mission seemed only to have increased in the decades that followed. Never more so than today, Gregory thought to himself. Everywhere he turned there was trouble. The United Nations had suddenly and without explanation terminated the Vatican's observer status, and withdrawn its recognition of the city-state as a sovereign entity. The European Union too was moving to eliminate the special privileges of the Vatican while shutting off its access to its financial resources. And the IMF was funding organizations dedicated to fighting the Church's moral and social teachings.

Worst of all, a powerful group of cardinals had publicly declared their sharp dissent from the pope's teachings. There were even rumors of an impending palace coup to force Pope Gregory XVI into retirement, unheard of in the modern Catholic era.

If it was anyone other than Mother Philomena who brought the warning of Pope Leo's vision, Gregory would have shrugged off this odd comment as one among the hundreds of unsolicited requests, demands, and suggestions directed to him on a regular basis. But Mother Philomena was not just a crusty old nun, although she was that. She was a great mystic revered by millions of the faithful. Although her critics called her "the female Jonah", no one disputed the remarkable match between her many dire warnings and the events that followed right after

As if to add to this chronicle of woe, Mother Philomena affirmed that the Holy Father was indeed a target of the Dark Forces. "There's a concerted, premeditated effort to destroy you," she warned, "not just materially but spiritually. Black masses, spells, curses, hexes. Everything is being brought to bear against you."

"Do you have only doom and gloom Mother?" Gregory sagged visibly. "No silver linings anywhere?"

"Holy Father, I suffer for you every day, as does my entire congregation. But I can only tell you what is shown to me, not what I want it to be." She paused for a moment, then continued. "There is one thing you could do that might slow things down. You could re-institute the St. Michael prayer after Mass."

The pope sadly shrugged his shoulders. "Mother, you know as well as I that this is impossible," he said, his voice weak. "Even my predecessor, who encouraged Raphael Aurelio to keep his army of exorcists intact in their battle against the demon in all his frightening forms, did not dare to support him publicly. There are too many prelates of the Church who fear Aurelio's power, and seek to suppress him and his fellow exorcists. Should I turn against these prelates and make the St. Michael's prayer mandatory, I too would lose what little support I still possess among the College of Cardinals. These are troubled times, dear Mother, unlike any we have faced before. I fear the words of Paul VI have come home to roost. 'The smoke of Satan has entered by some crack into the temple of God.'"

"Then I'm afraid things will just get worse," Mother Philomena said. "I can only suggest that you pray to our Father in Heaven for help. I know that he will respond, but if you don't cooperate with the response you receive, then—"

The nun was too overcome with emotion to continue. She turned and left the cavernous hall, leaving the frail pope alone to pray in silence.

Chapter 4

New Delhi one week later

The clatter of a dozen overlapping languages echoed through out Terminal II at Indira Gandhi International Airport as long queues of passengers waited in line under the ever watchful eye of airport security. Working his way slowly toward the ticket counter, Miguel craned to catch a glimpse of Santos, wearing red pants and a knitted green shirt, who was scurrying about the large, cavernous area. Even though they had been traveling together for almost six years, Miguel was only now starting to fully understand the peculiar habits and rampant idiosyncrasies that defined the enigmatic little man, one of which was to disappear in a snap when something of interest caught his eye, or in this case, to wander about in a distraught state at a sudden, unexpected, change in plans. Like an old dog tethered to an invisible chain, Santos would always show up at the proper moment — sometimes with only moments to spare, but always in the nick of time.

Today would be no different, Miguel thought. Still, in his particular state of mind, it would be better to have him nearby than off somewhere causing a ruckus. For all of Santos' selfless and endearing qualities, suffering in silence was certainly not one of them. Any change of any kind was always a cause for excessive angst for the quirky little priest, who saw life as an orderly progression with proper places for proper things. Actions were preceded by an ingrained respect for customs and traditions, which themselves were outgrowths of the faith and morals handed down from generation to generation through the inspired Word of God. Everything had a place, and there was a place for every thing. The only chaos permitted in Santos' world was that which he himself intentionally caused, mostly in an effort to confuse the Devil or his minions so that truth and justice could eventually triumph, restoring the expected order of things. But this change was by far the most troubling for Santos that Miguel had ever seen. It wasn't simply that the Congress had been moved to a different location, at the last minute no less. There was something deeper, something more troubling in the way Santos perceived this new state of affairs. Miguel could only hope that the short flight to Kathmandu, followed by a good night's rest once they landed, might put him in a better mood. It was a hope he often had that normally went unrealized. Nevertheless, Miguel held out the possibility that this time things would be different.

Or at least less frenetic.

Reaching the ticket counter, Miguel allowed his attention to return to the immediate task at hand. He gave the young female agent his travel packet who processed them with practiced efficiency, then handed the passports and vouchers back to Miguel. Her large, exotic eyes caught his for a moment, and he returned her gaze with equal interest. The thin, gangly frame of his youth had been replaced with a tall, muscular body, honed through years of travel with Santos as student, friend, and caretaker. Now a handsome, strapping young man in his early twenties, Miguel's striking physical features were matched by a kind, gentle nature that complemented and enhanced his personal appeal. Most people he met took an immediate liking to him, drawn by both his good looks and easy manner; qualities in himself about which Miguel seemed completely oblivious, further adding to his charm.

"Will you be returning to New Delhi soon?" she asked, trying not to sound too forward.

"I'm, er, not sure," he mumbled. The ticket agent smiled pleasantly while Miguel fumbled for a spare pocket, his clumsy manner endearing him even more. Finally he managed to place the tickets in an open flap pouch on his knapsack, and heft the heavy bag over his shoulder. "We don't really know where we'll be till we end up there."

"It sounds quite exciting."

"It can be," Miguel returned her smile.

"Rohini."

"What?"

"My name, it's Rohini."

"Oh!" he blushed. "I'm, er, Miguel."

"Yes, I know." Miguel looked at her, confused. "It was on your ticket."

"Oh yeah, right."

Buckling the last strap on his knapsack to brace it against his chest, Miguel lingered at the counter, uncertain what to say or do. Unfortunately, Santos' frenetic schedule had left little time for Miguel to develop relationships with the opposite sex, or with anyone outside the narrow circle of fellow exorcists with whom Santos had remained in regular contact. The celibate, at times cloistered life of a priest suited Santos well, but for a young man in his early twenties, it proved challenging at times. Never remaining in one place long enough to establish any outside relationships, surrounded by a world of middle aged and older men, there were occasions when Miguel doubted the wisdom of leaving his home to accompany Santos. Still, for all the hardships of the flesh, such inconveniences were more than balanced by a journey of education and self-awareness that took him to the far corners of the world. Friendships with other men or women, even the absence of physical contact with his own family, seemed a small price to pay for the privilege of accompanying Santos, and through him, growing spiritually and intellectually in ways a young boy from Dallas, Texas could only hope to dream.

"Well, er, it was nice meeting you, Rohini," Miguel said.

"You too, Miguel."

"I guess I've got a flight to catch."

"Yes, I know," the young woman smiled while Miguel continued to linger.

"Would you just get her number and get on with it?" an older man sighed, standing directly behind him in line. "I've got a plane to catch too!"

The pale, rosy glow already evident on his face turned a bright crimson red. Rohini smiled and silently passed a slip of paper to Miguel, who tucked it awkwardly in his jeans. With a stammered, barely intelligible reply he bade her farewell once again and pivoted, heading for the gate.

"Smooth, real smooth, kid," the man muttered under his breath.

Rome

"I must see the Holy Father," Mother Philomena said, reaching the door to the papal bedroom, only to be blocked from entering by Cardinal Fenucci, the pope's personal secretary.

"Pope Gregory lies gravely ill," the old, white haired Cardinal shook his head sadly. Though the pope's health had always been frail, the suddenness of his present decline was alarming, and relatively unexpected.

"All the more reason I must see him!" Mother Philomena pressed forward.

"The doctor has forbidden all visitors, Mother. He sleeps now, and must not be disturbed. Tell me what you want, and I will convey your message when the Holy Father awakes."

"A sacrilege was committed," the elderly woman sagged, as if confirming her worst fears about a future yet to pass. "A Eucharist was stolen from the Church of San Clemente in Belvedere Marittimo. In my dreams I saw it despoiled at the hands of a prelate of the Church, then used to invoke the unholy powers of Hell. The forces of Satan have been unleashed, and there is no one now to stop them, unless the Holy Father acts. He must publicly support the Holy Cross exorcists, and give primacy to their work. They are the only ones who can prevent the vision of Pope Leo from overtaking us all."

"I'm sorry, Mother," the Cardinal replied softly. "Opus Dei will soon be disbanded. Those who consider their extremist beliefs and practices to be dangerous in modern times have already taken the first steps. Their followers are no longer welcome in Rome. The pontiff was too weak to stop the Curia from issuing this decree, and now he is too ill to reverse their actions."

"No," Mother Philomena insisted, forcing herself past the elderly, white haired man. "I have seen what is to come, but the vision is not yet final. There is still time, if the Holy Father will act."

Pushing the heavy doors open, Mother Philomena dashed into the room. Pope Gregory lay in a wide, four post bed crowned with a canopy of spun golden lace, unconscious and breathing heavily. The old nun knelt at his side and took the pope's hand in hers, softly calling his name, but he did not stir. The color had drained from his face, and the aura of death was already about him.

"Please Mother," Cardinal Fenucci implored, his tear-filled eyes speaking more than words could convey.

Mother Philomena bowed her head, and let a small, soulful sigh escape her lips. "We are too late. The Holy Father will not recover. The power of Lucifer is mounting to a climax, and there is nothing to stop him now."

New Delhi

"Miguel, Miguel!" Santos scurried toward the young man standing near a row of orange vinyl chairs, his backpack on the floor and their other luggage deposited around him. A middle aged couple walking through the terminal had to scamper out of the way of his wildly flailing arms, made even more menacing by the thick wooden cane he wielded like a sword. "I can't find my passport! I must have left them with Father Dias!"

"I have it right here," Miguel replied nonchalantly.

"Hurry then! We must get our tickets before—"

"The plane doesn't board for another hour," Miguel held up the travel vouchers for Santos to see.

The little man sighed audibly, finding a nearby seat and resting his weary legs. Folding his hands across the top of his cane to help support his weight, he let out a small chuckle.

"Forgive me, Miguel. You know how much I hate to fly, and now this whole change of plans has gotten me flustered."

"I hadn't noticed," Miguel deadpanned, taking the seat beside him.

"I thought we'd be heading to Rome. Every year the International Society of Exorcists holds its Congress in the Holy City. But now, suddenly, the Curia revokes our privilege, without any explanation! Now we must go to Kathmandu? Travel to the Himalayas, at the last minute no less! This is all so disconcerting."

"I wonder what it's like, Santos?" Miguel could barely contain his enthusiasm. "We've traveled many places together, but never to the 'top of the world'. Have you been?"

"It's cold."

Miguel smiled. He leaned back to stretch his legs while Santos continued to fret, mumbling to himself about the sudden change in the location of the conference, and its topic: *The New Demonopathy*. What exactly was that, anyway? There would be time enough to find out, Miguel shrugged. For now, his only concern was getting Santos safely aboard the plane. This time, hopefully, without offending any of the passengers.

***

The plane was a three engine jet; one on its tail, the other two under each wing. Modern enough, Miguel thought, but still at least thirty years old.

An odd mixture of men and women filled the main cabin to capacity. Most were dressed in western attire, but a few wore the colorful native garb of the subcontinent. The most curious aspect was the absence of any children. Miguel, twenty-one, was the youngest person aboard.

"You're sure our luggage made it on safely," Santos worried, peering over Miguel to see outside the plane.

"Yes Santos. I'm sure it's there."

"I forgot to put my prayer books in my travel bag. I don't want to lose them. I need them for my work. You know how important they are."

"They'll be all right, really Santos," Miguel said. A woman across the aisle was already staring at the curious little man whose voice rose another octave with each plaintive question. Miguel touched Santos' arm and tried to calm him.

"What's the matter, Santos," he said softly. "I've never seen you this anxious before, airplane or not."

For a moment Santos did not react. His gaze was eerily distant, as if looking past the plane towards something unseen. "I have a troubled sense about this journey, Miguel," Santos finally answered.

"Why? Is Kathmandu that dangerous a place?"

"No more than any other we've been to," Santos shrugged. "There is always danger where the Devil lurks."

"But this time it's different?"

"It's not something I can express," Santos leaned back in his seat. "The world has become more evil these past few years. It leaves a palatable taste in my mouth, like the seed of a bitter root. Despite our work it never goes away, never lessens."

"You know that's not true, Santos. I've seen the good you've done."

"Grains of sand in an ocean of torment," Santos shook his head.

"You're being too hard on yourself," Miguel soothed. "Not everyone possessed can be saved, you said that yourself. There still has to be good within them that wants to break free of the Devil's grasp. Just because you couldn't help that woman last month—"

"No. I'm not speaking about myself, Miguel. The world is at a crossroads. History has driven us to a point where all of humanity is poised to fight or succumb to the forces of evil. This conference in Kathmandu, it's the focus of this somehow. I can't explain it Miguel, but I know that here the final battle begins. I can't tell you how or why, I just know it's true."

"You're still just upset about the last minute change in plans, Santos, that's all. I know you were looking forward to Rome."

"Yes, maybe that's it," Santos settled into the well-worn contours of his seat and closed his eyes, shutting out the world. His words were not convincing, but the crowded plane was no place to continue this conversation, particularly after the nervous, frenetic manner in which he had boarded the plane. He had already caused enough commotion for one day. Better to keep a low profile until they reached their destination.

The flight from New Delhi to Kathmandu would be over before he could take one of his usual catnaps, or so it would seem. Time, like great distances, had very little meaning in a world that seemed to re-invent itself on a daily basis.

Kathmandu

It was just after five in the afternoon when the aging jet landed at Kathmandu's Tribhuvan Airport.

The terminal building was modest by Western standards. It had all the amenities one would expect to find from a modern coffee shop to public lavatories, but still looked like something out of a 1950s movie. Exciting sights and smells assailed Miguel's nostrils, who tried to drink in every new sensation while shepherding the still brooding Santos through the arrivals area. A group of Nepalese soldiers standing near the baggage carousel caught his attention, and he offered a friendly smile that was not returned. Undaunted, he collected his and Santos' luggage, and with the feisty Filipino priest joined a line that was queuing to clear customs.

It took about twenty minutes for the long line to snake its way toward a row of wooden counters where several customs officials were stationed. Conspicuous as the only foreigners in line, Santos hobbled over to the middle desk, his wooden cane clacking on the polished airport floor, and waited while Miguel presented their passports. The official in charge took his time examining his Vatican credentials, casting a wary eye at Santos while he slowly thumbed through his travel documents and compared them to something out of view.

"You priest?" he finally asked in halting English.

"Yes," Santos said.

"Catholic priest?"

"That's right," Santos responded cautiously, an obvious edge to the official's tone.

"Buddha is the only way."

"At the name of Jesus every knee shall bow," Santos replied, his own voice becoming testy. Locking eyes with the man, he almost dared him to respond again, ready to press the point and defend his faith.

"This isn't the place for this, Santos," Miguel winced, his eyes darting nervously to a group of nearby soldiers.

"Only Buddha," the immigration official repeated, his free hand gesturing with a snap toward a pair of nearby soldiers.

Before either knew what was happening, the two soldiers approached Santos and Miguel. Words were exchanged between the soldiers and the customs official, their eyes flittering toward Santos and Miguel with each rise and fall of their voices.

"You come," one of the soldiers finally turned and spoke to Santos.

"Where?" Santos reacted angrily. "We've done nothing wrong."

"Come, now," the soldier repeated, this time gesturing with the barrel of his rifle. The surrounding area grew completely quiet as Santos and Miguel, baggage in hand, were led away to the opposite side of the airport complex, and ushered inside a small windowless room. Without ceremony, the two soldiers locked the door and left. Alone in the dim light of the musty storage room, Miguel turned to Santos, exasperated.

"Exactly *what* happened the last time you were here?"

"It was nothing really. A simple misunderstanding."

"'Misunderstandings' don't land you in jail!"

"I don't know what's going on, Miguel," Santos said, somewhat apologetically. "But I'm sure we'll get this all straightened out. We should pray to the Holy Virgin to watch over and protect us." He took out his Rosary and held the oval shaped beads, their texture and shine dulled by years of wear, and began to pray.

The worry and concern evident on his face seemed greater than normal, and it left Miguel with an uneasy feeling as he joined Santos in prayer. An hour later the door to the room was abruptly flung open. There in front of them was a tall thin Canadian Jesuit priest, accompanied by a short dapper man. The tall man, Father Morris Sanford, was the principal of Kathmandu's St. Joseph's School, the venue of the Congress. Sanford was beside himself with embarrassment.

"Father Santos? I came as soon as heard that you were detained. I can't imagine what prompted such a deplorable course of events. I trust you haven't been ill treated."

"No. We're both perfectly fine," Santos rose to his feet.

"Thankfully, I know the Airport Director, Mr. Subhash Subba. I asked him to intercede on your behalf and arrange for your release."

"I apologize for this indignity," Subba bowed to Santos. "An overzealous bureaucrat acted without proper authority in ordering your detention. Rest assured that the guilty party will be swiftly punished."

"There's no need to punish anyone," Santos smiled happily. "I'm sure it was a simple misunderstanding."

Subba snapped his fingers and a small throng of airport porters rushed in to collect their baggage.

"I would have been here sooner," Sanford explained, "but I'm afraid I've been quite distracted with this last minute request to hold your conference at St. Joseph's. We've been scrambling to accommodate everyone who's attending, almost one hundred and thirty of your fellow exorcists from all over the world. Thankfully, an anonymous last minute donation has helped our efforts immeasurably. I'm told everyone is here now that you've arrived, except for a few of the older priests who were too ill to make the trip."

"Yes, like Father Dias, Miguel said. "We stayed with him last night when we finally got to New Delhi. There were no rooms at the airport hotel, and he was kind enough to share his home with us. He told us to send you his regrets that he couldn't make the journey to see you again."

"I know Father Dias well," Sanford smiled approvingly. "There's no kinder, more honorable man anywhere on the subcontinent. I'll include him in my prayers tonight, that the Lord may speed his recovery. I'm just glad the two of you made it here safely. Mr. Subba tells me there is a strong weather front headed this way. Yours was the last flight to arrive from New Delhi. You made it just in time; the airport will be closed by tomorrow."

"We were on the island of Bohol in the Philippines," Santos explained. "I had been called to perform an exorcism in a remote village on the eastern shores. I thought there would be plenty of time to finish my work before leaving for Rome when word reached us that the Congress had been moved to Kathmandu, and a week earlier no less! It was all we could do to get to New Delhi last night to catch a plane today for Nepal."

"It would have been such a tragedy to reach Kathmandu, only to miss your conference," Subba said remorsefully. "I am thankful Father Morris alerted me to your situation, so I could be of help."

"I have known Subhash for many years, and count him among my friends," Sanford smiled, placing his hand on the man's shoulder.

Subba lowered his eyes self-consciously, as if embarrassed at the public praise. Soon the small group was heading toward the exit with Subba in the lead, proudly showing Santos the improvements to his airport.

"I didn't expect to see so many soldiers," Miguel whispered to Sanford as they passed by another group of armed men. "Rome, Paris, New York,

New Delhi — but not here." He was beginning to understand that Kathmandu was no oasis of peace, but to the casual observer its problems seemed to be on a far smaller scale than elsewhere in the world. Or so he hoped.

Before he could reply, Subba swung his arms around to show the group a new overhead lighting system, pulling Miguel and Sanford into the tour. When they reached the exit a car with a Nepalese driver pulled to the curb. As Santos, Miguel, and Sanford piled in, Subba leaned into the driver's window and spoke a few words which set the man to nodding vigorously. The colorful cab sputtered to a lurching start as the driver threw it into gear and sped away, leaving Subba behind with a friendly wave as the vehicle disappeared into traffic. Standing at a distance was a tall uniformed soldier who approached Subba once the car was out of sight. Subba frowned as the high ranking officer closed the distance between them.

"I gave strict orders that no one was to be detained," the man said angrily. "There were to be no unnecessary concerns raised! Lord Shaitana wants them all together, in one place. Why were my orders not followed?"

"An overzealous immigration official," Subba apologized profusely, "acting to protect Nepal from corrupt religious influences. The priest's name appeared on an immigration watch list as someone of interest. He was apparently involved in an altercation several years ago with local officials in Bhaktapur, something involving a prominent Buddhist family whose son he believed was possessed. Under normal times he would have been detained for questioning — but these are not 'normal' times. As soon as I learned of the unauthorized detention, I had him and his traveling companion released."

"I don't want to hear your excuses!" the officer raged. "Your carelessness is inexcusable! The actions of your man could have jeopardized everything."

"It was an unfortunate matter quickly resolved. When the Catholic priest Father Sanford alerted me to the situation, I immediately ordered their release. They are on their way now, with an interesting tale to tell, and no worse for the experience. Everything is proceeding just as you directed."

"Lord Shaitana must be informed of this at once," the officer stated indignantly.

"Yes, by all means," Subba appeared to agree. "And when you do, let him know that it was *your* soldiers who placed them in detention without notifying me. The priest and his young companion stayed there for two hours, under *your* guard, with no effort to free them until I ordered their release."

"Your people were responsible for this, not mine!" the officer angrily insisted.

"I'm sure there's enough blame for everyone," Subba replied nonchalantly. "We'll just let Lord Shaitana sort it all out, and punish those responsible. After all, I'm sure he has nothing better to do with his time than sort through an inconsequential bureaucratic snafu and assign blame to the guilty parties."

The officer blinked, his body shaking slightly as if recoiling from an invisible punch. "We, er, don't need to burden Lord Shaitana with this … incident," he reconsidered. "As you said, there is nothing consequential to report."

"A very wise decision," Subba agreed. "Now if you'll excuse me, I must attend to my duties. Please inform Lord Shaitana that the last of the exorcists has arrived in Kathmandu, and is on his way to the conference."

***

"What a wonderful city," Miguel strained to see as the car wound its way through Kathmandu's narrow congested streets. At its renowned Durbar Square they were greeted by a medley of pink-bricked pagodas and crowded bazaars, cobbled streets and cycle rickshaws, complete with tourists, gaily clad natives, and monkeys. There were no lanes for traffic, and no rules. People crossed the street at random, cars and all kinds of vehicles barreled past each other horns blaring. It seemed almost like a real-life bumper-car game.

"You've no doubt noticed the variety of people here," Sanford explained like a tour guide. Miguel's eyes darted from side-to-side while Santos watched the passing scenery with mild interest. "Kathmandu is made up of indigenous Nepalese who were the original inhabitants, and Nepalese of Tibeto-Mongol and Indian origin. The Tibeto-Mongols are the well-known Sherpas in the Mount Everest region. The Nepalese of Indian origin are primarily Hindu broken down into various castes, and the Newars, who descended from Mongol-Aryan inter-marriage. The Newars are the main inhabitants of Kathmandu. To give you some comparison, there are twenty-three million Nepalese all together. Ninety percent of the population are Hindus. The rest are Buddhists and Moslems, and some animists. Only six thousand of us are Catholic. Normally everyone exists in relative harmony. But these aren't normal times, I'm afraid."

"What's causing these tensions; religious or ethnic differences?" Miguel asked.

"Neither," Sanford said. Santos turned his head to listen while Sanford continued. "Most of the Nepalese royal family was gunned down by one of its sons some years ago. That weakened the ruling oligarchy and created a bit of a power vacuum. Now we have Maoist insurgents roaming the countryside terrorizing some of the smaller villages. They've even attacked the city once or twice, though more for symbolic than military reasons, I suspect. Still, they are a growing threat."

"Should we be concerned about them?" Miguel asked hesitantly.

"I think not," Sanford chuckled. "The real effect has been to allow a new political movement to form that's gained a fairly strong local foothold. You've seen those billboards we've passed with a picture of a tall, slender man with flowing dark hair and an elegant beard? They say that this is the 'Home of Lord Shaitana'. He's the spiritual leader of something called the Lumen Covenant. A rather incongruous name for his purposes, if you will."

"Lumen? That means light, doesn't it?"

"Yes," Sanford replied. "Shaitana believes that he, not Jesus Christ, is 'the Light', and only through a covenant with Shaitana and his Masters of Light will humankind fulfill its destiny. His teachings plagiarize the tenets of Christianity as well as those of the other major faiths, stripping them of their original meaning and producing an amalgam of self-serving syncretistic nonsense which puts him squarely at the head of God's mission on earth. If we have time, I will introduce you to my friend Lhundup Jinpa, a monk at the Buddhist Center near Hanuman Dhoka, the old Royal Palace. Shaitana is co-opting followers of Buddhism and other religions the same way he appeals to the Christian world. Lhundup Jinpa, more than anyone in Nepal, has fought against Shaitana's increasing political power, but I fear it may be a losing cause. A number of Buddhist monasteries were recently taken over by Shaitana's followers.

"What started out as an isolated cult in Nepal, no different than any other fringe religion, has literally been transformed into an international movement whose power and influence continues to grow with each passing day. Even the United Nations has granted his Lumen Covenant official observer status, equal to that of the Holy See. One can hardly read any publication or watch any satellite programming on television without some mention of Shaitana or his Covenant. Even Holy Mother Church is not immune to his influence. I learned only yesterday from Father Aurelio that Rykaard Cardinal Hindriks may be on his way to Kathmandu to meet with Shaitana."

"Hindriks!" Santos grew animated. "What in the name of all that is good would he want with Shaitana?"

Sanford exhaled slowly. "The good father is not sure, only that his presence can have no good attached to it. But fear not. I have asked Mr. Subba to alert me if Hindriks tries to enter the country, and he has promised me that he would."

"But surely people of faith won't be deceived by Shaitana," Miguel pressed, still trying to sort through the complexities of Sanford's comments.

"You are still young, my son," Sanford smiled benignly, "and full of grace from your companionship and travels with Father Machado, who watches over you with care. But many in the world are without such protection, and succumb to his deception. Shaitana has crafted his message so that everyone can pick and choose familiar elements from their own religious heritage, which gives them false comfort as they are seduced into betraying their true principles. They come to accept his perverted teachings as logical extensions of their own faith, never realizing that they are rejecting God instead of embracing Him. This is why Father Aurelio chose *The New Demonopathy* as the theme of the conference. The Church can no longer remain aloof from this growing threat, regardless of what the Curia in Rome believes. "

"And Shaitana — he lives here, in Nepal?"

"Yes, in a Buddhist monastery that was given to him when the monks who protected and cared for it pledged their allegiance to Shaitana. Like many others in Nepal, they were drawn to his Covenant when he said that he wanted to purify the world of all corrupt Western influences, including its religion. So far they've been empty threats, designed to appeal to some of the more xenophobic elements of this society. But as Shaitana's power keeps growing, he has begun to overshadow the Royal Family, and so he represents a grave danger. Even though he holds no elected office, his followers are so numerous that today he is virtually the ruler of the kingdom. I fear one day that he may close down St. Joseph's"

Reaching a row of tall, elegant buildings built in the colonial British style, the car passed through the front gate of St. Joseph's School, an oasis of Western civilization in the remote Himalayan mountains. Situated in a bowl-like valley a mile above sea level and surrounded by beautiful forested peaks, it was like walking into another world, another time, another moment in history. Though primarily a religious center for the minuscule Christian population of Nepal, it also offered the superior educational benefits typical of the Catholic school system found throughout the world. This drew the children of many leading Nepalese families to the compound, as well as their parents, where they had access to information and ideas not normally found elsewhere in the country.

While welcoming converts, Father Sanford and his staff took great care to separate the secular and religious aspects of their mission in Nepal so as not to foist Catholic doctrine on those of a different persuasion. This allowed St. Joseph's to exist in harmony with the broader community. Only since Shaitana's ascendancy had the campus become a lightning rod for local protests that had grown more frequent, and violent, with each passing day.

Santos seemed to perk up as they passed near the school chapel. "I can sense the presence of St. Joseph."

"Yes. We Jesuits have always been in the forefront of devotion to St. Joseph," Sanford replied. "Most of us are from Canada, where St. Joseph is our patron saint."

"No, it's more than that," Santos continued absently. "He's your guardian here."

Not quite knowing what to make of the comment, Sanford glanced at Miguel, who smiled whimsically and shrugged.

Winding their way along a tree-lined path, Santos shifted his gaze outside the car window. The setting sun cast long shadows across the ground, accentuating the beauty and grandeur of the compound, backlit against a multi-colored sky.

"Ah, here we are," Sanford chimed once the cab slowly rolled to a stop. Miguel and Santos' luggage was removed from the trunk and deposited on a cobblestone walkway. Sanford paid the driver, who nodded gratefully and left as two young boys collected the baggage.

"Let me show you to your rooms," Sanford offered, saying something in Nepali to the two boys who scrambled on ahead of them.

The walk toward their bungalow was slightly uphill. Santos, temporarily invigorated by the fresh, pristine air, was panting noticeably by the time they reached the top.

"I'm afraid the air here is a little thinner than what you're used to,"

Sanford said.

"I think it also says something about the shape you're in," Miguel added absently. Santos didn't appear amused, his round face furrowing in a frown though he did not reply. By now darkness had completely engulfed the compound. Reaching their bungalows, Sanford turned on a single, low wattage light. Both rooms were simple, but comfortable — a bed with blankets, a table, some framed pictures.

"Would you like to rest a bit before dinner," he asked, directing one of the young boys to place Santos's suitcase on the floor.

"Thank you, Father Sanford," Santos replied wearily. "I won't be joining you, tonight."

"I understand. As I said, the altitude can be quite taxing, even for a short journey. I'll have something sent to your room before we turn off our generators for the evening. We power down most of our electricity around 9:00 pm, so we'll bring your meal sometime before that."

"No, thank you," Santos' voice was drained of emotion. "I need to fast."

"Santos, I didn't mean to offend you," Miguel began to apologize.

"It isn't that," Santos shook his head. "Ever since we arrived in Kathmandu, I've felt a kind of dark energy surrounding me. I find it hard to think, even to pray. There is a respite from it here, in St. Joseph's. I want to use this time to fast and pray while my mind is clear."

"Certainly," Sanford nodded. "Come with me Miguel, and I'll show you to your quarters."

As Santos settled in, Miguel was taken to an identical room where he carefully unpacked his clothing and put his suitcase away. It was a ritual he practiced with each new room. For five years he had led the life of a transient, following Santos from one meeting to the other, from one exorcism to the next, always living a temporary existence. To compensate he would make each room his own, no matter how temporary, arranging its sometimes modest, sometimes elegant surroundings to his satisfaction.

Capping each effort, Miguel would place a careworn photograph of his parents beside his bed. With each passing day the notion of family was becoming more abstract than real, for in truth Santos was the only tangible connection Miguel still had to the outside world. And yet, despite the fact that he hadn't seen his parents in over two years — and only then for a brief, passing moment as he and Santos traveled through Dallas to a remote part of the state — he felt as strongly now about his family as he did the day he left with Santos. Perhaps even stronger. No matter how far he traveled, no matter how many months or years would pass before he could see them again, his love for his family did not lessen. Nor did their importance in his life.

Looking around the room, Miguel let a smile tug at the corner of his mouth. One of the true lessons he had learned during his journeys with Santos was that home, indeed, is where the heart was.

***

Awakening with a start, Miguel felt his bed hopping up and down, and the pictures on his wall shaking back and forth.

This can't be, he thought. He closed his eyes and prayed hard. The shaking stopped, and the room quieted. A quick look at his watch, bounced off the night stand and retrieved from the floor, read 3:01 am. Miguel lay his head back on his pillow and tried to get back to sleep, but thoughts of the supernatural flooded his brain and kept him awake. Finally, through sheer exhaustion, he was able to drift off to sleep.

When he arose the next morning Miguel wasn't sure if he dreamt about the strange phenomenon, or actually experienced it. To his surprise, Sanford met him after morning prayers, and spoke to him with a smile. "So did you feel the tremor last night?"

"Tremor?"

"Yes, Nepal is located on the Indian and Tibetan plates. We experience hundreds of quakes every year. The one last night was minor in comparison," Sanford explained, "but still able to move some furniture around. I trust it didn't startle you too much."

"Just a bit."

"My apologies for not letting you know about such things earlier. Well, nothing like a good meal to restore the constitution. Shall we go to breakfast? Our cook makes a wonderful *alu roti.* It's like a potato filled bread. Quite a mainstay here."

"It sounds delicious," Miguel said. Casting a glance toward the nearby mountains, he chuckled softly to himself. *So much for the supernatural,* Miguel thought, following Sanford toward the dining hall.

Chapter 5

Kathmandu

The crisp morning air held the scent of sweet, dew-filled flowers. Opening their petals to receive the first rays of the rising sun as it peaked across the tops of the nearby mountains, they formed a blanket of vivid reds, yellows, and oranges as far as the eye could see. The shapes and varieties of the flowers were almost too numerous to count, intermingled with other tall plants and manicured hedges covering more than an acre of hilly terrain. Strange, exotic birds chirped songs from the branches of nearby trees, and here and there the twitching snout or curious eyes of a small friendly animal would peek out from a cover of thick green leaves. It was as if the Garden of Eden itself had been magically recreated and transferred to this remote spot on the top of the world.

Walking through the ornate, carefully sculptured garden, Santos and Miguel made their way to the main conference hall. Neither spoke, their eyes drinking in the rich colors, and their other senses taking in the touch and smells of their magnificent surroundings. It was like going back a hundred years in time to experience life among the privileged gentry who long ago settled down in this foreign land, bringing with them their advanced culture and superior technologies. All that remained were the vestiges of the past, hollow shells of imperial grandeur that had been converted into more useful dwellings housing educators, civil servants, businessmen, or missionaries, all of whom now tried to assimilate into a society they once sought to dominate.

"Are you still troubled, Santos?" Miguel asked as they neared a row of buildings at the edge of the garden. The normally gregarious priest had missed morning prayers with Father Sanford, and equally uncharacteristically, had not shown up for breakfast. Miguel had gone to his quarters to check on him fearing that something sinister might have happened to Santos, only to find him still deeply engaged in prayer. It was only with great prompting that he persuaded Santos to leave his room and attend the conference.

"I thought we were in for a spell of bad weather," Santos thought aloud, his eyes cast upward.

Miguel glanced at the bright, cloudless sky, not quite sure what to make of the comment. "Maybe it's still on the other side of the mountains," he shrugged.

"Yes, I suppose so. Still, it's awfully pleasant, don't you think, for bad weather?"

"What is it Santos?" Miguel pressed. "You've been acting very strangely ever since we left India. What was it you and Father Dias spoke about the other night? Your whole demeanor changed after that?"

"There is an evil presence here, Miguel, unlike anything I've sensed before. It suffuses everything, like a foul stench staining whatever it touches. I can feel it in my bones, even now at St. Joseph's."

Miguel had seen Santos act this way a handful of times before when the Devil had been in strong possession of some tortured soul. But there was something odd about this occasion, and it caused Miguel to suppress an involuntary tremble. The remote mountain setting was serene, like a beautiful painting invoking images of heavenly paradise. There was nothing to suggest that anything but the presence of God permeated the surroundings. But deep down Miguel had to face a similar dread. For all its peaceful majesty, he too felt a terrible sense of foreboding, even at St. Joseph's.

And that sense grew with intensity in proximity to Santos.

20,000 feet above Italy

Ralston Hastings eased back in the soft leather seat and glanced out the window of his Gulfstream V long range jet. Beneath him the magnificent snow-capped Alps, looking like a mosaic of white and grey curves set against a background of sharply contrasting angles, had given way to patches of green and brown farmland interrupted by occasional valleys and streams. The only signs of civilization below were some barely visible roads and a smattering of bridges that dotted the landscape.

Inside the spacious private airplane, all of the sixteen passenger seats were occupied. Several high ranking business and political leaders, and an equal number of female companions considerably younger in age, relaxed in an atmosphere of decadent pleasure. Exotic edibles and fine vintage wine flowed freely, and music from a sophisticated, state-of-the-art entertainment system piped through the interior of the aircraft, but it was only so much background noise to the otherwise preoccupied middle aged men.

Hastings took in the women's flirtation and the men's loud, raucous laughter with measured indifference. They had stopped in Brussels to pick up the last of their guests, Henri Cousteau, the Principal Director and General Manager of one of the largest private banks in Europe. Sixty, balding, and significantly overweight, he was patting the leg of a shapely twenty-four year old brunette, who feigned rapt attention while he showered her with ponderous stories of mystery and intrigue in the arena of high finance.

While his wife, and the wives of the others on board, enjoyed themselves on a Mediterranean cruise sponsored by Hastings Communications, Cousteau and his counterparts were just beginning a week long sabbatical underwritten by one of Hastings' many public interest foundations. The itinerary was purposefully designed so that the participants — each of whom controlled substantial political and economic resources in their home countries — could set their own pace, and establish their own schedules. All Hastings required was their attendance at private dinner scheduled for the following day, where he would lay out in simple form his vision for a better world: a vision he intended to publicize through the international holdings of Hastings Communications, supported by the collateral efforts of like-minded political leaders and captains of industry.

"We should arrive in Rome in about fifteen minutes, Sir," an attractive young blonde in a neatly tailored stewardess uniform leaned forward and whispered into Hastings' ear.

"Thank you, Colleen," Hastings replied, sorting through a small pile of binders and briefing folders on the table in front of his seat.

"Your European bureau chiefs are all waiting at the Piazza Navona Communication Center as you directed. Will you be requiring anything else during your stay in Rome, for your guests — or yourself?"

Hastings looked into the young blonde's eyes. Her demeanor was completely professional, but the implications of her seemingly innocent question were all too clear. His attention returned to a thick leather binder which he thumbed through while he spoke.

"Yes, reservations for two at El Toula, nine o'clock. My usual table. And wear something black, with pearls."

"Certainly Sir," the young woman smiled, righting herself.

As she made her way back down the center aisle, a well dressed man in his forties sat in the empty seat beside Hastings. Vincent Stout glanced backward at the laughing, carousing men who had long since dropped any pretense of decorum or respectability as they mauled at the young women beside them.

"You don't approve of my methods, do you Vincent?" Hastings said without emotion, his eyes never leaving the binder.

"It's not my position to question your actions or your judgment, Mr. Hastings," Stout replied.

Hastings set the binder aside, and smiled thinly. "Which is why I continue to have confidence in your abilities, Vincent. It's important for a man to know his place. The world would be much better off if everyone understood the role they were meant to play. Do we have any word from our friends in Nepal?"

"Everything is proceeding as planned, Sir."

"Everything?"

"Yes Sir. Not a single hiccup."

"There are always hiccups, Vincent," Hastings lectured. "What about those who didn't make it to Kathmandu?"

"There were only five, Sir. Three are in their nineties, and confined to hospital. None of them are ambulatory. Their prognosis is terminal; they'll be dead of natural causes within the month."

"And the remaining two?"

"One lives in Guayaquil, Ecuador, and the other in New Delhi. Both are in their seventies. They will be dealt with individually, once the main plan is executed."

"Tell me Vincent," Hastings continued without emotion. "What do you think of a man who would murder a priest? Do you expect to rot in Hell for committing such a sacrilegious act?"

"I'm not murdering anyone Sir," Stout answered.

"Nor am I. The question was purely philosophical."

"Well, in that case," Stout continued, "I'd say there's not a lot of difference between killing a priest, and killing any other human being. The consequences depend entirely upon the circumstances at hand. If killing a man makes the world a better place for humanity, then it's a sin *not* to do it. As for the question of Hell, it seems to me there has to be a Hell before one can go to it, Sir."

"Shaitana might dispute you on that last point."

"The Devil's a bogey-man created to scare weak minded people into acting against their own interests," Stout dismissed the remark. "He no more exists than the man in the moon. Shaitana plays on the fears of children to convince them he's Lucifer's right hand man, so they'll fear and obey him. But I suspect you already know that, Sir."

"It is a convincing little show, you must admit," Hastings chuckled. "The Secretary General of the United Nations found it credible enough to sell his 'immortal soul' for more wealth and power, along with others."

"People believe what they want to believe. Shaitana winds them up and shakes them down like the TV preachers do. They think the Devil is controlling them, but it's just a self-fulfilling prophecy."

"And what do you believe in, Vincent?"

"Me Sir? I believe in myself."

Hastings settled back in his seat, the barest hint of an approving smile evident on his face. Shaitana was indeed a charlatan of the worst kind, he thought to himself. But he was also a man with millions of followers. It was one thing to control a world-wide communications network spanning every corner of the globe, which Hastings used to promote his own views and analyses. But it was quite another to force people to act on these beliefs. The lessons of previous elections was not lost on Ralston Hastings, where the mainstream media attempted to shape public opinion through distorted, one-sided reporting, only to find the masses rejecting their message because it conflicted with their core values.

Shaitana solved that problem. Dependent on Hastings' empire both for influence and protection, his values — and by extension those of his followers — could be shaped by Hastings to serve his own interests. The son of a poor servant girl was no match for a man of Hastings' brilliance, or so he reasoned. Shaitana could manufacture all the contrived parlor room theatrics he wanted to build his following, but Hastings would always control the message. As long as Shaitana served Hastings' purposes, he was free to invoke the mythical powers of Hell for whatever pseudo-religious purpose he chose. He could reign supreme in his own corrupt world and build a movement that spanned the globe, but he would always be kept on a short leash, dancing to whatever tune Hastings played.

It was, Hastings believed, the perfect marriage of convenience; enough to tip the balance of power in Hastings' direction, and give him, through Shaitana, the army he lacked to reach his objectives.

Kathmandu

Entering the assembly hall, Santos took his seat near the rear of the auditorium. Miguel and other laymen were forbidden to attend the private conference, which was restricted to members of the International Society of Exorcists. Only Father Morris Sanford, their host, was present for the opening ceremony. Then he too would depart, leaving the hundred and thirty or so middle aged and elderly priests to conduct their affairs in private.

The room was still busy with activity as the last of the participants entered, greeting old friends while milling about their seats as they waited for the conference to begin. Standing at the podium, Sanford caught sight of Santos and acknowledged him with a nod and smile, which the chunky little Filipino silently returned. Even at a distance of a dozen yards or more, it was plainly evident on Santos' face that he was still deeply troubled. A night of prayer and fasting had not seemed to help, but with the conference about to start there was little Sanford could do at the present moment. He resolved to seek Santos out at the first appropriate opportunity and see what he could do to help unburden his soul.

In front of each row of chairs was a long table with notepads, pencils, and binders filled with information about the conference. Still lost in his thoughts, Santos absently thumbed through his packet while a young Nepalese man in a waiter's coat filled his drinking glass from a carafe he carried. Neither Santos, nor anyone else in attendance, paid any attention to a small linen-covered cart that was wheeled into the room and left near the base of the podium. A tray of pastries lay invitingly on top, but its position directly in front of the speaker's platform made it impractical to sample the delicacies during the proceedings. To anyone who gave it more than a passing thought, it looked as if the cart was stationed to be at hand when the conference members took their break.

"May I have your attention," Father Sanford's voice rang out over the public address system. "If you will all please take your seats, we can get under way. I understand that you have a full day ahead of you, and it's already a little past nine."

The buzzing hum of overlapping conversation quickly came to a stop as each black clad participant settled into his chair. A prayer for humility and guidance was recited by Father Sanford to officially open the proceedings. Then he looked out over the assembled crowd, and spoke in a deep, welcoming voice.

"It is my great pleasure, as principal of St. Joseph's School, to host this annual conference of the International Society of Exorcists. When I received a call just days ago from my good friend and personal confessor, Father Raphael Aurelio, seeking a new location for your unfortunate last minute change in venue, I was more than happy to offer him the hospitality of St. Joseph's. He knew that few, if any, other places in the world could accommodate you on such short notice, and we are honored to fulfill his request. We are also honored by your tireless efforts on behalf of Holy Mother Church. It is you who today stand at the forefront in the fight against evil. In doing this you follow in the footsteps of the greatest exorcist of all, our Blessed Lord. The Gospels make it clear that exorcism, and delivery from demonic possession, was a primary ministry of Christ. He empowered his followers with the specific ability to cast out demons in his name. And yet those who think of Christ as peacemaker or teacher rarely mention, or even seem to be aware of, his focus on the battle against the diabolic. I believe, like my good friend Father Aurelio, that so-called Catholic theologians have caused untold damage to the faithful through their skepticism about the supernatural, which has led them to dismiss the very existence of the Devil. But the Devil doesn't cease to be because man doesn't believe in him. In fact he prefers that we don't. This allows him to prosper in our midst, right under our very noses, as society turns a blind eye to his presence.

"Our bishops have an obligation to appoint exorcists in their dioceses, but many have failed to do so. Through this omission, they provide no avenue of relief for those who are possessed. Many of our clergy have failed to warn the faithful about the dangers of the occult. Belief in astrology, the use of tarot cards and Ouija boards, and the practice of so-called white magic have now become mainstream. These seemingly harmless pastimes gradually drag the soul into satanic slavery, but few warnings are ever heard from the pulpit. An epidemic of superstition and diabolic oppression is taking place before their eyes, during their watch — and they seem entirely unaware of it.

"In this you are fortunate to have among you someone who does not shrink from his duty of doing the Lord's Will in season and out. When asked if he was ever afraid of taking on the Devil, or if he had ever faced retaliation from the Church bureaucracy that sought to diminish his work, he laughed and said, 'It is precisely this fear that stops many priests from performing exorcisms. They forget that Satan is after you regardless of whether or not you try to stop him. Fear is pointless and paralyzing. As for me, I had entrusted myself and my work to the Blessed Virgin from the very beginning and I have never once been bothered by the demon.'" Sanford smiled and looked at the tall, distinguished man seated to his right. "I present to you now the author of these words, Father Raphael Aurelio, my teacher, my confessor, and my friend of twenty-five years."

Raphael Aurelio, exorcist extraordinaire of the diocese of Rome and President of the International Society of Exorcists, stood to receive the warm applause of the delegates as Sanford left the auditorium for his office adjacent to the conference room, overlooking the garden. The balding, seventy-five-year-old Italian priest was reputed to have performed over twenty thousand exorcisms — as many as ten a day. It was rumored that Pope Paul VI, at the recommendation of Opus Dei, had personally commissioned the young Aurelio to coordinate the battle against "the demon with all his frightening plurality." It was a rumor Father Aurelio would neither confirm nor deny. As a young priest in the Archdiocese of Venice he had joined Opus Dei, *the Work of God.* Founded in 1928 by the Spanish priest Josemaría Escrivá, Opus Dei required its members to commit to a life of mortification and exemplary service to the Church. Its enemies called it a fascist dictatorial enclave and sought to suppress its activities, but were unable to counter the overwhelming support of its members and friends in high places within the Catholic Church, who saw it as a vehicle for encouraging Christians of all social classes "to live consistently with their faith, in the middle of the ordinary circumstances of their lives, especially through the sanctification of their work."

When he wasn't exorcising the possessed, Aurelio was excoriating bishops, priests, and theologians for their blindness with respect to the spiritual world, and their consequent inability to help the thousands who were suffering from diabolic oppression, obsession, infestation, or possession. Aurelio believed that he could not make progress in his battle against the dark side if he entered an ecclesiastical popularity contest, or as he bluntly stated on more than one occasion, murmur "sweet nothings" to the powers that be. Consequently, the outspoken priest did not endear himself to the bureaucrats of the Vatican Curia, who restricted his access to the pope. Nevertheless, Aurelio believed that he had a strong silent ally in Gregory XVII, who though unable to profess his public support for Aurelio's efforts, prevented any disciplinary action from being taken against him or his followers.

With Pope Gregory now near death, and his successor unclear, Aurelio felt that he and his fellow exorcists were operating on borrowed time. Like himself, many of his fellow exorcists were advanced in years. Each year death claimed a small, but growing number of the dwindling cadre, which had not been replenished to any significant degree since Santos Machado joined the society in 1962, immediately upon his ordination. Complicating their work, the Vatican's 1999 update to the Rite of Exorcism made the overall ritual all but toothless, according to a widely circulated controversial criticism by Aurelio that only added to his legion of enemies. Several of the most ancient and effective prayers had been taken out of the New Exorcism Rite. With biting sarcasm, Aurelio proclaimed that the theologians who updated the Rite had never performed an exorcism, or even been present at one, which made the new Rite as compelling as a primer on heart surgery written by non-doctors who had never even witnessed the surgical procedure. The enraged officials sought a formal censure of the irrepressible exorcist, but again found their efforts blocked by papal inaction.

"I am humbled by your confidence in my continued leadership of the Society," Aurelio began. "The theme of this Congress is *The New Demonopathy*. It is 'new', because the challenge we confront today is unlike any other humanity has faced since the time of Christ. Human history cannot be understood if we don't recognize the role of the occult and the diabolic. Human life and history as a whole is replete with interventions of evil spirits. To understand both the Old and New Testaments, and the mission of Jesus, we need to know about the Devil. The single greatest source of God's anger in Old Testament times is the worship of idols and strange deities. This is not because He is the "jealous Jehovah", but because this is enslavement to Satan and to demons. That path leads only to destruction and damnation. God's people are constantly seduced by the lure of idolatry.

"Also forbidden on pain of death is sorcery, magic, and all forms of the occult. In the New Testament, if you look at the life and ministry of Christ, again you see the sub-theme of diabolic intervention. Jesus is constantly casting demons out of people. There are sharp exchanges between the demons and Jesus, and Jesus warns us frequently of Satan's power, his presence and activity. Many modern scholars have either downplayed or dismissed these accounts, but this means ignoring what is patently obvious in the biblical texts.

"A new light is shed on all this through the experience of you, my fellow exorcists. You go beyond scientists and theologians because you are not dealing with theories or abstractions. You touch and feel the powers of darkness."

As the Bible recognizes, and Jesus and the Church plainly saw from the beginning, our main enemy is the Devil. Every resource should be utilized to combat this danger. However today theologians, liturgists, and ecclesiastics have all downplayed or even eliminated the very awareness of this reality. An entire dimension of reality is no longer recognized. But ignorance is not bliss in this case, because neither the Devil nor his demons cease to act because we don't acknowledge them. In fact, they are far more effective in this situation.

"Now all this is a deadly serious matter. It affects our lives, our families, the entire world. If we don't recognize the existence of evil spirits and their activity, we are unprotected. Is there a danger of being obsessed with the Devil? No. Our focus is not on evil spirits, but on protection from them that we receive from God. To be in touch with the real world and to benefit from all the resources that Christ has given us, we must first recognize the reality of the spiritual world, of powers and principalities that transcend the material order. The evil spirits hate us with a cold fury that does not change with mood or feeling. They do not have emotions or passions. They are pure spirits focused entirely on our destruction.

"Only an understanding of the demonic helps us further appreciate the importance of the sacraments, of the saints and angels, of the Name of Jesus. The hard fact is that there are people who manifest extraordinary symptoms that cannot be explained scientifically, understood psychiatrically, or treated medically. These include superhuman strength, levitation, and inexplicable knowledge in the subjects, among others. Only exorcism offers a way to heal these tortured souls.

"Some would say, 'Why bother since the victims of possession are few and far between?' Evil grows when Good is absent, through ignorance or neglect. Left uncontested, the Devil and his legions will seek to entrap all people without exception, in some fashion or other. Possession is only the most extreme example. Seemingly harmless occultic practices are becoming widely available and acceptable in common society. Wiccan societies and satanic music, fortune-telling, tarot cards, and sorcery are everywhere.

"Once infected through these innocuous sources, you are in dire danger of losing your soul to the Devil. Once you step into the spiritual underworld, getting back could be well-nigh impossible. For our own spiritual well-being and of those we love, it is urgent that we have a clear awareness of the Satanic forces openly at work in modern society. Even more important, it is critical to remember that Jesus, the Blessed Virgin, the angels and saints are always available to protect us in this world. The evil spirits are especially afraid of the Virgin, the Archangel Michael, and of the Name of Jesus. But if we don't call on them for assistance, they will not force themselves on us."

The hall was quiet, each delegate mesmerized by Aurelio's speech. Santos closed his eyes as the terrible feeling that was building in side him threatened to spill out in an involuntary cry. Aurelio's words seemed to stab at his very soul, as if they were directed specifically to him. His hands trembling with a fear he had never felt before, Santos rose from his seat and left the room, seeking the solitude of the garden to brace his nerves through additional prayer. No one noticed him slip out the rear door as Aurelio brought his comments to a close.

"In the nineteenth century we were warned that a new and powerful demonic invasion would strike the modern world — the world of the last century and this new millennium. From Anne Catherine Emmerich to Leo XIII, Heaven showed us what was to come. And it has come. Throughout the world we are called on to perform exorcisms at record rates, but we find that the Church hierarchy is skeptical not simply about possession, but of the very existence of Satan. Satan does exist, and he will win the battle for the souls of all the living, if we do not—"

The final words of Raphael Aurelio were lost in a deafening explosion that sent shards of jagged metal careening through the hall. Fire erupted when the combustible material was ignited by a secondary explosion from the gas lines heating the auditorium, bringing down the roof and collapsing part of the outer walls. Within seconds those not killed by the initial blast were consumed in an inferno that quickly engulfed the nearby buildings.

The initial explosion was so powerful that it knocked Santos from his knees while he prayed in the nearby garden. Righting himself, he looked at the conference hall, now blanketed in flames, and thought he saw the face of the Beast rising out of the thick black smoke enveloping the structure. Wordlessly, the orange red eyes seemed to seek him out, then disappear in the smoke and fire that consumed the building.

***

Roland Blavatasky opened the door to the private conference room and stepped inside. Seated across a table from Shaitana was the head of the Nepalese Army, flanked by two of his aides. Papers strewn about the table made it seem as if an intensive planning session was nearing its end. Only a large stack of foreign currency visible inside the General's briefcase seemed curiously out of place.

"Your Holiness. Forgive my intrusion," Blavatasky bowed. "I bring disturbing news. Guerillas have attacked the Christian school of St. Joseph. There were reports of an explosion and fire, with many dead."

"This is precisely what I feared," Shaitana spoke to the General. "The Royal Family has lost control of the nation's security. The Maoists have been emboldened by their weakness, and have attacked the city."

General Bal Bahadur Tamang stood and nodded respectfully to Shaitana. "Yes, you are correct; the government cannot protect our people, so the military must assume that responsibility. I will order an immediate state of martial law. Your wisdom is great, Lord Shaitana. I pledge my services and loyalty to your charge."

"Fortunately, the assault was only against the Western intruders who maintain a continuing presence here, in contravention to the rituals and beliefs we have venerated for centuries," Shaitana said. "Still, the guerillas represent a growing threat."

"They will be dealt with," the general replied.

One of the aides closed the briefcase, cuffing it to his wrist as an added measure of security as Tamang and the two soldiers left the room. Shaitana, resplendent in his long robe and manicured beard, waited for Blavatasky to close the door.

"See to it that evidence of the guerillas culpability is found at the site of the explosion," Shaitana said while sifting through a stack of papers.

"That has been done, my Lord."

"Good. And arrange for another payment to General Tamang's private account once the Royal Family has been quarantined. He will need the additional resources to ensure that loyalty is maintained among his junior officers."

"Yes, my Lord," Blavatasky bowed, departing as swiftly, and deferentially, as he entered.

***

"Santos, Father Santos!" Miguel screamed as he raced toward the burning building, finding his path blocked by several Nepalese who pushed him back from the danger.

"No go you," one of them said. "Many danger."

"What happened?" Miguel shouted.

"Boom. Many boom. All dead."

"Santos!" Miguel wailed, falling to his knees. Sobbing uncontrollably, he was oblivious to the sound of sirens converging on the campus. Fire trucks raced to douse the flames while a squadron of fierce looking soldiers began shouting orders to the dazed priests and workers who milled about the complex in a state of shock.

Slowly, as if fighting his way through a nightmarish dream, Miguel rose to his feet, and turned his back on the horrible images assaulting his eyes. Not knowing what to do, he made his way toward the chapel to pray for the soul of his mentor, and friend, who must surely have perished with the others.

Rome

The knock on the hotel suite door brought the sleepy face of a pretty young blonde out from the bedroom to investigate. Swaddled in a sheer silk robe that hugged her sinewy legs and torso, she peered through the peephole, then opened the door. Vincent Stout looked at her admiringly before stepping inside, his demeanor professional despite his obvious attraction to her beauty.

"Is he awake?" Stout asked, directing his gaze to the closed bedroom door.

"It was a late night," Colleen answered discretely. "I don't think he wants to be disturbed."

Stout nodded understandingly. "When Mr. Hastings awakes, please tell him that the package was delivered on time, with expected results."

The pretty blonde nodded not understanding the message, but giving it little concern. She had been one of 'Hastings' harem' long enough to know that it didn't serve her interests to be too curious about his private matters. Under no illusion about the role she served, she contented herself with thoughts about the jewelry and other expensive presents that always followed a night in his service, rather than esoteric business matters for which she had little real interest, even under the best of circumstances.

Without speaking, the young woman turned and headed back to the bedroom as Stout let himself out of the suite, his eyes lingering on her shapely form before closing the door behind him.

Kathmandu

Cut and bleeding from his close proximity to the explosion, Father Sanford stumbled through a row of hedges, reaching Santos as he was about to leave the sanctuary of the garden. Spotting him as he left the auditorium, Sanford had earlier watched him enter the peaceful sanctum and kneel at a prayer bench near a statue of the Virgin Mary. He resisted the temptation to leave his office and follow the troubled man and offer his friendship and counsel, hoping to ease his mind and allow him to return to the conference. Instead, he decided to let Santos find his answers through continued prayer. In the aftermath of the explosion that devastated the auditorium hall, and in light of the other knowledge he was now only beginning to fully comprehend, he was convinced that an Act of God had spared Santos life.

"Father Sanford," Santos cried as the tall man staggered then collapsed into his arms. "Are you hurt badly? Lie here while I get a doctor."

"Must … talk," Sanford wheezed. "Warn you."

"You're in no condition—"

"Everyone is dead. Father Aurelio … everyone. Assassinated."

"W-who?" Santos stammered. "Who did this? Why?"

"Aurelio … told me last night," Sanford gasped the words, "of an evil presence here … in Nepal. The Devil is using him … as his vessel … to consummate the vision of Pope Leo … in his favor. Aurelio did not know … the name, but I am certain … he spoke … of Shaitana."

Sanford coughed up a spasm of blood, but waved Santos away when he tried to help him.

"There is a formula … from Heaven, a series of Secrets … Divine Truths … that has been handed down. Aurelio said … only the Secrets can stop Shaitana … keep him from controlling the third millennium. Only you are left to find them. Find Father Lanciani … at the San Giuseppe Church … in Rome. He will tell you what … you need to know. You are the Final Exorcist, Santos. The fate of the world … rests in your hands."

Gunfire from Nepalese troops filled the air, along with indistinguishable shouts combined with cries of fear. General Tamang's soldiers set up a perimeter around the burning building and warned away any would be rescuers brave enough to venture close to the flames.

"They will say … it was guerillas … who did this. But it's not. Leave now, Santos. Leave Nepal. Trust no one in authority."

"But how? How can I leave? I-I don't know what to do. There's no one to help me. I don't have anywhere to go."

"Lhundup Jinpa … will help you."

"How will I know him? Where do I find him?"

"Go to the … Buddhist Center. He will … find you. Now leave … immediately."

"I can't leave without Miguel."

"He is no threat … to Shaitana. Only you … the Last Exorcist. Go now. Miguel will be … all right."

His body convulsing, Father Sanford took a final, pain-filled breath. Santos held his broken, blood-stained body in his arms as tears of anguish welled in his eyes until the sound of more gunfire and threatening shouts snapped him back to reality.

Righting himself, he blessed the departed soul of Father Sanford before making his way back through the garden to the safety of the nearby hills.

Chapter 6

Kathmandu

Bowing respectfully, Roland Blavatasky entered the ornately decorated study where Shaitana was seated at a large ceremonial desk, his attention divided between a satellite television feed of the atrocity in Kathmandu and a large stack of documents spread out before him.

Almost immediately following the explosion at St. Joseph's, the international news media had begun broadcasting definitive reports about communist guerilla activity in the remote Himalayan nation. A declaration of martial law was formally declared by the military, which had placed the Royal Family in 'protective custody' until the insurgent threat had passed. Spearheaded by Hastings Communications, the news was inflammatory and full of wildly speculative rumors disguised as fact. To the outside world it looked as if full blown civil war had broken out in a once peaceful nation that had been struggling with a chronic insurgency, which was precisely the image Shaitana and Hastings wished to convey.

"Your Excellency. Seventy bodies have been removed from the ruins of the heathen sanctuary. At least fifty more are still buried inside the rubble. Nine Jesuits were also killed in the explosion, including the principal of the Christian school. Another ten Nepalese workers were—"

"I am not interested in mortality statistics, Blavatasky," Shaitana dismissed his report with a wave. "I want to know that my orders have been carried out, completely and without exception. I want to know that every exorcist is dead, or soon will be."

"Certainly your Holiness. Our agents are in place to deal with the five who did not attend the conference. They are to act once news of the calamity has been broadcast. The situation will be fully resolved within a matter of days. There will be no one left to harm you."

"No one?" Shaitana fixed him with a spine-chilling stare.

Blavatasky swallowed hard. "There has been a report that one of the exorcists was not in the conference room. A priest named Santos Machado. A waiter said he left moments before the explosion."

"I said I wanted *everyone* dead!" Shaitana raged, slamming his desk.

"Those were my instructions! Were they not clear?" Blavatasky kept his head bowed while Shaitana angrily paced about the room, his dark hair and elegant, manicured beard swaying to the rhythm of his movements.

"General Tamang's soldiers searched the entire compound but could not find him, nor anyone who has seen him alive. The priest Machado is dead, I am certain of it."

"No, he is alive," Shaitana hissed. "I can feel his presence somewhere in Kathmandu. Find him, and send him off to his god! I can't take the chance of even a single exorcist staying alive."

"He is a foreign priest alone in a strange land. There's no one to help him. If he survived, he'll be captured and end up in the Buri Gandaki gorge with our other enemies. All is under control, your Holiness. You have my promise."

"This is one promise you had better keep."

"Of course, Your Holiness," Blavatasky hid his trembling hands and shuffled out of the room, sealing the door behind him.

***

Shedding his cassock and cleric's collar soon after leaving the St. Joseph's campus, Santos Machado picked his way through the narrow back alleys of Kathmandu. His three mile trek over hilly, sometimes rocky terrain left him winded and out of breath, and there were several times that he had to stop and rest before continuing on toward the city. Having stumbled through a thicket of brambles somewhere along the way, his feet were blistered and his trousers torn by the time he reached the outskirts of Kathmandu.

Fortunately for Santos, his by now disheveled appearance helped him blend into the ebb and flow of city life. Only western tourists in their designer jeans and bulging backpacks stuck out from the crowd of swarthy skinned natives, many of whom wore dated, brightly colored clothing. His garish, red striped shirt with wide, white lapels was reminiscent of the 1970s, and melded perfectly with street merchants and native shoppers alike. Even his dark skin and mottled complexion helped make him indistinguishable from the others around him.

Wandering through the city, Santos picked his way past the sprawl of beggars, shopkeepers, and diesel powered motorcycles and cars jamming the streets. The sweet, pungent scent of incense wafted through the air. Everywhere he turned there seemed to be another prayer wheel, another temple, another robed monk seeking alms for the poor. Digging into his pocket, Santos took out a few coins and deposited them in an earthen bowl at the foot of a legless man, receiving a toothless smile for his kind act. Around and above him throngs of long tailed monkeys acted as if the ancient city was their own personal playground, mixing with the tourists and shoppers while they scampered along the cobblestone walkways or dashed from one rooftop pagoda to the next.

Kathmandu was a cacophony of noises and smells, some pleasant, others overpowering, all crushed into a compact Third World theme park. The confusing array of cramped, often unmarked streets left Santos struggling to get his bearings. He was no stranger to this part of the world, but it had been more than a dozen years since his last visit to Nepal, and even then he had little time to enjoy the sights and flavor of the bustling city. It seemed as if the number of hawkers, rickshaw wallahs and souvenir sellers doubled as he moved closer to its center, making the confusing task of locating the Buddhist Center even more difficult.

Exhausted, Santos finally rested at the base of a small public fountain. Leaning wearily against his cane he prayed for guidance, having used his last 200 rupees to purchase a small plate of Bada — black lentil deep fried patties — to curb his stabbing hunger. The unappetizing meal was barely nourishing for a man who hadn't eaten much in the last twenty-four hours, and only aggravated the misery of his sore feet and aching muscles. Nearby, a loudspeaker from a passing military truck blared a harsh, tersely worded message about the imposition of martial law that Santos couldn't understand. The shopkeepers around him reacted with measured indifference to the announcement of a curfew and locked up their stores. Soon the milling crowds began to dwindle, and Santos found himself virtually alone in a deserted city, uncertain what to do or where to go. Struggling to his feet, he continued to wander the streets aimlessly, praying silently to himself as he desperately sought a familiar landmark to gauge his bearings.

By now it was late in the afternoon. The sun was beginning to descend behind the peaks of the mountain tops surrounding Kathmandu, casting long, angry shadows across the empty streets. He could hear the sounds of military vehicles patrolling the main thoroughfares of the city as he kept to the side streets and back alleys. Preying eyes peered out from partially opened windows to watch him without offering any help. Santos fought a growing sense of panic as the shock from the day's earlier events began to wear off, and he contemplated his present, increasingly desperate situation.

Just when he was about to surrender to despair, a strong pair of hands grasped his shoulders and turned him around. Santos looked into the face of a blue uniformed policeman with a red beret and fought to maintain his composure.

"Please, I—" Santos began, uncertain what to say or do.

"You leave now. Go," the policeman said in broken English.

"Very bad place here. Many problems. Not get hurt ."

"I don't know where I am," Santos said.

"Go now. Hurry leave."

"But—" Santos began to respond, then caught a glimpse of an imposing four column structure not more than two blocks away. The Old Royal palace looked like something out of Greek architecture, giving it a distinctly western appearance among the carved wood and pink stone buildings that populated most of the city. The Buddhist Center had to be close by.

"Leave, quickly," the policeman repeated, casting a furtive glance at a squad of soldiers farther down the street.

"Thank you," Santos whispered to the stern-faced man, whose attention remained focused on the approaching soldiers. Racing through the back alleys of Durbar Square as quickly as his aching legs would take him, he could hear the policeman and soldiers speaking in animated terms. The words faded once he turned a corner and found himself staring at an inviting, open door. Not bothering to stop and figure out where he was, Santos dashed through the entranceway. The heavy wooden door closed solidly behind him, leaving the stunned priest momentarily in the dark.

For a moment Santos wasn't sure if he had made his situation better or worse, and he instinctively clutched his cane like sword to use as a weapon. A single light from a flickering candle gradually began to illuminate the face of a benevolent, bald headed man in glasses and a flowing golden robe. In a sing-song voice he bowed slightly and spoke to Santos in reassuring terms.

"The soldiers will not enter this place. You have nothing to fear, Father Machado."

"Y-you know who I am?" Santos gasped.

"Certainly," the man smiled. "I brought you here."

"You're Lhundup Jinpa," Santos said. "Father Sanford said you would find me. But how? That policeman, was he—"

"You have had many friends looking for you," Jinpa spoke in perfect

English.

Sagging with fatigue, Santos allowed himself to relax for the first time since the explosion at St. Joseph's. Two acolytes of Lhundup Jinpa rushed to brace him against falling and guided Santos into a chair. Jinpa spoke to others unseen in the dim interior light, and water and food were immediately brought to him.

"The bomb," Santos said softly. "Father Sanford was killed ... and the others."

"We will speak of this again in the morning," Jinpa placed his hand on Santos' shoulder. "For now, nourish yourself and rest."

"Thank you," Santos mumbled, allowing himself the first luxury of the day as he scooped up a large helping of *Alu Dum* — boiled potatoes in curry — and ate voraciously.

***

Subhash Subba sat in the hard vinyl seat across from Miguel, comforting the young man whose red, puffy eyes and tear stained cheeks spoke volumes about his love for the quirky Filipino priest he regarded as a second father. Following an intense period of questioning by Nepalese police and military about the events of that morning, his possessions were quickly retrieved from his quarters, and the dazed young man was promptly escorted to the airport. There he was met by the outwardly sympathetic airport director who took him to a private lounge away from the milling droves of stranded passengers.

"Those responsible for this unspeakable tragedy will be found and punished," Subba said, grasping Miguel's hand. "Of this you can be assured, my young friend."

"Thank you, Mr. Subba," was all that Miguel could manage to say.

In his mind's eye he still saw Santos the last time they were together, reluctantly entering the conference hall at Miguel's urging. Years of travel and close companionship with the strange little Filipino priest had numbed him to the constant drama, angst, and last minute deviations from established plans that were a constant part of life with Santos. He had learned to ignore the seemingly changing whims of the enigmatic little man, for whom life appeared to be a constant series of crises. Kathmandu was no different than Columbia, Ceylon, The Baja, or the depths of Appalachia. It was Miguel's job to see that manufactured problems did not overshadow the very real ones he and Santos faced in their pursuit of the Devil. They had come to Kathmandu to attend the Exorcists' Congress, and it was up to Miguel to make sure that Santos was there on time. Now, he punished himself, if only he had not interrupted Santos and allowed him to continue his fasting and prayers, he would still be alive today.

Once again tears began to flow in a cascade of loud, wrenching sobs. Subba studied Miguel's face carefully, forming his next words slowly.

"Our police and military are combing through the debris of St. Joseph's for the mortal remains of those who were killed, so they can have a proper Christian burial. Some bodies were very badly burned, and not everyone has been recovered. Your Father Santos, you are quite sure he was in the conference hall?"

"I … took him there myself," Miguel choked. "Made sure … he went inside. Santos … is gone, may the Lord embrace him, and bless his soul."

"Yes, yes," Subba closed his eyes and lowered his head as if in reverence. "I will pray for him too. You're quite sure he's dead?"

Miguel looked at the man with a curious stare while Subba continued to study his face for any hint of contradiction. Santos' luggage lay at his feet along with his own. Miguel had explained that he returned to Santos' room after the explosion, hoping against hope to find him there, but the room was empty. After a tortured hour of prayer and contemplation, he packed up Santos' meager belongings and, with his own clothing and personal effects, was taken by the military to Tribhuvan Airport.

Satisfied that he was telling the truth, Subba rose from his seat and spoke to a nearby porter, who rushed forward to collect the luggage.

"The military has imposed martial law in Kathmandu and closed all the borders. All flights into Nepal have been suspended, but a limited number of aircraft will be allowed out of the country tomorrow. I have made arrangements to return you to New Delhi on one of the first flights. In the meantime, we have set up a cot for you in a room near my office. My assistant will bring you some food, and I suggest that you try and get some sleep, as difficult as it may be."

"Thank you, Mr. Subba," Miguel was genuinely grateful.

"Please, do not concern yourself dear boy. Father Sanford, who also perished, was my friend, too. Allow me to be your benefactor and protector until you leave Nepal."

Miguel gave the man an emotional hug, and followed the Nepalese porter down the hall. Subba headed for his office where he closed the door and dialed a number on the phone on his desk. A familiar voice answered on the other line.

"My Lord, I have questioned the young man called Miguel, who was man servant to the missing priest. He is convinced that Machado is dead, I'm sure of it. I have made arrangements for him to stay here, at the airport, under my observation. If the priest is alive and tries to contact him, we will know. If not, he will be placed on a plane tomorrow to New Delhi and expelled from Nepal."

Subba allowed himself to smile as Shaitana expressed his satisfaction. Ending the call he relaxed in his chair, confident that the missing priest, if not already dead, would soon be apprehended. Everything was proceeding just as his Lord and Master had predicted. Soon the world would belong to the followers of Shaitana, and Subhash Subba would be among the lucky few who would run the whole show.

***

The straw mat on a hard wooden floor was not the type of bed Santos Machado normally preferred, but he nevertheless slept deeply and peacefully into the early morning hours. The aches and pains of the previous day had been soothed somewhat by a thick, pasty balm one of Jinpa's fellow monks had given him to apply to the affected muscles. Except for a slight earthen smell that lingered in the air around him, the balm had highly positive effects. He stood, stretching the remaining sleep from his limbs, and felt remarkably refreshed.

Lying on a chair next to the door leading out of his room was his pair of slacks, mended by some anonymous tailor during the night. Santos dressed and ventured out into the hallway, where he could hear soft sounds of repetitive chanting somewhere in the building. The Buddhist Center was part temple, and part living quarters to the dozen or so monks and their acolytes who maintained the facility. Lhundup Jinpa was the elder Buddhist priest who was spiritual leader to a significant portion of Kathmandu's 700,000 population. While some of the smaller sects had found their temples closed in the anti-clericalism that accompanied Shaitana's rise in influence, Jinpa had managed to stave off any such efforts. In fact, he had strengthened his position in the traditional religious community, who saw him as the only local figure able to temper Shaitana's new 'post-religious' ecumenical movement.

Jinpa recognized that one day the tide would turn in Shaitana's favor. One day the dark forces unleashed by Shaitana would overwhelm him and prevail, and he and his followers would face the same fate as all others who opposed Shaitana; imprisonment or assimilation. But that day had not yet come, and until it did, Jinpa would remain an enemy of Shaitana and continue to fight all that he represented.

Santos continued down the corridor, making his way toward the rhythmic chants. He soon found himself at the entrance to a large prayer hall, where Jinpa and the others sat in the lotus position engaged in prayer. Colorful tapestry framed the walls, one of which depicted the image of the four armed Buddha who had two hands folded in prayer, while the lower two held crystal prayer beads and a white lotus. On either side was a row of Tibetan Buddhist monks, led in prayer by Jinpa, whose chanting hymns were accompanied by occasional trumpets, horns, and drums.

"O*m mani padme hum,* o*m mani padme hum,"* the words echoed through the temple. Santos stood transfixed at the exotic images and sounds. To him, these were only so many sweet melodies, since he did not know the language. But for Jinpa, the thrice-daily prayers had become an incantation against Shaitana

I pray to you, perfect noble one, lord protector
O*m mani padme hum*

I pray to you, lord of love,
With the power of evil karma gathered from
beginningless time
O*m mani padme hum*

The Mara Shaitana is born as a hell being
Buddha of great compassion, we have no other
protector than you
O*m mani padme hum*

Slowly rising to his feet, Jinpa signaled the end to morning prayers. He beckoned Santos to enter the Temple's inner sanctum, which was normally not accessible to westerners and other non-believers.

"I am glad to that you have recovered from your difficult journey," Jinpa bowed respectfully.

"I have," Santos replied. "It was Heaven-sent that I found you when I did. I'm not sure I could have lasted much longer out there, alone. I'm certain I would have suffered the same fate as the others if I had been caught and taken into custody."

"The Enlightened One has looked over you and protected you from harm. We prayed for someone to aid us in our fight against the forces of darkness that threaten to envelop us all, and he has delivered you to us in our time of greatest need."

"I'm not sure I understand," Santos replied hesitantly. "How can I help you? I'm completely cut off from everyone I know. All my brother exorcists are dead, Miguel is out there, somewhere — I don't know where — I'm alone in a strange land, being hunted by the military. Of course I'll do whatever I can to repay your great kindness in giving me refuge, but what can I do to help you, really?"

Jinpa let a knowing smile settle across his face. He directed Santos' eyes to the large golden tapestries hanging on a far wall. Embodied in them were tenets of his faith, much like the magnificent paintings in Rome that told the story of Christianity.

"We Buddhists believe in the Four Noble Truths, and in the Eight-fold Path through which all can be enlightened. These are the four truths. Suffering is universal; we are the cause of our own suffering; we should stop doing that which causes ourselves to suffer; and we end our suffering through the enlightenment that comes from the Noble Eight-Fold Path. Through the Path, we come to possess the Right View about life through the eyes of Buddha, which is with wisdom and compassion; Right Thought; Right Speech; Right Conduct; Right Livelihood; Right Effort in showing goodwill to all; Right Mindfulness of our thoughts, words, and deeds; and Right Concentration on one thought or object at a time.

"Father Sanford and I spoke many times about the fight against the maras — the demons — and especially the new locus of evil in our midst, Shaitana. This man has defiled our religion by proclaiming himself as Maitreya, the incarnation of the Lord Buddha that had been foretold for the future. He calls himself Lord Shaitana, claiming that he is the Enlightened One. Many of my younger disciples have been snared by his wiles. He says he wants to make Nepal a holy place by driving out all vestiges of the West. But we know that he is an instrument of the maras who seeks dominion over humanity. Each day his power grows stronger, fed by the power of evil. The monstrous maras under his command must be suppressed, lest they take control of our souls and subject us all to the reign of darkness.

"It is to this purpose I have devoted my life these past years, to thwarting Shaitana and in doing so defeating his evil purpose. But I found myself unable to stem his growing power and influence, and I prayed that we would be given an instrument of retribution, one who will defeat the great Mara and return us to the Noble Path. In his wisdom the Enlightened One has delivered you into our midst. You will be the instrument of divine intervention."

Santos stared at Jinpa, wide-eyed and speechless. The kindly Buddhist monk placed his hand on Santos' shoulder, continuing to speak in a soft, but fervent tone.

"We are not unlike, you and I Father Santos, for in your own manner you also seek to cleanse the world of evil. We face the same enemy today, Shaitana, who will not stop until all humanity is enslaved. I have done all I can to stop him. Now you must lead the way. You must defeat the Maras. The fate of the world, of the souls of our brothers and sisters, rests with you."

Santos had fought the Devil in villages and towns, large cities and small, on virtually every continent of the planet. Always he felt the power of God imbuing him with strength and resolve, and he used this power to help break the Devil's grasp on some poor, tortured soul. But now he was being asked to confront Evil in its most formidable form, not individually, but on a global scale.

Santos wondered if he was truly up to the enormous task that Jinpa had laid before him. The vision of Pope Leo was manifesting itself before his eyes, yet Raphael Aurelio, the greatest exorcist of all, was dead. Every other exorcist had been killed, victims of the same unholy power that he, alone, must now face. Though God, in his mercy, had spared him a similar fate, he drew little comfort from this merciful Act. If the future of all mankind truly rested on his shoulders, he felt himself to be wholly inadequate for the task.

For the first time in his life, Santos Machado doubted himself, and his abilities.

Hills outside Kathmandu

Rajendra Shrestha was a small man with streaks of grey in his short cropped beard. The camouflage jacket he wore was stiff with extra packets of ammunition for his AK-47, never more than an arm's length from his side. Camped in a makeshift hut near the border with India, he kept a wary eye on the flickering screen of a black and white television set powered by a hand cranked generator. Images from the St. Joseph's massacre played over and over as a somber-toned announcer recounted the events that had shocked all of Nepal, and the world.

The satellite feed from the Hastings Communications Center in New Delhi featured an interview with local Nepalese officials who showcased the bodies of two Maoist guerillas propped up on an examining table, their familiar red star berets arranged on their chests over blood stained uniforms. Looking like something out of central casting, the two bullet-riddled bodies bore silent witness to the atrocities they committed — except for the fact that neither man was known to Commandant Shrestha or any of his subordinates who commanded the insurgent forces in Nepal.

"Military officials have confirmed that these Communist guerillas were part of a suicide team that attacked the Catholic enclave in Kathmandu," the announcer dutifully reported. "Another twenty or so escaped in the confusion following the explosion that killed over one hundred and thirty priests, and a number of local residents at the facility. A spokesman for Pope Gregory XVII condemned the plainly anti-religious attacks and called upon the world to renounce all forms of violence against their fellow men. In a related story, the gravely-ill pope is rumored to be in a coma at the Vatican. Prayer vigils continue throughout Christendom for his speedy recovery, just as speculation abounds as to who will eventually succeed him upon his death. The leading candidate is Cardinal Bruno Reinhard, a liberal theologian who was at the forefront of opposition to—"

"Enough!" Shrestha shouted, slamming his fist on a rough hewn table that threatened to knock the teetering, old vintage television set onto the hard packed floor. "Bring me Chettri, now!"

Padam Chettri, first lieutenant and aide-in-charge to the ragtag rebel commander, scrambled across the rocky campground to reach Shreshta's hut. Still in a rage, Shrestha flung his hand toward the images on the screen and bellowed loudly.

"These are lies!"

"Yes Commander," Chettri responded. "Our people in the city say the military has taken prisoners from jail and dressed them in our uniforms, then executed them and brought their bodies to the Christian site. They have used the fiction to impose martial law in Kathmandu and depose the Royal Family."

"The Royal Family is of no interest to me," Shrestha seethed. "But the generals will be emboldened by this deception and soon seize complete control of the country. We must prepare for an immediate counter-attack before the military consolidates its power."

"Not the military. Shaitana."

A quiet, sudden calm came over Shrestha. Chettri watched his face transform into a mask of deep introspection.

"Do we still have an agent in Durbar Square?"

"Yes Commander. He has informed us that Tamang is searching for a priest with magical powers who escaped death with the others. He walked through the explosion and fires without fear, and was not harmed. He has sought refuge in a temple with Lhundup Jinpa."

"I want to see this priest who death will not touch, and who consorts with a Buddhist monk. Bring him to me."

"As you order, Commander," Chettri bowed, and quickly left his quarters.

Chapter 7

Kathmandu

Dusk had begun to settle over the strangely quiet city, now patrolled by dozens of menacing armored vehicles accompanied by heavily armed soldiers on foot.

Inside the safety of the Buddhist Center Santos fidgeted with a sleek, golden robe that a young acolyte had handed him, hesitating momentarily to orient the garment before wrapping it around his body. A hooded shawl was fitted over his head as if to guard him against the crisp night air, but it was really meant to hide his face and hair. Leather sandals replaced his western shoes, and in place of his cane he was presented with a large walking stick. Finally, the slightly bemused Catholic priest was handed a ring of 108 brightly colored prayer beads — the traditional *mala*, or necklace, used by Buddhist monks to represent the number of mental conditions or sinful desires one had to overcome to reach nirvana.

Placing his clothing inside a linen sack to carry along with him, Santos glanced at his reflection in a nearby mirror and chuckled. Neither monk nor priest, he thought he looked more like a circus clown than someone who was supposed to be part of Jinpa's entourage. Still, in a city darkened by a military curfew, the Buddhist monk was convinced that Santos could easily pass for a member of his traveling party. Even armed soldiers weren't going to stop a religious pilgrimage to Bhaktapur to the famous Boudinath Stupa, one of the most holy centers of Tibetan Buddhism, regardless of the hour their journey began. Once free of the immediate cordon around Kathmandu, Santos could make his way safely out of the country with the additional help that had been arranged.

"Are you ready?" Jinpa asked. "We have friends who are waiting for us outside the city."

"These friends," Santos replied cautiously. "How well do you know them?"

"We have a common interest in seeing that Shaitana is defeated. You will be safe with them until you reach the border. Come now. We must go."

The tolling of a large, ceremonial bell signaled the beginning of the procession. A scent of incense filled the air as the large doors opened into a nearly empty public square. Emerging from the temple adjoining the Buddhist Center, Lhundup Jinpa led his entourage past a squad of soldiers, several of whom bowed respectfully before clearing the way for the chanting monks. Slowly and methodically, each step in rhythm with the next, the group made its way through the ancient city streets, leaving the military to search in vain for a missing Catholic priest that many of them no longer believed existed.

Rome

"Everyone?" Father Ignacio Maggiore hung his head, cradling his forehead in his hands while he wept great tears of sorrow.

"Aurelio, Testa, Nuccio, Ramirez, they were all massacred. Father Sanford and several other Jesuits died as well. The bomb was devastating."

"Was there no one who survived?" Maggiore lifted his eyes.

"One, perhaps. Santos Machado. His body has not been recovered, and the military is sweeping the city looking for him."

"One priest, from over one hundred."

"One exorcist," Salvatore Rotolo corrected. "I have his file here."

Rotolo placed the manila folder on the prelate's desk. The robust, grey haired, sixty year old man was the present-day successor to Monsignor Josemaria Escriva, who founded Opus Dei in 1928 as a stringent spiritual regimen for Catholic clergy and laypeople. Opus Dei, the "Work of God", went beyond the mainstream Church practices, requiring daily Mass and prayer and spiritual readings geared to bring its disciples closer to God through a life of singular focus and devotion. In 1982, the pope made Opus Dei a personal prelature — a diocese without boundaries that was identified by its global membership, rather than a specific region or territory. Raphael Aurelio, the best-known exorcist of the time, was a life-long member of the Priestly Society of the Holy Cross, the clerical arm of Opus Dei. Through his influence, a large portion of the dwindling cadre of exorcists found a home in the Society of the Holy Cross.

Opus Dei's network of priests, businessmen, and ordinary men and women from all walks of life were fiercely devoted to what many considered a strict and unforgiving way of life that they did not consider a sacrifice. Through their own actions they hoped to show, by example, the infinite joy that came from surrendering one's self to God, completely and unashamedly, without concern for the temporary corporal hardships such devotion might engender. The purpose of man's life on earth was not to seek fleeting personal pleasure, but to glorify God through a single-minded focus on carrying out his works. Over eighty thousand strong, their reach extended to every corner of the world, giving financial support and assistance to priests like Aurelio and others through the Priestly Society of the Holy Cross.

Maggiore turned the pages in the dog-eared manila file, reading about the diminutive Filipino priest who, although not a member of the Society of the Holy Cross, had been brought to Rome by Aurelio as one of his most trusted associates. At the request of local bishops, Aurelio had often sent Santos to perform difficult exorcisms around the world. For some special reason God had spared the life of this globetrotting exorcist from the slaughter that claimed so many others. While Maggiore continued to read, Rotolo opened another folder belonging to Raphiel Aurelio, and placed an envelope sealed with a wax impression on his desk.

"I found this in Father Aurelio's quarters," he said.

Maggiore set Santos' file aside and took the envelope in his hands. Opening it, he read a personal message of warning from Aurelio.

"Dark forces have assembled that threaten to consume us," the letter began. "I fear a new demonopathy has descended upon the world. It draws us to Nepal, where the servant of Lucifer will try his worst to silence our work. He must not succeed. I do not fear my own death, if that is what awaits me. But my death, or the death of others, must not stop our holy mission. Whoever survives must seek out the Divine Truths, the Seven forsaken Secrets. They, and they alone, will light the way."

Attached to the letter were the names and locations of seven holy places, each different in its significance, but all equal in importance. Together they formed an unbroken chain that would help mankind rediscover the lost truths that God had revealed; truths which men had either forgotten or ignored, allowing Satan to deceive and confuse, and through his deceptions, lead men's souls astray.

"Only one survived," Maggiore repeated.

"We must find him," Rotolo said. "Rescue him and protect him from harm — and lead him on his journey."

"No. The journey is one he must make alone. There is a reason only one exorcist survived. God will light his way, with our prayers to help guide him. But he must follow the path alone."

"At least let us protect him from any harm," Rotolo pleaded.

"Find him and protect him, but no one must know he is being watched over. We cannot interfere with his actions, or influence him in any way."

"I will call upon those who have helped us in the past," Rotolo said, retrieving Aurelio's letter. "They will watch over him like angels, never seen, but always present."

Maggiore closed the file in front of him. "I only pray that this simple man, who God has chosen for so great a task, will find the courage and strength he needs to lead the way."

New Delhi

The crowded plane was crammed to capacity when it left Tribhuvan Airport amid heightened security following the massacre at St. Joseph's, and the declaration of martial law in Kathmandu a day earlier. Among its passengers was Miguel Guerrero, still in a daze from the loss of Santos and so many others. The airport director, Subhash Subba, had maintained a watchful eye on the young companion to the missing Catholic priest, hoping that Santos would try to contact him if he was indeed alive. The night passed uneventfully, as well as most of the next day. Following a series of clandestine calls between Subba, the local military commander, and an uncharacteristically anxious Roland Blavatasky, the decisions was made to allow Miguel to leave Nepal. If Santos Machado was still alive, there would be one less person in Kathmandu to help him.

Security at Indira Gandhi International Airport was equally tight when the disembarking passengers were put through another heightened security screening. Miguel was questioned at length about his proximity to the explosion as the Indian authorities made certain that he was not involved in the incident. Eventually they were satisfied that that the still-distraught youth had no connection to the radical leftists who attacked the Catholic retreat house, and allowed him to leave the quarantine area.

Emerging into the near-empty terminal, Miguel sat on a hard backed bench, and set his knapsack and suitcase on the ground. With his head hanging between his legs, he tried to decide what to do next. Should he go to Rome and make a report to the Vatican about what he saw in Nepal? And if he did, what if any purpose would it serve? The entrenched bureaucracy of the Curia was hostile to the exorcists and their Opus Dei patrons. Other than lamenting the tragic loss of life, there would be no action taken, no rush to fill the void left by the deaths of the exorcists. Perhaps he should simply return home to Dallas, Texas, and begin his life anew? But a life of what? His devotion to Santos wasn't simply a job. It defined him, gave him purpose. Miguel had never felt more alone in his entire life than he did at this moment in time.

"Miguel?"

The sweet musical voice pulled him out of his haze. He looked up into a familiar face, but couldn't place it with a name. Dressed in a light blue attendant's uniform, the dark haired, brown eyed beauty stared back at him with puzzled concern.

"Miguel, are you all right?"

"Rohini?" he mumbled.

"I just got off work and was going home. I didn't expect to see you back in New Delhi so soon."

"Neither did I," Miguel said, choking back his emotions.

"Why then … oh dear God, you weren't involved in that terrorist bombing? Oh Miguel!" Rohini swung her head around, searching the terminal with her eyes. "Your friend, the man you were traveling with. Where is he?" she asked, fearing the worst.

"Santos … was killed," Miguel was barely able to speak the words.

Rohini sat beside him on the bench, placing her arm around Miguel's shoulder. "Were you … hurt too?" she asked tentatively.

"No," his voice was a whisper. "Only priests could attend the Congress. I was in my room writing a letter when I heard an explosion. I rushed out and saw the conference hall in flames. It was completely engulfed in fire. No one in there got out alive … including Santos."

Drawing him closer into her arms, Rohini stroked Miguel's hair as a series of deep, muffled sobs wracked his body. She allowed him to cry until the tears came no more. Finally, after several minutes, Miguel righted himself and dried his eyes.

"I'm so sorry," he said sheepishly. "I still can't believe … Santos is gone. It makes me weep, even when I try not to."

"I know, he was your friend," said Rohini softly.

"He was more than that. Santos was like another father to me. He deserved a better fate than to die … that way."

"It was his karma, Miguel. No one can change what fate has ordained for each of us. Your friend is now at peace. Remember him for the blessings he left you. This way you will honor his work, and his memory, as you continue with your life."

"That's a very beautiful sentiment, Rohini," Miguel managed a smile. "I'll try to remember Santos that way, for the things he taught me and the wonderful experiences we shared."

"What will you do now, Miguel?"

"I don't know," he sagged a bit. "Return to the U.S., maybe. Twenty-four hours ago my life was set, now everything's been turned upside down. I'm still trying to figure things out."

"The last international flights have already left, and the main terminal building is closing now so the police can conduct their regular security sweep like they do every evening. Everyone must leave. Where will you go?"

"I don't know. Try and find a hotel someplace, I guess."

"You won't find anything close by at this hour. The downtown hotels are very expensive. Do you have friends in New Delhi?"

"Not really."

"Then come home with me," Rohini smiled. "You can stay at my place until you decide what to do."

"Your place?"

"Yes. I'd enjoy the company. It can get very lonely at times."

"No, er, I can't impose on you like that," Miguel stammered, feeling his face begin to flush.

"Nonsense! It's no imposition at all. Sharing a bed is a common thing. The sleeping arrangements may be a little tight, but I'm sure we'll manage."

Before Miguel could respond Rohini picked up his suitcase and started for the exit. As he watched the beautiful young woman stride gracefully ahead of him, competing thoughts filled his mind and fed his imagination. He played out a variety of different scenarios, almost all of which ran counter to the manner he wished to live his life. Though chaste of heart and pure of mind, Miguel was also a normal male in his early twenties who had just been invited to go home with a beautiful, exotic woman. Certainly he had no improper intentions, but what of this young woman whom he hardly knew?

With his world spinning rapidly out of control, Miguel grabbed his knapsack and followed after her as if in a dream.

Kathmandu

A few miles outside Kathmandu the slowly moving procession came to a halt. The glint of steel off a brightly lit moon caught Santos' attention as a squad of camouflaged soldiers quickly and without warning surrounded the group, cutting off their forward movement and blocking their retreat.

Santos bowed his head and prayed silently, certain that he was about to die. At peace with his impending death, he watched while words were exchanged between Jinpa and a darkly silhouetted figure. None of the monks betrayed any emotion as the discussion continued, at times with animated gestures by the scraggly bearded soldier, until halting the conversation with a seemingly dismissive wave the man motioned to the others under his command to remove Santos from the procession.

"You, now," a soldier spoke in broken English, guiding Santos with the barrel of his gun.

It was at this point that he first noticed a red star on the soldier's uniform. It wasn't the Nepalese military that stopped them; it was a band of Maoist guerrillas that operated in the hills outside Kathmandu. *Out of the fire, into the frying pan,* was the only thought that came to Santos. He looked toward Jinpa, whose expression conveyed no alarm.

"There is an old saying from your culture," Jinpa said calmly. "Politics can make strange bedfellows. These men will take you to Rajendra Shrestha, their leader. He has agreed to provide you with safe passage out of the country. Go with them, they will do you no harm."

"They're Communist guerillas!" Santos protested. "Even if they didn't bomb St. Joseph's, they're still terrorists."

"It might be wise not to use such strong words in describing their actions," Jinpa said, "whatever their true nature. Right now they are but a means to a good end."

"These … people are going to help me escape from Nepal? Why?"

"Shaitana is as great a threat to them as he is to any others in my country. Shrestha will help you escape, because he believes that doing so will help bring about Shaitana's defeat. This is what I have told him."

"But, what if I can't—"

"This is what I believe. That your heart is filled with doubt only testifies to the truth of my assertion, for no man would profess to hold such power if he truly understood the nature of the challenge you face. Go my friend, and fulfill the destiny for which you have been uniquely chosen.

May the Enlightened One guide and protect you. *Om mani padme hum.*"

The lead soldier barked an order in Nepali. Santos didn't understand the words — but clearly understood the meaning — as the soldier motioned with his pistol for Santos to follow. Jinpa and the others in the procession continued chanting their blessing to the odd looking, golden robed figure now flanked on all sides by heavily armed guerrillas, who disappeared with him into the darknes

New Delhi

Miguel said very little during his ride with Rohini through the streets of New Delhi in a quaint, three-wheel auto-rickshaw.

Careening through spacious, tree-lined avenues lined with imposing government buildings, they made their way toward Rohini's home in Kamala Nagar on the northern outskirts of the city. The sixty minute ride from the airport in south-west Delhi to Rohini's home took them through the center of the city. Marble and stone buildings set in the late nineteenth century European style gave it an imperial grandeur unlike any other Indian city. New Delhi, the latest of the seven cities of Delhi constructed through the centuries, had been designed by the famed architect Edwin Lutyens under the British Raj. All around them were massive mementos in stone laid by the various Hindu and Islamic dynasties that had ruled Delhi through the ages. The centerpiece of the city, the Rashtrapati Bhawan, once housed the British viceroys, and was now the official residence of the Indian President.

The auto-rickshaw soon left the city center and made its way to Kamala Nagar. As it climbed a small hill a large two story home came into view, set amidst a smattering of fruit trees and shrubs. The imposing brick masonry house was surrounded by a high wall topped with wrought iron. Its red roof and smooth, white sand-face plastered walls, carefully sculptured porticos and balusters, and looming Victorian veranda made it look more like a miniature palace than a common domestic residence. The house was one of several similar homes on the winding, brightly lit road, and it wasn't until the auto-rickshaw pulled to a stop that Miguel was certain they had arrived at Rohini's home.

"You live here?" he asked, expecting to find an apartment building or small house that was more in keeping with her job as an airline ticket agent.

"Yes," Rohini said, emerging from the cab. "Come in, and make yourself comfortable. And don't feel that you need to be a on your best behavior! Just ask for anything you want, and I'll be glad to give it to you. You've had such a stressful time. I want to make your stay as pleasant as possible."

Miguel stood at the edge of the street, still in a daze, while the young woman paid the driver and sent him on his way. Seemingly oblivious to his lingering concern over the propriety of accepting her offer to stay with her that evening, she took his hand in hers and began leading him toward the darkened house.

"Are you hungry, Miguel? I can make you something before we go to bed."

"No, er — no need to do that," he stammered.

"It's no trouble really."

"No, no, I'm perfectly fine about all of this ... I think. If we go slow, and things don't get out of control."

Rohini thread her arm through Miguel's arms, almost pulling him along as he trudged forward with leadened feet. Sweat began to build on his brow, and a deep look of panic spread across his face the closer they got to the front door.

"Miguel, are you all right?"

"Rohini, um, are you sure I'm not putting you out?"

"Of course not!" she laughed with an easy smile.

"I don't want to be a bother."

Rohini paused, looking deep into Miguel's eyes. "You've been through so much, Miguel," she said with genuine emotion. "Let me help you take some of the tension away."

"I, er, maybe we shouldn't … I don't think we should —" Miguel began to respond, but was interrupted by the sound of a door opening. Out burst three boys under the age of ten who raced up Rohini and wrapped themselves around her legs, giggling happily while two other men, one in his late teens and the other in his early twenties, watched warily from the doorway.

"Who are these people?" Miguel blinked back his surprise.

"My family," Rohini replied with a puzzled shrug. "These are my three youngest brothers, Amit, Tarun and Anand. And over there at the door are my other brothers, Ravi and Vijay."

"Your family?"

"Of course. Mother and father are inside. My uncle Kapilbhai lives with us too, upstairs. You'll probably stay in Kapil uncle's room tonight. Like I said, the sleeping arrangements may be a little tight."

"Oh, now I understand!" Miguel breathed a visible sigh of relief.

"What did you think I meant?" Rohini's eyes narrowed slightly.

"I, er, you said you were lonely," he answered sheepishly.

"I'm the only girl in a house filled with men — all of whom are my relatives. I was speaking about friends. What was it you thought I meant?"

"I, er, never mind," Miguel blushed.

"Well, come along," Rohini smiled. "I want to introduce you to my parents and Kapil uncle. You won't mind sharing a bed with him, will you?"

"No, absolutely," Miguel said, relieved. "Not at all."

Chapter 8

Hills outside Kathmandu

The sun had barely risen when a soldier appeared at the entrance to Santos' tent. The robes he had worn the night before were neatly folded and laid on the ground next to him. In their place he had changed into his regular shoes and clothing, sleeping in them on the hard earthen floor once they reached the guerrilla's camp.

Using the walking stick to pull himself to his feet, Santos looked into the face of a boy who couldn't have been more than fifteen years old. The child, his skin and clothing dirtied with mud and grime, looked back at the strange Filipino priest with little apparent emotion. Gesturing to the outside, he invited Santos to come with him.

The encampment was a hodgepodge of tents and shacks, camouflaged with branches to hide them amongst the dense green growth of the surrounding hills. Men as old as sixty and boys even younger than the one who summoned him populated the makeshift village. The cries of a young infant directed Santos to a woman and her child washing at a nearby stream. Like some caricature of a Mexican village during the time of Pancho Villa, he soon found himself surrounded by dozens of men, women, and children of all ages, each of whom seemed to have a weapon of some kind either on them, or in close proximity.

The farther he walked, the louder the mutterings grew as many of the guerrillas pointed at Santos and spoke animatedly among themselves. The attention he was getting made Santos increasingly nervous, but there was little he could do except continue to traverse the rocky, uneven ground on their way to a row of careworn shacks hidden in the underbrush of a large, overhanging rock. Arriving at the largest of three cabins, the young boy motioned for Santos to enter, then walked away. Whoever or whatever was inside, Santos would be going in alone.

"Ah, the priest," Shrestha said in passable English, looking up from his rough hewn desk. "You here sit. Please."

Warily, Santos took his place in a chair opposite the handmade desk. Only he and Shrestha were in the room, but outside he could already see a growing number of guerrillas gathering together and speaking among themselves.

"You sleep well, priest?" Shrestha asked.

"Yes, thank you," Santos tried to be polite.

"Hunger?"

"A little."

"We later eat, after talk. My people think you are … I not know word. I think, ghost?"

"Ghost?"

"Shaitana kill all priest like you, much power, very bad boom. But he no kill you. Why?"

"I was in the garden at St. Joseph's, praying," Santos answered. "I left the conference before the explosion."

"No in boom?"

"No. I was in the garden."

"No hurt when boom kill many priests?"

"No," Santos repeated. "I wasn't there when the bomb went off."

"You walk through fire, break Shaitana's magic?"

"Of course not," Santos let his irritation begin to show, in spite of himself. "I told you, I was not in the conference hall when the bomb went off. I wasn't near the explosion. Why are you asking me about this, anyway? I thought Jinpa said you were going to help me get out of Nepal. This conversation is pointless. When do we leave?"

"Not go yet. Maybe never," Shrestha said. "This very bad. Shaitana magic very strong. Bullets no good to stop. Only strong magic, from priest. This what Jinpa say. But you no magic. You no can hurt Shaitana. But know where we are. Can hurt us. This very bad."

"I knew this was a mistake to trust a band of terrorists," Santos muttered under his breath loud enough for Shrestha to hear.

The angry commandant of the Maoist forces pulled back loudly in his chair. "We freedom fight, no terrorist!" he shouted. Calling to a guard outside his door, Shrestha ordered the man to enter with his pistol drawn. More words were exchanged between Shrestha and the guard, and Santos found himself being pulled to his feet.

"You no magic. You no stop Shaitana. You now die."

"It won't be magic that defeats Shaitana," Santos said forcefully, temporarily stopping the guard from taking him away. "The power of our Lord Jesus Christ and his Church will vanquish him and his minions."

"Your Christ make powerful magic?" Shrestha narrowed his gaze.

"The power of our Blessed Lord is supreme over all others. Through him I will cast out the forces of Hell that gives Shaitana his strength. Without Satan he will lose whatever power he now has. But to do this I must first leave Nepal, and seek the knowledge of the Seven Secrets to perform my task."

"Ah, great magic," Shrestha said, stroking his chin. He ordered the guard to release his grip on Santos. "Jinpa speak truth. Eat first now, then we leave. Army control much, but no all. We get you to border, cross and take train to India."

"Thank you," Santos sighed with relief.

Another guard entered the command hut and led Santos to a gathering place where a meal of potato and cucumber stew was dispensed to him from a large cast iron cauldron hanging over an open fire.

While Santos ate, Shrestha summoned his top commanders and briefed them on his conversation with Santos. The western priest who had taken refuge in a Buddhist temple claimed to have magical powers equal to, if not greater than, those of Shaitana. Their mission was to get him safely across the border so he could invoke the secrets of the demon world, which the shamans of his religion held in a secret vault in some inscrutable location, guarded by a hydra-headed monster answerable only to the little Filipino priest. Invoking his black magic, Santos would summon a great bird from beyond the heavens who possessed razor sharp claws and a jagged, piercing beak to pluck out Shaitana's eyes and devour his liver. While the otherworldly powers were preoccupied in battle, Shrestha and his army would attack and defeat the Nepalese military, and take control of the country.

Or at least, that was what Shrestha though his people wanted to hear. In truth, the grey haired commander of the rebel forces had little use for formal religion of any kind, but he knew that the poor, uneducated peasants who constituted the bulk of his forces were steeped in mythology and folklore. Whether the mysticism was of eastern or western origin, they would take comfort from the belief that Shaitana's great powers would soon be checked, leaving them free to move against a weakened government.

New Delhi

An uncomfortable night sharing the same bed with Rohini's portly uncle Kapilbhai left Miguel as tired when he arose as he was when he went to bed the night before. Fighting exhaustion, he dressed and left the room while

Kapilbhai was finishing his late morning shower, making his way down an ornately carved staircase to the main living area of the house.

Expecting to see something a bit more exotic, he was greeted with a sight that could have been straight from his own home in Dallas, Texas. Overhead a ceiling fan moved the air, creating a soft, gentle breeze that cooled the house. To the left was a bookshelf with all kinds of popular Western novels from the eighties and nineties. A video game was attached to a wide-screen television set in the main living area, and the two youngest boys lay side-by-side blasting space demons and intergalactic terrors off the screen.

Wandering through the home, Miguel bumped into Rohini who was emerging from the kitchen. She greeted him with a friendly smile.

"Good morning, Miguel. Did you sleep well last night with Kapil uncle?"

"It was fine," he avoided the question, not wanting to seem ungrateful.

"Lunch is almost ready. I'm helping my mother prepare the last dish. Why don't you join my family in the dining room and I'll be in shortly. I'm sure they're anxious to meet you."

Entering the dining area, Miguel took a seat at the crowded table. He tried to make pleasant conversation with Vijay Khanna, the oldest of her five brothers, who remained silent while studying him with a fixed, penetrating stare. Seated next to him was Deepak Khanna, Rohini's father, who seemed no more enthusiastic than his oldest son about Miguel's unexpected arrival at their home the night before. The rest of the family, including Rohini's grandmother Lakshmi and great aunt Purvi, who upon news of the young man's arrival invited themselves over to their home, were also seated around the dining table, as was uncle Kapilbhai fresh from his morning wash.

Arranged before them was a meal of *chappatis*, a wheat flour Indian tortilla, dhal — a kind of lentil curry — and all manner of curried vegetables, pickles, basmati rice, and home-made yogurt. It looked as if a great feast had been prepared for an honored guest, though in truth Miguel felt more like a man about to consume his last meal before facing a firing squad. Rohini smiled at Miguel from a distance while she and her mother Meera, an elegant middle-aged woman dressed in a brightly colored sari, cut and sliced the last of the food in the kitchen, ferrying it out in stages to the crowded dining area. The chatter around him made it impossible for Miguel to do anything other than smile feebly in return. Strains of English,

Hindi, and a strange combination of both languages melded into one continuous noise as the overflowing table of children and adults ate from the communal plates laid before them.

Just as Miguel was beginning to relax and enjoy the wonderfully inviting tastes, Deepak brought all conversation to an immediate stop in his high-pitched, halting voice. He looked at Miguel with a disturbing gaze, and spoke loudly.

"What are your intentions toward my daughter?" he asked abruptly.

Miguel had just been sampling the rice and lentils and the question caught him completely off guard. He choked and swallowed, his face flushed, mumbling his answer.

"Er, nothing, Sir?"

"You come to my home, sleep in my bed, eat my food, and you have no intentions toward Rohini?" Deepak's face was a mixture of confusion and horror. "I must ask you quite directly. What are you doing here, young man?"

"I met Rohini at the airport," Miguel started to explain.

"You work together?"

"No sir. We just met the other day."

"For the first time?" Deepak's voice tightened and his eyebrows raised. "And now you come with her to our home, like that? I am not liking this, I can tell you for certain. This is not our way. Again, I ask you, what are your intentions toward my daughter? They cannot be good."

"Daddy!" Rohini hurried into the dining area, blushing a deep crimson red. "What are you doing?"

"I think I have a right to know what this young man intends for you," Deepak's voice rose another octave.

"He has no intentions father! He's a friend I met, a person who needed a place to stay for the night, and I offered him our hospitality."

The conversation continued in Hindi with the two oldest boys, and Rohini's grandmother, great aunt, and mother, joining the debate. Only uncle Kapilbhai seemed unconcerned, helping himself to another generous portion of curried vegetables. He caught Miguel's eye and gave him a friendly wink.

"Rohini's father does not like her mixing with boys. She is his only daughter, and her honor must be protected. You understand, don't you?"

"I'm not … I didn't … I have no improper intentions," Miguel replied, flustered.

"Well, whether you do or not, Deepak will see to it that you don't. Welcome to the family, my young friend."

Around the table the debate continued with enthusiasm. Miguel watched, wide-eyed in amazement, as the discussion grew more and more animated. Finally Rohini grew completely flustered and reacted to something her father said. Shouting to everyone in English, she again brought the overlapping conversation to a sudden, immediate halt.

"I am not going to marry Ratan. I will choose my own husband, not someone who is arranged for me!"

"If it was good enough for your mother and me," Deepak huffed, "it is perfectly all right for my daughter. Ratan has a fine job and a good future. We have already discussed many of the details with his parents. Any involvement with this 'boy' could ruin your prospects, not just with Ratan, but with any others in the marriage market."

"This is the twenty-first century, *pitaji!* Women are not chattel to be bartered or sold."

"We have already discussed the dowry," Deepak held his ground. "You must show more respect to our traditions."

Again the conversation returned to Hindi. It seemed as if everyone at the table had an opinion to share except for uncle Kapilbhai, whose attention was focused on scooping another portion of lentils and rice onto his plate. Even after Rohini withdrew from the discussion, the back-and-forth continued as all the family members shouted and gestured, driving their points home with matching body language.

Looking as if she was about to cry from embarrassment, Rohini turned to Miguel. "I'm so sorry about this," she said. "I can't seem to make my father understand that I'm not going to marry a man I don't love, or even know! We have this argument at least once a month, and it never changes."

Instead of being offended, Miguel found himself strangely amused by the entire proceeding. He tried to reassure the tearful young woman with a broad, self-effacing smile.

"You have nothing to apologize for, Rohini. It's obvious that you have a loving family that cares very much about you."

"Maybe they could care a little less, or a little more quietly," she winced at the loud, ongoing debate. "I just wish they'd understand that there's no room in the modern world for these old ways."

"Traditions are very important, Rohini. They help ground people, and give meaning to their lives. Especially in times of trouble."

"You actually think I should go through with an arranged marriage?" she replied incredulously.

"No, not at all," Miguel laughed. "Just understand your father's perspective, and use it to find common ground to discuss your feelings. I can see he only wants the best for you, like any father would for his only daughter. You just need to help him recognize how to do that in a world that's so different from the one he grew up in. Honor, respect, tradition — they all go together. I know your parents will do the right thing by you, because it's obvious how much they love you."

The room grew gradually quieter while Miguel and Rohini talked as everyone at the table slowly directed their attention toward them, boldly listening in. Deepak looked at Miguel, not certain whether he was supporting his position or not. His face softened slightly as he contemplated the young man's remarks, deciding to give Miguel a second consideration after having judged him so harshly.

"Meera," he called to his wife. "Bring our young guest some *rasagoola*. It is a milk sweet, Miguel, very tasty."

"Thank you," Miguel nodded while the middle-aged woman left the table and hurried to bring him a bowl of the delicacy.

In the blink of an eye the entire atmosphere around the breakfast table had changed. Everyone's attention remained focused on Deepak, who acted as if nothing out of the ordinary had happened.

"Now Vijay," he said, patting his stomach. "If you will please pass me the dhal curry, I am quite hungry."

India-Nepal border

Curled up in the back of a vegetable hauler belching great clouds of diesel fumes from its rusted exhaust pipes, Santos was ferried a hundred miles to the border with India. Only about a fifth of the hilly road was paved, and those sections that were contained plenty of axel-breaking potholes. Barely two lanes wide, it was strewn with the carcasses of broken down vehicles, some little more than skeletal frames as a result of prolonged exposure to the harsh elements. Interspersed here and there along the route were tiny houses here that seemed to spring up in the middle of nowhere. Peering through wooden slats in the side of the truck, the terrain was about as desolate and unforgiving as Santos could imagine. He half-wondered if the Maoist guerrillas were actually taking him to safety, or were transporting him instead to some remote mountain gully to be summarily executed, with his mortal remains dumped where they would never be found.

Any questions about his impending fate were soon answered when the noisy truck came to a lurching stop. The driver opened the back gate and let him out, then pointed toward a small village on the other side of a gently sloping hill.

"There you train," he gestured with the barrel of his AK-47.

"Thank you," Santos replied appreciatively, receiving only a slight nod in return.

Without anything being said the driver climbed back into the truck, turned around, and headed back into Nepal. Santos watched it bounce along the old dirt road until it was completely out of sight. Then, with his walking stick in hand, enough currency in his pocket from Jinpa, and a wedge of *Alu Roti* — potato filled bread — given to him by the guerillas at the camp, he crossed the border and made his way along the rocky terrain toward the remote Indian village.

Nestled in the valley of a barren, rock-strewn gorge, it seemed as if the world had passed the little town by. Except for a dilapidated old train depot built well into the last century, there was nothing to mark it as a place of any significance. A few peasants stood on the platform selling prayer beads and other religious amulets, occasionally producing sticks of dried curried beef or other exotic foodstuff from underneath ragged cloaks that they offered to the gathered crowd. It looked as if many in the station had walked for miles from even smaller hamlets scattered throughout the countryside to reach the depot. Many brought their own food, even some small farm animals, but enough purchased the marginally sanitary snacks or religious artifacts to make the exercise profitable for these enterprising merchants.

Blending in with the others milling about the train depot, Santos bought a ticket and sat down on a rickety old bench. A young Western couple, their designer backpacks and Michelin travel guides setting them apart from everyone else, stood at the opposite end of the platform drinking in the local flavor. It seemed as if no more than a minute would go by without one of them posing for another photograph against the lush mountainous backdrop of the India-Nepal border. Santos smiled sadly while he watched them go about their carefree ways. The sandy-haired man was only a few years older than Miguel, and he wondered if his young companion had made it safely out of Kathmandu or was still trapped in Nepal. Or worse. The forces of darkness that sought to destroy him and the other exorcists would not hesitate to take another innocent life if it served their unholy purposes.

Santos tried to block the image from his mind, knowing that there was nothing he could do to help Miguel at the moment. His main focus was on returning to New Delhi, and from there to Rome and the Church of San Giuseppe. He wasn't sure exactly what awaited him, and the uncertainty only added to his doubts about his ability to stop Shaitana from completing his diabolic mission that began with the murder of his fellow exorcists at St. Joseph. Before he left for Rome, however, he would return to see Father Dias who had sheltered him and Miguel the night they first arrived in New Delhi. Though sickly and frail, the elderly priest was still an exorcist, and Santos wanted to warn him of the possible danger he faced if Shaitana truly sought to reach out beyond Nepal and murder every living practitioner of this ancient rite.

A blaring whistle caused Santos looked up as an old steam engine train puffed its way into the station. Boarding the second class passenger car, he found one of the last open seats and sat down warily. The din of conversation in a dozen different dialects, mixed with the unsanitary conditions and scents of strange foods, all melded into a numbing blur broken only by another piercing shriek of the train whistle as the old wooden car lurched forward to resume its slow, stop-and-go journey across the northern territories toward the New Delhi Railway station.

Undaunted, Santos settled back and relaxed for the first time in two days amid the noise and smell of the crowded compartment. Closing his eyes, he prayed silently for the strength to see him through the next few days, then drifted off into a deep, consuming sleep.

New Delhi

With her grandmother and great aunt trailing a few steps behind them, and her brother Vijay keeping a respectful, but watchful eye on his sister from the vantage point of a second story veranda, Miguel and Rohini strolled along a garden path behind her suburban home.

Miguel had spent the day getting to know her extended family as all manner of aunts, uncles, cousins, and distant relatives dropped by to visit. It was a lively, circus-like atmosphere that somehow seemed vaguely appropriate, despite the manufactured chaos that came hand-in-tow with such a great influx of people. For a young man who was the only child of poor

Mexican immigrants, and had spent the last five years of his life cloistered from most of the world as the traveling companion to a quirky, frenetic little Filipino priest, it was Disneyland and the Fourth of July all rolled into one enormous indoor jamboree. Rohini would periodically appear to rescue Miguel from the onslaught of attention showered upon him, only to be pulled away by her mother, aunts or grandmother and forced to leave him to fend for himself. Since much of the conversation was in Hindi when not directed toward him, Miguel could only surmise that the answers he gave, or the composure he showed, had left a good impression. Even Deepak seemed to warm up to him as the day went on, inviting Miguel into his study to show him his prized collection of 1970's LP records, a few of which he played for his guest on a scratchy old record player from the 1950s.

By nightfall, after another fine meal prepared by Rohini and her female relatives, Miguel and the young woman managed to steal a few moments to themselves and go for a walk under the protective supervision of her extended family. In the clear, cool night air, the sky was alive with brilliant pinpoints of light that looked like tiny crystals on a velvet curtain. Walking and staring at the sky, Miguel let his thoughts drift to Santos, wondering if Heaven was truly nestled among the stars as the old stories imagined. Wherever it was, he hoped that Santos was finally at peace, and doing more of God's work by watching over him from his vantage point above.

"You're very quiet, Miguel," Rohini said after a long, quiet stretch.

"I was just thinking about my friend," Miguel replied sadly. "I know we can never truly understand God's ways, but it seems so wrong for Santos to be taken from this world before we had a chance to say goodbye."

"It's all karma," Rohini said gently. "Everything that happens to us is a result of our actions in our past lives. But I'm sure all the good things he has done in this life will ensure that in his next rebirth he will be in a higher state, closer to moksha, to liberation from the cycle of birth and rebirth."

Miguel didn't respond to the strange and challenging notions that ran contrary to his faith. Instead, he accepted Rohini's comments for what they were, a gesture of kindness among friends of different cultures, meant to console him during a time of great pain.

"I know. I'm just being selfish," he said in a low voice. "Santos wasn't only my friend, he was my teacher. There was so much more he had to give, for me to learn, I wish he was still here with me. You would have enjoyed knowing him, Rohini. He was a man of great inner strength and wisdom, even if things were often somewhat chaotic whenever he was around."

"'Chaos' is a concept I understand quite well," Rohini smiled, glancing back toward her house.

"Yes, I can see that," Miguel chuckled before turning somber once again. "I guess I'm just feeling all alone, for the very first time. Now I have to face the world without Santos, and it's a sobering thought. I don't quite know what to do."

"You could … stay here for a while longer, in New Delhi," she suggested hesitantly. "It might give us a chance to get to know each other better."

"This is all still very confusing to me," Miguel turned to face the striking beautiful young woman who looked nervously into his eyes. "I've never really had someone like you, I mean, with Santos we were always on the go. There was never any time to, you know, develop friendships."

"You are unlike anyone I've ever met before too, Miguel," Rohini said softly. "You must have thought I was so forward, giving you my telephone number that day I first saw you. I've never done that with anyone, not even men I've known for a long time. There was just something about you, the kindness in your eyes, the way you spoke, things I can't describe that told me you were quite unlike anyone I've ever met. I want to get to know you better, Miguel. Stay here, in New Delhi, until you decide what you need to do."

"You are very different too, Rohini. Very kind, very beautiful. I'd be less than honest if I didn't say your offer had great appeal."

"But—"

"But there is something terrible going on, even more than the death of Santos and the other priests at St. Joseph. I don't know what it is, but I know it's still lurking out there. I spent most of my adult life fighting the dark forces with Santos. What happened at St. Joseph's is part of all of this, but only the beginning. I need to let others know what I have seen, and what I fear may be still to come. I'm going to Rome. Santos had friends there, and maybe they'll be able to make some sense of this."

"So you're leaving?" Rohini said sadly.

"Tomorrow. But before I go, I need to visit a priest in New Delhi, someone Santos and I stayed with the night we first arrived. I was so distraught I didn't even think about going to him when I got back from Kathmandu."

"I'm glad," Rohini squeezed his hand and smiled.

"I am too," Miguel kissed her softly on the cheek.

For a long time neither spoke, continuing to walk in the darkness under a glimmering sheet of stars made even more brilliant by the company they kept. Wherever he went, whatever direction life might take him, Miguel would not forget the simple pleasure of a starlit walk with a person as kind and sweet as Rohini. In another time, another life, he might have surrendered to the temptation to stay with her and see where their relationship would develop. But these were not ordinary times, and Miguel felt a duty to Santos' memory to continue in his path, even if he thought he felt wholly inadequate for the task.

It was the least he could do for this most remarkable man, who was both his friend and mentor.

Rome

Mother Philomena awoke from a fitful sleep.

Across the room light from a single candle burned dimly, its wick almost exhausted. A crucifix on the wall cast a slim, almost imperceptible shadow across the prayer table below it, streaking the pages of an open Bible left there by the elderly nun. The only other object on the table was a simple rosary made of ordinary polished stones and worn metal clasps, a silent testament to the life of sacrifice and devotion led by the woman Pope Gregory XVII called "The Conscience of the Papacy."

Focusing her eyes on the flickering pinpoint of light, Mother Philomena watched the tiny flame grow smaller until it was snuffed out in a last, dying gasp, extinguishing itself in the melted wax. Climbing out of bed, she hastily dressed in her white-robed habit before venturing past the Swiss Guards through a courtyard and then into a corridor leading to the papal quarters. The still night air hung over her like a pall, seeming to drain the energy from her limbs while she made her way down the long, marble floored hallway to the chambers where Pope Gregory lay.

With trembling hands, Mother Philomena pushed the ornately-carved, heavy wooden doors open. In the dull light she could see Cardinal Fenucci kneeling at the pope's side. Drawing nearer to the bed, she heard the whispered prayers of the quietly sobbing man, and knew that the moment she dreaded had now come.

"The Holy Father has left this world, to join our Father in Heaven,"

Fenucci slowly lifted himself from his knees.

"Already the vultures swarm to pick at his bones," Mother Philomena said, shocking the white haired man. She looked impassively at Fenucci, then knelt to kiss the pope's cold, lifeless hand. "Pope Gregory is in Heaven, but he has left much unfinished business on Earth, horrifying business."

"I must inform the College of Cardinals," Fenucci said as he watched her warily, not quite knowing what to make of the elderly nun's strange behavior.

"I will pray for us all," Mother Philomena said, remaining beside the lifeless body. "May God deliver us from the evil that surrounds this holy place."

The clatter of his shoes on the smoothly polished floor was the only sound Mother Philomena heard as Cardinal Fenucci left the room. Closing the doors after him, the pope's personal secretary could only shake his head in wonder at the meaning of her words. Whatever cataclysmic images Mother Philomena foresaw, there were still duties to be performed. A successor to the now deceased pope had to be selected. Competing factions within the College of Cardinals had already begun to maneuver for position, their efforts intensifying with each new decline in the pope's health. Whoever it was they selected to assume the mantle of Christ's representative on Earth, Cardinal Fenucci wanted to remain in the enclave of power that embodied personal service to the Holy See. It was a calling he had answered a long time ago, and one he would not easily abandon.

Ritual and tradition would prescribe the manner by which the new pope would be selected. But now more than in other times, it was politics and palace intrigue that would define the outcome.

Chapter 9

New Delhi

The cab arrived early the next morning to pick up Miguel. Deepak Khanna, his wife Meera, sons Amit, Tarun, Anand, Ravi and Vijay, and the rest of his extended family, all joined Rohini in their front yard to bid the young American boy goodbye.

"You are a welcomed guest in my home on any occasion," Deepak took Miguel's hand and shook it firmly, drawing whispered purrs of approval from the elderly women who nodded while they spoke among themselves. "Next time you come we will listen to some of my 8-track tapes. My favorite is a singer called 'Conway Twitty'. He has a most pleasant way of performing. I hope he is still popular back in America."

"I'm sure he is," Miguel smiled.

"This is a fine young man," Deepak turned and spoke to his family. "Very intelligent, very thoughtful. Now we let Rohini say her final goodbye. All of you, into the house. Right now." Dutifully, the family returned to the home, though Miguel could see their eyes peering out from parted curtains.

Through muted tears Rohini squeezed his hand and struggled to maintain her smile. "I know we may never see each other again, Miguel. But I want you to know I'll always remember you."

"I won't forget you either, Rohini."

"Please write me when you can."

"I will. I don't know where I'll be, so I don't know when the letters might come."

"I understand," Rohini laced her fingers through his, drawing his eyes toward hers. "You will always know where you can find me, Miguel."

The simple kiss was a first for the nervous young man, and it left him delightfully light-headed. He loaded his backpack and luggage into the cab, his gaze lingering on Rohini as the rickety old car pulled away from the curb. With a final wave and smile his beautiful friend disappeared from view, leaving Miguel to wonder if they would ever meet again.

Rome

"It's confirmed, Sir," Vincent Stout handed a sheet of paper to Ralston Hastings, who was relaxing in his suite after a late night dinner with the Italian Minister of Finance. "Pope Gregory died in his sleep last night at 3:30 am."

"Tell all our outlets worldwide to run the obituary I had them prepare. I want his legacy defined properly. Gregory was an obstacle to reform who used the Church to block progressive policies where they were needed most. Birth control, abortion, same-sex marriage — the guy set social progress back a hundred years. I want the people to know just how much damage he did."

"Yes Sir."

"Who's in line to succeed him?"

"There are two leading candidates," Stout read from a file he carried, anticipating the question. "Cardinal Francesco Orsini is the chief candidate of the traditionalists. He says he wants to strengthen the conservative power base of the Church, even going so far as to reinstate the Tridentine Latin Mass. I'd say he's the leading contender at the moment, but he does have organized opposition from the more liberal wing of the Church. Their candidate seems to be the Belgian Cardinal Bruno Reinhard. Our research indicates that he's more of a diplomat than a theologian, though he did lead a pretty serious 'palace revolt' of sorts last year that forced to pope to rescind one of his papal edicts. He sees the 'big picture', particularly in the third world where he supports progressive family planning policies, but also internationally. He's said that he wants to bring Rome back 'into sync with the world'. We have a couple of his public pronouncements where he said he wants to eradicate fundamentalism both within and outside the Church. It's all here in this dossier Sir."

Stout handed the folder to Hastings, who glanced at it briefly then put it aside. "I've seen enough. Tell our people to put our efforts behind Reinhard. I want to make sure he's the next pope."

Stout looked at Hastings with a mixture of hesitation and confusion. "The pope isn't ... elected," he proceeded cautiously, "not in the way you're implying Sir."

"You still don't understand, do you Vincent," Hastings chuckled sarcastically. "The Catholic Church is more of a political institution than most governments. They control great wealth and property, they tax their parishioners every Sunday, they run schools and hospitals and attempt to influence national legislation, and they make political appointments to their own internal bureaucracy just like any other institution. There's a pecking order at the Vatican just like in any governing body. The people on the lowest rung are always looking for a way to get to the top, even if they have to claw their way over everyone ahead of them. Religion is just the sideshow that keeps it all together, and lets them maintain their power over the ignorant masses.

"No Vincent, there's a campaign already under way to see who gets the ring, and it's going to be vicious, even if it's behind closed doors. And we're going to help direct the outcome by talking up Reinhard while tearing down Orsini. You can't tell me the Cardinals don't listen to the press. The Church has been rocked with every kind of scandal, and they're still reeling from where it hurts them the most — the pocketbook. We're going to get every Catholic in the world to threaten a boycott if the Church appoints anyone but a compassionate, visionary leader to replace that old dinosaur, one who looks to the twenty-first century for answers, not the fifteenth. And we're going to tell them who that is. Bruno Reinhard."

"Yes Sir."

"You see, Vincent," Hastings smiled, relaxing in his chair while he lit up a cigar. "The people rely on us to help them navigate the complexities of life. Without us they'd never see the frauds for who they really are. We're going to usher in a new era of enlightenment where man controls his own destiny instead of entrusting his life to the capricious master plan of an imaginary God. We're going to get rid of all the 'keepers of the faith', and replace them with men and women of sound mind and healthy psyche who understand the difference between myth and reality.

"The era of religious dogma is over. The age of rationality is now upon us. Boogey men, ghosts, and the devil have no place in this world; only science and reason. If we can't touch it, feel it, smell it, or examine it with our own senses, it doesn't exist. I'm not saying people shouldn't believe in God. I'm sure there's something out there, somewhere, that got things started. But we don't need to waste our lives worshiping that, whatever it is, when we could all be using our time to build a better world. Once we get rid of the irrational belief that one religion or another has a monopoly on the truth, and recognize that all religions are equal — once they understand their proper place — we'll set the stage for the greatest advancement mankind has ever seen. Once their minds are freed from this clutter, all the people will lack is direction. And I'm going to guide them toward the proper path. The Catholic Church isn't the biggest, but it's the most influential, and when the dominos start to fall it will take all the others with it. Think of this as a public service, Vincent. We're going to help those old fossils in the College of Cardinals do the right thing and select a man who fits our time."

"I understand perfectly, Sir," Stout nodded.

"Good. Now when we run our piece on Reinhard, I want Shaitana to gear up his people to promote the same cause. He's got 30 million followers in every country on this planet. It's time to put them to use. And I don't want to hear any excuses about the time 'not being right'. I've bankrolled him long enough. I want to see a tangible return on my investment, starting today. I want rallies for social justice in all the major capitals. I want protests against religious zealots in the target areas we selected: restrictions on abortion, opposition to gay marriage, state funding of religious activities, the Boy Scouts, the whole nine yards. We're going to drive a wedge between these crazies who get their marching orders directly from God and the rest of civilization. I want Shaitana to use his standing at the United Nations to brand any fundamentalist religious activity a hate crime subject to sanction by the World Court. By the time we've finished, there won't be a decent person left anywhere in the world who will have the guts to publicly support those causes. It'll be more popular to be a Nazi SS guard than a god-fearing, bible thumping Christian."

Nodding respectfully, Stout left the room to execute Hastings orders. When the door closed a pretty young redhead dressed in a sheer silk robe emerged from the bedroom, and poured herself a gin and tonic from the bar in the suite. Standing in the light streaming through an open window, Hastings could see every curve of her voluptuous body. She smiled provocatively, then moved closer to his desk, sitting on its edge and crossing her legs.

"You can really do all that?" she smiled, sipping her drink.

"And more. Didn't anyone ever tell you it wasn't polite to listen in on other people's conversations, Gina," Hastings asked with a thin smile.

"There's a lot of things people told me never to do," she slipped from the edge of the table onto his lap, and nibbled at his ear. "But it never seemed to have much of an impact on me."

"Yes, I can see that," Hastings grinned when her hands found his chest. The telephone on his desk rang, and he tapped the speaker button. "Hold my calls for the next hour. And have the Gulfstream fueled and ready to return to New York this evening. I have some things I need to attend to."

"Yes Sir," the disembodied voice returned, leaving Ralston Hastings to pursue matters of other interest until his noontime speech before the power brokers of Europe he brought to his retreat.

It was now time to collect on the markers so many of them had willingly volunteered, in exchange for inducements of privilege and opportunity, when they joined his crusade to remake the world in an image more to Hastings' liking.

New Delhi

Father Francis Xavier Dias lived in a walled-off section of the city known as 'Old' Delhi, the capital of Muslim India between the mid-seventeenth and late nineteenth centuries. Full of mosques, monuments, and gated entranceways, its narrow streets and ancient buildings were home to throngs of street bazaars and sidewalk merchants hawking all manner of items from fifth-hand apparel, to exotic sweets and spices, to bootleg video games.

None of the streets were marked. Traffic took whatever direction the natural flow of cars, trucks, buses, and scooters seemed to follow, making a bewildering trip even more confusing. Miguel marveled at the sights while the micro-mini cab he rode in maneuvered through the densely packed streets with a dexterity and grace that made it all seem like an intricately choreographed ballet. He knew that Father Dias' house was near the astonishing thirteenth century Qutab Minar, a five-storey fluted red sandstone tower laced with verses from the Qur'an that rose about 250 feet from the ground. Spotting a familiar landmark every once and a while, as soon as he thought he had his bearings the cab would disappear into another jumble of streets, buildings, and people. Hopelessly lost, Miguel decided to simply sit back and enjoy the ride for the experience it was, satisfied that the driver, at least, knew ultimately how to get him to his destination.

"We are arrived here, young man," the toothless cabbie smiled, pointing with the palm of his hand to a relatively modern building at the corner of the street within sight of the Qutb Minar. "That will be 500 rupees my good friend."

Fishing through his pocket, Miguel handed the man an extra 100, and retrieved his luggage from the trunk. With a wave and a smile the cab driver sped back into the flow of traffic to search for another fare. Miguel hefted his backpack over his shoulder, and with suitcase in tow headed toward the door to the one-bedroom flat.

"Father Dias," he knocked, trying to make himself heard over the cacophony of noises above and around him. "It's me, Miguel Guerrero. I was here the other day, with Father Santos. Are you home?"

There was no response. Miguel shouted again, this time louder, but again only silence returned from inside the apartment. Testing the door knob, he found it unlocked. Curious, he opened the door slightly and called again. This time he could hear the faint voice of someone speaking on the other side of the flat. The voice was too low to make out the words, but they seemed to be in Latin.

"Father Dias?" Miguel called, opening the door wider. Gasping in shock, he saw an overturned bookcase with its contents spilled across the floor. Elsewhere in the room there were signs of a struggle with pictures knocked crooked and a lamp broken on a table.

A long, thick stick lay on the floor amid all the debris. Miguel picked it up, thinking that he might need a weapon, and proceeded farther inside the apartment.

The strangely-familiar voice grew louder when he approached the bedroom. The window shades were drawn and it was dark inside, masking the appearance of a short little man bending over a bloody, prostrate body sprawled on the carpet. Miguel gasped when he recognized the face of the battered man as the kindly Father Dias.

"Who are you?" Miguel shouted, lifting the club-like stick. "What are you doing here! What did you do to Father Dias!"

It was only then that Miguel got a good look at the little man's face, who stopped his prayers and turned to look in his direction. For all his happiness at seeing Miguel again, Santos Machado found it difficult to express his joy. Beneath him was the bludgeoned body of his friend Father Dias, another exorcist killed by some unknown intruder in the most vicious manner. The words of Father Sanford played in his mind as Santos realized, with absolute finality, that he, truly, was now the only one left alive.

"Santos!" Miguel shouted. Still holding the walking stick above his head like an executioner's club, he quickly dropped it and rushed to embrace his friend, sobbing loudly and joyfully. "I-I thought you were dead! They told me you died in the explosion, like the others."

"God spared my life, Miguel."

"I'm so happy to see you again," he tightened his arms around him. "How did you get here?"

"We'll have time to talk about that later, Miguel. I must finish saying my final prayers for Father Dias, and then we must leave here, quickly."

"Shouldn't we call the police?"

"No. The forces of darkness behind this answer to no man. They may still be watching this place. He was killed only hours ago, his body is barely cold. We may be next if we don't leave soon."

"Where will we go?"

"To Rome, to the Church of San Giuseppe."

"Not the Vatican?"

"Pope Gregory is gravely ill, and the Curia is hostile to our ways. There is another path for us to follow. Now kneel with me and pray for the soul of Father Dias, that God the Father may welcome him into his embrace, and reward him with eternal life."

Across the street a tall figure in black, with short cropped hair and a pock-marked face watched Santos and Miguel as they left the flat. Taking one of Father Dias' canes to replace the cumbersome walking stick, Santos hailed a passing cab and, with Miguel at his side, headed toward the bus station. They would go to Calcutta where an airline would take them to Rome. If whoever killed Father Dias was watching for Santos, the airport at New Delhi would be the most logical place to find him. Travel to Calcutta by way of a cramped, ramshackle jitney bus was the best way to hide in plain sight.

Or so Santos hoped.

New York

In his flowing robe and manicured beard as elegant as ever, Shaitana sat in the office of UN Secretary General Axel Olsson. Next to him Roland Blavatasky read from a private message sent through the diplomatic service of the Secretary General, who listened respectfully while the news was read.

"The priests Dias in New Delhi, and Ramon in Guayaquil, have been killed my Lord. The other exorcists are near death from natural causes, and present no challenge. The path is now clear to invoke the powers of the Lumen Covenant."

"You presume to tell me my course of action, Blavatasky?" Shaitana replied coldly.

"No my lord," Blavatasky bowed respectfully. "I only report that all obstacles are free to invoke the Covenant, and assume your rightful place as sovereign of this world."

"Then all the exorcists are dead? Is that what you are telling me, Blavatasky?"

"Yes my Lord?"

"And the priest Machado?"

"He perished in Kathmandu with the others."

"Liar!" Shaitana raged, slamming his fist on the Secretary General's desk.

"It has been three days my Lord," Blavatasky said, his voice trembling. "There is no sign of the priest anywhere in Nepal. No one has seen him, no one has knowledge of his whereabouts. He must be dead. I am sure of it."

"Are you willing to match that with your life?" Shaitana seethed

Blavatasky's throat tightened. "My Lord, I—"

"The exorcist Machado is alive."

"But my Lord, how can you know—"

"I feel his wretched presence here, in my gut. Like the foul stench of a rotting carcass it hangs over me, cramping and confining me. Until he is dead, the power of the Lumen Covenant cannot be released. Everything I have done, everything I have planned, remains in jeopardy."

"My Lord, I—" Blavatasky started to respond.

Olsson watched in stunned disbelief as Blavatasky's body began to quiver. He reached for his face, only to pull back layers of decaying skin when his body began to decompose literally before his eyes. With an other-worldly scream the terrified man dropped to his knees and begged Shaitana for mercy, but there would be no compassion for the man who had pledged his loyalty to Lucifer's servant. Loyalty would not protect Blavatasky, who had failed his Master, and now his Master would take his revenge.

With the power of Hell coursing through his veins, Shaitana unleashed the full force of his fury against the hapless man. Bones cracked, and worms dug through his still-living body, as Blavatasky was reduced before Olsson's eyes to the dust from which all men came. The last pitiful groan of the decomposing man was accompanied by a sudden streak of immaterial energy as the soul of Roland Blavatasky left his body, briefly to glimpse the wonders of Paradise before being sucked back into a timeless, pitiless void from which it would never emerge.

"My Lord Shaitana," Olsson bowed respectfully as the last grains of dust swirled across the floor. "Your power is great. Tell me how I can serve you?"

"Find the priest Santos Machado. Or suffer the same fate as the others who fail me."

"Thy will be done," Olsson said.

"Now leave. I want to use your office."

As Olsson left the room and closed the door, Shaitana slumped in his chair. All the energy he had used to dispatch Blavatasky had completely drained him. Without the full force of the Lumen Covenant, through which Lucifer would ultimately channel his diabolical powers using Shaitana for his earthly instrument, he was limited to what Roland Hastings had derisively labeled as 'parlor tricks'.

Once Santos was dead, there would be no one to stop him. Hastings, the Church, and all others who stood in his way would be swept aside in a single stroke. The vision of Pope Leo would reach its climax when billions of souls came under the sway of evil incarnate.

Chapter 10

Rome

The Mass had barely concluded, the first since the news of Pope Gregory's death during the night, when several Cardinal Bishops broke off into a small enclave to continue their discussion begun earlier that morning.

Cardinal Francesco Orsini, his shock of thick white hair blowing in a gentle breeze, strode along a vine covered walkway inside the Vatican grounds with two of his fellow electors from the College of Cardinals, Cardinal Thomas O'Riley of Chicago, a heavy set, pugnacious man who looked more like a longshoreman than a Prince of the Catholic Church, and Cardinal Carlos Bacagalupe-Ojeda, a distinguished, balding, highly educated prelate from Argentina. Two others, both Italians like Orsini, followed them at a respectful distance. Though all were part of the Cardinal's inner circle, O'Riley and Bacagalupe-Ojeda were his principal advisors, and it was to him the future, potential pope looked for advice and guidance.

"We can count on the support of no more than a third of the College, your Eminence," Bacagalupe-Ojeda began. "Another ten, perhaps, can be persuaded to support you at the conclave, if the Africans will declare their support publicly. But that still leaves you short by a dozen votes."

"Reinhard is already lobbying the Africans," Orsini said somewhat dismissively. "Even before the Cardinal Camerlengo has declared the pope dead before the Apostolic Camera. I won't submit to the same desecration of *the Universi Dominici Gregis.* We will wait until *sede vacante* has been declared. Then we will present our vision for the papacy, but discreetly."

"Waiting only strengthens Reinhard," O'Riley stated bluntly. A rough, cantankerous streetfighter born on the lower east side of New York City, he kept many of these same traits after entering the priesthood. Like Orsini, he was a fervent traditionalist who longed for a return to the simpler, more straightforward times of the past, when the Catholic faith expressed itself through age-old ceremonies and time-tested practices. The "watering down" of the faith, as he derisively termed it, to keep the Catholic Church in sync with modern society, downplayed these traditions, and in so doing took away much of its distinctiveness. From that deliberate homogenization with other Christian communities came a Church weakened in moral authority, and ultimately unprepared to assume the mantle of leadership that Christ intended when he ceded its earthly control to the successors of Peter. "Reinhard has been cultivating support among the so-called progressives for years. I've seen him work the Curia like a big city ward healer, and he's impressive. If you let him get out ahead of you, he won't be stopped."

"The Church of Peter is not a Chicago political machine," Orsini smiled in gentle rebuke. "We have traditions of succession to be followed, and respected. How can I hope to lead a resurgence of faith if I ascend to the papal throne by violating those very principles?"

"We're talking about a level playing field, your Eminence," O'Riley pressed. "If the vote was taken today, Reinhard knows you would be the acknowledged leader. That would give you the momentum you need to bring enough of the others around, and eventually assume leadership of the Holy See. But the vote won't take place today. In six days Pope Gregory will be laid to rest, followed by the *novemdiales* — nine days of mourning. That's an eternity to someone like Reinhard. If you don't meet his every move now, by the time the conclave meets there won't be any question who will be the next successor to the throne of St. Peter."

"My friend," Orsini put his hand on O'Riley's shoulder. "I know, in your heart, you offer only what you believe is best. But the Church has already made too many compromises, forsaken too many of its customs and traditions in the name of expediency. We will meet as a conclave in fifteen days to seek God's wisdom and blessing in choosing a new pope. Until then, we will mourn the loss of Pope Gregory XVII, whom the Heavenly Father has released from the pain of his suffering."

"At least let me answer some of the scurrilous attacks being leveled against you in the press," O'Riley said. "The pope is only hours dead, and they're already anointing Reinhard his successor. You're being called a 'throwback' and 'reactionary', and there are innuendos that you've misused your position with the Church for personal gain. We have to set the record straight. No one will support a tainted candidate, not in these times. Even if the charges are patently absurd, they must be answered."

"No," Orsini shook his head. "My service to the Church is above reproach. I won't allow those with questionable motives to force me into abandoning my principles, which are rooted in my faith. Every member of the conclave must pledge an oath to disregard all secular influences as they cast their vote. I cannot sanction your effort, no matter how well intended."

"As you wish, then, your Eminence," O'Riley nodded.

As Orsini continued on with the remaining two Cardinals, O'Riley and Bacagalupe-Ojeda remained behind in the garden.

"He is a great man, truly blessed," Bacagalupe-Ojeda said to O'Riley as they watched Cardinal Orsini continue on his way.

"Yes," O'Riley fixed his gaze on the disappearing figure, responding sadly. "But it is Reinhard who will become the next pope."

Both men were steeped in the arcane, sometimes incomprehensible practices of the Vatican Curia, which could be as political an institution as any secular body. It was naïve to follow Orsini's prescription, and yet his refusal to yield to expediency was precisely the reason both men so adamantly supported his candidacy.

The modern Church bore little resemblance to its predecessors of earlier centuries. Too many accommodations had been made for ardent traditionalists like Orsini, O'Riley, and Bacagalupe-Ojeda to feel that its fundamental beliefs and practices were still being properly promulgated into the twenty-first century. Orsini, an intellect of enormous talent, was in their eyes — and the eyes of many other traditionalists — the last hope for the Church to return again to a solid foundation. But, beginning with the first Vatican Council, the College of Cardinals had become more flexible over the years in recognizing the grey areas in what had once been, for the Catholic Church, a more straightforward "black and white" world. To some, false opinions, contaminated thinking, and other presumably anti-Catholic errors had become commonplace and accepted. To them, the liturgy of the Church was secularized and stripped of its divine inspiration. Mass was celebrated in the common vernacular instead of the traditional Latin in a misguided attempt to make the Church more relevant to the contemporary world. In doing so it lost much of its distinctive majesty and a sense of the sacred, which further clouded its clarity of vision. The supernatural world, the vision of Paradise, even the notion of Hell were downplayed or omitted all together in an attempt to make the Church acceptable to all. Transubstantiation and the propriatory character of the Holy Sacrifice were barely mentioned, if at all.

The true irony was that as revolutionary and ecumenical as these nascent reforms were, to many outside the Church they were nothing more than window dressing for an already too-repressive religious philosophy. Birth control, abortion, the ordination of women priests, the sanctification of same sex marriage — none of these fundamental issues had been altered in any significant way. To Ralston Hastings, who despised everything about the faith he had once embraced as a child, only to reject later in life following the horrific deaths of his parents, the Catholic Church was a repressive, anachronistic scourge on humanity whose efforts and influence had to be curtailed, if not entirely eliminated.

Under attack from within and without, for being too conservative and not conservative enough, the Church faced its greatest crisis in the days following Pope Gregory's death. The 100 year curse on the Church, the Lucifer Covenant, seemed to be insurmountable. Shaitana, the anointed agent of Lucifer, was determined to bring this crisis, shown in the vision of Pope Leo XIII, to a terrifying end, accomplishing ultimately the enslavement of every human soul. Only one person still stood between Shaitana and his unholy vision of conquest. It wasn't a world leader, or a captain of industry, or even a would-be pope. It was, to Shaitana, the most terrifying and intractable obstacle of all.

A simple man of faith, with a clear vision and a mission from God.

***

While their plane taxied on the tarmac at Fiumicino's Leonardo da Vinci International Airport, Santos' thoughts were on Raphael Aurelio. *How many times had he come to Rome to consult with the kindly, yet fiery old priest?* When he wasn't performing exorcisms, Aurelio was speaking about them — to magazines, conferences, churchmen, whomever might give him an audience. Though dismissed by the Vatican bureaucracy, and ridiculed in the press, no one had done as much to awaken public awareness of the drift toward the occult as Aurelio. There was no better proof of the effectiveness of his efforts than the fact that he, and his fellow exorcists, were brutally assassinated in Nepal. Yet, even this travesty did little to turn public opinion in favor of Aurelio's work. Touted as a clash between extremist ideologies -— Western religious fanatics who were killed by fanatical communist guerillas — it was quickly relegated to the back pages of every major newspaper once the shocking details were reported, and then forgotten all together. By the time Miguel and Santos arrived in Rome, the story had long since been replaced by another celebrity divorce, a sensational serial killing, and one of a dozen political scandals de jour.

Noticing a black band on the custom official's arm as he and Miguel moved closer to him in line, Santos paid little attention to it until he spotted another black armband on a passenger disembarking from a different flight. A quick look around the terminal revealed at least two other people wearing identical signs of mourning, all in dissimilar attire or in obviously different occupations. Curious, Santos asked the customs official the reason for his armband once they reached the small square booth where he was stationed. The man gave Santos, dressed in his cassock, a curious look while examining his Vatican passport, as if not understanding the need for so obvious a question, then replied in a soft, sad voice.

"To honor the memory of del Santo Padre."

"The memory—" Santos gasped.

"I-I'm sorry father," the man seemed genuinely startled. "You didn't know? Pope Gregory died last night, in his sleep. I thought that was why you had come to Rome, to pay your respects."

"The pope is … dead," Santos could barely repeat the words. "First Aurelio and the others, then Father Dias," he turned to Miguel. "It is the work of Satan, I'm more convinced of it than ever. Come, we must make our way to Father Lanciani at the Church of San Giuseppe! Hurry!"

The customs official watched in stunned amazement as Santos literally snatched his passport from the man's hands and headed toward the exit, the stuttering clap-clap-clap of his cane reverberating off the smooth linoleum floor.

"I'm so sorry," Miguel shrugged and smiled awkwardly.

The man handed him his passport so he could follow after the rapidly disappearing little priest, who had already cleared the terminal and was somewhere outside. In fractured Italian Santos commandeered a passing cab, bypassing a long line of tourists who were queuing for a ride. With Miguel quickly piling inside, they headed toward the Roman Forum and the church of San Giuseppe *dei Falegnami* — St. Joseph's of the Carpenters.

Their brief stay in Calcutta had allowed Santos to replenish their cash, which he now waved as bribe to urge on the taxi driver's already reckless race through the city. Up and down hills, through narrow twisting streets, the battered cab dodged pedestrians and other vehicles alike to arrive at a magnificent baroque church with a pink marbled façade, built in the late fifteen-hundreds and dedicated to St. Joseph the Carpenter, the foster-father of Jesus Christ.

The Church of San Giuseppe sat atop an old Roman jail. Excavated between the floor of the church and the almost three thousand year old prison for condemned enemies of the Roman state was the Chapel of the Crucifix. According to legend, it was the place where St. Peter was imprisoned before his death. As the heir to Christ's work on earth Peter decided, after a vision, that he should return to Rome and emulate Christ's sacrifice. He was arrested as soon as he crossed the Aurelian Gate, and was taken to the prison. While there he continued to convert non-believers, among them two prisoners, Processus and Martinianum. Without water to perform their baptism, Peter touched the ground and a spring miraculously appeared. He then baptized them and other repenting prisoners before he himself was martyred at the Circus of Nero and Caligula.

For a moment Miguel wasn't sure if the frenetic little priest, having dashed from the taxi cab the moment it stopped, was even at the right church. He paid the driver and hurried inside after Santos, who was already lost among the throngs of tourists milling about taking photographs. Only when he saw the gilt coffered ceiling displaying a carving of the Nativity, with frescoes of the life of St. Joseph adorning the Carpenters' Guild chapel, was he certain they were at the Church of San Giuseppe. But where was Santos?

Hushed conversation in a far corner brought Miguel toward a short, gray-haired priest with a waist-length beard. Miguel kept a respectful distance while Father Rocco Lanciani, an Oblate of St. Joseph, held back tears as he and Santos discussed the death of their friend Raphael Aurelio.

"This is far worse than I had imagined," Lanciani said in good, but halting English. "Aurelio told me before leaving Rome that he expected the Devil to do his worst. When I heard the news of the terror bombing, I knew at that moment Aurelio had been received into our Heavenly Father's arms, may God rest his soul." Looking at Santos, he cocked his head and continued quizzically. "But we were told that all the exorcists had been killed. Not a single one survived."

"I was the only one," Santos said softly.

"And now you bring me news that Father Dias was murdered!"

"By the same evil forces behind the attack on St. Joseph's, I believe."

"Then it is good that you have come to the Church of Joseph the Carpenter," Lanciani placed his arm around Santos' shoulder. "But I don't know why Aurelio told you to come to me. I am not Opus Dei. I shared only the friendship of a great and wonderful man. This church, so close to Peter, was always a special place for him. He often sought refuge in its solace. Perhaps that is why you were directed here?"

"Perhaps," Santos repeated.

"I was about to celebrate Mass when you arrived, Father Santos. Would you join me? You'll find extra vestments in the rectory."

"Yes thank you, I will."

"Follow that door, down the stairs, then to your left. We shall celebrate *Dies Irae*, the Mass for the dead, for Father Aurelio."

While Miguel waited in the hard wooden pews, Santos left the upper floor in search of the rectory. The lower level was a maze of narrow passageways, some carved out of solid stone, and despite the simple directions Santos soon found himself lost. Unable to retrace his steps, he felt as if he was wandering in endless circles, even though he couldn't possibly have covered so great a distance in such a short time. His frustration grew when the already-muffled sounds from the Church above faded all together, and he now roamed the hallways in total silence.

Turning a corner, Santos spotted a statue of the Virgin Mary resting on a pedestal. Lit by a crest of candles, it seemed to glow with an otherworldly sheen, drawing Santos toward it. Suddenly he felt more than saw another presence in the shadows ahead. The frail, elderly figure was swaddled in priestly robes, presenting a regal image in the dim ambient light. In his hands was a scroll of some kind, partially unraveled, as if the figure had been expecting Santos and was waiting for him to draw closer.

"Forgive me," Santos apologized, coming nearer. "I've lost my direction some how. I was looking for the rectory—"

Whether it was from memories of historical pictures or sheer intuition, Santos stopped short, staring at the frail, delicate ecclesiastic he now recognized as Pope Leo XIII.

"My son, you have done well in your service to the Church of God," the ghostly figure spoke. "Now you are called to an even greater mission."

Thunderstruck, Santos dropped to his knees, his hands folded in prayer, as the vision of Pope Leo opened his arms and gestured for him to rise.

"The fate of humanity, of the Church, depends on following the Plan of God, the Plan that was given but not received," Leo spoke in a voice both rich and soft. "The Beast has been loosed from the Abyss. And the Beast seeks to swallow its prey."

"Is this is why I was sent here?" Santos spoke reverently. "To teach me what I must know to fight the Beast?"

Now backlit against a bright, glowing light, the elderly pontiff blessed Santos with the sign of the cross, then began to speak. "Then I saw an angel come down from heaven, holding in his hand the key to the abyss and a heavy chain. He seized the dragon, the ancient serpent, which is the Devil or Satan, and tied it up for a thousand years and threw it into the abyss, which he locked over it and sealed, so that it could no longer lead the nations astray until the thousand years are completed. After this, it is to be released for a short time."

Immediately Santos saw the image of Shaitana emerging from a monstrous void, surrounded by hordes of hideous creatures.

"I heard a voice from heaven say, 'At the time when you hear the seventh angel blow his trumpet, the mysterious plan of God shall be fulfilled, as he promised to his servants the prophets.' Then the voice that I had heard from heaven spoke to me again and said, 'Go, take the scroll that lies open in the hand of the angel who is standing on the sea and on the land.' So I went up to the angel and told him to give me the small scroll. He said to me, 'Take and swallow it. It will turn your stomach sour, but in your mouth it will taste as sweet as honey.' I took the small scroll from the angel's hand and swallowed it. In my mouth it was like sweet honey, but when I had eaten it, my stomach turned sour. Then someone said to me, 'You must prophesy again about many peoples, nations, tongues, and kings.'"

The sweet smell of incense now filled the air as the statue of the Virgin came to life. The snake under her feet was breaking free.

"Then the dragon became angry with the woman and went off to wage war against the rest of her offspring, those who keep God's commandments and bear witness to Jesus." Leo looked directly at Santos. "Know this. For two millennia the war has been waged. The Woman appears in every age and place, warning her offspring, protecting them from the Dragon. Here in the twelfth chapter, the Mother of the Messiah appears in the heavens, clothed with the sun and crowned with stars, but also shows herself present in the world and in the struggles of her children. And yet too many have been blind to her presence and her messages. Too many know nothing of the Just Man who protected the Holy Family, the Heir of David. Too many have denied their Son and been lost to the Dragon. Know now the Seven Secrets, the Divine Truths, that God has bequeathed to humanity, that you may chain the Beast, and return him to the Abyss."

Santos listened in stunned silence while Leo began to read from the parchment Scroll. There were seven strange verses on it.

Where the Savior's line began, the Times fulfilled,

Where the sainted Family fled in haste, returned,
Where the fires of Hell leapt out, the sun plunged down,
Where the Family's silence spoke, the End in sight,
Where the Hebrew Mother showed the nations' fate,
Where the rising sun erupts, the Virgin wept,
Where the stairway came from Heaven, ask the one who knows.

"Follow these remedies given by God," Leo said. "They are the only way out, the only rescue from the present crisis."

"Wait!" Santos pleaded. "I-I don't understand. What do the verses mean?"

"Humanity has already been told what they mean, but the Church has not acted. And God will not interfere with free will by acting again without a human response. Since Heaven has already spoken, it is up to you to rediscover the divine answers."

"Why me?" asked Santos asked, as confused as he was humbled. "I'm just a simple man. Nothing I've ever done has prepared me for this."

"You are the one who has been chosen," the ghostly figure began to fade. His hand extended, Leo offered the parchment to Santos, who hesitated. "You must accept the Scroll, and all that it embodies, of your own free will. There it shall remain, in your guard, until the time comes to release its holy powers. Once you accept the Scroll, no one can pry it from your grasp unless you surrender it willingly."

"I-I do accept," Santos said, his mouth dry. He took the Scroll from the vanishing figure, whose words echoed faintly through the darkened hall until they, too, finally disappeared.

"When the seals on the Scroll have been removed, when the instructions of the Secrets have been understood and acted upon, the curse upon this generation will be removed, and the Beast will be forced back into the Abyss."

A visibly shaken Santos emerged from the lower level of the church, still clutching the parchment Scroll, to find Father Lanciani and Miguel exactly where he left them.

"Did you forget something?" Lanciani asked with a puzzled frown.

"Forget?" Santos repeated.

"You barely closed the door and opened it again. I thought perhaps you left something behind, something you needed before you headed to the rectory."

"I've been gone for twenty minutes," Santos said incredulously.

"Forgive me Father Machado, my English is not that good. I heard you say *minuto* — minute, not *secondo* — seconds."

"I couldn't find my way. I was wandering in the halls, when I came upon a statue of the Blessed Virgin —"

"The Blessed Virgin?"

"It beckoned me forward. Then he was there."

"Who?"

"Pope Leo XIII. He appeared in a vision and spoke to me, told me what I must do."

"Like Peter, you have been visited from Heaven," Lanciani dropped to his knees and blessed himself with the sign of the cross. "This is why you came to the church of San Giuseppe, to receive the gift of knowledge to guide you on your quest."

"Santos, what is it?" Miguel approached, noticing his curious, abrupt return. "Is something wrong?"

"Miguel," Santos became energized. "We must leave at once."

"Leave? But we just got here?"

"Bless you, Father Machado," Lanciani said. "Bless you and God speed on your way."

"Hurry Miguel," Santos charged toward the exit, his wooden cane tapping the way. Tourists parted like Moses before the Red Sea while they danced out of the path of the chubby little man.

"Hurry, where?"

"To where the Savior's line began. To Jerusalem!"

"Jerusalem? But I thought—"

Before he could finish the sentence, Santos was already out the door and hailing another cab.

Miguel lifted his eyes toward the gilded ceiling and breathed a heavy sigh, collecting their luggage and trudging out the door to join him.

New York

"Italian customs confirmed what you suspected, My Lord," Olsson said behind the closed doors of his private conference room. "The exorcist Santos Machado escaped from Nepal. He landed at Leonardo da Vinci airport at nine o'clock this morning local time on a flight from Calcutta, India, accompanied by his young charge Miguel Guerrero."

"Then he is in Rome, no doubt to elicit the protection of Opus Dei," Shaitana said through clenched teeth.

"By eleven, he and Guerrero were aboard a flight to Jerusalem, alone."

"Alone? You're certain?"

"Yes my Lord. Our agents watching the Vatican detected nothing. Wherever Machado went during those two hours, it was not to seek the help of Opus Dei."

"He is alone then, good. Alert our people in Jerusalem," Shaitana spoke tersely. "Give them the information they need to identify him and track his movements. I want him killed, but first I want to know where he travels and who he sees. I want to know if his choice of Jerusalem is happenstance, or something more … troubling. Now go."

"Yes my Lord," the grey haired man nodded silently, hiding his quivering hands while he closed the door behind him.

Chapter 11

Rome

Santos caught a glimpse of the cockpit while they boarded the crowded plane to Jerusalem. *Twenty-five*, he thought to himself. *Maybe twenty-eight. Too young to be a pilot.* And a woman at his side, no less.

There were more unsettling images when a tall, thin man directed him and Santos to their seats, offering them each a pillow and blanket, and reminding them to buckle the short stubby belts securely across their laps. The world was upside down in the span of twenty paces. These people were children playing at a game of life, challenging preconceived notions of their proper roles and responsibilities, and it only added to the general unease that he always felt when flying.

And yet, for all the incongruities, as he looked around the cabin Santos could sense that this was truly the proper order of things. "Better to pick your fights wisely," he chuckled under his breath, remembering the sage advice of his father, a man for whom change too had come with great difficulty. Growing up in a small provincial village in the Philippines, the years blended into a slowly flowing stream that helped fasten images of life and labor with more firmness than they deserved. But isolated as they were, his family could not escape the clash with modern society. Not during the turbulent years of the twentieth century where many ways of life were changed. The misery and troubles of the outside world had invaded their sanctuary with a drumbeat of heavy leather boots and terrible weapons. But it had also brought new ways to treat the ill, and improve the lives of a poor peasant family. So it was that his father had learned to adapt to new methods and ideas, not the least of which was to allow his only son to leave the simple, structured harmony of their village, and join the priesthood where he would explore the world in ways he himself could never imagine.

Settling back in his seat, Santos closed his eyes. The flight from Rome to Jerusalem would be long and taxing. The challenges he faced were enormous, both physically and emotionally. No longer was he a simple exorcist doing God's work by casting out the Devil from some poor, unfortunate soul. The fate of mankind literally rested on his shoulders, and his alone, if the vision of Pope Leo was to be believed.

The vision, Santos repeated in his mind. Was it a vision that handed him the parchment Scroll, or Pope Leo XIII, sent to Earth by God to deliver the instrument of a divine rescue operation to him, Santos Machado, a lowly priest who never sought power, never sought glory for its own sake? Though he doubted his own worth at having been given so overwhelming a task, he also knew that God would not charge him with such an important undertaking unless he, Santos, had within him the ability to succeed. The difference would be how Santos himself utilized the talents given to him by God, strengthened by his unyielding faith, to pry open the seven secrets that would bring forth the full power and glory of God.

He prayed that he was up to the task, this simple priest from a distant land. He prayed that he would be given the courage to fulfill his duties, even at the cost of his own life. He prayed that God would look over and protect him, and his young companion Miguel, for he knew that what lay ahead would be more horrific and terrifying than any demon they had ever faced. What Santos Machado was about to do would strike at the very heart of Pope Leo's prophecy. His failure would not be his alone, but that of all humanity, and it was a terrible burden to bear.

With a heavy heart and in solemn prayer, Santos steeled himself against the maelstrom he knew was coming. Whatever the outcome, whatever the consequences of his actions in pursuit of the seven divine remedies, Santos was certain of at least one thing. Success or failure, victory or defeat, he would do his best to force the Beast back into the Abyss. It was all God could ask.

And all that he could give.

Tel Aviv

Security was unusually tight at Ben-Gurion airport outside Tel Aviv, the transit point to Jerusalem.

Changing into his cassock shortly before they landed, Santos placed the parchment Scroll inside one of his pockets and waited for the plane to come to a stop. Like cattle filing through a narrowing chute, the passengers on the flight from Rome collected their belongings and disembarked after the bumpy, but otherwise inauspicious landing. Again herded into a collecting room, the diverse group of travelers were segmented into separate lines, each leading to a different immigration officer.

Santos, tired from his second long flight in as many days, and his face still showing the strain of contemplating the words and visage of Pope Leo, trudged up to the immigration desk where a middle-aged woman began to examine his credentials. The woman in her starched blue uniform and crisply knotted tie was friendly at first, but after looking through his passport and seeing the unusual pattern of travel, she began to frown.

"So you've been to the Sudan," she said.

"I have," replied Santos.

"And Nigeria, Nepal, the Philippines."

"I was born in Cebu, outside Manila."

"And you've traveled to the Middle East. Five times in the last two years."

"Yes," Santos drew the word out slowly, his eyes meeting hers.

"And yet you come again. Now to the State of Israel."

Miguel, behind Santos in line, could see his neck tense and shoulders begin to stiffen. Santos brought his hands to the counter, folding them almost in prayer as he looked at her with unblinking eyes. "To the Holy Land of our Good Lord," he corrected.

The woman met his gaze with a stone-like stare. He didn't care for the tone of her question, but his response had only steeled her resolve. With a silent nod she drew two uniformed soldiers closer to her booth.

"We have had warnings about a terrorist ring based in Manila," she barely completed the sentence before Santos erupted in a furious screed.

"I'm a Catholic priest! How dare you insult me in this sacred place!"

"Santos! *para te!* " Miguel tried to calm his friend as the two soldiers quickly moved to intervene.

Against the far wall a tall, gray-haired man who had been observing the confrontation walked over to the immigration officer and whispered a few words to her partially turned face. After a moment's hesitation, and another silent nod from the woman, the soldiers relaxed.

"A misunderstanding," the stranger smiled to everyone and no one. The immigration officer stamped Santos' passport and allowed him through, performing only a cursory review of Miguel's documents before permitting him to join his friend.

"I am Ehud Hasharon," the man said, extending his hand to the two of them.

"Father Santos Machado," Santos replied.

"Yes, I know who you are," the man smiled. "And you must be Miguel

Guerrero."

"I am," Miguel replied, confused. "Do we know you, Sir?"

"Oh no," Hasharon laughed easily. "But I certainly know you. Both of you. If you'd be so kind as to accompany me, I have a car waiting for us outside."

"Who, er, exactly are you?" Miguel asked suspiciously.

"We can discuss that in private."

"I think I'd rather discuss it now," Santos said.

"Let's say I'm someone with enough influence to clear you through customs, even though your names appear on a security watch list."

"Why?" Miguel reacted, startled.

"You're the only two Western survivors from a terror bombing in Nepal. One of you, the resourceful Father Machado, seems to have entered India after that without going through the necessary customs checkpoints at Kathmandu or New Delhi, where you just happen to turn up at the home of another murdered priest."

"You think we're involved in all of that?" Miguel's mouth went dry.

"I work for Israeli Intelligence," Hasharon pulled back his waistcoat to reveal the butt of a pistol. "It's my job to find out exactly who and what I should believe, and who or what I should suspect. Now if you will please both accompany me, I'm certain we can clear up this little matter rather quickly."

As they left the airport the pair was taken under armed escort to a windowless building in a walled-off compound a short distance away. There in separate rooms Miguel and Santos were questioned at length about the events of the preceding days, and their travels together over the past six years. Minutes dragged into hours as the interrogation continued; always the same questions, and always the same answers. Finally, as dawn arrived on the following day, a haggard looking Ehud Hasharon met up with Moishe Silverman outside the adjoining interrogation rooms, an expatriate American Jew who emigrated to Israel in the aftermath of the Seven Day war.

"Well, what do you think?" Hasharon lit a cigarette and took a deep draw.

"This boy has been his traveling companion since he was sixteen. He's part student, and part nursemaid to hear him tell it, but no complaints. He seems genuinely attached to the old guy, and kept asking me to make sure he was all right. He thought the priest was killed in Kathmandu and only discovered he was alive when they met up in India at the dead man's home."

"Some coincidence," Hasharon grunted.

"I don't think so. Everything I've been told hangs together, weird as it is. This priest Machado, he's an exorcist?"

"Claims to be."

"And how does his story hold up?"

"Fine, if you believe that the Devil is about to take over the world, and only he can stop him."

"And he knows this how?" Silverman chuckled.

"The pope told him."

"The pope's dead, I thought."

"This one was too, for about a hundred years."

"What?"

"Believe me, you don't want to hear it."

"Well, speaking of dead popes, we got a real mess on our hands here, Ehud."

"What? How?"

"All we need is some kind of international incident involving a Catholic priest detained by Israeli intelligence immediately following the death of their pope. CNN will put another bureau chief in Tel Aviv just to handle the overflow of world condemnation when they manufacture another 'atrocity' to pin on us. You forget, I used to live in the States. There's nothing the press likes as much as condemning Israel for being mean to the terrorists murdering our children. It's a whole new level of crap they'll throw our way if they can spin this into us taking on the Catholic Church too — particularly in their time of mourning. Better to just deport him and be done with it."

"Well, if you believe what you say, we can't really do that either. There's nothing to tie him to any terrorist group, if you don't count the Maoists he broke bread with in Nepal. But they seemed as interested in getting rid of him as he was to get out of the country. If we throw him out of Israel, he'll make some kind of stink and end up on the front pages just the same. The U.N. has already made an inquiry about his detention. There's no telling what kind of influence this guy has. No, we either keep him locked up, or let him go to this Church he wants to visit. Those are the only choices."

"You're senior, Ehud," Silverman sat back in his chair. "It's your call."

"Personally, I think he's a flake, but a harmless one. He thinks he's some kind of mystic or whatever, and we get enough of those to know what we're dealing with. I say let 'em both go. Maybe they'll hook up with

Madonna on one of her Kabbalah excursions and they can read their Ouiji boards together."

"I'll make arrangements to have them followed, then."

"No," Hasharon took a final puff and stubbed out his cigarette. "We've got more important things to do with our time. Give them a 48 hour visa and directions to the Church of the Holy Sepulcher, and get them out of my hair. Assuming they don't get themselves killed by wandering into a refugee camp and getting their throats slit by Hezbollah or Hamas, we'll be rid of them soon enough."

"Right."

"I tell you Moishe," Hasharon called to his friend as he started towards Miguel's cell. "These are either two of the greatest liars I've ever seen, or the luckiest unlucky pair I'll ever meet. Either way, in two days they won't be my problem."

New York

"I have everything here that you asked for, Mr. Hastings," Henry Stimpson, a scrawny little man said, walking into the empty board room with a bundle of leather bound books and overflowing file folders tucked under his arms.

Hastings watched warily as Stimpson laid the documents out on the table, each book marked with dozens of post-it notes, and each file folder brimming with different sized papers peaking out of both ends.

"It's all right here sir," Stimpson said. "A most unusual request, if I say so, but a delightful challenge to research."

"I'm not interested in your job satisfaction quotient," Hastings barked.

"Oh, certainly Sir," the biting remark seemed to go right over Stimpson's head. "Where would you like me to begin?"

"At the beginning, Stimpson," Hastings rolled his eyes and poured a large brandy from a crystal decanter.

"Yes Sir, very well Sir. I completely understand. I received this request over the secured line from a Mr. Prithvi Shah, an employee of the Lumen Foundation headquartered in Nepal. Normally, these types of inquiries come from a Mr. Roland Blavatasky, but upon checking I learned that his services were recently terminated, and he is no longer in the employment of —"

"Can we just get to the meat of this, Stimpson?" Hastings sighed.

"Yes Sir. Sorry Sir. I'll get right to it. Well, as you know, my department has standing orders to alert me if any, shall we say, unusual requests come to us from any of the Hastings affiliate organizations that are allowed access to our database and staff of professionals. Those orders were from you, directly, Sir."

"I know that Stimpson," Hastings fought to keep his calm.

"This request was to research the genealogy of Jesus Christ."

Hastings sat upright in his chair, focusing on Stimpson with renewed interest. "Why that particular subject?" he asked.

"I'm not entirely certain, other than it came from the head of the Lumen Foundation himself, a Mr. Shaitana I believe. I'm not personally acquainted with the gentleman. I can only speculate as to the reason."

It took all of Hastings resolve to keep from leaving his chair and physically attacking the scrawny, spectacled little man who stood at the end of the table, his face a blank mask, waiting for Hastings to ask the most obvious of questions. If it was not for the remarkable brilliance of the Savant-like academic who headed his research department, Hastings would have fired him years ago. But despite his misanthropic, maladjusted, socially reclusive nature which made social interactions with others an inordinately painful experience, Henry Stimpson had an exceptionally gifted talent for ferreting out the most obscure data and compiling it into the best industrial espionage money could buy. Whatever Hastings needed to know to keep himself, or his organization, on top of his competitors, Stimpson could provide. Now Hastings would use these same talents to understand the nature of Shaitana's request, and with it increase his leverage over the one man who — if left to his own devices — could one day pose a genuine threat to Hastings' empire. That is, if only he could get him to come to the point.

"Would you … speculate then?" Hastings said through gritted teeth.

"With pleasure," Stimpson smiled. "It all comes down to the myth of the Holy Grail and those who guard its secrets, the Priory of Scion. Now, as I'm sure you know from Hollywood, if no one else, the Holy Grail is supposedly the chalice used by Christ at the Last Supper, the same chalice which collected drops of his blood as he lay on the cross. The pursuit of the miraculous, but missing Grail inspired great literary and artistic works in the Middle Ages. Historically speaking, the Grail is purely a figment of the creative imagination. You can consult the great Grail scholar Richard Barber on this. There's no mention of the Grail anywhere prior to 1190 when it appeared in Perceval, an incomplete work by the French writer Chretien de Troyes. Within five decades of this first appearance, the Grail became a major theme of popular romantic works that tied it to King Arthur and the Knights of the Round Table. The most famous English version of the myth is the fifteenth century Le Morte d Arthur by Sir Thomas Malory."

"What does this have to do with—" Hastings started to interrupt, but Stimpson continued.

"These medieval myths were powerful, though innocuous. But a bizarre new twist was created in the eighteenth and nineteenth centuries. One author claimed that the Grail had an occult origin and linked it to everyone from the Knights Templar to the Rosicrucians. Another suggested that the Grail idea derived from pre-Christian Celtic myths of a miraculous cup. Of course, scholars have long since discredited these fanciful ideas. To begin with, the notion of a Grail first emerged in a novel written over a thousand years after the death of Christ. So I ask, how can one build a whole theory of occult conspiracies around something that was purely a work of fiction? The Holy Grail exists only in a series of romantic novels written in the Middle Ages. There's no ancient tradition, no historical account of a mysterious Grail hidden away. It's a literary artifact. You might as well ask me where we can find the gods of Mount Olympus."

"So you're saying that Shaitana is after the Holy Grail, which doesn't exist?" Hastings said, confused.

"Certainly not," Stimpson replied to the exasperated man.

"But why then all this focus on—"

"The story of the Grail gets us to the Priory of Scion, that fanciful organization sworn to protect it and its secrets. But you see, according to the proponents of this theory, it isn't an object that one seeks in searching for the Grail. The Holy Grail refers to the royal bloodline of Jesus Christ and Mary Magdalene and their descendants. The most notable of the supposed progeny was the Merovingian dynasty that ruled France from 476-750 A.D. The mysterious Priory of Scion and the Knights Templar were sworn to protect the descendants of the dynasty. Of course, in this view official historians, under pressure from the Catholic Church, covered up the truth. But here's the real cover-up. The source of the bloodline story was the biggest con artist in the history of modern France, Pierre Plantard, a convicted embezzler and admitted forger and also the founder of the so-called Priory of Scion.

"Were it not for the shoddy scholarship of *The Da Vinci Code,* which has perpetuated this myth, no one would be talking about the Holy Grail or

Priory of Scion at all! Plantard is a thief, con man, and Nazi collaborator who claimed, among other things, that he was a Merovingian with a rightful claim to the throne of France. Plantard founded the Priory of Scion in 1956 to advocate low-cost housing. He disbanded it in the same year after being sent to prison. He revived the Priory again in 1960, but resigned in 1984 when a French journalist exposed his fabrications. He restarted the Priory in 1989 then terminated it finally in 1993 when he admitted his impostures to a magistrate. He died in 2000."

"So now you're telling me the Priory of Scion is a fraud too, and the man behind this con is dead?"

"Precisely!"

"And you couldn't have just come out and said this?"

"Ah, but there's more," Stimpson chortled.

"Of course there is," Hastings sat back and poured himself another drink.

"As a historian, I can confirm that there is no historical evidence for a relationship between Jesus Christ and Mary Magdalene. As for the alleged bloodline, that's demonstrably a pure concoction. This, of course, begs the question in reverse. Rather than inquire into the mythical lineage of Jesus' descendants, one might look instead into the Line of David, examining the Covenant and its implications for today. Israel and the Gentiles, Jews and the Church, all fascinating subjects. How the Old Testament Joseph is identified with the New Testament Joseph in terms of power and role? In certain circles Joseph is seen as the bridge between Judaism and Christianity. Here, the Throne of David comes to the center —"

"Enough!" Hastings finally threw up his hands.

"Sir?"

"More religious nonsense and prattle! I should have known, coming from Shaitana. Next he'll be having you research the connection between the Sermon on the Mount and the first moon landing."

"No Sir," Stimpson replied seriously. "I don't believe there's any real linkages —"

"Thank you Henry," Hastings interrupted politely, stopping him in mid-sentence. "Another excellent report, as always."

"Should I send this Mr. Shaitana my research?" Stimpson asked.

"Yes, by all means. I'm sure it's quite important to him, God knows why, but I'm sure it is. Anything to keep our friends happy."

"Certainly sir."

"And Henry," Hastings said as the little man gathered his books and folders and prepared to leave. "If you receive any additional requests for more ... substantive matters, please bring them right to my attention."

"I will Sir. Yes indeed."

When the door closed Ralston Hastings reached for the half-empty decanter and shook his head, chucking under his breath. As a man of science, a man governed by reason, he couldn't fathom the enormous waste of time and talent it took to ponder such inanely superfluous issues. Whether it was the nature of Christ's parentage, the descendants of his mythical progeny, or how many angels could dance on the head of a pin, it was all so much distraction from real world problems and solutions. Only escapists and cowards took refuge in the superstition of faith, and only fools wasted their time on such discussions. The world had enough problems to be solved without creating new ones in our minds.

Let Shaitana revel in the mire of superstition and the occult, he thought. The question of Jesus' origin, or the implications it might carry, had absolutely no meaning for a man of Hasting's intellect and ambition.

Tel Aviv

"Why is it Santos?" Miguel rubbed the tiredness from his eyes after being reunited with their luggage, which had been thoroughly searched by Israeli authorities and deposited haphazardly back inside their suitcases, "that lately every time we travel to a new country, we end up in jail."

"'Detention'," Santos corrected. "It's not the same thing."

"I can't take much more of this," Miguel groaned, searching for and finding the framed photograph of his parents, now disassembled into its component parts.

"Fear not, my young friend," Santos seemed uncharacteristically cheerful for the ordeal they had just been through. Tucked away safely in his cassock pocket was the parchment Scroll Leo had given him at the Church of San Giuseppe. Though interrogated by Israeli Intelligence, he was never perceived to be enough of a threat to have his body searched, his status as a Catholic priest adding to the reluctance to violate his privacy. "My guardian angel always looks over me when I'm in trouble. Now I have even higher powers watching over us."

"Pope Leo told you to come here, to Jerusalem." Miguel said. "But where? We only have two days to find what you're after, and then we have to leave."

"We won't need two days," Santos smiled reassuringly. "I know exactly where to go. Israel is 'where the Savior's line began'. And the Church of the Holy Sepulcher, the site of the crucifixion of Christ, is the place where he became the Savior."

Chapter 12

Jerusalem

The Church of the Holy Sepulcher, first built in the third century AD by the mother of the Emperor Constantine, commemorated the site of the crucifixion and burial of Jesus Christ. Replacing a pagan temple built by the Roman Emperor Hadrian, from its earliest days the Church became a place of spiritual affirmation for the pilgrims who traveled great distances to worship at the most sacred spot in Christendom. The original Byzantine church was destroyed by the Persians three centuries later, then rebuilt shortly after that. Destroyed again in 1009 by the Egyptian caliph al-Hakim, it was subsequently restored by the Crusaders. Since that time the Church has remained standing, though divided, as competing religious factions each claimed authority over the site.

The great round domes of the ancient church sprouted above the compact, surrounding buildings like beacons guiding a caravan of old. Converging on the site, Santos ordered the cab to stop and opened his door.

"We're getting out here, Santos?" Miguel asked.

"No Miguel. You stay here. This I must do alone."

Miguel watched as Santos struggled up the inclined hill. On his way he passed a tall man with short cropped hair and a pock-scarred face. Dressed in black, he stood out from the rest of the tourists not only for his distinctive attire in the warm noonday sun, but for the piercing gaze that seemed to follow every step of Santos' movements.

Intent on reaching the church now looming before him, Santos didn't notice the inordinate attention he was attracting from this man who had tracked his movements from India to Rome, and now to Jerusalem.

30,000 feet over India

On his plane heading back to Nepal, Shaitana received a coded message that Prithvi Shah, an elegantly dressed thirty-year-old man in a black mustache and goatee, translated and read to him.

"It's from our operative in Jerusalem. The priest and his young bodyguard were detained by Israeli authorities immediately upon their arrival at the airport in Tel Aviv. Through our offices at the United Nations, we were able to apply pressure to have him released, so that we might track his movements in Jerusalem as you instructed. They were freed sometime that following morning, and headed directly to the shrine known as Golgotha."

"The Church of the Holy Sepulcher," Shaitana hissed.

"Yes my Lord."

"He is there now."

"He has been given the knowledge, but he doesn't know how to use it yet," Shaitana's voice was cold and hard.

"Knowledge, my Lord?"

"Once he unlocks the key to the divine remedies', all that I have planned, all that I have worked for, will be destroyed. The priest Machado must be eliminated right away."

"I will see to it, my Lord."

"Do not fail me Prithvi. I am not a man to be trifled with."

"Nor am I, my Lord," the man replied calmly. "The priest is as good as dead."

Jerusalem

Entering the site called Golgotha, *the place of a skull,* Santos fell to his knees and knelt on the ground where Jesus was crucified. Reciting a verse from Matthew, he began to pray for Divine guidance. "And when they were come unto a place called Golgotha, that is to say, a place of a skull, they gave him vinegar to drink mingled with gall: and when he had tasted thereof, he would not drink. And they crucified him, and parted his garments, casting lots: that it might be fulfilled which was spoken by the prophet. They parted my garments among them, and upon my vesture did they cast lots."

"I've always loved that passage from Matthew," a kindly white haired man said.

Santos rose to his feet and nodded to the Armenian Orthodox priest, one of the multiple custodians of the Church of the Holy Sepulcher. "I am Patriarch Tereneg Vazken, prelate of the Governing Council. Our holy charge is to watch over this sainted Church and all that it prescribes with our Roman Catholic and Greek Orthodox brethren."

"Father Santos Machado," Santos extended his hand.

"Why have you come here, Father Machado?"

Santos looked at the fellow priest quizzically. The church was filled with tourists and clergy from all over the world. Nothing about Santos singled him out as a person of distinction. He didn't know how to respond.

"You are here because you seek knowledge," Vazken said, answering his own question. "Knowledge that is above and beyond that sought by others who come here."

"H-how did you know?" Santos gasped.

"I can see it in your eyes. They are the same eyes that came to me in a dream last evening. I was told that a man of faith would seek me out. He would come to the Church of the Holy Sepulcher to retrace the path of our Lord, to where I do not know. For this I was to be his guide, and serve him any way I could. Until I saw you at this moment, I did not know that you were the one whom I sought. I'm glad to have found you, Father Machado. There is much I have to tell."

Sitting on a carved stone bench, the elderly man drew Santos closer. In soft, compelling words he spoke of the history of the Jews. Salvation would come from the Jews, Jesus said, in the gospel of John. And out of Israel emerged the New and Everlasting Covenant. Inspired by their conviction that God was spiritual, not material, and bound to God in an irrevocable partnership or "covenant", Israel, unlike any other nation then or since, built both a national identity, as well as individual lives, around direct divine instructions. By its very existence, the nation of Israel was testimony to a power and a presence that transcended time and space. Israel's history was the tale of God's own family, his Chosen People. Above all it was a story of supernatural covenants and archetypal leaders, sacrifice and sacrilege, exodus and exile.

As Santos knew, a covenant is an agreement, an oath which brings down curses on those who break it and blessings on those who observe it. The history of Israel, the prophecies of the holy messengers of God, and the covenantal saga of God and his people suddenly entered a new order of being with the appearance of Jesus of Nazareth, the Christ, the "Anointed One" of God and the Messiah King of Israel. In him, with him and through him, all the great prophecies, premonitions and promises were fulfilled, and the Old Testament covenant itself came to a climax.

This Jesus of Nazareth identified himself with the God of Israel, claiming the authority to forgive sins, cleanse God's temple, and determine the eternal destiny of every human person. His words, he said, would last beyond the passing of heaven and earth, and his authority was greater than that of the Old Testament. He was Lord of the Sabbath, the personal embodiment of the Torah, a king with an everlasting kingdom and the ultimate judge of all. As Colossians told, His followers held that "in him dwells the whole fullness of the deity bodily."

At the crux of the Christian story was the claim that Christ rose from the dead after his crucifixion. It was this claim that led to the genesis and growth of the Christian movement in first century Palestine began. Jesus' identity as a Davidic King comes through both his foster-father and the queen-mother Mary. God had promised David that "your house and your kingdom shall endure forever before me; your throne shall stand firm forever." Joseph was descended from David's son Solomon, and Mary from his brother Nathan. Although God had promised David that his "line" would reign forever, Solomon's branch had been cursed for its disobedience, and its last ruler was Jeconiah.

According to Mosaic law in the Book of Numbers, a woman could receive her inheritance if she married within the same tribe. Joseph's biological children could not inherit the throne, but a son born solely of Mary would not be subject to the Curse of Jeconiah, and could lay claim to the Davidic throne because his mother's marriage to Joseph had secured her rights of inheritance. Thus the Angel Gabriel announced to Mary, "The Lord God will give him the throne of David his father and he will rule over the house of Jacob forever and of his kingdom there will be no end."

"And so the Davidic dynasty was restored as promised by God to the prophet Ezekiel. As prince-regent, Joseph was the protector of the royal family and its Kingdom. Under direct divine guidance, it was he who protected the Virgin-Mother and the Holy Child against the forces of evil. With the coming of the Christ, it became apparent that every major milestone in the odyssey of Israel had a counterpart in the world without end. Why was it then that Israel did not, and does not to this day, acknowledge Jesus as Messiah and King?" Vazken asked rhetorically.

Santos, a simple man schooled in the basics of his faith, but not a religious scholar, listened in rapt attention. The knowledge he needed to seek out and understand the divine remedies of Pope Leo's vision was being laid out before him, piece by piece, brick by brick.

"Even though Jesus and his family," Vazken began to answer his own question, "as well as the Apostles and the early leaders of the Church were all Jewish, the vast majority of the nation of Israel rejected their Messiah. But given the past history of both Israel and humanity as a whole, this rejection was all but inevitable. From Adam onward, the human race has rejected every gift of God, and chosen instead what is self-destructive. In Israel, the persistent rebellions against Moses and the other prophets, and the bondage to idolatry and other sin, weakened both mind and will. Clearly the obsession with idolatry had been stamped out by the time of Christ, but the habit of rejecting prophetic messages and messengers of God was deeply ingrained. This meant death for the Messiah-King. It was a death that implicates us all for it was sin that crucified Christ, the sin in every human soul.

"But God works around our sin, and his victory always mirrors the seeming defeat. The first step to destruction comes through a woman who, enticed by an evil angel, disobeys a divine command. The first step of restoration comes through a woman who listens to a good angel and accepts the divine invitation. Damnation is consummated by the disobedience of one man, redemption by the obedience of another man. Likewise, though Israel rejected her Christ, the Royal Family of Israel will rule the world forever. And at the end of time Israel herself will accept her Messiah as King. So we are told and so it will be."

"But what bearing does this have on today?" Santos asked. "Is there a final chapter to this story, to the end of the world?"

"If you look at the New Testament, two key phenomena come to pass at the climax of history. Jesus says about the 'last days', they will 'fall by the edge of the sword and be taken as captives to all the Gentiles; and Jerusalem will be trampled underfoot by the Gentiles until the times of the Gentiles are fulfilled.' St. Paul wrote that 'a hardening has come upon Israel in part, until the full number of the Gentiles comes in, and thus all Israel will be saved.' So there is a 'time of the Gentiles' that ends at some point. It would seem this happens when Jerusalem was in Jewish hands. From 70 A.D. to 1967, Jerusalem was ruled by Gentiles, but Israel has ruled it ever since the Six Day war.

"At the first coming of Christ, there is the apostasy of the Jews and the acceptance of the Messiah by the Gentiles. At his Second Coming, there is an apostasy of the Gentiles and the acceptance of the Messiah by the Jews. The great Fathers of the Church have written about the apostasy of the Gentiles. St. Jerome said, 'the incredulity of the Gentiles will occasion the conversion of Israel.' St. John told us that 'seeing the Gentiles abusing little by little their grace, God will recall a second time the Jews.'

"In modern times popes like Leo XIII and Pius X have said the same thing. In the view of many Christians, the apostasy of the gentiles began in the eighteenth century with the Enlightenment in France, and reached its darkest depths in the Holocaust. Today gentile Europe holds that humanity is unrelated to anything transcendent. Morality is entirely a matter of economics and biology, and history is directionless and meaningless. This is the Great Apostasy, and Europe is no longer a Christian continent. At the same time, with the end of the Six Day War, the Jews took possession of Jerusalem. If we go by the New Testament timetable, we can at some point expect the final fulfillment of Judaism, the coming into the Church of the People Israel."

"You're speaking of the end-times," Santos said.

"All of history before the Incarnation was moving toward the coming of the Messiah. All of history after Christ is oriented toward his Second Coming. And both Scripture and the consistent tradition of the Church teach that the world will be ruled by an Antichrist before the Second Coming of Christ. Now, of course, events such as these have in some sense been taking place in every age since the first coming of Christ. So on their own they don't prove anything. But my interest is specifically the destiny of Israel as it relates to God's plans in history. And I think the astonishing return of the Jews to their homeland and to Jerusalem seem related to biblical prophecy.

"Now this is what I find most interesting. According to St. Paul, God permitted the Jews to initially reject Christ because this brought about salvation to the Gentiles. The New Covenant is the fulfillment of the Old. But then the people of the Old Covenant turn up again at the climax of the New. At the beginning there is the apostasy of the Jews, and at the end the apostasy of the Gentiles. When the Gentiles have fallen away, the Jews will come into their own. And the apostasy of the Gentiles marks the end of their age. It's now the "time" of the Jews. And, of course, the Second Coming will take place only after the Jews finally turn in faith to their once and future Messiah-King. Hebrew Catholics believe this is why Satan is behind attempts to exterminate the Jews as in the Holocaust. If there are no Jews, there is no Second Coming."

Santos' interest peaked at the mention of Satan, and his eyes remained riveted on Vazken.

"The hatred for Jews goes beyond anything that's natural," Vazken continued. "Anti-Semitism is no different from any other form of racism. But the passion of the Jew-haters is so embedded and irrational, it seems to be a form of possession. It's a kind of hatred that transcends national and racial boundaries, with a focus purely on the fact of one being Jewish. Since the people of Israel were chosen by God and play a central role in his plans, Satan has a special hatred for them and will stop at nothing to destroy them. He awakens the same sort of hatred in the enemies of the Jews. This ingrained hatred often masks itself as loathing for their economic dominance, or unbelief, or perversity. It is the hatred that ended up as the Holocaust, which Satan, acting through the occultist Hitler, thought was his 'final solution'.

"But instead of exterminating the Jews, in fairly short order the Jews were able to regain control first of their homeland, then Jerusalem. And I think this has set the stage for the next turning point in world history. I hope this has been useful to you, Father Machado. I only know that God has given you a task of enormous importance, the first step of which we have taken together, but now it is a journey you must continue alone."

Santos sat in silent contemplation as Vazken rose and began to leave.

"One last thing, Father Machado," he called out. "The Church through which the Apostles of Christ minister should not to be thought of as a different religion from Judaism. It is, in fact, the fulfillment of Judaism. The Chair of Moses becomes the Chair of Peter. There is a symbiotic link between Judaism and early Christian liturgies, practices, and structures. The Jews saw the Temple as a unique locus of encounter between God and the human being. The Christians have a similar understanding of the sacred space that is the altar where, in the celebration of the Eucharist, they enter into the divine life of Christ. And, of course, the Jewish Passover is the foundation for the celebration of the Catholic Mass. I believe it is also no coincidence that synagogues and ancient churches alike reproduce the proportions of the temple laid out by Ezekiel. It has been a great blessing to meet you, Father Machado. God protect you and look over you, and speed you on your way."

Alone, Santos knelt before the image of Christ on the cross at the site of the crucifixion and prayed for the inspiration that could only come from God to guide his way. Around him the chapel grew quiet and the people seemed to fade. Not sure whether he was dreaming or hallucinating, or experiencing another vision, in his mind he saw the spear that pierced the side of Christ, blood spurting out in great dark pools that were immediately absorbed into the earth. An unseen hand held the spear, and as he struggled to give it a face, the image of Hitler in mesmerizing speech came into focus. His face, violent and distorted by hate and rage, transformed into Satan's, and then Shaitana's, completing a cycle that brought the Devil back into man's life in the most hideous of ways.

Looking up, a Star of David blended with the cross as two Scriptural passages floated in the air, sweeping and swirling, vanishing and forming again, presenting themselves for him to read before disappearing in an ethereal mist.

> "Simon has declared how God at the first visited the Gentiles to take out of them a people for His name. And with this the words of the prophets agree, just as it is written: 'After this I will return And will rebuild the tabernacle of David, which has fallen down; I will rebuild its ruins, And
> I will set it up.'" (Acts 15:14-16)

> "For I do not desire, brethren, that you should be ignorant of this mystery, lest you should be wise in your own opinion, that blindness in part has happened to Israel until the fullness of the Gentiles has come in. And so all Israel will be saved, as it is written: 'The Deliverer will come out of Zion, and He will turn away ungodliness from Jacob.'" (Romans 11:25-26)

At that moment Santos understood the first Secret. Israel and the Line of David were central to human history. Now that the times of the Gentiles had been fulfilled with their great apostasy, the world was heading toward the climax of history and the return of Christ. The final step required for the coming of Christ was the Jewish acceptance of their Messiah and his Family. When Jesus said, "The Son of Man is to be handed over to men, and they will kill him, and he will be raised on the third day," he was prophesying his own destiny, as well as the future of his Church and of his own people, the Jewish nation. Only by sharing in his suffering, abandonment and death, could his people be shaped into His image and thus accept him as their Messiah.

With the destruction of the Temple in 70 A.D, the Jewish people were scattered around the world until finally "dying" in the Holocaust. But God does not allow man to do away with his covenants, and the people of Israel rose again as an independent nation. But for them now to make the final ascension, the Church must open the door to Nation Israel by removing all obstacles to the ingathering of the Jews. The Church, headed by the Bishop of Rome, must formally recognize Hebrew Catholics as a distinctive national community, marked by an irrevocable divine election, and enable them to maintain their God-given identity within the Church. Jews baptized into Christ's Church who accept the Law of Christ would remain Jewish in culture, custom, and race, and would marry among themselves.

In doing so the Church would recognize "where the Savior's Line began, the Times fulfilled," and erect the first barrier to the demonic plans of the Enemy.

***

After an hour of waiting inside the sweltering cab, Miguel saw a familiar figure emerge over the crest of a hill and begin walking down the sloping inclined street. Alone on the cobblestone street, Santos tapped his cane along the uneven surface to steady himself as he walked. Drained from the highly emotional ordeal, he appeared lost in his thoughts. He didn't notice when behind him, closing at a rapid speed, a dark grey Mercedes suddenly came out of nowhere, and seemed to speed up as it headed in his direction.

"Santos! Watch out!" Miguel called frantically.

Startled by Miguel's shout and the simultaneous screech of automobile tires, Santos stepped aside just as the speeding car brushed by him in a blur, missing him only by inches. The sudden movement sent him tumbling to the ground, though unhurt. Farther down the street the driver stopped abruptly, his face hidden behind tinted glass. Hesitating for a moment as if uncertain what to do next, he put the car in gear and sped off down an adjoining street.

"Santos! Are you all right?" Miguel raced to his side, helping to lift him to his feet.

Santos brushed off his trousers and dismissed Miguel's concern with a wave. "I'm fine, nothing broken."

"You could have been killed! Did you see that? He came straight for you!"

"Now Miguel, don't exaggerate," Santos gently chided. "I've been to the Holy Land a dozen times. The truth is, everyone drives this way."

"Not that way, Santos," Miguel remained firm. "He was headed straight for you."

"Well then, once again it's fortunate my guardian angel was with me," Santos laughed.

"This is no joke, Santos."

"No it's not, Miguel," Santos smiled. "But the fact is I'm unhurt, and the driver has left as hurriedly as he came. There's nothing to be served by dwelling on the incident, except to make us both unhinged. Now come, we must follow the path where the Sainted family 'fled in haste, returned'. It's off to Cairo. If we're lucky, we can be there before the evening is out. But first I need to find a telephone."

Chapter 13

Cairo

Egypt was the wellspring of many pre-Christian mystery-religions and the birthplace of most of the world's occult practices, some of which have survived from ancient times and still exist in the twenty-first century.

In the Old Testament, Egypt is contrasted with Israel as the oppressor of the People of God and the source of countless diabolic practices. On the other hand, it was also a country specially chosen by God to be of pivotal importance in the spread of Christianity to the nations of the world. This duality is reflected in the Old Testament, where it was the home of the Patriarch Joseph who was able to feed his people because of his authority under the Pharaoh. In the New Testament, Egypt was the country that provided refuge for Jesus and the Holy Family as they fled Herod's forces.

Egypt was where Jesus first confronted the diabolic and the occult. During his time on earth it was a center of idol worship, and as such an affront to the belief in the one true God, the God of Christians and Jews. Condemnation of the worship of "demons and idols made from gold, silver, bronze, stone, and wood, which cannot see or hear or talk," was a centerpiece in the Book of Revelation, which equated "the dogs, the sorcerers, the unchaste, the murderers, the idol-worshipers," with all who "love and practice deceit." Isaiah in the Old Testament had prophesied the impending destruction of these false gods and idols, and it was Jesus' stay in Egypt that ultimately led to their destruction. "In that day there will be an altar to the Lord in the midst of the land of Egypt; and a Pillar to the Lord, at its border. And it will be for a sign and for a witness to the Lord of hosts in the land of Egypt."

According to the traditions of the Coptic Church, 'the altar' mentioned by Isaiah was the Church of the Virgin Mary in Al-Muharraq Monastery. This was the site where the Holy Family settled after fleeing Herod, with the altar-stone the 'bed' upon which the Infant Jesus lay. Located in the geographic center of Egypt, Al Muharraq Monastery was, quite literally, "in the midst of the land of Egypt". It was this connection, this rich tradition of Egypt as Christ's first battleground against the occult, that led Santos

Machado to search for the second Secret in the land of the Pharaohs now transformed into a modern-day battle ground of Good and Evil.

***

"Santos! Santos Machado!"

Santos turned toward the sound of his name, but all he could make out was a sea of unfamiliar faces in the crowded airport terminal.

"Santos! Over here!" the voice rang out again.

Ramses Nazour, a plump, though muscular, curly-haired man with a full white beard, always cheerful, always laughing, pushed his way through the throng of people separating him from Santos, and embraced his friend of thirty years with a crushing hug.

"You haven't changed a bit," Ramses laughed, patting Santo's belly, and then his own. "And as you can see, neither have I. We were two fat old men when I last saw you, and we're two fat old men now that you've returned to Egypt! I've missed you, you old reprobate."

"Miguel, meet Ramses Nazour, a Copic Orthodox priest and a descendant of the pharaohs. At least, that's what he tells me," Santos smiled, "and who am I to disagree?"

"Young Miguel!" Ramses literally picked him up by the waist and embraced him. "I have heard much about you. I see you are taking good care of my friend Santos, the Demon-chaser."

"You and Santos are old friends?" Miguel caught his breath once Ramses released him. Dressed in a white cassock that was similar, but not identical to Santos, standing side-by-side they looked like negative images of each other. Except for the beard and Ramses' taller frame, they could have been brothers.

"Yes, very good friends," Ramses said fondly, picking up Santos' and his luggage. "Now come. A fine meal is awaiting us. You must both be tired after your long flight from Rome and unexpected visit with the Israelis. We'll eat, catch up on old times, and then the two of you get a good night's sleep. Tomorrow I take you to the Church at Zeitoun, just as you asked, Santos."

***

After dining on a meal of lamb tagine with prunes, Miguel and Santos reclined on the old tattered couch in Ramses' surprisingly spacious home on the outskirts of Cairo. Adorned with familiar religious paraphernalia — a portrait of the Virgin Mary, Christ on the Crucifix and other symbols of his faith — the room looked as if it could have belonged to Miguel's parents or any other Catholic family. Even the furnishings were surprisingly modern in design, though most of them showed a great deal of wear and tear.

"So, how do you know Santos?" Miguel asked, finally able to work a word in edgewise amid the laughter and friendly banter of two old friends catching up with each other.

"Santos the Demon-chaser?" Ramses chuckled. "Before I was ordained, when I was but a mere wisp of the man I am today, I met a young priest on a pilgrimage to the Holy Land. This priest, he was very young and not so fat as he is today," Ramses winked, "but he still commanded great presence. He was not like the others who came to worship in the footsteps of our Savior. Though these were men of devotion, you could see in his eyes, in his demeanor, that his piety was far greater, his faith so much deeper, than any of the others. I was drawn to this man like a moth to fire, to bask in the light and drink in the sweet taste of his communion with God. I watched as he laid his hands upon the body of a poor, tortured soul whom all others had forsaken, both men of science and men of faith, and saw him drive the Devil away. I watched as the stricken man was literally reborn in the arms of Christ, and I wept with joy. It was then, through that singular act of mercy, that I found my own calling to serve our Lord. I have never forgotten this young priest, who I am proud to call 'friend'. It has been more than thirty years, but every day before I sleep, and then again when I rise, I thank our Lord for the many gifts he has given me throughout my life. But I thank him most of all for allowing me to share a few moments of my life with the young priest, who touched my soul that day as well."

The tears in Santos' eyes as he listened to the words that were spoken by Ramses both humbled and invigorated him. Whatever doubts he had about himself, or his abilities, to carry forward the holy mission given to him by Pope Leo, vanished in that moment. God had given him one of the greatest gifts allowed to man, to see himself through the eyes of another. If he was half the man Ramses Nazour believed him to be, then with the continued help of God, he would succeed.

Tomorrow he would seek the wisdom of the second Secret, and with the others revealed, use them to send the Devil back to Hell.

Aswan

The Isis Temple, on the island of Agilkia in the Aswan, was home to the modern day devotees of that ancient Egyptian goddess.

Of all the mythical deities of that period, the most popular and widely worshiped was the goddess Isis. Revered as the Queen of Heaven, Earth and the Underworld, she was also known as "The Great One Who Initiated Existence, and First Among the Goddesses; Goddess of the Sun, the Moon, and the Stars". To the Egyptians, she was Iset. To the Greeks and the Romans, she was known as "Isis of the Ten Thousand Names." At the height of her worship, temples of Isis could be found from Egypt to Germany, and from India to England.

Meeting in a torch lit tent near the Temple of Isis, Harold Boyle, a one-time amateur British archaeologist and now prominent secular humanist whose work was funded by the Lumen Foundation, addressed a group of modern day worshipers of the goddess Isis. The emergence of Shaitaanism as a credible intellectual and religious movement, thanks in no small part to the relentless efforts of Hastings Communications to swaddle it in the cloak of legitimacy, had spurred a collateral rise in neo-paganist worship for those individuals for whom traditional religions — even watered down ecumenical ones — held no great appeal. Like the Druids in England who flocked to Stonehenge for the summer solstice, or the Wiccans of the world who practiced modern-day witchcraft , they prayed to no single god, recognized no central religious authority, other than that which the human mind itself created. They were, in short, the perfect vehicle for Shaitana to use when it suited his purposes, since both held the same common enemy: established, traditional religions, particularly those audacious enough to believe that they actually represented the one true Word of God.

"And so it is with great trepidation that I must give you this warning," Boyle said in a voice filled with drama while handing out a handful of photographs to the odd collection of men and women seated before him. "The Vatican has sent an agent to Cairo for the express purpose of banishing the worship of *She of Ten Thousand Names.* He seeks to impose the Authority of Rome over all other practices and beliefs, and will stop at nothing to deny you your natural right to worship the god or gods of your own choosing. Already, in his wake, he has left a trail of cruelty and destruction by attacking all manner of Wiccans, paganists, and others who dare challenge Rome. He carries with him large sums of money to bribe every manner of official until his dastardly deed is accomplished. But fear not. The hour of fortune is at hand. We shall smite him and all that he represents, and drive his kind from these hallowed shores, if we act now with resolve and purpose."

"So what you're saying," a distinctly American-accented voice interrupted, "is that they're gunna try and close us down if we don't stop 'em?"

"That is precisely my point," Boyle exclaimed.

He looked over the rag tag group of drop outs, drifters, and what in another era might have been called beatniks or hippies, mumbling angrily among themselves. Flocking to Egypt after Internet rumors failed to materialize that an intergalactic spaceship would land somewhere on the Isle of Capri on the first day of the new millennium and whisk them all to their new home world, they gravitated toward a replacement cult-de-jour, this one based on supposedly time-tested Egyptian mythology. The "Sons and Daughters of Isis," as these children of wealthy, indulgent parents preferred to be called, became a magnet for every social deviant and confused agnostic on the planet, collecting in such great numbers that the Egyptian government simply consigned them to Agilkia where they posed no real threat to the social order, content to use their parents' money to help prime the local economy.

"This really sucks," the American said. "I just got here."

"All is not lost," Boyle raised his hands to quiet the murmuring. "I have passed along photographs of the chief agent of the Vatican, a priest by the name of Santos Machado. He's in Cairo somewhere, and he must be located before he can work his damage."

"Cairo's a big place," the American whistled. "How are we gonna find him?"

"Hey, maybe we should ask Isis to guide us?" another voice chimed.

"Yeah, that's a good idea. We'll make some sacrifices and drink a lot of wine, and things like that, get it going really good!"

"And we need a roasted fowl, too," a third person offered. "And some different kinds of fruits. That's really important, I think."

"Okay fruits, but no dates," the American grunted. "I've still got the runs from the last time I ate them."

"All right, no dates. We'll go with bananas."

"Bananas are fine. And maybe some mangos too."

"Wait, you're missing the point—" Boyle stammered, but his protest was quickly drowned out in the overlapping voices of plans and counter-ideas, most of which seemed to have drinking, drugs, or sex as their main component.

"That went well," a shadowy figure said sarcastically as the group, now lost in their own deliberations, traded ideas back and forth at a dizzying rate. "I told you this wouldn't work. These idiots couldn't find their way out of a one story house if you gave them a map and flashlight. They're either brain dead from drugs, or too self-indulgent to think about anything other than getting laid."

"Then just what do you expect us to do?" Boyle countered. "You got the same call I did. Find this chap Machado and dispose of him, or away goes my funding, and yours too no doubt. Besides, I'm no killer. I wouldn't have the foggiest notion of what to do, or the gall to do it."

"Listen, you're the archeologist. They said Machado's looking for something of historical significance, so figure it out. Tell me where he'll be, and I take care of him."

"Do you realize how many places of significance there are to the Catholic religion in Egypt? He could go anywhere from the shrine to St. Athanasius to the Church at Zeitoun. I wouldn't know where to begin."

"Well you better think of something quick," the man said gruffly. "Use that brain of yours to come up with a logical connection to that research we got sent. Which one of these places has the most to do with the genealogy of Jesus Christ."

"If I had to guess, and it's only a guess," Boyle breathed heavily, "I'd focus on the Church at Zeitoun. That's where Mary was said to have appeared in 1968. Thousands reportedly saw her. The sick were cured, the blind could see again —"

"Yeah, yeah, I get the point. It's as good a place as any to look. Okay, I'll go there first thing after sunrise and keep my eyes open. If he's there, I'll get him. If not, at least we can report back that we did everything we could to find him. I mean, they'll understand we did our best, won't they? That's all they can ask. Right?"

"Right old boy."

"Okay, then."

With the sounds of flutes and homemade drums banging out a primitive rhythm, Boyle and the man watched the impromptu Festival of Isis begin amid the swaying bodies of half naked women, open barrels of rich fermented wine, and the pungent smell of the cannabis plant wafting through the still desert air.

Chapter 14

Rome

The pope's burial was a solemn and auspicious occasion, watched by millions of viewers worldwide in addition to the throngs of the faithful who crowded St. Peter's Basilica.

Before the funeral began, the "Fisherman's Ring" of Pope Gregory XVII was removed by the Cardinal Camerlengo. The gold signet ring with the name of the Pontiff engraved around the circumference, and the figure of Saint Peter engraved in the center casting his net from a fisherman's boat engraved in the center, more than any other item signified papal authority. Its destruction in front of the other cardinals by the Cardinal Camerlengo signified that no such authority presently existed. It would now fall upon the College of Cardinals to choose one of their own to take up this mantle and lead the Church in the new millennium.

Dressed by his Penitentiaries, or the priest confessors of Saint Peter's, in his papal robes with two veils of white silk resting over his face and hands, the body of Pope Gregory was placed inside three coffins, each one encased one within another. The first coffin was of cypress wood, which was then inside a coffin made of lead. On the lead coffin there was an inscription of the pope's name and the dates of his pontificate. That lead coffin was then placed within a coffin made of elm. It was this closed, unadorned coffin that rested on steps to Saint Peter's Basilica for the hundreds of thousands of people who came to the Square to pay their last respects to a great steward of the Church, and to pray for the repose of his immortal soul.

"Norman Cavanaugh here, reporting for the European Bureau of Hastings Communications Worldwide," the serious faced reporter intoned, standing on a platform overlooking the entrance to St. Peter's. "Today a few thousand of the faithful came to this lavish, ornate monument to Christianity to pay their respects to a flawed, but humble man who assumed this holy office a mere dozen years before. In an era of human cloning, manned spaceflight to the moon, and recombinant DNA technology, this one-time peasant priest was sadly out of step with the great advances in human development. His election after a contentious battle within that elderly male bastion known as the College of Cardinals marked a turning point for the Catholic Church. Where it once stood on the precipice of genuine global leadership, under the disastrous reign of Pope Gregory XVII the Church of Rome descended into an abyss of irrelevancy from which it has yet to recover. On the wrong side of almost every important social issue, its legacy of the past twelve years is one of anachronistic obstructionism, fighting every step of human progress with ill-conceived, superstition-laden papal edicts that sought to return its followers to the primitive existence of the sixteenth century."

The camera showed a wide shot of more than a hundred thousand people, men and women of all ages and nationalities, huddled together in prayer and respect for their fallen pope. Cavanaugh brushed the imagery aside as he continued to paint an entirely different picture, one directed by his superiors at Hastings Communications headquarters in New York City.

"Sadly, for the misguided souls who come here today, who are few in number and bereft of most outward signs of grief, this truth is all too evident. Today the Catholic Church faces its greatest challenge, how to win back the hearts and minds — and most importantly the pocketbooks — of its disillusioned parishioners. The next pope must be a man with the singular vision to correct the errors of the past and place the Church back on the long road to social relevancy. For this we go to Jerry Rather in our Washington D.C. bureau, who has prepared a report on the leading candidate to succeed Pope Gregory, Cardinal Bruno Reinhard."

"All right, cut," the producer said, killing the power to Cavanaugh's camera.

The smarmy, bow-tied reporter set his microphone down and glanced over his shoulder again at the mass of humanity filling St. Peter's square. He turned to a young woman standing off to his right, clipboard in hand, and spoke to her with a puzzled frown.

"Just how many people do you think are out there, Leslie?"

"A hundred and fifty thousand, by last count," she said without looking up. "Another fifty to a hundred thousand outside the Piazza San Pietro."

"I daresay that's more than a 'few thousand'," Cavanaugh looked concerned.

"Probably."

"Doesn't do a lot for my credibility, Leslie, to have me read the teleprompter about a 'small crowd' while the Second Coming is assembling right behind me."

"Look Norman," the young, attractive woman with a decidedly East Coast American accent said. "You're paid to read the news, not to make it. I've got my marching orders straight from our New York office. I'll write the script, and you read it."

"Yes, but —"

"There's no 'buts'. You pull down two hundred thousand euros a year to stand in front of the camera and get people to listen to you. That's a lot of money, even over here. If you don't like your job, there's a dozen other pretty faces waiting in the wings to take over for you."

"No, it's not a problem," Cavanaugh quickly backpedaled. "I have no opinion on the matter, you know that. If you say the pope was a Neanderthal, I believe you. I'm simply saying, when I'm reporting on a crowd turnout and the evidence behind me contradicts what I'm saying, you might consider switching to a different camera so the viewer isn't presented with contradictory images."

"Okay, that's a good point," Leslie agreed.

"So, when is my next report?"

"In about two hours. We're going to have you interview a woman who claims Pope Gregory fathered her illegitimate child back in Slovakia when he was a parish priest."

"Really?"

"Please, Norman," the woman smirked. "What difference does it make? It's good theater. As long as we beat our competitors in the ratings, that's the only thing that counts."

"And getting out the proper message," Cavanaugh said nonchalantly.

"That, Norman, goes without saying," the young woman smiled, returning to her work as the relieved reporter headed off to his mobile dressing room.

Cairo

The Church of the Virgin Mary in Zeitoun was built in 1924, and consecrated by Athanasious, bishop of Beni Suef, in 1925. In ancient times, Zeitoun was known as Mataria and it was to this city that Joseph, Mary and the infant Jesus came when they escaped from Herod. St. Mary's Church, an ancient shrine, had been built on the precise spot where the Holy Family had been living in exile. The shrine had disappeared and was then rebuilt several times until finally the current church came up in 1924. It was here, on April 2, 1968, that an apparition of the Virgin Mary was said to have appeared on the dome of the church. The international press coverage that resulted soon made the church a destination point for the faithful throughout Christendom.

According to witnesses, an hour and a half after sunset a young woman dressed in white appeared on the church dome. At first thinking she was about to fall, bystanders on the street called out, then realized that the dome was curved, and no person could possibly walk on it. At this point several recognized the apparition as the Virgin Mary. Millions witnessed the sight in person or though the media, and it quickly became a holy shrine. Its elegant Italian-style architecture and neo-Coptic paintings suffered under the onslaught of religious pilgrims, many of whom burned candles to the Virgin Mary in such quantities that it blackened the church's interior walls and caused other damages. A restoration project was begun to repair the interior including its domes, and it was through just such a maze of scaffolds that Santos first entered the church.

Miguel and Ramses kept a respectful distance as Santos approached a statue of the Virgin Mary. He knelt in prayer, and shut out the world around him while he asked the Blessed Virgin for her help. Again another Bible verse appeared before him, visible to no one but himself.

> "The woman herself fled into the desert where she had a place prepared by God, that there she might be taken care of for twelve hundred and sixty days. Then war broke out in heaven: Michael and his angels battled against the dragon. The dragon and its angels fought back, but they did not prevail and there was no longer any place for them in heaven. The huge dragon, the ancient serpent, who is called the Devil and Satan, who deceived the whole world, was thrown down to earth, and its angels were thrown down with it. … When the dragon saw that it had been thrown down to the earth, it pursued the woman who had given birth to the male child. But the woman was given the two wings of the great eagle, so that she could fly to her place in the desert, where far from the serpent, she was taken care of for a year, two years and a half year."
> (Revelation 12:7-9,13-14)

Images of a cosmic battle of darkness and light swirled about him. Then an image of the Virgin Mary as the Lady of Zeitoun, and then again an image of Joseph, Mary and the infant Jesus traveling through the desert.

As the ethereal display began to dissolve, Santos felt someone nudging him gently. He turned to see a young man with soft, golden hair smiling benevolently. The clothing he wore looked more like the garb of ancient times, but his words were modern. Santos looked at him, uncertain if he was real or imaginary, as the young man began to speak.

"I am Michael," he said. "You have traveled far, Santos, in the Name of God. But your journey has only begun."

"You know me?" Santos asked.

"I have been with you your whole life."

"My whole life? I don't understand. Who are you?"

"I was sent to speak to you, to reveal to you the secret you seek in this land. Remember a time when you were five years old, and you went to Mass with your mother. When the priest said, 'santos, santos, santos' before the Eucharistic prayer. You thought he was speaking to you, and went up to the altar. From that day, you felt a calling to the priesthood. God has rewarded your lifelong devotion to the Holy Angels by assigning me as your guardian along this path."

"You are ... the Archangel Michael," tears began pouring down Santos' cheeks. Watching him sob, Ramses and Michael could only wonder at what miracle might be taking place. Intuitively, the old Orthodox priest moved a step closer to Santos, as if something compelled him forward. Also fixating on the praying priest, was another man, Harold Boyle, who signaled to the shadows of the dome high above them where another pair of eyes watched Santos intently.

"I have come here to tell you the story of Christ's journey, where the sainted Family fled in haste, and then returned. Egypt was a stronghold of Satan before the coming of Christ, the center of the diabolic mystery-religions," Michael began. "It was here that Ham, one of the three sons of Noah, led the rebellion against God. His descendants were the Babylonians, Philistines, Egyptians, Canaanites, and Assyrians who became the enemies of Abraham and the Israelites, the descendants of Shem. But Egypt was also specially blessed. Of Ishmael, the son of Abraham by his Egyptian concubine Hagar, God said, 'I hereby bless him. He shall become the father of twelve chieftains, and I will make of him a great nation.'"

"The Ishmaelites rescued Joseph, the son of the Patriarch Jacob. It was Joseph who later became the Pharaoh's viceroy and led his kingdom through a great famine, and eventually made Egypt the home of the Israelites. But within four centuries the Egyptians had enslaved the Israelites, and inducted them into their idol-worship and other evil practices. When the Pharaoh would not heed God's command to release the Israelites, both he and his nation were severely punished. But the Israelites were punished in the desert as well when they returned to the occult practices of Egypt. To cleanse their souls, God asked them to daily kill and sacrifice rams and bulls, the very animals worshipped as gods by the Egyptians, and to treat as unclean any creature that the Egyptians worshipped.

"Once the Chosen People had been purified of idolatry and sorcery, the divine blueprint was to liberate Egypt. Thus Isaiah prophesied, "The Lord shall make himself known to Egypt and the Egyptians shall know the Lord in that day; they shall offer sacrifices and oblations, and fulfill the vows they make to the Lord. Although the Lord shall smite Egypt severely, he shall heal them, they shall turn to the Lord and he shall be won over and heal them." The prophetic day arrived when the Christ-Child and his family made their way through the desert to receive the homage and hospitality of Egypt. During their three years here, idols across the land crumbled in the wake of the family. So great was the impact that Lucifer was furiously enraged, but could not resist because he was restrained by the divine power. This cleansing of Egypt was followed in successive years by the conversion of the entire nation with churches built in all the places visited by the Holy Family.

"You have been brought here, Santos, to the Cathedral of Zeitun the Blessed Virgin appeared to people of all faiths, to witness again the cosmic battle between God and his angels and the Evil One. Learn well the message for the Church of this age. Teach the reality of the Devil and his demons, and of the cosmic battle for every soul. Condemn all idolatry and all that is occult. Tell the faithful to entrust themselves to the protection of Jesus, Mary, and Joseph, and the nine choirs of angels — the Seraphim, Cherubim, Thrones, Dominions, Powers, Principalities, Archangels and Angels. And after every Mass the faithful must recite the prayer of Leo: 'Saint Michael the Archangel, defend us in battle; be our defense against the wickedness and snares of the devil. May God rebuke him, we humbly pray; and do you, O Prince of the heavenly host, by the power of God, thrust into hell Satan and the other evil spirits who prowl about the world for the ruin of souls. Amen'."

"I will do this," Santos said.

"You must know one other thing," Michael continued. "Angels are but purely spiritual beings. We have no bodies, only pure intellect and will. We are 'present' only in the sense that we apply our power and mind to one place, as I do now here in this shrine to the Blessed Mother. We can travel from one place to another in the same way in which you move from one thought to another. Because we are not human, because we were never born with men's souls, we know things instantly. We don't have to weigh our decisions before we act, we make all the choices of our lives in an instant, as I have already done with you this day. Our decisions are immediate and immutable."

"I don't understand," Santos said, sensing there was more to Michael's words than he could comprehend.

"At the moment of our creation, every Angel decided whether or not we would serve our Creator. God will not force his love on any of his creations, even those who are ethereal beings. A free creature can be good only if it chooses to be so, and to be good means to freely choose what is right. Each of us individually was given that choice, to love and serve God and all that he intends, or follow a different path. The greatest of the angels, the most brilliant and powerful of us all, rejected the divine blueprint because he was not to be at the summit of creation in the plans of Providence. Instantly and forever he became the Enemy of God, the Adversary, the vilest and most malefic being imaginable. He was not alone in his rejection. Multitudes upon multitudes of the angels threw their lot in with him, offered the prospect of unlimited freedom outside the divine milieu.

"But freedom comes at a price. In rejecting God he did not lose his power and intelligence. He simply turned them into instruments of his evil will. Once created, angels never die. Those angels who defied God condemned themselves to everlasting misery since they could not have what they needed above all, the God they rejected totally and forever. Their misery can't be escaped through sleep or death since they're subject to neither. The only salve to their endless suffering is the prospect of bringing others into the Abyss with them. That's why these malefic angels are your enemies and seek nothing but your eternal doom.

"But we, the angels who chose God, love you as much as they hate you. We are messengers of the divine love and the invisible spiritual directors of your souls. We do all we can to protect you from your relentless adversaries, and rejoice over every one of you that dies in union with the divine will."

Santos swallowed hard. It wasn't clear if the message he was given was that he would not survive the ordeal before him, but in truth it didn't matter. He would do his best, and accept whatever fate God had in store for him. Closing his eyes, he watched the image of the Archangel fade, until once again he was alone with his prayers.

High above the floor, hidden in the shadows, a man dressed in black watched Santos continue to kneel in prayer. The arches and columns of the Church were framed in marble, and some of the slabs had been loosened for cleaning and repair. The man moved silently along one scaffold directly underneath Santos. With straining muscles he worked a marble panel back and forth until it finally came free.

The tourists and pilgrims below were too intent on admiring the beautiful wall paintings, or themselves so deep in prayer, that no one noticed the small flakes of crumbling mortar from the loosened panel sprinkle to the ground. Only Ramses, who caught a glint of light coming from the dome area as a ray of sun penetrating the darkness reflected off the man's watch, turned his head upward. Still too dark to make out the black clad figure, he did see the large marble panel begin its fall.

Striking one of the scaffolding panels as it dropped, it slowed its descent long enough to allow him to act. Dashing toward Santos, still lost in his communion with God, he pushed his friend roughly aside just as the heavy stone slab came crashing to the floor. It caught the right side of his head and with a terrible, sickening snap, killed him instead of Santos.

"Ramses!" Miguel cried.

Santos, stunned and confused, righted himself to see his friend lying in a pool of blood. He rushed to his side and lifted Ramses' head, cradling it in his lap while Miguel and others surrounded them.

"Someone call a doctor!" one tourist said, backing away at the grisly sight.

"No," Santos replied quietly. "The time for man has passed. Ramses is with the Lord, may God bless his soul and welcome him into the Kingdom of Heaven." With Miguel choking back tears, Santos made the sign of the cross on Ramses' eyes, nose, mouth, and body. "By this Holy Unction may God pardon thee whatever sins thou hast committed by the evil use of sight, smell or touch."

For what seemed like hours, but were only minutes, Santos remained with the body until medical officials came and transported it to the local mortuary. His cassock stained with blood, Miguel helped him to his feet. The interior of the Church was now deserted, emptied by the authorities of all except for a smattering of people who managed to slip through the now cordoned off area and wander through the empty church. One of them was the English amateur archaeologist who had watched the near miss of the falling slab that almost took Santos' life. Though his companion had vanished into the crowds, he remained to watch and observe, hoping to learn something from the quiet conversation between Santos and Miguel that would redeem him in their failure.

"This wasn't an accident, Santos," Miguel let his eyes drift skyward toward the domed ceiling.

"Look at this church, Miguel," Santos said softly. "There is construction and repairs everywhere."

"And a big stone slab just happens to fall directly towards you?"

"You dwell on the wrong matters, my young friend," Santos smiled weakly. "It's not for us to question God's plan for our lives. Accident or intentional, once again my life was spared to continue with the task I was given."

"Ramses' dead, your friend, Santos!" Miguel's voice rose sharply. "What about him?"

"We live this life not for earthly reward, but to prepare ourselves for eternal judgment and life everlasting. My sorrow at the loss of my friend must be tempered with the knowledge that he is now in Heaven, receiving his just reward for a life well spent in the service of Our Lord. It was his time, Miguel, not of his choosing, but of God's; not by his manner, but as the Lord willed. Who are we to question God's plan for each of us? We are but to do our best with the time we are given, until one day we too are called to the service of Our Lord."

"I-I'm sorry Santos," Miguel said softly.

"You are a young man," Santos brushed his hair lovingly. "Time will teach you what your heart already knows, but cannot yet express."

"Did you … find what you were looking for?" Miguel asked.

"Yes," Santos replied. "But not until this moment, not until we spoke, did I truly understand."

Miguel's face scrunched, not sure what Santos meant. As Boyle listened from nearby, pretending to drink in the rich flavor of the shrine's interior, Santos continued.

"The Holy Family faced the murder of children under Herod, just as we faced death here today. It is not possible to imagine the magnitude of the horrors of hell that ranged against the Holy Family when they were in Egypt.

All that stood between the success or failure of the mission of Jesus was one man, to whom God had entrusted the future. Joseph, the guardian of the Holy Family. Like his namesake, the Patriarch Joseph of the Old Testament, the New Testament Joseph was forced by circumstances to go to Egypt, just as God has placed me here today. Both men were guided by God through dreams, as the Heavenly Father has led me in this quest. I know what I must do with the knowledge I have been given, which comes to me in suffering and pain, just as it did to Our Lord those many centuries ago."

"Where do we go now, Santos?"

"'To the land where the fires of Hell leapt out, the sun plunged down'," Santos replied. "To Lisbon."

Withdrawing from the cathedral, Boyle walked into an adjoining courtyard and used his phone to make his report. As they left the church and passed through the crowd outside waiting for a chance to enter, they passed a tall, pock-faced man with short cropped hair. Catching him out of the corner of his eye, Santos thought he recognized him, but was uncertain from when or where. Not giving it another thought, he continued on with Miguel, never noticing that the hard faced man continued to track his every step.

Kathmandu

"The priest still lives," Shaitana seethed.

"Yes my Lord," Prithvi Shah answered without emotion. "Our operatives in Cairo were unable to find him," he lied.

"Incompetent fools."

"But an airline agent who belongs to our movement reported that Machado and his companion purchased two tickets to Lisbon. They should be there in the morning."

"Do you have any idea of the significance of their travels?" Shaitana hissed, not expecting an answer. "There is no doubt where they go now, and what the priest intends to do. He must be stopped at all costs."

"I will send—"

"No!" Shaitana erupted. "You will go there yourself, and see to it personally. Kill Machado with your own hands if you must, but kill him you will!"

"Yes my Lord," Prithvi bowed.

"All that I have worked for, all that I am, can be blocked by this man. There is no more important task."

Without another word Prithvi left the room. Shaitana strode to a window and looked out on the serene landscape before him, and raised his hands in prayer. "My Lord Lucifer, Prince of Darkness and all that is Unholy, the prophecy of Leo will be fulfilled, but in your favor."

The tranquil scene began to boil with darkening clouds and sweeping winds that transformed it into a hellish scene. Shaitana lowered his arms and looked out the window, pleased. His Lord and master had heard his prayer, and renewed his faith in him to lead his charge on earth. Shaitana was convinced that victory would be theirs. He had only one small obstacle still in his way, and that would soon be removed.

Chapter 15

New York

The burial of Pope Gregory XIII marked the start of a nine day official period of mourning, after which the College of Cardinals would meet to begin their deliberations to choose the next pope.

Hastings was pleased by the level of coverage the pope's death and succession battle had already received, but it was no time to rest on his laurels. CNN, ABC, NBC, CBS, the BBC, and most of the other major international media outlets, both visual and print, had picked up on the false stories and rumors he planted about Pope Gregory and Cardinal Francesco Orsini. Like a mindless pack of automatons, the traditional mainstream media followed the lead of Hastings Communications and never deviated from the twin themes of Pope Gregory's failure and Cardinal Orsini's incompetence — or worse, his supposed abject dishonesty. Only a few of what were derisively labeled "right wing" media outlets tried to present a more balanced view, but they were routinely dismissed by the media powers that be as simple stooges and lackeys of the Christian Right. Only the world as Ralston Hastings saw it was unbiased; all other views were by definition "tainted," and had to be suppressed.

Seated at his conference table, Hastings reviewed the current production schedule with his senior staff. Mary Maples, his executive producer of the nightly news, spoke first.

"We're going to lead with a story tonight on the U.N.'s efforts to brand Christian fundamentalism as hate speech. The U.S. and Britain vetoed the resolution yesterday, but the General Assembly is going to hold a plebiscite today, and we expect an overwhelmingly favorable vote. Syria and the Sudan are leading the way, with support from France and Germany. That makes it a truly international effort."

"What are we doing to condemn the U.S. and Britain as obstructionists?" Hasting asked.

"Ron Sawyer is going to run another piece on the British P.M.'s war record, and one of our correspondents in Ohio dug up an old elementary school transcript on the President. It looks like there may have been an unauthorized grade change in primary school that turned a B-minus into a B-plus. We're getting ready to slam him as a fraud and demand that college scholarships be rescinded retroactively. Of course it's all symbolic since he graduated Phi Beta Kappa, but test marketing shows this kind of hit piece has great appeal to certain demographics, and should give him some trouble in the Senate with a few of its more liberal members."

"Keep the pressure on," Hastings said. "You know the drill. If they don't see it our way at first, we'll explain it to them in terms they can understand."

Everyone laughed as Hastings lit a cigar, relaxing in his chair while Maples continued.

"We'll follow the U.N. story with another about the protests around the world over the rumors about Orsini's personal life and real estate dealings. Our molestation witnessed backed out at the last minute, so that's a scrub until we can find someone to replace him. Unfortunately, Orsini spent most of his priesthood in a monastery, so there isn't a lot of contact with young children, but we are working a 'monk' angle that may still pan out. That ties in with another rumor that he tried to sell some monastic property to a real estate developer a few years back. Again, we're pretty thin on facts here, but we've got enough invested in the piece to put something out now, and fill in the missing details later."

"Excellent."

"As for Cardinal Reinhard, we couldn't get him to give an interview on camera. Seems he's drawn the line at public lobbying for the top spot, but we were able to assemble enough of his past speeches into a half hour special that we're running tonight, and repeating every few hours over the next nine days. It shows him as a true man of faith and a great visionary who appreciates the secular nature of things as much as the religious. We're going with his own words for the most part, but we have had to water down some of his pronouncements to avoid offending our French and German friends. It seems he really does believe in the divinity of Christ, go figure? But there's still enough to work with to make him a compelling alternative to Orsini."

"Good," Hastings nodded. He turned to a bald headed man in a three piece suit sitting at the end of the table. "Wilson, what about freezing the Vatican's accounts until this whole matter is resolved."

"Well, we looked into that, Mr. Hastings," the banker replied. "France is willing to take the first step if Germany will follow. We're still negotiating with Berlin, but I think we'll get there in another day or so. Both governments will freeze all Catholic Church bank accounts and put a lien on church property using the subterfuge that the selection process for the pope violates their countries' human rights laws."

"How?" Hastings puzzled. "I like the idea, but what's the connection?"

"Not a single woman is to be found in the College of Cardinals. That's discriminatory on the face of it, if nothing else."

"All right, great," Hastings laughed.

"Unfortunately, there's precious little international law to support such a bold move. But it will take the courts months to decide the matter, and during that time the Church's assets will be frozen. We've begun a similar outreach to other friendly countries to magnify this opportunity. It's unclear how many will follow suit, but the intention is really to send a message to the Vatican to make the correct selection when the conclave convenes. If they do, the effort will be, shall we say, amicably resolved in short order. It will, however, have the salutary after-effect of laying a legal foundation to tax church property in those nations participating in the action. This would lead to a corresponding diminution of Church power, which is a clear, related goal."

"Excellent," Hastings applauded. "Call in some additional markers from the offices of the European Economic Union. They can add some clout and credibility to your efforts. And see what you can get out of the Italian Minister of Finance. Italy won't join the suit, at least not yet. The country's still tied too closely to the Vatican. But he can make some 'helpful' statements about the need to examine the issue. If he balks, which he will, remind him of a certain young lady he was introduced to a few nights ago."

"I will indeed, Sir," Wilson chuckled.

"All right, boys and girls," Hastings stood and stretched, pleased with the meeting. "You all know what you have to do. I'm proud of you, every one of you. You've put in long hours and worked very hard to get us where we are today. It hasn't been easy exposing these fundamentalist lunatics for who and what they are, but each of you has made a real difference in bringing the truth to light. We're a little more than a week away from replacing that old dinosaur in Rome with a man who can lead the Catholic Church out of the Dark Ages and into the twenty-first century. I don't have to tell you how important this is. There are a lot of people in this world still ruled by superstition, and the Catholic Church is at the forefront of promoting this travesty. If we can turn it to see the light, then the domino effect will take place world wide. Politicians who hide behind the church to oppose a women's right to choose won't have anyplace to go. They'll be exposed for the throwbacks to the stone age they really are. Embryonic stem cell research will be common place and fully funded by all governments. Social progress won't depend on the whims of a few old impotent men who derive their guidance from the two thousand year old writings of a few delusional religious fanatics who purport to speak for God. No, the world will be a truly wonderful place, where every man and woman can achieve their full potential without the fetters of somebody else's morality getting in their way. And you people, sitting around this table, will help make this all happen."

The reaction of support and appreciation for Hastings' words and efforts was universal and overwhelming as the table erupted in sustained applause. Imbued with renewed vigor, each man and woman left the table vowing to do his best to make the great man's dream a reality.

Whether God existed or not, whether the Catholic Church or anyone else spoke on his behalf, was a comparatively insignificant concern to the task at hand, to literally remake human history in a way that focused on the here and now, instead of some abstract, esoteric notion of rewards in a mythical thereafter.

Lisbon

The Lisbon hotel was a short distance from Cais do Sodre Station along the shores of the Tagus River. The seedy, run down neighborhood was home to hundreds of vagrants and beggars who squatted in abandoned buildings, or made their homes in the alleyways or crevices of any man-made structure large enough to shelter them against the elements.

Miguel looked at the dangerous surroundings as they made their way toward the Hotel Alfonso VI, a grandly-named boardinghouse that must have been, at one time, worthy of its name. Now age and neglect had reduced it to little more than a patchwork roof and crumbling walls. It was, nevertheless, a place to stay that would not tax Santos' dwindling resources, and like Mary and Joseph seeking refuge in a foreign land, they approached the innkeeper and asked him for a room.

"Two thousand Escudos," the man said in broken English, barely looking up from his newspaper.

"Two thousand!" Miguel gasped. "We don't have that kind of money! We've just about exhausted every account we have getting here, and there's still four more places we need to go. We'll never make it at this —"

"Two thousand Escudos is thirty eight dollars," Santos smiled benignly.

"Towels fifty Escudos extra," the innkeeper interjected, his eyes still focused on his paper.

"All right, Santos," Miguel relaxed a bit. "But even still, we need a lot more money than you've got in the bank to take us everywhere we need to be. Maybe I should stay here, and let you travel on alone. At least that way we can stretch the money farther."

"No Miguel. I need you at my side. You are my angel here on earth, just as your namesake watches over me in Heaven. We have all the material possessions that we need to complete this holy mission."

"If you say so, Santos," Miguel replied, not entirely convinced.

Lifting their bags, Miguel followed Santos down the hall and into the cramped, dimly lit room where both men, exhausted from their journey, curled up on their beds and fell into a deep, consuming sleep.

Asleep and snoring soundly, Santos wasn't sure if the images that filled his head were real, or a dream. He could sense that his physical body was still in the room sleeping on the bed, but his other senses painted an entirely different picture. It was as if his soul had been freed from the corporal world to float freely above.

He looked down on Miguel to his left, and his own body directly beneath him, and pondered the strange, but wonderful feeling of existing in a completely different realm. Like a dream where he knew he was still asleep, but couldn't awake, he let his spirit soar out the room, flying through walls and speeding through the air. Magically he dashed from location to location, some nearby, others thousands of miles apart, reveling in the freedom of his new found powers. But then, just as suddenly, the dream — if that's what it really was — came crashing down upon him. Instead of pristine skies, he found himself caught up in a maelstrom of angry black clouds swirling around him. Lightning bolts and flames shot through the air, some coming dangerously close to him, and he felt the stinging prickle of electricity crawl along his skin. But as unnerving as that sensation was, Santos was not prepared for the next sensation; searing, white hot heat that burned the flesh on an outstretched palm he instinctively raised to block the fireball coming right at him.

"You are no match for my powers," the image of Shaitana bellowed, rising from the pits of Hell beneath him.

The pain from the fire was real, and intense. Santos grasped his hand and looked at the flesh begin to bubble and corrode. Another fireball was hurled his way, and he swatted it aside, doubling the pain he now felt.

"Your God is the God of weakness and lies," Shaitana seethed. "He is no match for the powers of Hell!"

"Stop your blasphemy!" Santos shouted. "'Whoever is begotten by God conquers the world.'"

"There is nothing you can do to stop me. The world is already mine."

"No, it is NOT!" Santos erupted in fury. Charging toward the hovering figure, he grabbed Shaitana in a death lock and began to wrestle with him while crashing through the air. Below them the tortured souls of millions of the damned urged Shaitana on, while above him Santos could hear the heavenly voices of Michael, and the angels and saints, praying for him. It seemed as if the struggle went on for hours, each side gaining temporary advantage over the other, only to have the battle then swing the other way.

Finally, with neither side enjoying the advantage, both Santos and Shaitana broke free. Staring at Santos, circling his foe like a wounded beast, Shaitana slowly began to retreat.

"This is not over, priest," he said, now surrounded by an army of minions who cackled and growled at the lone figure hovering before them. "The next time we meet, I will destroy you, and everything you hold dear."

"Do your worst, Shaitana," Santos said bravely. "I don't fear you, or the master you serve."

"You will," Shaitana's voice faded in the darkness. "And the others who follow your wretched path. You will."

Drenched in sweat, Santos sat up in bed and looked around the dingy room. It was already nightfall. He and Miguel had been sleeping for hours, and the young man still showed no signs of stirring. Better to let him continue to rest through the night, Santos thought, and be fresh for the morning.

Rising to use the bathroom, Santos felt his legs quiver as he walked the short distance aided by his cane. He turned on the light hanging from a cord above him, and looked at his reflection in the mirror. The vividness of the dream was still fresh in his memory, and he touched his face with his hands and winced unexpectedly. Turning his palm over, he saw a red, angry sore on his hand. The bubble blister was painful, and he stared at it almost in disbelief.

"It wasn't a dream," he whispered in awe.

Slowly, the magnitude of his epic battle now intensified in his mind, Santos turned off the light and returned to his bed. Like the apparition at Fatima, he had seen his own vision of Hell. Lucifer's agent Shaitana would stop at nothing to keep him from his holy task, but Santos knew that no powers of the Devil could hurt him. The Archangel Michael had promised him protection, but that same armor did not extend to others who helped him on his way. "We do all we can to protect you from your relentless adversaries," Michael said, "and rejoice over every one of you that dies in union with the divine will."

Ramses had given his life for Santos, nobly sacrificing himself to keep Santos from being struck by the falling slab of marble. He looked at Miguel sleeping peacefully on the bed, and wondered if he too would suffer the same fate.

New York

"Well, would you look at that!" Jerry Rucker laughed, motioning with his head toward a shabbily dressed man waiting for a bus on the corner of West 57th street. "Isn't that Mike McConnell? My, how the mighty have fallen."

"By Jove, you're right," Vincent Stout stared at the man. "I haven't seen him since, well —"

"—since Hastings went off on him a couple of years ago," Rucker finished the sentence. "I heard he lost everything, even his wife."

"She divorced him?" Stout puzzled. "I can't believe that. They'd been married twenty years, at least. She didn't strike me as the kind to dump her husband over a financial reversal."

"Not divorced, dead. Cancer or something. No job, her husband blackballed from every company on the planet who didn't want to get on Hastings' bad side, no money for expensive doctors. You know how it is."

"What was it Mike did anyway to tick Hastings off and get himself fired?" Stout replied, holding his emotions in check.

"Something about the company dress code, or something stupid like that," Rucker tried to remember. "He was pretty senior in the news department. He should have known better than to question the big guy's decision."

"Yeah, I remember now. It was about the same time the French banned religious symbols in their schools. Hastings thought it would be a great idea to ban necklaces with crosses, and those Jewish skullcaps, in all our offices here and abroad. Raised quite a stir in our Tel Aviv bureau, if I remember correctly. Didn't we have a number of people quit?"

"About half the office," Rucker laughed. "But it gave the old man the excuse he was looking for to move the bureau to Ramallah."

"As I remember, the standards weren't quite as strict there as they were everywhere else," Stout mused. "Something about not offending local sensibilities?"

"Yeah, so there's a double standard, what's new?" Rucker shrugged. "The point is, McConnell should have kept his mouth shut. I mean, it's Hastings' company. If he doesn't want to see a bunch of religious fanatics walking around his buildings wearing their little crosses or beanie caps, it's his decision. Mike only made things worse for himself by challenging Hastings, at a board meeting no less. I mean, what was he thinking? It's not like he was some kind of religious nut himself."

"No, he was just a fair man."

"Fairly stupid, if you ask me. Look what it got him. No job and a dead wife. And for what? Defending a few holy rollers who came bitching to him, and who can't seem to understand the world is a better place if we all moderate our beliefs for the common good."

"Hastings isn't around now," Stout chuckled to his friend. "You don't have to make 'the speech'."

"I'm not posturing," Rucker became defensive. "The fact is, it's men like Hastings who've made the world what it is today. I'd rather hitch my star to his wagon than to those religious zealots who think embryonic stem cell research is a sin, even if it means letting people like Christopher Reeve rot his life away in a wheelchair."

"Cultivating stem cells from embryos doesn't have anything to do with spinal chord injuries."

"Well, that's not the point," Rucker said, flustered. "Science and technology shouldn't be constrained by religion and politics. Wasn't it Caesar who said something about giving things to himself and letting the other people take what they want?"

"Are you talking about the Bible quote that says "render unto Caesar—"

"Yeah, exactly! Hastings should run his own business the way he wants.

And people like Mike McConnell should know enough to keep their mouth shut about it, or suffer the consequences."

"A dead wife is a pretty big consequence."

"He brought it on himself," Rucker shrugged. "I say good riddance to him, and his kind. So, where do you want to eat?"

"You know Jerry," Stout sucked in his breath, "I'm not really all that hungry. Maybe some other time?"

"Sure. Catch you around."

"Yeah," he said, watching McConnell board a bus. "I'll see you back at the office."

Chapter 16

Fatima

Fatima was like an oasis in the middle of a wilderness.

Two hours north of Lisbon, it was a long, hard ride through desolate terrain. While Miguel drove the rental car, Santos let his mind play over the miraculous events of almost one hundred years earlier, when an apparition of the Virgin Mary was revealed to three small children, Lucia dos Santos, Francisco Marto, and Jacinta Marto.

Fatima was, without question, the greatest of the twentieth century apparitions, one which had a profound impact both on the faith of millions and on central events of the twentieth century, so it was no mystery to Santos Machado that he would be directed to this remote spot on the Iberian Peninsula to retrace the path given to him through the Vision of Pope Leo.

The Fatima apparitions were preceded by three appearances of the Guardian Angel of Portugal, in which he prepared the three tiny sheepherder visionaries for the coming of the Mother of God. After the overthrow of the Portuguese monarchy shortly after the turn of the twentieth century, Portugal was ruled by anti-Christian groups who killed hundreds of Christian priests, nuns, and monks. Public religious ceremonies were forbidden, and a general persecution began against anyone in the country professing to believe in the Christian faith. It was into this unpromising environment that the Lady of the Rosary made her world-changing entrance

Lucia, Francisco, and Jacinto had taken their sheep to a hilly area called the Chousa Velha. At this time, Lucia later recounted, "a strong wind shook the trees and above them a light appeared, whiter than the driven snow. As it approached, it took the form of a young man, transparent and resplendent with light. He began to speak. 'Fear not. I am the Angel of Peace. Pray with me.' He knelt on the ground, bowed low, and three times recited a prayer: 'My God, I believe, I adore, I hope and I love You. I ask pardon of You for those who do not believe, do not adore, do not hope and do not love you.' Then he arose and said: 'Pray this way. The Hearts of Jesus and Mary are attentive to the voice of your supplications.'"

On another occasion the angel appeared again and told them, "The Hearts of Jesus and Mary have designs of mercy for you. Offer unceasingly to the

Most High prayer and sacrifices. Offer up everything within your power as a sacrifice to the Lord in reparation for the sins by which he is so much offended and of supplication for the conversion of sinners. Thus bring down peace upon your country. I am the Guardian Angel of Portugal. More than all else, accept and bear with resignation the sufferings that God may send you." The apparitions of the angel were followed by six apparitions of the Virgin Mary to the three children, and numerous subsequent appearances and messages to Lucia. The apparitions themselves were public events, so that even onlookers were aware of something extraordinary taking place, especially in October of 1917.

Russia, the soon-to-be godless Communist state, was the initial focus of the Fatima predictions. The Virgin predicted first that Russia would spread its errors around the world, and then that Russia would be "converted". The first prediction was made before the Communists came to power. As implausible as the prediction seemed at first that the actions of a backward, semi-feudal, agrarian country would come to dominate world politics for most of that century, once coming to power it seemed equally implausible that, once coming to power, the Communist state would simply wither away, not through violent revolution, but from its own internal collapse.

The apparitions of the Virgin Mary at Fatima in 1917 were in some respects a direct response to a plea from Pope Gregory XV, who implored the intercession of the Blessed Mother in bringing the Great War to a halt. Within eight days of a pastoral letter by Pope Gregory XV imploring the faithful to pray to Mary, the Mother of Mercy, the Blessed Virgin appeared at Fatima with her own plan of peace for the world. As if to show the difference between her and the diabolic world, she spread out her hands and the light that poured out from them went into the depths of the earth to show a sea of fire filled with demons and the damned. Uncounted numbers of devils and lost souls were lost in a vast and fiery ocean. The devils, hideous creatures, dark and animal-like, filled the air with shrieks and howls. The lost souls had kept their human form and were twisting and turning in the flames, screaming in terror. Neither the devils nor the lost souls seemed to have an instant's peace as fire swirled around each of them and poured out of their bodies.

It was then that the Virgin Mary, the Lady of Fatima, told the children that God wanted to establish devotion to her Immaculate Heart to bring more souls to salvation. She warned that an even greater war than the last one would soon consume the world if people did not stop offending God. When an unknown light illumined the night, it would be a sign that the divine chastisement would soon begin. She also asked for a consecration of Russia to her Immaculate Heart to be issued by the Pope. If this were not done, Russia would spread its errors and entire nations would be annihilated. But in the end her Immaculate Heart would triumph, because a new Pope would consecrate Russia to her, and the country would be converted followed by a short time of peace.

By the middle of October 1917, the entire country had heard of Fatima, despite efforts by the civil authorities to suppress news of the apparitions, and to force the children to recant their stories. Seventy thousand people had arrived at the Cova to witness the last apparition, whose time and date had been given to the children in advance of each new occurrence. The night before, a terrible — some said diabolic — storm swept through Europe, and it was still raining hard by noon of the next day. When the Lady appeared to the visionaries, she said that she wanted a chapel built at the Cova, and warned that people must amend their lives so as not offend the Lord, since He was already greatly offended.

Then she stretched out her hands, and rays of light went toward the sun. The sun shone like a silver disk, and the multitudes of faithful who had followed the three visionary children to the Cova could look straight into it without shading their eyes. Suddenly it started shooting off different colored rays in all directions and spinning on its axis. And then, just as suddenly, it seemed to hurtle towards the earth. The terrified onlookers dropped to their knees, convinced that the end had come, and many sought forgiveness for their sins. Just when it seemed that there would be a cataclysmic collision, the sun returned to its normal position and everything was as before.

While the crowds were gazing at the solar phenomenon, the three children were witnessing various scenes in the heavens, Jesus in a red costume, Joseph and the infant Jesus blessing the crowds, and finally Mary in the brown robes of Our Lady of Mount Carmel. With this magnificent display the apparitions of Fatima came to an end, but its impact on the century had only just begun.

In early 1989 Sister Lucia, one of the three visionary children who became a Carmelite nun, sent a communication to the world announcing that the consecration of Russia and the world to the Immaculate Heart, made by Pope John Paul II in 1984, had been accepted by God, and that its results would become apparent later that year. Later that year the Berlin Wall fell, and within two years the Soviet Union collapsed as well.

"You're awfully quiet, Santos," Miguel said, winding through a barren patch of road as they closed in on their destination, the shrine at Fatima. "Is everything all right?"

"The Devil is much stronger than I thought, Miguel," he replied, almost without emotion. "His stranglehold over the lives of men is great, and growing with each day. He feeds off the wickedness of the world, and there is much for him to feast."

"Whatever it is, whatever you have to do, Santos, I know you'll succeed. I've seen you face great challenges in the past. The Devil is no match for the power of God that flows through you. Don't doubt yourself."

"My doubts have been replaced with conviction, Miguel," Santos smiled benignly. "I know that the Lord is watching over me with all that He commands. He has given me the strength and wisdom to prevail, and I will do as He intended. But the cost of these efforts weigh on me, I will confess."

"You're thinking of your friend Ramses?"

"Yes. And others."

"I didn't know him, but I do know him," Miguel struggled to find the right words. "He was a man of great faith, like you, who devoted his life to the service of God. There's no greater expression of faith or love for our Creator than to give your life to save another. You taught me that, Santos."

"Yes, and I believe it as fervently today as I always have. It's the one thing that gives me comfort for all that we face."

"I'm glad you said 'we', Santos," Miguel smiled. "I want to be as vital a part of this as I can. I'll be there for you, like always. Whatever you face, we'll face it together. I want you to know that you can always count on me, now more than ever."

"I do know that Miguel," Santos said sadly, remembering the image and words of Shaitana, and fearing what they may foreshadow. "I know that all too well."

***

Almost as if it was directed by some unseen force, the small car came to a stop not at the impressive shrine to Our Lady of Fatima, but at the area where the three young sheepherders were shown the vision of Hell.

Exiting the car, Santos walked over the grassy field and stood silently under a tree, his eyes closed in prayer. Around him he felt the presence of another, but when he looked he saw only a single white dove floating through the gentle breeze as it came to land on a nearby branch. He watched it preen, cooing melodically while it went about its task. The peaceful, almost tranquil sounds were like a balm to his soul, and he soon became lost in the pure pleasure of the moment.

"Santos, my son," he heard the sound of a woman's voice calling his name, more beautiful than any song, softer and more fragrant than the sweetest memory his mind could recall.

A great light began to grow in front of him. Through it he could see a lady in a blue dress wearing a star-studded crown, smiling with a love that melted him to the core of his very being. He knew instantly it was the Blessed Virgin.

"Santos, my son," she said again, holding out her hand. "I have come to help you on your holy mission."

With a trepidation borne from overwhelming emotion at being in the presence of the Mother of God, Santos took her outstretched hand. Immediately the ground beneath seemed to disappear, and he plunged into an endless void of total darkness beset by despairing howls, shrieks of fiendish laughter, and menacing growls. The stench of decayed carcasses and excrement made him sick to the stomach. Slimy creatures slithered around his legs, and he felt as if all hope was lost. His only consolation was the hand that held him, leading him through the nightmarish scene.

Suddenly a verse from Scripture appeared in front of them: "For what shall it profit a man, if he shall gain the whole world, and lose his own soul?" In the glow of the verse, he saw that the darkness was actually an ocean of ethereal flames. All around were monstrous spirit-beings peering balefully at him. The Virgin Mary began to weep as she and Santos watched two people walk into a tidal wave of flames. One was a stunningly attractive woman whose face was contorted in a grotesque grimace, the other a stodgy old man with worldly-wise eyes and a hardened face. As they passed through the flames they were instantly transformed into unearthly beasts roaring at each other. The spirit-beings turned their attention to the new arrivals in their midst, fiercely gnawing at them in what seemed like a feeding frenzy.

The tear-stained Virgin now spoke to Santos. "This is why I have appeared so many times in so many places, as a Mother who cannot bear to lose any one of her children. This is what I came to warn about. This is what all the Secrets are for, to warn the world about the possibility of losing God and all that is good forever."

"I know that my God is an infinitely loving Father," Santos said with great compassion as he watched more damned souls descend into the bowels of Hell. "But how could a loving Father allow any of his children to perish in this manner, to suffer forever?"

"It is because you love that you ask, my son," the Blessed Virgin said with a gentle smile. "And if you love, how much more so does the God of infinite love who created you from nothing for the endless joy that comes from union with him? Love is the center of being. It is the unconditional love of the Three-in-One that brought the cosmos into being, and breathed life into humankind, the same love that redeemed a race in rebellion and unleashed the life of God in every open heart. Love is truly the energy behind everything. You were born to love. But you can only love if you are free. God cannot force you to love Him, and it is this that makes the loss of God inevitable.

"God did not create Hell. The spirits in Hell created Hell. Hell is a mystery not of God's love, but of the terrifying reality of freedom. Every man and woman is given the freedom to determine their own destiny. Ultimately, it is free will that makes the choices, not one's intellect. At the end of life, these choices fuse into one — either eternal rejection or acceptance of God. God is always there to help guide you on your journey through life so that you will make the right choices, but you must reach out and hold the Hand he extends to you, and accept and embrace His love. So great was the Good Shepherd's desire that not one sheep be lost that he took on a human nature, subjected Himself to the torment of the Devil and his human instruments, and underwent the most intense suffering possible, a suffering driven by every human choice against God. He did this for us, to show us the way to salvation so there would be no doubt as to which choices each of us should make. God gave you his Church and the sacraments to assist you on this journey of life.

"Those condemned to Hell are not sent there for committing a series of evil acts, just as those who enter Heaven are not rewarded for a specific number of good deeds. You are condemned to Hell because, at the moment of death, your will is fixed in total and permanent rejection of God. Throughout their lives these people chose love of self over love of God. If you choose to serve only your own needs and pleasures, then you are on a road away from God. At Fatima I warned about the grave danger of sins of the flesh. Sex like every human faculty and pleasure is a creation of God and therefore good. But the Fall has disordered the will and with it control of your faculties. The ravenous pursuit of sexual pleasure stains the soul reducing you to a slave of your appetites and hardening your will against all that is good. For the soul that loves only itself, there is no room for love of God. To be separated from God is to be separated from everything that your true nature needs, physical and spiritual. Hunger, thirst, and physical pain are all conditions that result from the needs of physical nature. Loneliness and anguish overcome you when you are separated from what your spirit requires. If you choose to be separated forever from that which your physical and spiritual natures need most of all — God — then your suffering is the greatest imaginable and it is unending, relieved neither by sleep nor death."

A crucifix stood in front of the ocean of flame, visible to the long, winding line of lost souls plunging into Hell. Beneath it was the Fatima prayer. "O My Jesus forgive us our sins, save us from the fires of Hell, lead all souls to Heaven especially those most in need of your mercy."

"This is the message that you must take from here," the Blessed Virgin said. "Humanity lives not on the brink of nothingness but the edge of eternity. You are not zeroes but infinities. Your lives have a purpose, union with God, but a union that has to be chosen or rejected. Hell, the loss of God, is real and a dread possibility for every human being. How easy it is to lose your soul, to choose damnation over salvation, to worship the Devil and turn your back on God! Since your choices in the brief sojourn between womb and tomb will decide your eternal destiny, every one of your intentions and actions is of the utmost importance."

Then, as suddenly as she appeared the Virgin vanished, and with her the terrifying images of Hell.

"Did you have another Vision, Santos?" Miguel asked. Santos, still beneath the same tree where he started his journey, turned to see the concerned young man now standing beside him. "You didn't move for such a long time, I got worried."

"How long?" Santos asked, confused. What seemed like minutes when he spoke with Pope Leo was actually only a matter of seconds.

"Two hours, at least. Maybe more. I thought you were meditating at first, but then you took out the Scroll."

"The Scroll?"

"The one you're holding in your hands right now."

Santos looked down, and to his amazement found that the parchment given to him by Pope Leo was unfolded as if being read. He looked at the strange Hebrew letters and gasped. The language, completely unknown to him, was somehow easily understood. The first three passages relating to the secrets of Jerusalem, Cairo and Fatima were completely comprehensible. Miguel looked at the same sections and blinked in amazement as he too could read the words without difficulty.

"God truly works in wondrous ways," Santos smiled, rolling up the Scroll and placing it back in his pocket.

"It's getting late," Miguel looked to the west toward the setting sun. "We're still a few miles from the Fatima shrine. We'd better get going soon, before it's too dark."

"Our task is done here, Miguel. I have what I came for."

"Is it something to do with the words of Sister Lucia?" Miguel asked. "You were repeating them when I approached you. 'Are you willing to offer yourselves to God and bear all the sufferings He wills to send you, as an act of reparation for the sins by which He is offended, and of supplication for the conversion of sinners? Then you are going to have much to suffer, but the grace of God will be your comfort.'"

Again Santos looked at Miguel in stunned silence. Not only was he unaware of the great lapse in time he experienced, his conscious mind had somehow operated independently from the rest of his body. The words were hauntingly prophetic, not simply for what he had already been trough, but for what he feared was yet to come.

"No my young friend," he placed his hand on Miguel's shoulder. "I believe that was a different message from the Blessed Virgin, one meant to remind me that the task ahead will challenge us all in ways we cannot comprehend at this moment. The grasp of the Devil on man's soul is strong. We will face difficult times in the days ahead, but they should not deter us. The cost of failure is too great."

"If anyone can beat the Devil, it will be you Santos," Miguel said with boyish enthusiasm.

Santos didn't reply, the hateful words of Shaitana still fresh in his mind. Together with Miguel they left the holy site, and headed back to Lisbon.

Lisbon

The city was already dark by the time Miguel pulled onto the street leading to their hotel. Dimly lit and now filled with vagrants, the area looked threatening but not dangerous. Still, the warning signs of trouble were clearly there, and it gave Miguel pause as he pulled the car over to the corner.

"I should take you right up to the hotel and drop you off, Santos," Miguel said, looking around warily.

"Nonsense. It's a short walk from here, and you have to return the rental car. I'll be perfectly fine."

"Still, I think it's better to—"

Santos was out the door before Miguel could complete the sentence. Mumbling under his breath, he shook his head at Santos' stubbornness and chuckled half-heartedly, knowing that there was little he could do to influence his friend once Santos had his mind set on anything.

Putting the car back in gear, he was about to pull away when he noticed a dark colored automobile several yards ahead turn on its lights and begin to move slowly away from the curb. Curious, he watched it pull into the center of the street and pause, as if lining itself up with some unseen target. Small trash fires dotted the litter strewn street, illuminating the men and women who skittered in and out of its shadows.

Miguel strained to see Santos, spotting him just as the car revved its engine and screeched forward at a high rate of speed. He jumped out of his own car and screamed a warning to Santos, but his shouts couldn't be heard over the noise and clatter of the surrounding street. Santos did hear the squealing tires, and turned to see the late model car hurtling toward him. Unable to escape its path, he watched helplessly while its headlights grew brighter and bigger as the car closed in on him.

"Santos, NO!" Miguel gasped.

The sickening crash of metal sent Miguel to his knees, but when he looked up again he saw a different sight from the one he expected. At the last possible moment a second car, parked in front of the hotel, had swerved out into the street and collided broadside with the approaching vehicle. The force of the impact was enough to send the first car rolling over on its side and into one of the kettle drum fires lining the street. Gasoline spilled from its ruptured tank and exploded in a fireball that sent Santos to his knees. The driver of the car screamed in agony as his body was consumed by the spreading flames, but there was nothing anyone could do help him.

The driver of the car who saved Santos' life still sat behind the wheel, his face cut and bleeding from the shattered glass of his exploded windshield. Santos used his cane to raise himself to his feet again and raced to the man's aid. Opening his door he tried to pull him out, but the force of the impact had crushed his legs and trapped him inside.

"My son, are you hurt badly," Santos grasped the man's hand. His blond hair and pock-marked face were visible in the flickering light.

"You are safe," the man said, blood spilling from his mouth.

"Santos! Are you all right?" Miguel shouted out of breath as he ran toward the car.

"This man needs a doctor."

"That car, he tried to run you down! This was no accident."

"I'm all right Miguel. Go quickly, this man is badly injured. Get a doctor. Hurry!"

As Miguel dashed toward the hotel entrance, pushing his way through the curious vagrants who stood around watching, Santos leaned forward and used a corner of his sleeve to wipe some blood away from his mouth to help the man breathe. "I'm a Catholic priest," Santos said. "I'll stay with you until help arrives."

"Santos … Machado," the man coughed painfully.

"You — you know me?" Santos stammered.

"Opus Dei … watches over you."

"But how —"

"There are many … who will give their lives … to protect you," the man gasped. He was having trouble breathing and Santos tried to quiet him, but the man shook his head. "Leave me … don't get involved. Tickets are waiting … at the airport."

"Tickets? To where?"

"Where the Family's silence … spoke, the End … in sight."

"You, you know about the Divine Truths?" Santos whispered.

"Only that you … are chosen. Opus Dei … the Work of God … watches over you. Go … please now."

The distant sound of a siren punctuated the air. Santos kissed the man's hand and blessed him for his deed, then slowly withdrew. The man smiled through his bloody face and closed his eyes, still breathing but in intense pain.

"The hotel manager called an ambulance," Miguel raced back to Santos side. "Is he going to make it?"

"I don't know."

Santos looked at the faces ringing the car who peered at the man with detached curiosity. One of the vagrants caught his eye. The man, outwardly disheveled, stared back at Santos with keen, penetrating eyes. With a silent nod he signaled that he was more than just another nameless soul lost among the debris of society.

Surrounded by him and others from Opus Dei who had taken up strategic positions around the hotel, Santos returned to his room, praying that the man who had risked his life to save his would recover, and that God would watch over all the others who helped safeguard him.

Chapter 17

Rome

"We are all assembled, your Eminence."

Cardinal Francisco Ramirez spoke for the small group of Cardinals gathered at the home of Benito Giacalone, an Italian industrialist who was an outspoken critic of Vatican social policy, and a personal friend of its most prominent antagonist, Cardinal Bruno Reinhard. Six others, including the African Cardinal Ode Ojomu from Nigeria, formed a voting block that controlled almost fifty percent of the conclave that would elect a new pope. This meeting of Reinhard's "kitchen cabinet," as his detractors at the College of Cardinals derisively labeled the seven politically ambitious men who supported Reinhard's public and private attacks against established Church traditions, was the second in five days. Like the ward healers of a well-oiled political machine, they had been making deals, dispensing favors, and counting votes among their fellow delegates. With less than a week remaining until the full body of Cardinals met to begin the conclave, optimism was running high that a first ballot victory for Reinhard was within their grasp.

"We have received excellent press worldwide," Ramirez began his report. "The sentiment is near universally favorable for your election as our next pope."

"I have sought none of this influence," Reinhard said, almost apologetically.

"Of course not, your Eminence," Ramirez responded. "But it does show the depth of spontaneous support around the world for the new vision you will bring to the papacy. Even non-Catholics and non-Christians have joined in expressing their love for you and support for your candidacy."

"There is some support I could just as well do without."

"Yes, the Shaitaans. A very odd, ecumenical movement, I agree. But one that shares many of the same goals we seek, to set the Church of Peter on a new path relevant to today's world, just as the Lord Himself created a church two millennia ago that spoke to the pressing matters of his time."

"But I am not Christ," Reinhard said, his voice devoid of emotion.

Ramirez paused, aware that the skilled diplomat-priest and leading intellectual of his time would press a point simply to gauge the reaction, and in so doing help hone his own position for public discussion at a later time.

"But as pope, you would be Christ's representative on earth, and as such instituted by him to lead the Church as a shepherd does his flock. It is a poor steward who, when given such great responsibility, ignores the true nature of the world in which he lives to carry on ancient traditions that are no longer relevant to humanity's present needs."

Reinhard nodded without responding, a signal that Ramirez's words were well received and mirrored Reinhard's own position. The Nicaraguan Cardinal, emboldened by his approval, continued his report with increased enthusiasm.

"Cardinal Ojomu has told us that a block of the Africans will support your candidacy. They wish to receive certain dispensations from the new Pope regarding established Church practices in birth control and polygamy, and more financial support for the Church's mission in Africa."

"You know my position on these social matters," Reinhard spoke directly to Ojomu. "The birth rate in Africa is not a matter for Rome to decide. And we cannot pronounce on indigenous practices. These matters are addressed, but it will take time to change enough minds to go further than this, so our efforts will not be undercut by resistance from traditionalists within the Curia and the College of Cardinals. Medical science has given us great new insights into the definition of life, both at the moment of conception, and long after the brain has ceased functioning even though the body lives on. We will incorporate these truths into a new papal edict that will re-define the parameters of acceptable behavior in the twenty-first century. As for the matter of opening the Church's coffers to Africa and other parts of the world, I would make that one of my first acts."

"Would Rome continue to direct how these new funds are spent?" Ojomu asked.

"No," Reinhard smiled. "Like many other matters, that is one best left to the conscience of the local parish, its bishops, and ultimately to its Primates and Cardinal protectors."

Ojomu seemed pleased with the answer. Ramirez opened a folder, and continued his report.

"We need only five additional members of the conclave to pledge their support to you, and Orsini's supporters will see that there is no hope for him. You will be selected pope on the first ballot. I have a list of nine whom I believe can be persuaded. All of them are concerned about recent actions by the French and German governments to freeze Church assets and declare the Vatican hostile to human rights. So far it has remained only a threat, but enough of one that these Cardinals fear the same tactic spreading to other parts of the world. Certain decisions have been made by the governing authority during the *sede vacante* to assuage this concern by contributing to a reparations fund controlled by the French and German finance ministries that will reach out to women and minorities who suffered persecution because of the Rome's intransigence on social issues. For now, this action appears to have stalled any further efforts by France or Germany to make good on their threat, but these Cardinals fear that the election of the wrong pope will send a financially disastrous message to Paris and Berlin, if not the rest of the world. It would be wise, your Eminence, to send a signal of conciliation when you celebrate your next Mass. Several media have asked permission to televise it, and it gives you an opportunity to reach out to the world without appearing to do so politically."

"I will consider your request," Reinhard said, bringing the meeting to a close. The small group stood and kissed Reinhard's outstretched hand before departing, one-by-one, leaving him to ponder his next moves in the fulfillment of a life-long quest, one that he expected to have as profound an effect on the future course of world events as did Peter's assumption of the papal throne nearly two millennia earlier.

Ireland

The flight to London was long, but uneventful.

Tickets for the trip were waiting for Santos and Miguel when they arrived at the airport, as well as enough funds through a wire transfer to ensure that their accommodations in Ireland, their ultimate destination, would be considerably less dangerous than those in Lisbon. Despite his best efforts to check on the health of the man who had saved his life, neither he nor Miguel could find any information on his whereabouts or condition. Not a single hospital reported receiving an accident victim matching his description, and there was no record of the event itself at the local police station. It was as if it never happened. Even the body in the burned out car seemed to have vanished from history. The reach of Opus Dei was far and sweeping, and Santos gave silent thanks to their noble sacrifices in watching over him and Miguel. Looking at the faces of his fellow passengers both at the airport in Lisbon and on the plane, he knew that some of them must be Opus Dei, but there was no way to tell who. Like his guardian angel they were always there with him, silent and unseen but vigilant and protective, insuring that he would not be attacked again.

The short trip to Ireland was equally uneventful, except for a rough, bumpy landing in Dublin that left Santos's nerves frayed and again fore-swearing any future flying. Tired, they unloaded their bags at the nearest hotel and immediately boarded a bus to Knock, the Western Ireland site of a famous apparition in 1879 of Mary, Joseph, John the Evangelist, and Jesus in the form of a Lamb with a cross behind him.

Located in a small village in Galway in the northwestern part of Ireland, the apparition at Knock was unique in that it was entirely silent. Witnessed at the time by fifteen people, a chapel was soon erected at the site, drawing millions of worshipers in the ensuing years. Because, unlike Fatima, no message was delivered, the significance of the apparition has remained a source of ongoing debate. Many felt it was a warning that the end-times had begun. In the vision John the Evangelist, the author of the Book of Revelation, reads from the Bible with his hand held up as if gesturing in mid-speech while proclaiming the truth of the book. But the message, God's chastisement of the world, was also a reminder that humanity is still living in the Hour of Mercy, with one last chance to seek out God's mercy.

Arriving amid the devoted pilgrims who came to Knock by the thousands daily, Santos and Miguel entered the Apparition Chapel, where a Mass was being conducted. Seating themselves in a wooden pew, they joined the service shortly before the Eucharist was about to be consecrated. Still weary from the frenetic pace of travel that was exacting a heavy toll on his already frail body, Santos closed his eyes and listened to the familiar words of the parish priest transform the colorless wafer and sacramental wine into the transubstantiated body and blood of Christ.

As he listened and prayed, other words seemed to mix in his mind along with the priest's. The book of Revelation came alive, its message there in form and substance, drifting through a turbulent void as it materialized in his thoughts.

> In my vision, I heard the sound of an immense number of angels gathered around the throne. There were ten thousand times ten thousand of them and thousands upon thousands, shouting, 'The Lamb that was sacrificed is worthy to be given power, riches, wis-

dom, strength, honor, glory and blessing'. Then I heard all the living things in creation …crying, 'To the One who is sitting on the throne and to the Lamb, be all praise, honor, glory and power, for ever and ever'. (Revelation 5/11-13)

Santos blinked his eyes open. It was he now, not the parish priest, saying Mass before a church that held millions within its walls. A sea of humanity stretched as far as the eye could see, all kneeling in devotion, all waiting in anticipation for Santos to offer them communion.

Consecrating the bread and wine, Santos broke the Host and, to his astonishment, found that it had turned into actual flesh. Blood gushed from it in an endless stream, spurting to the ceiling and staining the altar. As the blood continued to pour forth, a stately man in the vestments of a bishop with a short miter ascended to the pulpit. It was St. John the Evangelist, author of the Fourth Gospel and the Book of Revelation. With an open Bible in his left hand, he raised his right hand and spoke to the congregation.

"In the beginning was the Word, and the Word was with God, and the Word was God. And the Word became flesh and made his dwelling among us." Gesturing toward the flesh and the blood, he continued. "Unless you eat the flesh of the Son of Man and drink his blood, you do not have life within you." Then, pointing at the statue of the Lamb behind the altar, his words grew louder and seemed to echo from all corners of the immense, transformed chapel. "Behold the Lamb slain from the foundation of the world. Like a sheep he was led to the slaughter, and as a lamb before its shearer is silent, so he opened not his mouth. Our paschal lamb, Christ, has been sacrificed. Therefore let us celebrate the feast. Blessed are those who have been called to the wedding feast of the Lamb."

Turning toward Santos, the Evangelist approached him and spoke to him directly.

"The end is at hand. Satan is active. Hell is real. What you have witnessed until now is the crisis that faces the world. Now you will be shown the solution, which begins with the Flesh of the Son of Man. What, many ask, is different about the Host before and after consecration? The answer, in a word, is the Life that is now present in it. The Eucharist throbs, pulsates, explodes with the infinite Energy of the Divine Life. But this Energy can only be experienced by the soul. The sacrament of the Eucharist retains the appearance of food and drink because it does for the soul what bread and wine do for the body — it sustains, builds up, restores. And each instance of the physical reception of the Eucharist, if accompanied by a receptivity of the soul, replenishes and intensifies the divine Life that is already present in us. Every encounter with the Divine Life that is in the Eucharist is simultaneously an encounter with Him Who possesses that Life, the Risen Christ. So Santos, this is the truth that the Church must continue to teach in the face of unbelief and doubt. The Eucharist is the vehicle of the divine life, the life that you need for all eternity. All the faithful should be exhorted to receive this very Life of God as often as possible for their own protection and sanctification both in the end-times and at all times."

The Evangelist knelt at Santos' feet, and waited for him to serve the Eucharist. With humility and resolve he offered him the consecrated Host and chalice, knowing that the first step had now been taken on a long, difficult path that would not end until the doubting and unfaithful were convinced to end their wicked ways, and the forces of Satan had been crushed.

Kathmandu

"Your Holiness," a frightened servant approached Shaitana, fearsome in a consuming rage at the news he delivered. "I exist but to serve you. Tell me what you desire, and I will —"

"Enough!" Shaitana thundered, sending the man recoiling in fear. "This man is a priest, not a god! He suffers and bleeds like any other man. Why is he not dead!"

"Opus Dei has surrounded and protected him. They killed Prithvi Shah, murdered him and set his body afire as a warning to you, my Lord. They are numerous and well appointed, with connections that run deep throughout corrupt governments and civil societies. They are ruthless in their determination to protect the priest Machado and his young companion. Every effort we have made has been blocked."

"Every minute that passes saps more of my strength," Shaitana hissed. "I weaken while the priest grows stronger. He must be stopped, but not by other mortals. This I understand now. Only I can fulfill my own destiny. I must be the one to stop him, and everything he represents."

"We know where he is now, my Lord," the servant said, "and where he will go next, to the place where the Hebrew Mother showed the nation's fate — Amsterdam."

"No," Shaitana said. "It will not be Amsterdam, or any other site of false prophecy. I will meet him at the one place his death, and my victory, will be the most meaningful. I will meet him at his final destination, when he believes that his journey is over, and his guard is down. I will meet him on the only real field of battle. I will meet him in Rome."

Chapter 18

New York

"You look worried, Mr. Stout," the young woman said, handing him the second dispatch in as many hours from Nepal. "Is everything okay, if you don't mind my asking?"

"Just fine, Cynthia," he grunted. "Everything's perfect."

"Mr. Hastings wants—"

"I know what he wants," Stout replied more gruffly than he intended. The young woman caught her breath and stepped back involuntarily, not sure whether to leave his office or wait for a reply to the message marked 'urgent'. Stout saw the look in her eyes and grinned awkwardly, putting her at ease. "Don't mind me," he half-apologized. "It's been a long week and I'm a little tired, that's all."

"I understand perfectly Sir," she smiled. "You have such a stressful job, and Mr. Hastings can be very, well, you know — demanding."

"You don't know the half of it, Cynthia," he shook his head. "I've been with him for almost ten years, ever since he grabbed Bergseth Communications in a hostile takeover and completely remade this company. That launched his international news operation, if that's what you want to call it, and made us what we are today."

"I don't understand, Mr. Stout," Cynthia furrowed her brow, taking the statement literally. "We're the largest news organization in the world. Even CNN takes our feeds and rebroadcasts them. The New York Times has been making our lead story their next day headline for as long as I can remember. I've even heard rumors that we're about to acquire CBS. What else would you call us? 'It isn't news until we report it,' isn't that what you always say?"

"Yeah, that's what I say," Stout repeated.

"So, I don't understand."

For a long moment Stout looked out the window of his corner office, one floor directly below Ralston Hastings. He held many titles during his mercuric rise up the corporate ladder, overseeing everything from operations to accounting, where he watched Hastings creatively apply arcane corporate tax law to shelter the majority of his assets that gave him the resources to continue to grow his company. Now one of the wealthiest men in the world, his Hastings Communications Worldwide was so large and so powerful that few governments, including the United States, dared challenge him. With an almost completely unfettered hand he supported his friends and crushed his rivals, both competitors and politicians, leaving him alone at the top of an international organization accountable to no one but himself.

As with many corporations, the more power and responsibility Stout acquired in furthering Hastings' interests, the less descriptive his title became. Known now only by the innocuous description "Assistant to the Chairman", he was arguably one of the most influential people in the Hastings empire. Valued for his loyalty and above all, his discretion, he was privy to the secrets and inner workings Hastings's mind. It gave him access and power well beyond the formal responsibilities of his office, and the fear in people's eyes was not lost on him when he visited political officials, or met with the leaders of corporations who might one day become targets of a Hastings investigative report. Throughout it all he tried to maintain a personal balance that didn't overtly abuse his authority the way lesser men might succumb to money and women as inducements of favor, though he was not completely immune to certain temptations that occasionally came his way. Hastings recognized this attribute and rewarded him with a privileged position in his inner circle, a reward that Stout returned through his complete and unquestioning loyalty to Hastings.

That loyalty had never been shaken, not through the bribery and corruption of international officials, the malicious sabotage of rival news operations, or even Hastings' petty personal piques which ruined the lives of the people who offended him. These were the normal, if unpleasant, collateral issues confronting any great man of power. Like Hastings, Stout saw little difference between government officials who profited personally from a dictator's oil, and his actions in bribing or rewarding these same officials. Gathering and reporting the news was a cutthroat business, and in this sense little had changed since the time of William Randolph Hearst, if not earlier.

But the thing that bothered Stout the most, which is to say, the only thing that truly tugged at his conscience, was Hastings penchant for personal vendetta. No action was too small, no slight too insignificant, to see the full force of Hastings' resources brought to bear against the offending party. Women who refused his sexual advances were investigated and their personal life exposed for public humiliation. Politicians who questioned

Hastings' activities or ethics would become the subject of personal attack or worse, criminal investigation by friendly authorities. No one was safe from Hastings' rage, and no amount of counter-pressure was sufficient to make him to moderate his actions. Where he didn't control the courts, lawsuits would drag through the courts for years, fed by a barrage of frivolous motions that caused further delays, and often bankrupted the suing party. Where the presiding judge was friendly, the verdict was swift and always in Hastings' favor, laying the foundation for a counter suit that would drain his accuser's savings before ever coming to trial.

Now, in a world threatened by terrorism, challenged by true social injustice — not simply the convenient, agenda-driven slogans of a political philosophies — and plagued with the corruption of many international officials who lined their own pockets rather than addressing the needs of their people, Hastings Communications had zeroed in on a new target: people of faith. And not just any faith. Not the faith of those who killed others indiscriminately for political gain. Not those who cared little for the lives of unborn children. The enemy, in the eyes of Ralston Hastings, were people who held fundamental, Judeo-Christian religious values. These people, who believed there was an objective 'right and wrong', who believed that morality stemmed from a relationship between God and man, and not from men alone, and who sought little more than to practice their faith without oppression, they were the main threats to society in the eyes of Ralston Hastings. And Vincent Stout was the primary vehicle through which Hastings would execute his vendetta against the faithful.

He wasn't sure when the doubts first entered his mind; he only knew they were there. Perhaps it was when he had to confront the fact on their flight to Rome that Hastings had graduated from intimidation to condoning murder. Perhaps it was when he read the overseas cables from the charlatan in Nepal that Hastings was promoting, who spewed a visceral hate for Christianity and all it stood for that was so deep it made Stout cringe just to read it. Perhaps it was nothing more than the accumulated effect of ten years of lies and deception weighing on his soul. But whatever it was, the gnawing, troubling feeling that tugged at what little conscience still remained locked away in his mind had broken free, not enough to completely alter his behavior, but enough to introduce the first semblance of doubt. And doubt was the one thing that could not survive if his loyalty to Hastings were to remain intact.

Vincent Stout, sitting in his office and staring out the window as his secretary waited for his reply, had a long way to go on his journey of personal redemption. It was a journey that would lead him away from the trappings of wealth and power he still coveted, but whose luster had begun to tarnish. He wasn't even sure if the feeling in his gut was real, or a temporary distraction brought on by fatigue and stress. But he knew that, whatever its source, disturbing thoughts had entered his mind, and they weren't going to go away until he reasoned them through. The journey of his own rebirth had begun not with a thundering crash of lightning from above, and not with a seminal life changing event. But it *had* begun, and in taking the first step, he knew it would not end until he had the answers he sought.

"Thank you Cynthia," Stout finally turned in his chair, facing the young woman again. "That will be all for today."

"Certainly Sir. If I get any more dispatches from Nepal —"

"— you can tell communications to send them directly to my office and I'll attend to them. Thank you, Cynthia. Now, go home and see your family," he smiled.

"Yes Sir," she brightened. "Good night, Sir."

The door closed, and Stout found himself alone with another request from Shaitana to increase surveillance on the Vatican in his search for a quirky little Filipino priest who escaped his murderous plot in Kathmandu. Hastings had left strict instructions that any such cables from Shaitana were to be reviewed immediately, with Stout's recommendation for action. No matter how outwardly foolish the request, if it served a larger purpose in the alliance between Hastings and Shaitana it would be approved, particularly at this critical juncture when a full scale effort had been mounted to influence the selection of the next pope.

This time, though, the overseas dispatch would not make it to the top floor office. Crumpling the paper, Stout tossed it into a nearby trash basket.

"Request denied," he grunted, then returned to his work.

Amsterdam

The city of Anne Frank, Van Gogh, and a notorious red light district known the world over was also home to Ida Peerdeman, a forty-year-old, single woman who resided in a small, suburban apartment on Diepenbrock Street during the waning days of World War II.

There was nothing particularly remarkable about the life of this daughter of a textile salesman born in 1905, whose mother died when she was only eight years old. The youngest of five children, she was raised by her older siblings in a home where, like many of her generation, God and family life formed the central core of their purpose and well being. As the war in Europe was drawing to an end, she sat in her living room with her sisters and her local parish priest talking about the future while the Allied armies advanced upon Nazi occupied Holland. It was the Feast of the Annunciation, the day that Mary gave her consent to God to bear his only begotten Son so that mankind could be saved. A mysterious light emanating from an adjoining room drew her toward the figure of a young Hebrew girl, whom she instantly recognized as the Virgin Mary. Thus began a series of revelations that continued for more than a dozen years, revealing truths and conveying warnings that continued to shake the foundations of Western Christianity into the present day.

Unlike Fatima, Zeitoun, or even Knock, Amsterdam held none of the fascination of other nineteenth and twentieth century apparitions. There was no meeting of a luminous figure in the woods or on a hillside, no dazzling display of celestial forces, no crowds watching the visionary in ecstasy. Yet the apparition made up for its lack of a glamorous setting with substance of a different kind, momentous prophecies touching on world history and theological teaching.

Initially, details about the apparition were shared only with a few friends and clergy, and the visionary herself remained anonymous for many years. The Virgin Mary appeared sixty times from 1945 through 1959 with a variety of prophecies and messages for the Church and the world. An image of her appearance as a woman clad in white, wearing a sash with her arms lowered and the palms of her hands turned outward, was produced later to commemorate the event. Eventually word spread of the miraculous apparition of "Our Lady of All Nations," and by the end of the twentieth century millions of people around the world had heard of and received her messages.

Many detailed and specific prophecies were made by the Virgin Mary at Amsterdam, which began precisely on the same day that a great Eucharistic miracle took place in Amsterdam six hundred years earlier. The messages she delivered were a blend of moral exhortation, theological exposition, prophecy and history. All were concerned with the link between moral and spiritual lives and the state of the world. Her messages focused on the need to come back to the Creator, the Cross — the crucified Christ — and the Holy Spirit. Without this no true peace was possible, and the world would sink into greater degeneration.

One prophesy in particular said that the Church in Rome would face a terrible struggle. She predicted that there would be a faction in Rome against the Pope, and because of it the Church was in danger of a schism. False theories would be propagated to deceive people about the sacraments, Church doctrine, the priesthood, even marriage and family-planning. Satan would lead people astray by confusing them with ideas of modernism that ran contrary to the Divine teaching and laws, which were valid for all time and applicable to every period.

A second series of prophesies foresaw world catastrophes and political turmoil, often with specific reference to China, Korea, Vietnam, the Balkans, Russia and America, even foretelling the rise of a New Israel three years before the Jewish state was formed. The Virgin said that mankind would endure even greater suffering and hardship as the century progressed, but she also offered hope. All humanity was under the protection of The Lady of All Nations. If they called upon her as their advocate, asked her to stave off disasters and banish degeneration from the world, she would intercede. The world had lost its bearings and must put its trust in its Mother, who had never forsaken her children.

So it was at Fatima and elsewhere, the purpose of the prophecies was not to terrify, but to instruct. Like the Old Testament prophets, Our Lady of All Nations pointed to a cause-and-effect relationship between human sin and its inevitable consequences in the natural order. But beyond pointing out the correlation between sin and suffering, she offered herself to assist humanity at its most critical time. But humanity had to accept and cooperate with God's messenger if she was to be effective.

God the Father had sent his only son, Jesus Christ, as the Redeemer of all Nations. Mary, the Handmaid of the Lord, was chosen by the Father and the Holy Spirit to be the Advocate of all Nations. She gave the world a simple prayer to be recited in front of a crucifix, one that would guide the faithful in their daily lives. "*Lord Jesus Christ, Son of the Father, send now Your Spirit over the earth. Let the Holy Spirit live in the hearts of all Nations, that they may be preserved from degeneration, disasters and war. May the Lady of all nations, who once was Mary, be our Advocate. Amen.*"

Arriving at the house and chapel at 3 Diepenbrock Street where Ida Peerdeman had lived, Santos knelt in prayer before the image of Our Lady of All Nations. Miguel watched him with concern, not knowing how and when the next Vision would occur, but certain that he would experience another spiritual event like he had in every shrine they had visited before. Each experience seemed to invigorate him at that moment the Vision took place, leaving him exuberant and empowered by new knowledge and a greater, more focused, sense of purpose. But it also took a terrible toll on him physically in the hours after the Visions passed, and Miguel began to fear that his friend and mentor might not survive the ordeal once his mission was completed.

Slowly and quietly a small voice began to work its way inside Santos' thoughts. He looked around, waiting for the Vision to appear, but saw nothing or no one.

"Santos," the voice grew stronger. It was angelic, forceful, but also tranquil and relaxed. It seemed everywhere at once — inside his mind, outside his body, in the air and the walls. The words were like a soothing balm that made him almost giddy with ecstasy. It was the voice of the Holy Spirit speaking to him, not through any physical medium, but within his soul.

"Santos, my son. You are here to learn about the day the very life of God entered the bloodstream of man. It was the re-start of history, the inauguration of a new order, the blueprint of the final age. From that day, a new kind of force was at work in the world, a new state of being descended on humanity. And this God-Force was also a Person, the Spirit of God, the Holy Spirit. On the day of the descent you know as Pentecost, history itself was baptized by the Holy Spirit with the Blood of the Son and in the Name of the Father. The destiny to which all men and women are called is to share in this divine nature, to participate in the life of God. All of eternity awaits those who accept it."

Santos trembled at the words, which he didn't hear as much as feel, their meaning so completely comprehensible he saw the mysteries of God's work in its unmistakable form.

"When the Spirit touches a soul it acts with a divine power. To be divinized is to live with the Life of God, and to know and love with the Power of God. It is to become *like* God, but you cannot *be* God. Ultimately, it is to become like Jesus who was the Anointed One, because he was filled with the Holy Spirit. Divinization was understood and taught by the Apostles of Christ and the Fathers of the early church, but today it is the forgotten mystery. The unifying doctrine has all but disappeared from the Christian consciousness. It is this Secret you have come here to learn and share with your fellow men. God took on a human nature so that humans may take on the divine nature. God 'humanized' himself so humans could be divinized. This is the central truth that makes sense of all the natural and supernatural phenomena of history.

"Five pillars support the platform of divinization. They are five incarnations of the Spirit. First, the vehicles of the divine life known as the *sacraments.* Second, the *supernatural virtues* — faith, hope and charity — that are brought into being by the divine life. Third, the *divinizing gifts of the Spirit*, wisdom and fortitude, sanctify and enlighten your soul. Fourth, there are custom-tailored gifts of the Spirit known as *charisms*, and finally the effects on you of the indwelling Spirit that are called *fruits of the Spirit.*

Divinization proceeds through the two human faculties that image God — intellect and will. All vehicles of the Spirit are designed to divinize your knowledge and love, through which you will find clues to what God is like. To be divinized is to receive eternal life here and now, to live with the life of God, to be filled with the Holy Spirit. This is the fundamental secret that makes sense of all Christian doctrines and devotions, in fact, of Christian experience as a whole.

"Now, no human being played as great a role in mankind's salvation as the Virgin Mary. When the human race used its freedom to turn away from God, it was an offense against an infinite being, and only an infinite being could make sufficient reparation to bring man back into God's fold. But for the incarnation of God as the man Jesus, and his subsequent death in reparation, there needed to be a freely willed acceptance of God's invitation to himself become human. That acceptance came from Mary, who was called the New Eve by the first Christians because she untied the knot of Eve's disobedience.

"Herein lies her ultimate glory, and the fullness of the divine victory. Satan's defeat was total because the divine triumph was begun from 'inside', through a human person, namely the Virgin Mary, and then consummated by Jesus, who was a divine person with a human nature.

"So this is the Secret that has been waiting for you here. Proclaim anew the ancient doctrine of divinization to unify all Christians in the truth and power of the Spirit of God. It is this Spirit who directs history, and the goal of the history of every person is union with God in eternity.

"That union has to begin in time if it is to happen at all. Only those who are divinized here and now will enjoy eternal life with God. It is the Spirit who divinizes through his agents and channels, and it is the Spirit who acts through history as a whole and in the history of each person to make the divine invitation. He directs and produces the play but the actors determine their ultimate roles. Proclaim also the great truth of the Virgin's role as Spouse of the Spirit, the New Eve with the New Adam and Mother of all Christians. It is no accident that the Lady of All Nations first appeared her on the feast of her Yes to God."

With that the sweet, gentle voice faded.

Santos stood and looked at Miguel in awe. He retained the clarity of the message, though only in terms his mind could comprehend. Where before he had spoken with saints of the Church, now he had felt the very hand of God.

Overcome with emotion, Santos collapsed on the floor beneath the portrait of Our Lady of All Nations, and fell into what seemed to be a coma.

Chapter 19

Amsterdam

"How's the patient in 219 doing today?" the young doctor asked, beginning his early morning rounds with a review of the night activity log at the head nurse's station.

The nurse in charge looked up from her desk, her reading glasses perched on the edge of her nose, as if weighing her thoughts before responding to the question. The middle aged woman in a white starched uniform took another sip of her coffee, and let out a long, slow breath.

"Irascible."

The young doctor laughed. "You know, I learn a new word from you every day," he smiled.

"Here's his chart," she handed him a clip board. "You might want to visit with that young man over there first, the one sleeping on the couch. He came in with him the other day; says he's his traveling companion. I was able to get a better medical history from him than 'I'm all right, let me out of here'."

"His name's ... Guerrero?" the doctor puzzled, looking at the chart.

"Yes. He's very devoted to the man. He won't leave Mr. Machado's side. I made him go back to his hotel yesterday to get some rest, but he returned late last night and wouldn't leave, so I gave him the couch."

The doctor walked over to Miguel, sprawled out on a red naugahyde couch that was several inches shorter than his six foot tall frame. He tapped the sleeping man gently on the shoulder, stirring Miguel who immediately sat upright and rubbed the sleep from his eyes.

"Mr. Guerrero, I'm Doctor Osterhoudt," he said in slightly accented English. "I understand you travel with Mr. Machado."

"Yes, Father Machado. I help care for him."

"Father Machado?" he glanced at the chart again. "He's a Catholic priest?"

"Yes. An Exorcist."

"Exorcist," the man's eyes widened. "I suppose that makes sense. I see he collapsed at the Peerdeman house. We get one or two charismatics a month who are overcome by the experience. Mostly elderly people, like your Father Machado. The ordeal is just a bit more than they can handle. All that mysticism and the supernatural, I suppose."

"Is Santos all right?" Miguel asked, bringing the conversation back to focus.

"Well, I haven't examined him yet, but his chart says he was stable last night, and the head nurse reported no problems this morning, unless you count a somewhat forceful personality, if that's the correct word."

"'Forceful' will do just fine," Miguel smiled.

"Your Father Machado is a difficult patient. Perhaps you can help calm him so he can heal and be discharged."

"Is he very sick, doctor?"

"Well, actually," the doctor glanced at his chart again, "he's in remarkably good shape for an overweight, sixty-five-year-old man with borderline diabetes, high blood pressure, and some emerging problems with his liver, not to mention the circulatory problems in his left leg."

"What about his collapse at the shrine of Our Lady of All Nations?"

"Oh that? Simple dehydration, I think, and stress."

"Then he's all right?"

"I'd like to keep him a few more days, maybe get his blood work under better control. And it wouldn't hurt for him to lose a few pounds."

"But he's all right," Miguel pressed. "He's not in any immediate danger."

"No, I don't think so," the doctor said. "But he's clearly exhausted, and could use a good rest."

"Have you actually met Santos?" Miguel hid his smile.

"Not exactly. I'm covering for his admitting physician today. But I have his chart, and I have heard some things about him. Tell me, is he always this, er, stubborn?"

"No," Miguel replied. "Sometimes he's worse. When Santos has his mind fixed on something, it's best to just go along or get out of his way."

"Yes, but his health—"

"I don't mean to argue, doctor," Miguel said politely, "but Santos isn't going to change the way he lives no matter how long you keep him here. Unless he's in real danger, I'd like him released. We have important business in Tokyo, and then Rome, and it can't wait any longer than necessary."

"Well," the young doctor mused, "I can't do any more than give you my best medical advice. I think he should stay a few more days, but if you insist, I will discharge him."

"Yes, thank you."

"Before I do, though," he said, flipping through the chart, "there is one curiosity perhaps you could explain. The admitting physician noted blisters on his right palm. The burn looks recent. Was he in an accident of some sort?"

"I don't know," Miguel puzzled. "I wasn't aware of any injury to his hand."

"Well, it's just a minor detail. Still, it is curious. The blister doesn't seem to respond to medication. It's as fresh today as when he was first admitted. You might want to have his regular physician follow up on that after you finish your travels."

"I will, thank you."

"I'll visit Mr. Machado in a few minutes, and if everything looks the same, I'll see that he's discharged promptly."

The doctor returned to the nurse's station, preparing to begin his rounds. Miguel thought about his final comment, and wondered if Santos was keeping anything else from him. The two had grown extremely close over the past several years, and there was little each didn't know about the other. The only time Santos withheld information was when he believed it might endanger Miguel. When they first began to travel together, Santos was overly protective of his new young charge, shielding him from many of the more difficult, and threatening aspects of exorcising the Devil from some poor unfortunate soul. But as the years passed and Miguel grew in body and spirit, there was little he didn't experience as Santos' helper and companion, and his overly-protective instincts all but disappeared.

But these were not normal times. The power of the Devil was magnified a thousand fold over ages past. And, Santos was no longer just one more of God's many agents on earth. He was the last man left who could carry out a mission of unprecedented danger and discovery. Miguel knew that Santos would try to shield him from the threat of injury as much as possible, but he also knew that the time would come when such dangers could not be avoided, and in fact must be confronted no matter the risk to him or anyone else.

When that day came Miguel would be at Santos' side, like always, facing the unknown together.

Rome

The Conclave was a centuries-old tradition of the Catholic Church, first instituted in the late thirteenth century by Pope Gregory X. Its purpose was to forestall another repeat of the interminable delay that occurred in selecting him as the new pope, something that put the Church at great risk during the two years the College of Cardinals deliberated his selection. From that point forward, within a short, specified period following the death of a reigning pope, every member of the College of Cardinals would be sequestered in a closed off hall until they reached their decision. Inside this hall walled-off spaces for small apartments were created, each with three or four small rooms or cells. In each room was a crucifix, bed, table, and a few chairs. Access to the conclave was through one door only, locked from without and guarded so that no one may leave or enter.

Cut off from the remainder of the Vatican and the world, the College of Cardinals would debate, cajole, and compromise until one of their number was elevated to the throne of St. Peter. By modern times, the failure to reach consensus was signaled by burning the discarded ballots in a stove mixed with straw whose chimney extended through a window of the Sistine Chapel, producing a thick dark smoke. When a new pope was chosen the smoke was pure white, a signal to the faithful that another link in the unbroken chain that began with Peter had been selected.

Honed through years of tradition codified through a papal Bull, and refined over the ages by subsequent popes who both modified and streamlined the process, the procedure, prayers, and time frame for action by the Conclave were specific and unyielding. A successful candidate would receive two-thirds of the votes cast, exclusive of his own, depositing his ballot in the chalice on an altar and proclaiming *Testor Christum Dominum qui me judicaturus est me eligere quem secundum Deum judice eligi debere et quod idem in accessu præstabo* — "I call to witness the Lord Christ, Who will be my judge, that I am electing the one whom according to God I think ought to be elected." Two votes were taken every day, one in the morning and one before dark. A successful candidate will signify his acceptance of election by taking a new name, one that will symbolically represent his papacy and all that he hopes to accomplish. The Cardinal Camerlengo then puts the Fisherman's Ring upon his finger, and a proclamation is made announcing the new pope to the world.

It was within this august setting that the Belgian Cardinal Bruno Reinhart entered the Vatican halls for the last time as a Prince of the Catholic Church, certain that he would leave them as the Supreme Pontiff. In the televised mass he conducted, broadcast worldwide by Hastings Communications, he had preached a sermon of tolerance and understanding, of the need to accommodate traditional Church doctrine to ever changing realities in a worldwide, pluralistic society. The outpouring of public support was overwhelming both in its overall scale, and depth of passion. Rallies appeared to spring up spontaneously, as if the people had been waiting hungrily for a new man of vision to take his place among the world's secular and parochial leaders. There was no longer any question which person the masses would chose, Catholic and Protestant, Moslem and Jew, and every other religion included, if only they had a right to vote.

At least, that was the message carried by the leading news organizations, following a carefully built trail manufactured by Ralston Hastings and supported through the nihilistic adherents to the newest purported religion, a self-described ecumenical movement known as Shaitanism. It was a message reinforced through economic blackmail against a church weakened by scandal, and confused as to its ultimate purpose in a changing world — to remain firm in its fundamental teachings, or adapt its message to reflect the exigencies of a new social order.

Whether Bruno Reinhardt was aware of the extent to which unseen forces were manipulating events to ensure his election, or simply believed that a beneficent God had looked favorably upon his well-reasoned challenges to existing Church dogma, mattered little in the end. He aspired to the papal throne not for glory in the service of God, but for the power it brought to implement his own vision of the world.

Tokyo

The 747 touched down in Tokyo thirty minutes ahead of schedule. The long flight, covering almost half the world, was an unexpectedly welcome respite for Santos, for whom air travel of any distance was an unpleasant, but necessary sacrifice he often had to make. With the financial support of Opus Dei, both he and Miguel had the unaccustomed pleasure of travel in wider seats with better food, instead of being relegated to the cramped, cattle car-like conditions they often found themselves in.

Still weak from his short stay in a Dutch hospital, he decided to take Miguel's advice and purchase the more expensive tickets. His green polyester shirt and recycled plaid pants made him stand out noticeably from the middle class passengers, who eyed the little man curiously. Both he and Miguel laughed at the rampant speculation running through the cabin that he was either an eccentric millionaire, a recent lottery winner, or an aging rock star who was traveling the world living off the proceeds of his record sales and concert tours, completely unconcerned about what people now thought of him. One sixteen-year-old girl even asked him for his autograph, which he happily obliged, though she left his seat as confused as she came when she couldn't decipher his illegible scrawl.

By the time their plane landed in Japan, Santos felt thoroughly refreshed and ready to travel to the Akita shrine. He was up and heading toward the exit before Miguel pulled him back and asked him to wait until the crowded aisles cleared.

"I know you feel better, Santos, but I'm still worried that you're pushing yourself too hard. We still have another long flight ahead of us before we head back to Rome. I think you should pace yourself a little."

"I can still feel the power of the Holy Spirit surging through me, Miguel," Santos said. "It's wonderful, invigorating."

"And it also put you in the hospital. You're not in the best of health, Santos. I told you what the doctor said about your blood pressure and other conditions."

"I feel fine."

"I know you do, but you're not. And if you continue to ignore that fact, the next time you collapse you may not be so lucky."

"Really Miguel, I—"

"You asked me to help you, to see that you're properly cared for so you can continue to do God's work. But you won't listen to what I say," Miguel let his frustration show. "Why have me along if you're just going to do things your own way, regardless of what I think?"

A smile began to work its way across Santos's face. He put his arm around the young man's shoulder whose concern for him was deep and obvious, and bobbed his head. "You're right, Miguel. I will need to pace myself better to get through the next few days. I know I can be impulsive on occasion, maybe even a little overbearing at times. But you help keep me centered, and without you I would be lost. I'm sorry."

"I didn't mean to be so abrupt, Santos," Miguel began to apologize before Santos cut him off.

"You were no more abrupt than I deserved. The truth is, I look to you for many things Miguel — advice, a sense of structure for my chaotic life, even companionship during our long and difficult journeys. But what I look to you for most, what I have come to count as a blessing these past many years as we've traveled together, is your friendship Miguel. And with that friendship comes a responsibility to speak one's mind, fully and completely, just as you have done, and just as I have come to appreciate once again."

"Thank you, Santos," Miguel choked with emotion.

"Now, it looks as if the lines have thinned. If you can get me through customs one more time without us landing in detention," he winked, "I will be most grateful."

Both he and Miguel shared a hearty laugh as a nervous stewardess approached with another request for Santos' autograph, this time from a passenger who swore he remembered seeing him play at Woodstock, or as warm up to the Beatles at Shea Stadium, or at some other famous concert from the 1960s.

With a flourish Santos signed the scrap of paper, penciling in a large, flamboyant cross in place of the 't' in 'Santos', and with Miguel in the lead headed toward the exit.

***

The Akita shrine to the Blessed Virgin was unique in the Orient. In 1969, Agnes Sasagawa, a postulant in the Order of the Handmaids of the Eucharist, saw the Vision of an angel while praying the Rosary. The heavenly being told her to recite the prayer from the children of Fatima at specific times over the following years, "O My Jesus, forgive us our sins; save us from the fire of hell; lead all souls to heaven, especially those most in need."

Sister Agnes Sasagawa followed the instructions precisely. Four years later, in the Japanese town of Akita, she was unwrapping bandages from her hand which had mysteriously started to bleed when she suddenly heard a voice directing her to a chapel where an apparition of the Blessed Virgin appeared. Then, and in the months that followed, she was given messages by the Virgin Mary requesting prayer, sacrifice, and abandonment to God not only from those who had already devoted their lives to the Church, but from the secular world as well.

Each time her voice seemed to come from a wooden statue of the Blessed

Virgin that was bathed in a brilliant light whenever an apparition occurred. The statue began to emit a clear liquid from its eyes resembling tears whenever Mary spoke. Just as remarkably, though completely deaf Sister Agnes could clearly hear the Virgin Mary. In the last apparition at Akita, the Virgin Mary warned that the Devil would soon infiltrate the Church pitting Cardinals against Cardinals, and bishops against other bishops. The Church would then be full of those "who accept compromises and the demon will press many priests and consecrated souls to leave the service of the Lord."

After immersing himself in prayer at the chapel of Akita, Santos walked out into the courtyard, trying to shake off a deep sense of melancholy. Unlike Amsterdam, Fatima, or any of his previous encounters, there was no communion with the Holy Spirit, no appearance from a messenger of God revealing another of the Divine Truths. Instead, he was left only with thoughts of sorrow and foreboding. He was in a land that had seen centuries of martyrdom, and experienced the horror of a nuclear war. It was here that humanity had received the severest possible warning from the Virgin on October 13, 1973 — the very same day on which Leo XIII had his vision of God and Satan, and the sun came hurtling down to earth at Fatima. "In order that the world might know the wrath of the Heavenly Father toward today's world," the Blessed Virgin spoke to Sister Agnes, "He is preparing to inflict a great chastisement on all mankind. If men do not repent and better themselves, the Heavenly Father will inflict a great punishment on all humanity. It will definitely be a punishment greater than the Deluge, such as has never been seen before. Fire will plunge from the sky and a large part of humanity will perish. The good as well as the bad will perish, sparing neither priests nor the faithful. The survivors will find themselves plunged into such terrible hardships that they will envy the dead."

It was a conditional warning to be sure. It could be averted if men repented. But he wondered if man had really changed since the time of the Old Testament, when God constantly gave his chosen people the opportunity to obey his commands, but they rarely did no matter how severe the consequences. Through his infinite generosity he made salvation possible to all through the Great Sacrifice. But even that was not enough to convince mankind to change its evil ways, and through the twenty centuries that followed innumerous plagues, pestilence, wars, and other chastisements were visited upon the world.

As he sat despondently on a bench, Santos was joined by a man of taller than medium height, with dark brown hair and a slight beard, and dark piercing eyes. He had a white robe that reached his ankles, with a cloak that covered his shoulders and was draped over each arm. The cloak was brown, sometimes purple, and he wore gold colored sandals. He was youthful and yet looked mature with an air of strength, purpose and serenity.

"Do not be sad, my son," he said to Santos. Santos looked up, so shocked by the comment that he didn't know what to say. "I am the father of your Savior and your father. As I once protected the Child Jesus and his Mother, the Holy Family, I now protect the human family."

Santos felt strangely re-assured. He instinctively felt that the man sitting next to him had been at his side all along. Emboldened, he now asked how mankind could avoid what seemed so inevitable?

"God wants nothing but for his children to turn back to him," St. Joseph said. "Heaven has spoken about this many times. Today I want to tell you about the messages given to three women consecrated to the religious life in the last century. My Son spoke of his divine Mercy to Sister Faustina Kowalska of Poland. He told her, 'In the Old Covenant I sent prophets wielding thunderbolts to My people. Today I am sending you with My mercy to the people of the whole world. I do not want to punish aching mankind, but I desire to heal it, pressing it to My Merciful Heart. I use punishment when they themselves force Me to do so; My hand is reluctant to take hold of the sword of justice. Before the Day of Justice I am sending the Day of Mercy.'

"I myself spoke of my role in the divine plan for humanity to Sister Mildred Mary Neuzil. 'I bring to souls the purity of my life and the obedience that crowned it. All fatherhood is blest in me whom the Eternal Father chose as His representative on earth, the Virgin-Father of His own Divine Son. Through me the Heavenly Father has blessed all fatherhood, and through me He continues and will continue to do so till the end of time. My spiritual fatherhood extends to all God's children, and together with my Virgin Spouse I watch over them with great love and solicitude. Mine was perfect obedience to the Divine Will. To be careless in this is most displeasing to God and will be severely punished in the next world. I desire souls to come to my heart that they may learn true union with the Divine Will.'

"'My child, I desire a day to be set aside to honor my fatherhood. The privilege of being chosen by God to be the Virgin-Father of His Son was mine alone, and no honor, excluding that bestowed upon my Holy Spouse, was ever, or will ever, be as sublime or as high as this. The Holy Trinity desires thus to honor me that in my unique fatherhood all fatherhood might be blessed. I am the protector of the Church and the home, as I was the protector of Christ and His Mother while I lived upon earth. Jesus and Mary desire that my pure heart, so long hidden and unknown, be now honored in a special way. Let my children honor my most pure heart in memory of my life with Jesus and Mary and the love I bore them, the sorrow I suffered with them.'

"Finally, God the Father himself spoke to Mother Eugenia Ravasio. 'I am stooping down to the poorest of My creatures to talk to her, and through her, to all men. I know your needs, your desires, and everything in your hearts. But how happy and grateful I would be if I saw you coming to me and confiding in Me your needs, like a son who has total trust in his father. How could I refuse you the smallest or biggest thing if you asked Me? I desire only this: I desire that one day be dedicated to honoring Me in a special way under the title of Father of All Mankind. For this feast, I would like a special Mass and Office. If you prefer a Sunday, I choose the first Sunday of August.'

"So this is the message you must take from Akita. The Church must institute a feast honoring the fatherhood of St. Joseph. The Church must institute a feast in honor of God the Father of humanity on the first Sunday of August. And, finally, the Church must implore the Mercy of the Father so as to avert the horrendous consequences here on earth of the terrible sins committed constantly by the human family."

With that the gentle man rose and faced the setting sun. As it dipped below the horizon, his image faded along with it, leaving Santos to ponder the final task still awaiting him, to search "where the stairway came from Heaven, ask the one who knows."

Rome

After fewer than twenty-four hours, on the first ballot of the Conclave, a new pope was elected. The world did not know his name, only that white smoke billowed from the chimney to the Sistine Chapel. Catholics around the world rejoiced, while business and political leaders waited anxiously to see who would soon appear on the world stage to speak on behalf of the largest segment of the Christian community.

The news was of particularly interest to two individuals, separated by great distances and divided by conflicting cultures, but united in their singular devotion to the same villainous cause. The new pope would be their enemy or ally — perhaps even both — and they waited impatiently along with everyone else for the announcement of his name. The only clue to the new pope's identity was a strange, confusing sight that caught Vatican observers completely off guard, and instantly set theologians and lay people alike wondering about its significance.

Mixed with the bilious white smoke announcing his selection, was an ominous streak of black.

Chapter 20

Rome

The new pope moved swiftly to put his stamp on the Church.

Taking the name of Martin VI, Martin the Reformer, he moved to replace key officials in the Italian Curia with Prefects closer to his own ecumenical views. Institutions like Opus Dei, already relegated to the sidelines during the reign of Pope Gregory XVII, were now threatened with outright banishment. The new Belgian Pope had made clear his intention to radically alter the manner in which the Catholic Church operated both internally, and in relation to the rest of the world. Gone was a sense of moral superiority informed by two thousand years of rites and traditions. In its place was a broader, more understanding view of the conflicting truths which influenced human behavior. The need for adherence to a set of rigid moral values was balanced with biological imperatives inherent in every human being to propagate the species and control his own destiny. The ethno-centric, European bias of Church doctrine would, under the stewardship of Pope Martin, draw strength from the wisdom of other cultures and religions. Instead of dividing the world along artificial lines, the Church of Rome would now seek to unite it through a common denominator of compromise and logic. Relevance, in the twenty-first century, was no longer the realm of superstitious practices. The modern world required modern thinking, and that was to be the hallmark of a new millennium, a fundamental rebirth, of the Catholic Church and the Catholicism it practiced.

Cardinal Bruno Reinhard, now Pope Martin VI, did not wait for his formal installation as the new Pontiff to begin making these changes. His first act in the moments after his election, even before he appeared on the balcony at St. Peter's Basilica to wave to the crowds below who had come to pledge their fealty and devotion, was to call Alex Olsson, the Secretary General of the United Nations, and promise to begin a new era of global responsibility for the Holy See. Not every change he desired could be enacted overnight, the new pope explained. A cumbersome Vatican bureaucracy still held great sway over the day-to-day affairs of the Church. The replacement of its senior most officials would begin the process of change, but there were many months ahead — even years — to fully realize the vision.

The appointed spokesman for the world's secular powers expressed his support for the new pope and his confidence in his actions, and pledged to bring all the resources he had to bear to help facilitate the necessary, long-overdue transition. Martin thanked him and ended the conversation, satisfied that a new period of enlightenment had begun for the Church and its mission on Earth. He then consented to don the white vestments of a new pope and greet his flock, who needed his firm guidance and leadership more than they possibly knew.

Olsson too ended the call immensely pleased with their conversation. The last clear threat of moral condemnation for his actions, and those of the block of member nations whose interests he represented, had been removed. He immediately reached for his private line to inform Shaitana that path ahead was now clear to proceed.

Dallas

Weary but still energized, Santos and Miguel arrived in Dallas Fort Worth International Airport on their way to Santa Fe New Mexico. As they passed through the terminal the headline from a local paper caught his attention. It announced the election of a new pope, a reform-minded Belgian who vowed to make the Church more relevant to modern times.

Santos stared at the paper, his thoughts returning to Akita and the warning of the Devil infiltrating the Church. "The Church will be full of those who accept compromises and the demon will tempt many priests and consecrated souls to leave the service of the Lord."

Santos shuddered involuntarily, and continued on his way. The hour of judgment was fast approaching, and he wondered if anything he did could alter the outcome. Only the sight of Esteban and Marisol Guerrero anxiously waiting for them once they passed through customs diverted his thoughts. Realizing that they would be passing through Dallas, Santos had sent them a telegram, unknown to Miguel, telling them of their expected arrival. Miguel hadn't been back to his parents' home in over two years, and was overjoyed to see them. Rushing into his mother's arms he was smothered with kisses, then embraced by his father, who spoke to his son proudly.

"How wonderful you look, Miguel! You left us as a child, but every time you return, we see you more and more as a man."

"Speak for yourself, Esteban," Marisol brushed the hair from Miguel's eyes and straightened his collar. "My little Miguel will never be far from my heart."

"Please mother," Miguel blushed as she continued to fuss over his appearance. "Not in front of Santos."

Santos laughed heartily, as did Esteban, at the sight of the small grey haired woman fretting over her child, bombarding him with questions about his health, diet, even his social life, such as it was. Miguel resigned himself to being sixteen years old again and dutifully answered her questions, soon joining in the self-deprecating laughter as her mental checklist of worries and concerns were addressed one-by-one. Only a perplexed Marisol, who didn't see the humor in the situation, was left to puzzle over the men's supposedly strange behavior.

"It was wonderful to see you again," Miguel said to his parents, finally satisfying his mother that he was getting enough food, and rest, and other life essentials. He glanced at Santos, nodding his appreciation for the unexpected surprise, then turned back to his parents. "I wish we could stay longer, but we have to get to Santa Fe."

"So quickly?" Esteban frowned, speaking to Santos. "Can't you and Miguel stay another day, at least? Marisol started cooking the minute we got your message from Tokyo that you'd be traveling through Dallas. We have such a feast prepared in your honor!"

"It would be a shame to miss such a fine meal," Santos lamented. "But I must get to New Mexico as quickly as I can. But," he continued, winking at Miguel, "your son has taken such good care of me that I can spare him for another day while go on by myself."

"No, Santos," Miguel's eyes darted between Santos and his parents. "I can't leave you now."

During their flight from Japan he thought briefly about asking Santos for just such a favor, but kept the thought close to himself. As much as he wanted to be with his family again after so long a separation, this was not the time to abandon Santos. The little Filipino priest, however, had other plans. Before leaving Tokyo he pondered the final steps he would need to take, and the immense consequences they portended. Throughout the last two weeks Miguel had been at his side, ready to help him whenever he could, but it was always Santos to whom God's messengers spoke. It would be a blessing for Miguel to visit with his family again, and they could rejoin each other when he returned to Dallas for their final flight to Rome.

"I will be fine, Miguel," Santos said, his words brightening Marisol and Esteban's faces. "You are a great help to me Miguel, but I am still quite capable of fending for myself when I have to, as I did those many years before you became my assistant. Your family is important too, and they have sacrificed much these last five years by allowing you to be at my side. I know how difficult this has been for you too. Go with them. I have a plane to catch."

Tears welled in Miguel's eyes, and he embraced the rotund little man with all his strength. Santos grunted at the forceful hug, and laughed approvingly. Marisol quickly gathered her son and began walking him toward the exit while Esteban, his voice choked with emotion, reached for Santos' hand and shook it warmly.

"Thank you, Santos," he said.

"You have a wonderful son, Esteban. He has a fine character and strong, kind heart. He has been a blessing to me."

"He writes us often about you too, Santos. Miguel left us a troubled, confused boy. You have helped to make him a fine young man."

"No, Esteban," Santos shook his head. "I did nothing more than let the values you and Marisol taught him by your own example strengthen and emerge. I wish I had time to tell you just how remarkable your son is. Perhaps one day I can, but until then, know that everything I do now, everything I accomplish, is as much through the effort of Miguel as myself. Without him I would be truly lost."

Drawing Esteban closer, Santos glanced at Miguel and his mother still talking and hugging each other a short distance away. He took out his tickets and showed them to his Esteban.

"Could you, er, tell me what gate I'm supposed to go to? I haven't got the slightest idea."

Miguel wondered what the great, uproarious laugh was coming from his father, a laugh shared equally by Santos. He watched Esteban physically turn the chubby little man and send him down the busy corridor. He knew that his and Santos' mission to discover the Seven Secrets was coming to an end, but once it did an even greater challenge would confront them. He was thankful for the opportunity to be with his parents again, even if it was only for twenty-four hours. Once Santos returned to Dallas, they would immediately head to Rome, where the forces of Hell would do their worst to prevent Santos from delivering the Holy message.

It was by no means certain that Santos would succeed, or whether the two of them would survive the ordeal alive. All he knew was that he and Santos would do their best, even if it meant surrendering their lives in the process. Until then, he intended to enjoy this reunion with his parents, for it might be the last time he saw them until they were united again in Heaven.

Rome

The top three floors of the Hotel Majestic on the Via Veneto were reserved for Shaitana and the extensive entourage that traveled with him. The odd group consisted of bureaucrats and devoted followers, frail looking scribes who translated his thoughts into scriptural dogma, and heavily armed bodyguards. Though constantly surrounded by his sycophants and protectors, ultimately Shaitana was alone in the world. His only true companion was the Devil with whom he had struck his bargain many years ago. It gave him power, glory, wealth and influence, but did nothing to soothe the void in his soul that left him an empty shell of a man. His only purpose was to do Satan's bidding. Life, in this world or the next, had no other meaning for him.

As he looked out over the city of Rome, seeing the crest of St. Peter's Basilica off in the distance, Shaitana felt a renewed sense of power surge through his body. He was fast approaching success, and it filled him with a strength he had never known before. The only obstacle that still remained was an insignificant Filipino priest off on a futile quest to discern the seven holy secrets — the seven Divine Truths — that would be used to stop him. He wondered just how much magic the little priest could conjure if the Pope himself in Rome would not act on his rantings. Victory was within his grasp, and the world would soon know the power of the only true god expressed through his loyal servant, the power of Satan as manifest through Shaitana.

Santos Machado was little more than an annoying flea. But even a tiny flea could make an animal scratch. Nothing would be left to chance, not even an exorcist's prayers that would fall on a pontiff's deaf ears. When Santos Machado arrived in Rome, Shaitana would be waiting. With his death the world would be reborn, not in the image of God, but as a vessel of pure evil. This Shaitana swore with his own life, for his soul had long since been committed to the service of his Master.

Santa Fe

The desk clerk at the Adobe Inn looked up from his morning paper and blinked his eyes in faux disbelief at the sight of a rotund little man in a wild shirt and outdated pants walking through his lobby. Santos, resting on his wooden cane, stood at the check in counter and presented his Vatican passport as his only means of identification.

"Santos Machado. I believe I have a reservation."

The desk clerk looked through his computer files and pulled up the name, glancing again at Santos whose head barely seemed to clear the top of the counter.

"It says here you're a priest," the man said suspiciously.

"I am."

"What kind of priest?" he asked, his eyes drawn to the brightly flowered shirt Santos wore.

"I'm a Catholic priest. An exorcist."

"Exorcist!" the man replied, startled. "Really?"

"As God is my witness," Santos raised his right hand theatrically.

"Wow, man. Hey Margie, come here," he called to the back office. "I've never met a real exorcist before."

"What is it Greg?" a middle-aged woman emerged from the rear of the hotel. Her eyes caught a look at Santos. She frowned, and spoke to her fellow clerk in a hushed voice.

"You want me to call the police?"

"No, man!" Greg exclaimed. "This guy here, he's a priest. An exorcist!"

"Exorcist, really?" the woman said.

"So did you come here to fight the Devil?" Greg asked enthusiastically.

"Yes, in a manner of speaking."

"So, like, when are we going to see some heads spinning?"

"It doesn't really work that way," Santos chuckled, seeing the disappointment in the man's eyes, "but if you'd like, I can shake my head back and forth really fast."

"What?"

"Just give the man a room, Greg," Margie said, turning around and walking back into the office while Santos continued to chuckle under his breath.

Rome

"I must see Pope Martin," Mother Philomena said, finding her way blocked to the new pontiff's private chambers.

Carlo Giordano, the new head of the Vatican Curia, stood his ground and refused to let the old nun pass.

"His Holiness cannot be disturbed," Giordano said, contempt dripping from his voice. Slender, white-haired, he had the look of a petty bureaucrat elevated to a position well above his own abilities. For years he had been Bruno Reinhard's eyes and ears within the Vatican, reporting on intrigue and ordinary activities alike so that the Belgian theologian could gauge his support and keep watch over his detractors. His reward for years of loyal service was to extend this same surveillance and protection to the man who now was pope. No one, not even a revered mystic like Sister Philomena, would be permitted unfettered access to the Holy Father, unless it served Pope Martin or Carlo Giordano's personal interest.

"You don't understand," Mother Philomena pressed. "I have come to warn him about a great convergence. The hour is fast approaching when the Devil will make his play. The Pope must —"

"Enough, old woman!" Giordano shouted. "We'll have no more of your superstitious prattle! The Pope will not see you, now or tomorrow, this week or next. Leave! Return to your prayers and your 'Visions', and do not bother us again."

The old nun stared at the unctuous, imperious man who continued to block her way. With great sadness she turned and headed back to her quarters. There she would pray for God to intercede and somehow bring the Pope to reason. If not, the last of her Visions, the most terrible one of all, would surely consume the world. It was this Vision which came to her in a waking dream as the Pope stood on the balcony in St. Peter's square that terrified her the most. The shining light of Heaven was slowly blocked out by a dark, consuming shadow that swept over the newly elected pontiff, strangling him and the Church he led, until there was nothing but a black, pitiless void left in its place.

The end-times had begun. There was still enough time to stop its advance, and return the world to the state it once had, but that time was rapidly coming to a close. Soon the only light that would shine upon man would come from the bitter, scorching, fires of Hell.

Santa Fe

The Chapel of Loretto was built by the Sisters of Loretto in the late nineteenth century, the first order of nuns in America dedicated to teaching. Inside is a twenty-foot-tall staircase that makes two 360-degree turns without any center support. Made of wood, it was built using only square wooden pegs without glue, nails, or any other bonding material.

What makes the staircase memorable is both its unique form of construction, which has never been successfully explained or duplicated, and its mysterious appearance in the small frontier church. When the Chapel was initially completed, the sisters found that there was no way to reach a choir loft at the rear of the structure. Several local carpenters were asked to design a staircase, but every design required the use of a ladder that would cut into the interior space of the small Chapel.

The sisters made a novena to St. Joseph, the patron saint of carpenters, seeking a solution to their dilemma. On their final day of prayer a man arrived at the chapel with his tools and a donkey, seeking work. He was hired to build a circular staircase, which he completed after several months of labor. Then, as mysteriously as he arrived, he disappeared, never asking for or receiving his pay, or the gratitude of the nuns who marveled at his magnificent design. The Sisters of Loretto came to believe that it was Joseph himself, the foster father of Jesus, who appeared and answered their prayers.

No longer a Christian Church, the little chapel was now a private museum. Santos arrived at the building only to find its doors locked and a sign indicating that it was closed to the public. A small fire in an adjacent structure had filled it with smoke, and there was some water damage from a precautionary soaking the local fire department had given its roof. The damages were minor and easily reparable, but the sign said it would be two weeks until the chapel re-opened.

For a long while Santos stood at the entrance to the chapel, wondering what to do. He had traveled half way around the world to reach the Loretto Chapel, only to find himself now barred from entering. Was it a sign from God that his mission was over now that a new, unsympathetic Pope in Rome had been selected? Or worse, was it because he had somehow failed, that his faith and piety were not enough to complete God's work.

He stood on the steps, wondering what to think and what to do, when an old beat up station wagon drove up and stopped at the curb. A man in his forties with a wife and young child peered out the open window.

"Say Mister," he called. "Kin you tell me if this is the church with that magical stairway?

"The Chapel of Loretto, yes," Santos answered.

"Great!" the man answered. Opening the door, he got out of the car and called to his wife. "Maria, you and Chris come on out. We finally made it."

The man, dressed shabbily in workman's clothes, bounded through the wrought iron gate and headed toward the chapel entrance, only to see the same sign blocking his path that Santos had read.

"Well, ain't that a kick," he grumbled. "We come all the way from Piney Bluff to see this here magical staircase, and we can't get in."

"Hello," the little boy said shyly, smiling at Santos while holding onto his mother's hand.

"This here's my son Chris, and my wife Maria."

"Hello," Santos smiled back at them.

"I don't rightly know what I'm gonna do now. I ain't got two weeks to set around waitin' for the door to open."

"I don't either," Santos lamented. "I have to get in there now, to pray, and seek guidance from the Lord."

"Well," the man thought for a long moment. "Seems I remember passin' another church a few blocks yonder. I guess you could always go there."

"No, it has to be this location," Santos insisted, "'where the stairway came from Heaven.' I must find the 'one who knows', and receive the final Secret. Without it, I can't complete my task."

"You on a secret mission or sumpin'?" the man asked. "Sounds pretty serious."

"It is. If I fail, all humanity will pay the price."

The man looked at Santos with a long, silent stare while he rubbed the stubble on his cheek. "What exactly is it yer lookin' fer?"

"The answer, the glue that holds the other secrets together. The knowledge that I need to return to Rome, and reveal God's plan for us on earth."

"God!" the man said. "So you're after that, understandin' God's mind. Seems to me like you outta already know that."

"What?"

"Now I'm not a religious man, mind you, but it seems to me the answer to what God's thinkin' has already been given to us. Knowin' and willin' something are the two most basic acts of any man, just like God. A human bein' has a mind and a will, and God is an infinite bein' with an infinite mind and an infinite will.

"Now, when an infinite bein' thinks, that thinkin' itself is a person. And when the bein' wills, the willin' too is a person. Just think of this bein' as the Father, the mind or knowin' as the Son, and the will or lovin' as the Spirit. But it's one God, because it's one Bein' that knows and loves. The Father gives all that he is to the Son, and the Son receives all that he is from the Father, and their love for each other 'breathes' forth the Spirit. We do the same too when you think about it, but in a different way. Every time we think, every time we love, and every time we bring a new person into bein', we're imitatin' the Holy Trinity. So it's not really much of a mystery, if you ask me, how God can be the Father, and Son, and the Holy Spirit all at once, because he lets us experience the same thing on a human level every day. The Father creates us, the Son redeems us, and the Spirit sanctifies us."

Santos looked at the man, unsure what to say. His little boy was playing with a small dog that wandered into the courtyard. Maria, his wife, was dutifully watching over him to make sure that no harm came to the boy. As she stroked her son's hair lovingly, she spoke to her husband, then Santos.

"I kin see he's still a might uncertain about what this all means," she said. "You wanna know how kin human eyes see, and our hearts understand, the Father, Son and Spirit? Jest look at the Holy Family. They was like a trinity on earth that represented in a certain way the Blessed Trinity in Heaven. Jesus was really the divine Son, and Mary was a portrait of the Holy Spirit, and Joseph was Shadow of the Father."

"So it all comes together both here on Earth and in Heaven," the man continued. "God's love for us, as his children, is the glue that holds it all together. God the Father loved us into bein'. God the Son loved us out of the wages of sin, and God the Holy Spirit loves us into choosin' life eternal. We do this for our children, lovin' them into bein', sacrificin' ourselves for 'em, formin' their characters as much as they let us. Now this don't make us God, mind you, but when we imitate his ways we do become god-like in our actions. So in the end, all that matters is the Love that will never let go of you. All that matters in this world is that we enter into a communion with the Life-giving Love of God. Isn't that right, son?"

The little boy looked toward his father, and then smiled lovingly at Santos. "Only God's love can destroy sin, and only his love can lead to joy."

"See," the man said proudly. "My boy knows this. In fact, in a way, he helped teach it to me."

"I-I understand now," Santos said, amazed. "I know the actions that must be taken to fulfill the Seventh Secret. The Church has to teach with clarity the doctrine of the Trinity, and The Holy Family must be seen as the image of the Holy Trinity. There's even a prayer we can recite to the Trinity that dwells within our souls: 'O my Love, my only good, Most Holy Trinity, I adore You, hidden in the depths of my soul. To You, to Your honor and glory, I dedicate my life. May every thought, word and deed of mine be an act of adoration and praise directed towards Your Divine Majesty enthroned in my heart. Through the Immaculate Heart of Mary and the pure heart of St. Joseph, I consecrate my life to Your adoration and glory.'"

"That's a good prayer," the man nodded. "Well, I guess we better git movin' along. We're just passin' through Santa Fe. We still gotta find us a place to stay for the night."

"Thank you for help, er —"

"My friends call me Joe."

"Thank you, Joe. I'm Santos."

"Santos, like the Saint! Well that's a good name for a feller too. You take care of yerself Santos. Sounds like you got a right powerful lot of trouble facin' you. Peoples get set in their ways and don't like to change, even when it's fer their own good. Now you take my cousin Marty. He's a good enough feller, but he keeps doing things he ought not even though he's been taught better. Sometimes it's ' cause he's just plain confused over what to do, but most likely it because he let's hisself think somethin's okay even when it's not. After a while a man can get pretty relaxed about his evil ways, and treat them like it's all normal and that. That's his free will shuttin' out his conscience, which is God's way of talkin' to us about what's right and wrong. He's a lot like that new pope of yers, if you ask me. He's a proud man full of hubris, but down deep he's still got a good soul — if you can reach it."

"Joe, how do you know—"

"You said yer goin' to Rome next, didn't you? Figures a man would need to git the Pope on his side if he had any chance of savin' the world."

The man began to walk away, beckoning his wife and children back into their old decrepit car, leaving Santos behind on the chapel steps to puzzle over his final remarks. Just as he turned the key and put it in gear, he poked his head outside the window and looked back at Santos. "When you git there, you might want to show 'em that parchment you got in yer pocket.

He kin read it all now. Anyone can who needs to understand it, 'lest their soul is already lost'."

With that the man pulled away from the corner and headed down the street. Santos watched in stunned silence, not sure what to make of the strange encounter. The only thing he knew for certain was that God had spoken to him through Joe and his family.

Silently, he fell to his knees and gave his thanks to God, who once again had shown him the way at the little chapel in Santa Fe.

Chapter 21

Rome

As darkness descended over Rome, Shaitana waited in his luxury suite for news of Santos Machado's arrival.

The invisible protection of Opus Dei had prevented him from striking down the little Filipino priest as he traveled throughout the world searching for the hidden secrets, the Divine Truths that he would use against him like a weapon. Instead, he waited for word of Santos Machado's arrival in Rome, passing the hours in slow, seething fury that threatened to explode at any moment. So close to his goal, he could feel it in his soul, what little of it still remained. He had long ago bartered away any hope of salvation, and only a deep, empty void remained where his immortal soul had once dwelled. With a mixture of venom and anticipation he waited in his room, prowling the walls like a trapped animal, until word finally came that the man he hated, the man he feared most, had finally arrived in the Eternal City.

"Shall I accompany you, my Lord?" a thick-necked, heavily muscled man asked.

No. I will handle this matter alone."

"But it could be dangerous, my Lord. Opus Dei still protects the priest. They are strong here in Rome."

"And I am now stronger," Shaitana said. "I can feel the power within me continue to grow with each new breath. Tonight, all prophesies will be fulfilled. Tonight, the world will be transformed."

The giant man bowed as Shaitana swept through the open door, leaving his entourage behind and disappeared into the night.

***

The Vatican was a city state, autonomous from the rest of Italy and governed by its own laws and procedures. Like any nation it had bureaucrats and public officials to oversee its many function. Most of these civilian employees attended to the important, but mundane affairs of state. But some had a greater responsibility, to guard the Vatican and protect the Pope, the same as any police force or army protected its leaders in any other country around the world.

Three men dressed in black suits — members of the Vatican's private security force that worked in coordination with the Swiss Guard — stood at their post outside a heavy bronze door that led inside the walled city. They watched with heightened interest as a quirky little man in a black cassock, his heavy cane tapping on the cobblestone walkway, approached their post with a young man at his side. Trotting, half-running as best he could, the priest made his way toward the lead guard. Beyond the great bronze door was a courtyard leading to the pontiff's quarters. With his shoulder pistol within easy grasp, and his military training on full alert, he was not a person to be reckoned with lightly if trouble was to come.

"Young man, open the gate," Santos called, waving his cane like a pointing stick. "I must see the pope!"

The guard placed his hand on the butt of his weapon, not quite sure what to make of the comical sight. Miguel saw that he was alarmed by Santos' actions and tried to slow him down, but the stiff-legged priest kept forging ahead.

"It's a matter of great urgency," Santos shouted again, drawing to within a few paces of the guard, who pulled his weapon from his holster and held it braced across his chest.

"The pope is not receiving any visitors," he said.

"But I must —"

"Please halt your advance," he commanded, his gun now at the ready. Santos saw the glint of steel and quickly complied.

"I am Santos Machado," he took the parchment Scroll from his pocket and held it out for the man to see, "and I have come to do God's work here tonight."

"I don't care if you're St. Nicholas, and that's a letter from John the Baptist," the guard replied gruffly, refusing to look at the Scroll. "This area is secured, and you will not be admitted. Now please leave, before this situation becomes unpleasant."

"Santos," Miguel tugged at his arm. "Do what he says."

"But I must see the pope!"

"You can put a request into the Secretariat of State's office first thing in the morning," a second guard replied. "I'm sure the pope will be happy to see you, but not tonight. Now go."

"Come on, Santos," Miguel started to lead him away. Reluctantly, Santos hobbled away from the gate, looking back forlornly before continuing down an alley at the rear of the walled city.

Holstering his weapon, the lead guard shook his head and fought to suppress a smile that nevertheless worked its way clearly across his face. The funny little man, if he was indeed a priest, was one of two dozen people that day who had 'urgent' business with the pope. They carried everything from baked goods, to petitions, to full-sized wooden crosses draped across their shoulders. The guards weren't sure if Santos was a crackpot, or just another overly exuberant petitioner who wanted to put his personal mark on the new Pope's administration. But in the end it didn't matter. They had been given their orders, which they intended to carry out fully. No one would get past that door, no matter how 'urgent' their business, unless they had the proper credentials.

Several minutes later another figure emerged from the shadows, this one a tall slender man with a manicured beard wearing a long, flowing cape. The lead guard sighed softly under his breath, his hand once again resting on the butt of his pistol, and waited for the man to close the distance between them.

"Open the gate," the approaching man commanded. "I have business with your pope."

"The Holy Father isn't taking any visitors tonight," the guard repeated dryly. "You can put a request —"

The guard stopped in mid-sentence, clutching his throat and dropping to his knees. His companions rushed to his side, only to be met with similar unexplained constrictions in their throats. Shaitana watched impassively as the air was sucked from their lungs, leaving each man dazed and gasping for breath.

Unable to breathe, unable to speak, the three guards collapsed in a heap in front of the door, unconscious but not dead. It was the only act of mercy Shaitana intended to show that evening. He would save his strength for more pressing concerns, once the renegade priest found his way into the papal quarters. He didn't know how Santos would cajole his way past the Vatican guards, but he knew that he would find a way. His God, who had protected him from harm these past many days, would now deliver him to Shaitana like a sacrificial lamb. It was a fitting, if ironic end to a great struggle that had lasted more than a century.

Stepping forward confidently, Shaitana walked through the solid bronze door as if it wasn't there and emerged inside the courtyard. With a contemptuous smirk he made his way toward the pope's private residence. As the Covenant foresaw, the confrontation between Good and Evil was nearing its climax. Not only would Shaitana ensure that Evil triumphed, he would make it happen in the very heart of the Christian world.

***

"I can't believe the guard wouldn't let me pass," Santos shook his head in disbelief. "I even showed him the Scroll."

"This isn't the way to do it, Santos," Miguel said. "I tried to tell you when we landed. They're not going to just let you barge into the Vatican and see the Pope! That first guard was going to shoot you!"

"I don't think he really intended to use his weapon," Santos weighed the question while he answered.

"The point is, Santos, there's got to be a better way to go about this."

"How?"

"Well, I don't know," Miguel admitted. "But storming the gates of the Vatican isn't going to get us anywhere."

"Perhaps I could help," a calm voice replied. Santos and Miguel turned to see Father Ignacio Maggiore, the head of Opus Dei, standing nearby. Santos recognized him instantly. "Your young friend is right. The guards won't let you pass. Not tonight, not tomorrow. Not at any time."

"Then how do we get inside?" Miguel asked.

Maggiore smiled. "We'll let the dead lead the way."

The robust, sixty-year-old man turned, preparing to guide them toward another entranceway, but Santos stopped him.

"Thank you, for watching over me," he grasped the man's hand, who seemed to choke with emotion at the tender gesture. "The young man in Lisbon, was he injured badly?"

"No. But he would have gladly given his life for yours, Father Machado, as would I or anyone else at Opus Dei. We seek to do God's work on earth, but you have actually done it."

"My work isn't complete."

"It soon will be," Maggiore smiled. "Now come with me. There's something I want to show you."

Deep beneath the Vatican were a series of ancient tunnels. Some were transit ways to distant points, others catacombs of the early Christian faithful. Within this labyrinth was a pathway leading to the papal quarters.

Rarely used and little known, it was the perfect way to breach Vatican security and take Santos directly to the pope.

Lit by hand-held lanterns, the three descended down a long winding staircase, and made their way through the dusty maze of musty smelling tunnels. Cobwebs hung from the soft stone walls, some with small pockets carved into them that still held the bones of early Christian martyrs. Lining the walls were occasional wooden crates covered with dust and age, or bottles of wine in crude glass containers that looked as if they were centuries old. It was like something out of central casting in an old horror movie, except for the absence of burning torches carried on a pole, or a hydra headed monster lurking somewhere in the shadows.

Twisting and turning their way through the ancient underground tunnels, following a confusing path of right and left turns that seemed to go around and then come back on themselves, they arrived at the bottom of narrow stone staircase where Maggiore paused. At first Santos thought he had taken the wrong turn, but as they stood in the dim light he and Miguel could hear muffled voices working their way through a thin wooden door at the top of the steps. Pope Martin was speaking with a man named Carlo who was discussing various matters of Vatican intrigue centered around the Curia and the College of Cardinals.

"What's wrong?" Miguel finally asked.

"I've come as far as I can. The rest of the way you must go alone."

"But won't it be better if you're with us?"

"You and Santos were chosen by God to make this journey. Opus Dei has sworn to protect you from harm and see that you arrive safely. We have now fulfilled that oath. The task ahead is yours, and yours alone. May God bless you and guide you on this holy mission."

Maggiore backed away, extinguishing his lantern, and disappeared into the darkness. With a determined sigh, Miguel started up the staircase to lead the way for Santos, hobbling closely behind him.

The creaking door opened to a surprised Pope Martin, now alone in his chambers. The vestments for his coronation on Sunday were laid out across a dressing table, and the room was filled with other adornments for the coming ceremony. The pope gasped audibly and staggered backward in shock at the sight of Miguel entering his apartment, relaxing only slightly when the familiar black cassock Santos wore came into view.

"W-who, who are you?" he stammered.

"Your Holiness," Santos said with a calming voice. "I am Father Santos

Machado, an exorcist who—"

"Get out of here!" the pope shouted. "How dare you break into my quarters?"

"It was the only way," Santos apologized, retrieving the Scroll from his pocket.

"Get out!"

"Please, you have to listen!" Miguel pleaded. "Santos escaped from Nepal after the others were killed, the exorcists who died at St. Joseph's. He was sent to our holiest shrines by a Vision from Pope Leo. We've traveled the world, recovering the Secrets that we've brought to you. Please hear him out."

"You're mad, both of you! Guards!"

The pope started for the door, only to stop suddenly when Santos unfurled the Scroll. A bright light began to illuminate the apartment, and the Hebrew words seemed to lift themselves off the parchment. The words spun out from the Scroll like an unfolding spiral, swirling about and changing into a recognizable language. The pope watched open-mouthed as a deep, rumbling voice emanating from everywhere and nowhere, from above and below and all around, read the words aloud.

Prepare a home where Hebrews meet their King.

Announce an end to deadly works of darkness.

Remind the world—for endless joy, the choice is now.

Let it be said the Life of God transforms the Bread and Wine, The divine Life indwells the soul.

Proclaim the Eve whose Yes brought Heaven down to earth, The Spirit's Spouse, the Mother of all peoples.

Observe the Father's Feast, enthrone the Protector of the Lord. Repent and cease all evil acts or taste their fatal fruit.

Let all adore the Three in One And see Their mirror: God's own Family.

"T-this, this can't be real," the pope sank to his knees, not in prayer but in terror. "This is some kind of magician's trick."

"No, your Holiness," Santos said with a firm, clear voice. "It is the messenger of God speaking to you, to all of us — but especially to you. These are the Seven Secrets, the divine truths for our time that will free us from the powers of darkness. The Secrets require nine actions from the Church, to be executed by its visible head on earth, the successor of St. Peter."

"W-what are they?" the pope asked in a quavering voice.

"Three doctrines must be taught. First, that the three persons of the Holy Family are images of the Holy Trinity; second, that Mary is the *New Eve* with Jesus the New Adam, and that she is *Panagia* — Spouse of the Spirit and Mediatrix of Grace — and *Mother of all Peoples,* hence the Advocate for humanity; and third, you must proclaim the truth of divinization, the ancient biblical and apostolic revelation that we can share the very life of God while remaining human.

"You must also reaffirm three traditional teachings. The reality and danger of the occult, the literal existence of Hell, and the inevitable impact of evildoing on the present world order. And you must institute two feasts and a new jurisdiction. Declare a feast in honor of God the Father of all humanity, and declare a feast honoring the Pure Heart of St. Joseph. Finally, you must proclaim Hebrew Catholics as a distinctive national community within the Church which will help make possible the ingathering of the Jews."

The pope, still in shock, struggled to absorb the message Santos delivered. He trembled as he listened, the world that he once thought he understood now turned on its head.

"Following this nine-fold Divine Path will restore God's glory on Earth," Santos continued.

"First, the definition of the relation between the Three Divine Persons and the Holy Family will provide humanity with a true idea of both the inner life of God and the meaning of human history.

"Second, the proclamation of Mary as the New Eve bears witness to the true triumph of God because it shows a creature freely cooperating with her Creator to achieve final victory despite the fiercest efforts of his foes.

"Third, the definition of divinization will help bring about the reunion of Christendom because it unveils the true relationship between human nature and the divine life, faith and works, freewill and grace.

"Fourth, the prohibition of occultism and idolatry will protect the human soul against its greatest enemies

"Fifth, the reaffirmation of Hell restores a proper perspective on the ultimate and eternal consequences of every human choice and action.

"Sixth, the warning of cause-and-effect relationships in the spiritual world will help show that every choice and action also affects life here and now.

"Seventh, a feast-day in honor of the Father will be the climax of the gradual recognition of each Person of the Blessed Trinity which began with the feast-days honoring the Son (Christmas and Easter) and the Spirit (Pentecost).

"Eighth, likewise, there is a climax to the progressive recognition of each member of the Holy Family starting with Jesus, moving to Mary and ending with Joseph.

"And finally, the institution of a home for the Hebrews within the Church aligns humanity with the plans of God by bringing the People of the Promise into union with their Messiah thus drawing history to its climax. The Secrets are vital both to the betterment of each individual person, and of the world as a whole," Santos explained. "They reveal the nature of God which is required for individuals to understand their own lives and the purpose of human history. They show the true role of the Family of God, the Holy Family, in the destiny of the human family, and they show the two ultimate possibilities open to every person: to be separated from God or divinized; they direct human history towards its climax.

"The Secrets are a bridge between Heaven and Earth, Time and Eternity. They tie each human soul to human history. The Secrets don't simply negate the power of Satan. They elevate and amplify the power of God in each receptive soul. The Secrets release divine graces into human history while it empowers all those who heed its message and protects them from harm.

Finished, Santos rolled up the Scroll and prepared to hand it to the pope, who was still on his knees, trembling. With an uncertain, unsteady hand he reached out to accept it when a brilliant flash of light disrupted the room. Shaitana, looking more like the Devil than a man, materialized near the pope and tried to grab the Scroll, screaming in pain as flames erupted from the parchment and burned his palm. Yanking his hand back, he stared in shock at the Scroll which was undamaged from the fire.

"Now we're even," Santos smiled.

"No," the evil man hissed. "We've just gotten started."

Chanting a curse that invoked the Devil's powers, Shaitana swept his hand across the room. Instantly Miguel and Pope Martin seemed paralyzed where they stood. Still breathing, neither blinked nor moved a muscle, leaving only Santos unaffected.

"Now the battle begins between the only true adversaries," Shaitana said. He looked at the pope and scoffed dismissively. "He has no power. He has no faith, only a belief in himself." Turning to Santos, his eyes seemed to glow like burning embers. "You are the one who believes. You are the one who can stop me — unless I stop you first."

"You'll have to kill me," Santos said without fear.

"That," Shaitana hissed like a snake, "is precisely what I intend to do."

"Then I'll send you back to Hell!" Santos held up a cross and began to pray. "I adjure you, ancient serpent, by the judge of the living and the dead, by your Creator, by Him who has the power to consign you to hell, to depart forthwith in fear along with your savage minions. It is God Himself who commands you; the majestic Christ who commands you. God the Father commands you; God the Son commands you; God the Holy Spirit commands you. The mystery of the cross commands you. The faith of the holy apostles Peter and Paul and of all the saints commands you. The blood of the martyrs commands you. The continence of the confessors commands you. The devout prayers of all holy men and women command you. The saving mysteries of our Christian faith command you."

"You're not strong enough to defeat me!" Shaitana roared, fighting off the words that seemed to paralyze him momentarily, before he broke free.

"I adjure you," Santos continued, "in the name of the spotless Lamb, tremble and flee as we call on the name of the Lord before whom the denizens of hell cower. I adjure you in His name, begone. It is futile to resist His will."

"My master is stronger than yours! My powers are greater than yours!"

Thrusting his hand forward, Shaitana seemed to block the words that Santos spoke. A wall of flame appeared, and accompanied by the terrifying screams of the lost souls in Hell, it muffled Santos speech. Closing his eyes and focusing his thoughts, Santos tried to overcome the barrier, but he couldn't break through. Shaitana pushed and redoubled his efforts, and the wall of flame grew closer to Santos, who dropped to his knees and tried desperately to hold it back.

"You've lost!" Shaitana boasted. "Your God is no match for my master!"

"Depart impious one," a voice called out. "Depart with all your deceits. It is He who judges you out. It is He who casts you out. It is He who has prepared everlasting hellfire for you. BEGONE!"

"NO!" Shaitana screamed as the wall of flame collapsed and a black, swirling void suddenly appeared behind him. With a terrifying shriek the man who would be Lucifer's incarnation on Earth was sucked into the bowels of darkness to join the damned as another soul locked forever in pain and misery.

"Miguel!" Santos whispered, looking up at the face of his loyal companion who now helped him to his feet. "The prayer, I could not … speak it, but someone … did. Who?"

"It was your young friend," Pope Martin said softly, now able to move.

"Miguel? How?"

"I-I don't know, Santos."

"I do," the pope said. "I see many things clearly now. Shaitana was wrong. Santos wasn't his adversary. It was all men of faith who put their lives, and trust, and love and devotion in the hands of God. As long as each of us follows the Path of God and are thereby divinized, the Devil is powerless. This I understand now. As the Shepherd of the Church of God, I will do all that the Lord has asked through you. I will proclaim the ancient teachings revealed for this new era, and invoke the protections offered by Heaven so that the hundred year curse is lifted."

His mission complete, with Miguel at his side Santos retrieved his cane, and quietly left the room.

Chapter 22

New York

The installation of Pope Martin VI was televised worldwide, but nowhere with more coverage, and a greater sense of disappointment, than by the international resources of Hastings Communications.

His first sermon as the new Pope was conciliatory toward traditional Catholic values, and sweeping in its support for the work of Opus Dei. The seemingly abrupt departure from the new ecumenical focus Hastings had expected enraged him at first. Feeling betrayed and humiliated by his outspoken support for the new pontiff, he gradually let his fury abate, but not his underlying anger.

"Let's dig up what you can on the new pope," he strummed his fingers on the conference room table of his lavish New York headquarters. "I made him, and I can break him, or at least take him down a peg or two. These people are all the same. They'll say anything to get elected, then turn their backs on you the moment they get in power."

"We've got a story about his uncle Friedrich from Bavaria we can go with," someone volunteered. "Hitler Youth, Nazi sympathizer, the standard stuff."

"Is any of it real?" Vincent Stout asked.

"Sure. Enough to keep us from getting sued, anyway."

"Kill the story," Stout said, directing his next comments to Hastings. "It didn't work the last time it was tried. Besides, he's not going anywhere. The pope's elected for life, and he doesn't resign when his health begins to fail. We've got him until he dies. Better to let him remember the help you gave him on the way up, than to attack him once he's reached the top."

For a long moment the room remained silent while Hastings mulled the thought over in his mind. "You're right," he softened to the relief of many, worried that another major battle was brewing within their headquarters. Only someone like Stout, who held the confidence of Ralston Hastings, could publicly disagree with his pronouncements without costing him his career — as long as he chose his battles wisely, and they were few and far in-between. "The pope's a fraud, like every other politician. So what else is new?"

"Speaking of frauds," Stout continued. "Has anybody heard from Shaitana?"

"He's in Rome," a young woman answered. "At the Majestic."

"How many floors?" Hastings asked through gritted teeth.

"Three, including the penthouse."

"I've about had it with this guy too," Hastings became angry again. "What did that Lumen Foundation cost me last year?"

"One point three million," Stout replied.

"Cut him off. I'm not going to pour any money down that rat hole. And tell Legal to put a lien on his property. Seize whatever assets you can, and get me back as much of my investment as possible."

"That will probably collapse his organization," the woman said.

"Good riddance to it. Three floors! Nobody makes a fool out of Ralston Hastings."

The meeting continued with discussions of how best to influence the upcoming U.S. presidential elections, and which public or private figure to make the target of their next hour long investigative program.

Chastised but not deterred, Hastings would continue to build his worldly empire, a task that was never ending, and ultimately never satisfying — but one that consumed every moment of every waking hour in the life of a man who had little else to show for his existence.

Rome

Tugging at his cleric's collar, Santos arrived at the bronze door a full half hour before his private audience with the pope.

After checking the appointment list, the guard made a phone call. Mother Philomena appeared in a moment and nodded to the rotund little priest, her aged, weathered face seeming bright and relaxed. She took him down the endless corridors to the papal apartment.

"The Holy Father will see you now," Pedro Ruiz, the pope's new personal secretary announced.

Santos lifted himself from his chair and bracing his weight with his cane, entered the ornate room. Standing at the pope's side was Ignacio Maggiore, his warm smile greeting Santos who knelt before the pope and kissed the papal ring. Righting himself, he was startled to find helped to his feet by the smiling pontiff.

"How are you feeling today, my dear Padre Santos?"

"Very well, your Holiness."

"Good! Are you up to another task?

Santos looked at Maggiore, who chuckled with anticipation as he waited for the pope to continue.

"Yes your Holiness. Whatever I can do, I will do gladly."

"Go then!" Pope Martin clasped his shoulder. "We have much to do, the three of us. The Monsignor and I were just discussing a most vexing problem. With the death of Father Aurelio, and those who followed in his path, the Church must rebuild its ranks. We need someone to train our young priests in the most ancient of all arts, one practiced by our Lord Jesus Christ so may years ago. Will you Santos? Will you accept the challenge, and fill Aurelio's chair."

"I-I would be honored," Santos felt his voice tighten with emotion.

"Good! The Monsignor will see to it that you have everything you need. Now before you begin, I want you to take a few days rest. Come back healthy and refreshed, and we begin anew — all of us."

"I will, your Holiness," Santos kissed his ring. "Thank you."

"No Santos," the pope said with deep sincerity. "It is I who must thank you, for opening the eyes of my soul."

Santos left the pope and Maggiore to continue their discussions, and returned to Miguel who was waiting for him in the vestibule outside his office.

"Mother Philomena told me all about it, Santos!" he exclaimed. "It's wonderful!"

"It is," Santos said with humility. "God works in truly wondrous ways."

Together they left the building, and began walking through the Piazza San Pietro. As they passed the flowing fountains, Miguel paused, turning to Santos with a look of concern.

"What is it Miguel?" Santos asked.

"There's just one thing, Santos. With your new responsibilities, I think it might be important, you know, to set the proper tone."

"What?" Santos replied, puzzled.

"I was unpacking your luggage last night, and I think, well, maybe you should consider buying some new clothes."

"All right," Santos laughed after a moment's pause, placing his arm around Miguel's shoulder. "We'll go shopping in the morning."

"Great!" Miguel sighed with relief.

"But nothing too expensive," he winked. "I still have an image to maintain."

— End —